Rabbit in a Bottle

Rabbit in a Bottle

R02.11

I welcome your comments, thoughts, and questions.
Write to: JimGuyer@JimGuyer.com

For updates, like "Rabbit in a Bottle" on Facebook

Available at
"The Coffee House" in Hutsonville, Il
Amazon.com
and other retailers

For Mom and Daddy. . . .

Lyle & Inge Guyer – June 1, 1947

<u>Many Thanks to</u>
Yeshua
Grand Master Lynn Stangle
Rachel Talbot
Sue Van Abs
Cathy Rakestraw
Becky Robinson
Frances Evans
Dave & Danielle Davolt
John York
Craig Stovall
Cathy Daugherty

Rabbit

- In a -

Bottle

A story by
Jim Patrick Guyer

Rabbit in a Bottle

Published 10/26/2012

ISBN-10: *0615677495 (Soft Cover)*
ISBN-13: *978-0615677491 (Soft Cover)*

Library of Congress Control Number: PENDING

Any people depicted in stock imagery provided by Thinkstock are models, and such images are being used for illustrative purposes only.

Certain stock imagery © Thinkstock.
This book is printed on acid-free paper.

Table of Contents

Rabbit in a Bottle

Chapter 1

Saturday, the Day I Died

The Accident

- My name is Gerald Camden. My story begins on the day I died. –

Gerald leaned his body deep into a curve as his skis cut across the surface of the water. His father steered the boat toward the dock, then cut a narrow arc to slingshot his son close to the pier. Gerald saw his mother say something to her husband then turn toward her son and put her hands around her mouth as she tried to be heard above the noise of the motor. Gerald cupped a hand to his ear, but he couldn't make out the words. Christine pointed off to the side.

Gerald saw the pier and realized he had held on to the tow rope too long. He dropped the handle and skidded across the surface as he gauged the distance and the angle of his approach. With a slight adjustment, he could miss it completely. He steered his skis gently to the side as his momentum started to run out. The turn wasn't sharp enough. He adjusted the angle of his skis, but without the tow rope, it was difficult to keep his weight balanced. One ski sank lower in the water and dragged his foot back. Gerald teetered forward and turned as he fell. The side of his head struck the corner post. There was a brilliant flash and then his world went black.

Sisters

- Her weapons were her crystal eyes. Making every man mad. Black as a dark night she was, got what no one else had. -

When Tammy Wells made her morning entrance at the high school, she glided down the halls. There was a science to her manner. Staying at the social center of the school required more than just being pretty, it was also about gait, facial expression, and style.

Male students who were digging in their lockers stopped to turn and peer around the gray metal doors to get a look. Hallway conversations about sports and automobiles stalled as she went by. Her large black curls lightly bounced off of the milky white skin as she strutted past. Tammy carried a faint smile to show her sparkling white teeth as she gazed forward with her large, round, dark blue eyes. It gave her an innocent appearance.

At the far end of the hall, she noticed her two sisters, Violet and Jean, coming toward her. Jean had sandy brown hair, while Violet's was jet black. Pretty girls, Tammy thought, but not quite as cute as herself. They weren't really sisters, even though that was what they had called themselves since grade school. The triangle made up their own exclusive little sorority, and Tammy was their ringleader. She liked having them as her consorts. They made a sort of barrier between her and the rest of the world. Tammy became a bit puzzled by the seriousness of their expressions and the tight, anxious way they walked toward her. Something was up. Something big.

"Sisters!" she said to them as they approached. "What is it? It can't be that bad."

The girls paused in the hallway as they met. Jean shifted her books under her arm. "It is bad. It's very bad."

"It's Gerald," Violet continued for her.

"Gerald?!" Tammy smiled faintly. "He's not going to dump me, is he?" She added a tone of sarcasm to her voice, as if to suggest that the idea was unthinkable. In the end, it came out sounding insecure.

"No, no! Nothing like that," Jean cut in. "He's in the hospital."

"He is?" Tammy caught her breath. "What's wrong with him?"

"He was in a boating accident," Violet explained.

"How bad is he?"

"He's like, brain dead or in a coma—something like that." Jean shook her head. "I am not really sure which one it is, or what any of it means."

Tammy shook her head. "I really don't know, either. I mean, I've seen it in movies and stuff. I know that it means you sleep for a long time, but I don't understand more than that. Poor Gerald! I suppose I should go see him."

"He's in ICU. They have him on a ventilator," Jean said. "You know," she made a pointing motion toward her throat, "where they put that tube down your throat to make you breathe."

Tammy shuddered, "Ugh! That kind of stuff creeps me out. Maybe I'll wait. Right now, he wouldn't even know I was there. I'll send him a card, and then go see him when he's awake." Tammy was quiet for a moment, "I suppose that's pretty selfish of me not wanting to visit him till later."

"No!" Jean hissed. "Don't be silly! It's perfectly natural. Like you said, he wouldn't know the difference."

"She's right," Violet touched Tammy's shoulder, "it wouldn't help him. You're just going through a turbulent time right now. Things are going to be a little off-track for a while. You'll snap back."

"Yeah," Tammy said, gazing off in the distance, "I guess you're right."

Pulling the Plug

- I will always regret the ordeal that they suffered. –

"Your son is not in a coma," Dr. Baker said gently. "He is brain dead. The two are not the same. With a coma, there is still some measure of neurological function and a recovery is possible. Your son has no brain activity. There is no chance of recovery."

Christine wept quietly as she gazed down at the body of her son lying in the hospital bed. It seemed as if there were tubes and wires entering every inch of his body. Her husband stood next to her as Dr. Baker rambled through an explanation of "brain dead," and the tests that had been done to confirm it. She felt a desperate desire to yank out all the tubes and wires, then scoop up her son and run away with him. The doctor's voice faded into a distant drone. She didn't understand half of what he said, but she knew what it meant. Her son was gone, and he wasn't ever coming back.

"The insurance will only pay for a week in a case where there is no hope of recovery."

"Then I'll pay," John answered firmly. "I don't care what it costs."

"Yes, yes, of course; that is a natural reaction, and it is one that I would recommend, if there was any hope at all. mUnfortunately, there is none. You will bankrupt yourself, and in the end, the machines will still be shut down." Dr. Baker gestured toward the bed, "Look at him. Do you think he would want to go on like this? I promise you, it will only get worse from here. He'll

3

start to wither, and then will come the bed sores. His ligaments will draw up. It's your decision, but if this were my son . . . ."

"No," John answered, "he wouldn't want this. We'll give him a few days, but after that I think it is best that we . . . ." John swallowed hard, reluctant to speak the words, "just let him slip away naturally."

Christine slid off the bed and turned around to confront them. "I don't think so," she said with a hint of threat in her voice.

Dr. Baker put a hand up. "Let's try not to get emotional about this."

"Don't be emotional? Is that what you're asking?" She pointed back toward the bed. "My son is lying there, fighting for his life! You want to pull the plug on him, and then you ask me to not be emotional? What kind of person are you?"

"I'm just a doctor," he answered resolutely. "I'm offering my professional opinion on the available options."

"And you!" Christine turned toward her husband. "You're ready to go along with this? Your son is hanging over the edge of a cliff, and you're ready to just let go of the rope? I told you that you were bringing him in too close to the pier! I tried to shout back to Gerald, to warn him to be careful!"

John nodded, "That may have been what distracted him."

"If you want to make this my fault, that's fine; but you are not going to pull the plug on my son!"

Dr. Baker nodded, "There's no need to rush to make a decision. We have some time." He spoke slowly, so as not to provoke her ire again, "Please, just consider that your son has no active brain waves. He's not fighting for his life; he has already left. Sometimes, people try to hang on too long as a crutch for their own grieving. I'm going to leave now, so you can think about it and talk things over. Feel free to stay as long as you need to."

When Dr. Baker left the room, Christine went back to sitting on the bed and holding her son's hand. "There's nothing to talk about. They're not pulling the plug on my son. I don't care if we have to mortgage the house and sell everything we have!"

John nodded and plopped down into the chair with resignation. Over the next couple of hours the room was silent, except for the quiet beep of the heart monitor and the click and hiss of the respirator cycling through air exchanges.

Eventually, a nurse entered the room, "I'm sorry folks, but visiting hours are over."

"I am not visiting," Christine answered softly, "I'm staying."

John stood up, "Maybe it's best if we go."

"You go on and get some rest. I'll be okay. I'm staying with my son. He needs me now."

John made eye contact with the nurse, and she nodded her approval. He bent over and gently rubbed Christine's back, and then kissed her cheek. He stood up and sighed, took a long last look at his son, then walked slowly out of the room.

Red Red Wine

- Red Red Wine, It's up to you. All I can do, I've done. -

The stereo system played UB40's "Red Red Wine" softly in the background as Amy Roberson sat at her kitchen table. It was draped in a white cotton tablecloth with gold embroidery. Her hair and makeup were perfect. She lit the candle in front of the gold-framed engagement portrait, and then uncorked the bottle of red wine.

- I just thought that with time, thoughts of you would leave my mind. –

The lyrics echoed in her ears. She poured the rose-colored fluid into the crystal wedding goblet. This was the start of the hardest seven days of the year. They had married on the first anniversary of the day they met. Two years and one week after the wedding, he was dead.

- I was wrong, now I find. Just one thing helps me forget. Red Red Wine. –

She raised the chalice to her lips. They had met at an ice skating rink. A novice skater, she had gone to the rink on a lark, and he was on the university hockey team. He helped her around the rink as this song was playing. Afterward, he offered to buy her a bottle of wine and take her to Grant Park to see Buckingham Fountain. She took a drink of the heavy fluid. The ironic thing was that neither of them actually drank wine. Neither of them liked the taste of liquor. A year later they bought a bottle of red wine to commemorate the first anniversary of their chance meeting. He had promised that they would carry on the ritual every year for the rest of their lives.

Rabbit in a Bottle

- Red Red Wine, stay close to me. –

Seven days after their second anniversary she found him dead. She swallowed the wine, and then reached out to run her fingertips over the glass that covered the photo. After the funeral, she had left Chicago. She had gotten rid of almost everything, sending it all to churches and Goodwill. She drove to her new job in downstate Illinois with little more than the clothes on her back and the car she came in. As soon as she got established, she threw out the clothes and traded the car in for a newer model. Her old life in Chicago now seemed like a distant memory. Looking at the portrait was like gazing into a window to her past life.

- Don't let me be in love. –

She picked up the bottle and traced the edge of the foil label with her thumb. She was tempted to drink it dry in an attempt to numb herself, but on the day of the funeral, she had vowed that she wouldn't rely on a crutch. It was a bargain she had made with herself, that she wouldn't let the tragedy destroy her. Her old life in Chicago would die and be forgotten, so she could start a new life in a rural area. She'd had no family. When she left Chicago, she'd broken all ties with his family and everyone she knew. Perhaps they had forgotten her by now. She hoped that was the case. She had always felt a little bad for deserting them without notice, but it was something she had to do. The old Amy Roberson had died, and a new person had risen in her place and started a new life.

- It's tearing apart. My blue blue heart. –

Amy put the bottle down, and then picked up her glass to drink the last swallow. She leaned forward to blow out the flame, and watched the thin grey stream of smoke rise up from the wick. The end glowed like a small red coal. She gently blew on it, trying to keep it alive. It lasted a bit longer for her efforts, but ultimately it winked out and went black. She recorked the bottle and gathered up the glasses. She took a last look at the portrait. "Happy anniversary," she spoke aloud. She got up from the seat and tucked the picture under her arm. Time to put away the old memories for another year.

Life Signs

- I felt a little sorry for Dr. Baker. He was thrust into an unfair situation. –

Sunday night had come. Christine stared at the clock and mentally willed the hands to stop before the dreaded 9:00 deadline. She held her son's hand as she gazed into his face and wished she could see him without the corrugated plastic hose in his mouth. Signing the papers was the hardest thing she had ever done. In the end, she decided that the putting her son's poor body through any more pain would be selfishly clinging to a crutch. It was time to let go.

A few minutes later, Dr. Baker arrived with a nurse, "I'm sorry folks, but it's time."

"But," Christine said in a soft, sad voice, "there's five minutes left."

"I know; Nurse Richards and I need to prep him. Please say your goodbyes and step out. I will come and talk with you in the waiting room when it's over."

"We'd like to stay with him." Christine glanced up at the doctor. "We'd like to see him through it."

"That's not a good idea." Dr. Baker grimaced, "This can be an ugly transition. There can be gasping and writhing in the bed. It's noble to want to stay, but it's really better if you don't."

"No," John said unequivocally, "he never quit on me. I am not going to quit on him." He stood at the edge of the bed and gazed down at his son. "You do what you have to do, but I'm staying."

"I'm staying, too," Christine said quietly.

"Very well, then," Dr. Baker sighed then turned and nodded toward Nurse Richards, "Let's start shutting down the equipment."

"Wait!" Christine exclaimed. "He just squeezed my hand!"

Nurse Richards shook her head and stared down at the floor.

John turned enthusiastically toward the nurse, "That's good news, isn't it?"

Nurse Richards turned back to him with resignation. "He didn't squeeze her hand." She paused, "If he twitched, it would only be a muscle spasm. This sort of thing happens all the time. It can be very frustrating. People always get cold feet at the last second, and start hoping for a miracle."

Christine turned to Nurse Richards. "Maybe there's still a chance he could recover!"

Nurse Richards gave a courteous smile and turned away.

Dr. Baker leaned toward Christine. "Nurse Richards is right. If you felt something, it would have only been a twitch caused by a muscle spasm."

"No, it wasn't just a twitch! I know what I felt! I'm telling you, he squeezed my hand!"

Nurse Richards exchanged a glance with Dr. Baker.

Dr. Baker put a hand up. "Let's all take a step back and relax. Nurse Richards, why don't you get a cup of coffee and let me talk to these nice folks alone for a while."

Nurse Richards nodded and walked out of the room.

Dr. Baker put an arm on Christine's shoulde, Sometimes when people want something so very desperately badly they start to imagine things. The mind play tricks on us and the tiniest thing becomes exaggerated."

Gerald let out a low moan. Dr. Baker turned to Gerald in astonishment.

"Did you hear that?" John asked.

"Yes," Dr. Baker quickly moved to the head of the bed. "I heard it," he said, trying to understand the impossible. "There was no brain activity; I personally ran the tests twice." Dr. Baker took a small silver penlight from his white lab coat, pulled back each of Gerald's eyelids, and shined the beam into his pupils. He turned toward John, "Go get Nurse Richards!" John nodded and bolted out of the door. Dr. Baker shook his head in disbelief, "Mrs. Camden, I need you to step out, so I can get this ventilator out."

"You're not going to shut the machines off!"

"Your son doesn't need the machines. He's alive, and he's starting to wake up!"

The Playoff Game

- When football came back to Hutsonville, it did so with a vengeance. –

Hutsonville had not had a football team since the 1920s. Students would thumb through the photos of the team in the old yearbooks kept in the library, and wonder why the program had come to an end. A widely spread rumor claimed that the team was dissolved when a player's neck was broken. The legend held that the incident prompted the school to embrace a gentler sport by building a basketball gymnasium and burying the football uniforms beneath it.

Principal Hawk adamantly denied these rumors, but no one seemed to know the real reason. This was the first year a football team had been reinstated.

Game night in Hutsonville was a big event. The stands were packed with spectators, and it was largely attributed to one person. Watching Tyler Banks on the field was more like watching a ballet or an old Bruce Lee movie than a football game. Every time the ball was snapped, Tyler seemed to wait for the defensive line to close in on him, so that he could nimbly dance around them before firing off a pass with laser accuracy.

The football field was brightly lit with artificial light. The game was a real nail biter. Hutsonville was five points behind. They had the ball. It was fourth down with eighty-two yards to go.

Tyler was larger than average and stronger than most his age, but that was not what gave him his extraordinary skills. His dexterity and reflexes were without equal. When someone had once commented to him that he was "superhuman," he had countered with "unhuman." It had been a private joke.

Tyler glanced up at the clock as the ball was about to be snapped. There were only twelve seconds left to make up the eighty-two yards, or the Lawrenceville team would go to the Regional Championships game in their place. He peered into the intense faces of the Lawrenceville offensive line. Victory seemed to be within their grasp. Tyler felt a bit bad for them. Maybe it was a shameful thing to tantalize them with the prospect of a victory, only to yank it away at the end of the game. Unfortunately, the only other way for his team to win would have been a total blowout.

The ball was snapped. Tyler danced left and right, as if trying to find an open receiver. It was a façade. Even if someone was wide open, and his throw was deadly accurate, he couldn't be assured that the catch would be made. Since this was the last play, he could leave nothing to chance. He would have to run the ball himself.

The defensive ends came from both sides, and the safety came up the middle. They were trying for a blitz. Tyler shifted from side to side, but they had him hopelessly boxed in. At the last second, he ducked under a flailing arm and broke through. When he ran across the line of scrimmage, every spectator in the stands was on their feet. The rest of the defensive line left their guarding positions and moved in to converge on him. Tyler ran close to the nearest one and at the last minute, squatted and spun around, letting the tackler fall past him. He made sure that his knee stayed a good six inches above the turf. He couldn't afford a fudged call by a referee. Tyler sprang to his feet and ran full steam. The other tacklers had to step over their teammate to chase him. It only cost them half a second, but it was too long. Tyler bolted down the center.

Only two opponents were left between him and the goal line. They headed in from both corners of the field to cut him off. Tyler feigned left and then right, to keep them guessing which way he would go. At the last minute, when they were a foot away, Tyler broke left and leapt into the air, rotating his body. His opponent's fingernails lightly skated off the white number "20" on the back of his orange jersey. His body made a complete rotation, and he hit the ground running. He raced for the goal line as the last few seconds ticked down. When Tyler's foot touched the other side of the goal line, he slammed the football to the ground, and looked up to see the clock click over to zero.

The crowd made a deafening roar and broke into pandemonium. Spectators flooded onto the field in droves. The Hutsonville team lifted Tyler up on their shoulders and began chanting his name and shaking their fists in the air. Tyler pointed to his teammates and shouted, "Team! Team! Team!" at the top of his lungs, to be heard over the noise. He glanced over at Coach Geoff Pensyl who rubbed his sandy moustache and nodded, then held up one finger. Tyler smiled back and nodded as he held up one finger, as well. Then he rolled his hand over to give Coach Pensyl a thumbs up, "I got you, Coach; I got you," he thought to himself. "One more game to get to the state championships. No worries. We'll get there."

Awakening

- I remember waking up in the hospital. It was like being born. –

Gerald sat up in the bed and rubbed his face. He stared at the palm of his hand and tried to focus his eyes. He scanned the room and saw three people. In front was a stocky older man with dark gray hair, black plastic glasses, and a white lab coat with a stethoscope strung around his neck. Behind him was a couple. The man was tall and slender with light brown hair. Beside him was a lady with blue eyes and dark yellow hair. Why was she crying?

Gerald started to speak, but his throat ached.

"Go slow," the man in the white lab coat stepped forward. "Take your time." He poured a cup of water from the white Styrofoam pitcher on the bed table, "Have a drink."

"Where am I?" Gerald's voice sounded scratchy and hoarse.

"You're at Union Hospital in Terre Haute, Indiana. I'm Dr. Baker. You've had a bad spill, but you're going to be fine. Do you know how you got here?"

Gerald tried to remember, but his mind was empty. "No." He looked past the doctor at the couple who eyed him anxiously. "Who are they?"

Dr. Baker gestured toward the couple behind him, "Don't you know them?" The lady with the blonde hair wrung her hands.

"No."

Christine let out a whimper and covered her mouth with her hands.

Dr. Baker put a hand on her arm, "Relax; this may take a little time." He turned back to Gerald, "These are your parents, John and Christine Camden. Are you sure you don't remember them?"

"No, I'm sorry, but I really can't."

"Do you know your name?"

"No. There's just nothing."

"It's Gerald. Your name is Gerald Camden."

"Gerald Camden," he repeated back to the doctor. The name sounded foreign to him.

"That's okay. Don't try too hard; just wait for it to come back easily." He turned back toward the Camdens, "I'll let you spend some time with him, but please don't stay long. He needs to get some rest. With any luck, his memory will be back to normal when he wakes up tomorrow."

Dr. Baker left the room, and Christine rushed forward to caress her son's face, "We were so scared. We thought we had lost you!"

"It's okay now, Mom."

John stepped forward to lay a hand on Christine's shoulder, "Welcome back, Son."

"Thanks, Dad." Gerald still had no memory of these people, but he wanted to offer them a small bit of comfort.

The Locker Room

- Eddy Leach was something of a mystery. His father had a successful business, so he wasn't poor. He had his own little apartment above the shop. I'd never heard of him being abused or mistreated. What made him so mean? They say there is some good in everyone. If there was any good in Eddy, it would be hard to find it. –

Eddy wore only a t-shirt and underwear as he went through the locker room of the Lincoln Trail College pool. Technically, they were sleep pants. They would pass for boxer shorts, but they had the benefit of having pockets. He had purchased them for this very use. He moved down the aisle, opening each of the red painted metal doors. It was a flawless plan that he had crafted himself. If anyone caught him rifling through the clothes, all he had to do was start putting on the pants as if they were his own. Odds were, it wouldn't be the real owner. Even if it was, he would just explain that it was a mistake, apologize, and pass them over. It was perfect.

In Eddy's mind, it wasn't really stealing. Anyone who was careless with their belongings deserved to have them pilfered. They were asking for it. He was the one who came up with the plan, and he was doing the work to execute it, so it was only fair that he should be the one reap the profit. He fancied himself a Darwinian type of person. The strong and intelligent should thrive, while the weak and careless must pay for their negligence. It was simple, and it was fair. Eddy saw himself as an apex predator and was determined to stay at the top of the food chain.

Eddy knew this was small-time. At best, he would probably only make a few hundred dollars by running the lockers, but he did it anyway. It was a way of saluting his roots and maintaining the discipline of a true businessman. The money was there, waiting to be harvested and should not be neglected.

He yanked open the next locker door and hit pay dirt. A pair of unfaded jeans and an embroidered shirt lay heaped onto a pair of pointed-toe black boots with diamond stitching down the sides. "Cowboys," he silently mused, "so tough, and so stupid." Eddy gave a quick look around, and then fished the wallet out of the back of the pants. He combed his wavy sandy-colored hair back from his face and shook his head in disgust. The brown rawhide wallet had strips of leather stitched along the sides. This guy had to be an idiot. He would bet that the fool had never even been on a horse. So much for "Cowboys."

Eddy plucked out three Benjamins, along with some smaller bills, then tucked the wallet back into the pants and tossed them back into the locker. "My friend, you should have invested in a padlock," he quietly chided his unseen victim. "This time it's going to cost you. Stupidity is expensive, and I'm here to collect." He stuffed the bills in his pocket. "Time to get my pants and go," he muttered to himself as he shut and latched the painted metal door.

As he turned around he saw a young kid, maybe eleven or twelve, watching him from a few feet away.

The kid pointed a finger at Eddy, "I saw what you just did!" The voice attempted to sound authoritative, but it had a slight quiver, "Now, you put that money back right now," he pointed to the walkway leading to the pool, "or I'm going to go back in there and tell the lifeguard what I just saw." He concluded by putting his hands on his hips and glaring at Eddy.

Eddy paused and smiled a little. The kid had stones. He had blonde hair with blue eyes and was slightly pudgy. He made Eddy think of a little blonde Easter egg. Nonetheless, he was a problem. Eddy was a professional, though, and he had come prepared for problems. He reached out and grabbed a handful of the Easter Egg's hair, then walked him back a few steps to press his face against the side of the white painted concrete wall. He smoothly reached into his pocket and brought out the handle of a switchblade.

Eddy leaned close as he lifted the knife into the air and snapped open the blade, "What's your name, kid?"

"Tommy," the boy gasped, watching the gleaming blade from the corner of his eye.

"What's your last name, Tommy?"

"Feldon," he swallowed, "Tommy Feldon."

"Yeah," Eddy nodded, "I thought so. Tommy Feldon. I know who you are. I know where you live." Eddy paused to lick his lips, "Here's the deal, Tommy. I don't think you saw anything. And," Eddy gestured toward him with the knife, "that is a very lucky thing for you. Because if I thought you had seen something," Eddy traced the flat of the point in an arc along the kid's cheekbone, "then I would have to take this knife and pluck out one of your eyes."

"No," the boy stammered, "I didn't see anything!"

"Good, good." He lifted the knife away from his face. "Are your parents here, Tommy?"

"My mom is going to be coming. I'm supposed to meet her out front."

"I'll tell you what, Tommy. You seem like a decent kid, and I am a man of good faith. You forget you ever saw me, and you won't have a bit of trouble. Do you think you can do that for me, Tommy?"

"Yes! I never saw you!"

"Otherwise, I'm going to come to your house one night, and I'm going to slit your mother's throat while she sleeps. And then," Eddy hovered the point over his pupil, "I'm going to come in your room, Tommy. I will pluck out the eye you owe me and then feed it to my pit bull."

"No, I promise you," he gasped. I will never say anything!"

"Okay." Eddy let go of his hair and stood up straight. "When are you supposed to meet your mother?"

"I just go out front when I finish my laps."

"Are you on the swim team, Tommy?"

"Sort of," Tommy rubbed his hands nervously together as he talked.

"Sort of? What is that supposed to mean?"

"I'm an alternate."

"Do you like being an alternate, Tommy?"

"No, it sucks."

"Then why be one?"

"I need to shave three seconds off my time to make the team."

"How many laps did you do?"

"Five."

"Well, Mom is going to have to wait a little longer. Go back in and do three more laps."

"I'm tired," Tommy said pleadingly.

"Listen, kid!" Eddy leaned the point of the knife back in his direction. "You owe me an eye! I'm just asking for three laps."

"Okay."

"Well," Eddy tipped his head to the door, "get to it!"

The kid didn't hesitate to take his leave and hurried to the door.

"And you better do eight laps every time from now on," Eddy called after him, "and you better make the team; otherwise, you and I are going to talk again!"

Eddy pursed his lips in frustration. He yanked the locker open again, then stabbed his knife into the crotch of the cowboy's jeans and slashed outward. Lousy cowboy. Let him go home with no crotch in his pants. Eddy went to the other side of the locker room to retrieve his jeans and shoes and slid them on, then made his way out of the building. It had been a good day. He had taught some mechanical bull-riding fool a lesson; he helped a kid make the swim team; and he turned a tidy little profit for himself.

As he walked out the front of the building, he saw a blonde lady waiting in a pale blue Honda Accord. That had to be Easter Egg's mama. He smiled and waved. She smiled and waved back. It was a flirtatious gesture. He would have liked to have stopped and talked to her, but that would have been an amateur move. He wasn't going to break discipline just for her. First and foremost, he was a professional.

Amnesia

- It never made sense to me how someone with amnesia could remember things like how to speak English or how to tie their shoes laces but couldn't remember their own name. –

It was Monday morning, and Dr. Baker walked into Gerald's room. Gerald's parents stood up when he entered. "Good news!" Dr. Baker laid a folder full of papers on the edge of the bed. "You're getting out this morning."

Christine eyed her son. She seemed a little uncertain, "Are you sure he's okay?"

John beamed, then walked over and patted Gerald on the shoulder, "He's fine."

"Physically, he's fine," Dr. Baker qualified the description. "He has retrograde amnesia, which means his procedural memory is intact," Dr. Baker crossed one arm and lightly tweaked his chin, "but he is currently suffering from the loss of his declarative memories. There's not a lot we can do to help him at this point. All we can do now is wait for his declarative memory to recover."

Christine scrutinized her son for a moment and then folded her jacket over her arm and turned toward the doctor. "I don't understand anything about procedural and declarative memory."

Dr. Baker nodded, "Declarative memories are memories which store his personal experiences. Procedural memories are

15

memories which are not personal in nature. They're stored in a different area of the brain, and aren't normally affected by amnesia. Gerald obviously remembers how to speak English. He knows what a bird is, and that it can fly, but if he ever had a pet bird, he doesn't remember it. You can seat him at a keyboard and he may be able to type, but he won't remember any letters he's ever written."

"Do you think his memory will return?" John glanced back at the doctor.

"Oh, yes. I'm quite confident it will." Dr. Baker adjusted his glasses. "It's just hard to say how long it will take. With any luck, he'll start to recall bits and pieces of memories in a week or two."

Christine eyed Gerald with trepidation. Something was strange about him; he was different, somehow. The way he sat in the bed, the way he turned his head, his facial expressions when he spoke—somehow he seemed very unlike her son. "Something doesn't seem right about him," she said over her shoulder to the doctor. She put her hand on Gerald's forehead, trying to reassure herself that he was the same. "He feels a little warm."

"He's running a slight fever, but there doesn't seem to be any cause for it. He doesn't appear to have an infection. Check it from time to time. As long as it stays below one-hundred degrees, I don't think it's anything to be concerned about."

She laid her palm on his cheek. "If you're really sure he's ready. . . . "

Dr. Baker smiled.

Christine still felt troubled, as she slid his shirt and pants out of a bag and handed them to Gerald.

"If you folks will follow me," Dr. Baker motioned to the parents, "we'll let him get dressed while you sign some release papers." Dr. Baker gave Gerald a last look over his shoulder, "Good luck, Son. Try to take things easy for a while."

"Thanks," Gerald answered, "I will."

Breakfast in America

- Lori Taylor belonged to a typical upper middle class American family. Despite being so normal, they had their share of quirks. -

Lori leaned over the kitchen counter. She was a lean girl, slightly tall. Her shoulder length hair was brown with a slight curl.

Dr. Taylor sat at the table behind the morning newspaper that tented around his body. Occasionally, a hand emerged between the paper and the table to grab a piece of toast.

When the toaster popped two disks out of its slots, Lori gathered them up on a dish and sat at the table.

Dr. Taylor dipped the paper to peer over the top, "Hey, is that a toasted waffle?" He had dark brown hair and a plump face; on his lumpy, oversized nose he wore a pair of half-moon reading glasses to aid his round brown eyes.

"Yes." Lori smiled and glanced down at the plate in front of her.

"Well, give me some." He stuck his hand under the paper and waved his fingers as if to motion them forward.

"No. Go fix your own, Fat Man."

"Frozen waffles aren't on your diet, dear," his wife chided him.

"Listen to that young girl sassing her sweet father. That sure does make the palm of my hand itch, and you know when my palm itches, there's only one thing that helps."

"I'm too big to spank, Daddy."

"They always think that, right up to the time they get bent over that knee."

"Oh, Daddy, you're so full of it! You never even spanked me when I was little. Mama had to do it."

"I probably should have. Maybe that's where I went wrong."

Lori took a bite of her waffle and deliberately smacked her lips as she chewed it, "Uhhhhmmmm. This sure is good, Daddy. Too bad you're on a diet."

"Give me some of that, you brat!"

Lori grinned and lifted a waffle by the edge to dangle it in the air. She waved it at him to waft the aroma in his direction. Then she tore off a piece the size of a half-dollar and dropped it on his plate. "There. You can have that."

"Your generosity knows no bounds." He grabbed up the meager portion and flipped it up into his mouth.

"Mama, why don't boys like me?" Lori asked.

"Oh dear," Mrs. Taylor shook her head. "Here comes the 'Why don't boys like me' conversation."

"I'm serious, Mama." She shifted her weight and picked at her waffle, "I'm a senior now, and I've never been out on a date."

Dr. Taylor stuck his head up over his paper, "What's the big hurry to start going out on dates?"

"I was talking to my mother. Don't you have to go to work?"

Dr. Taylor smiled, "Sorry, there's nothing but cleanings all morning. My first appointment is a drill and fill at 10:30."

Lori scowled, "Terrific."

"Lori, if you start a conversation in his presence, then he has a right to join in."

"You're right." She turned back to her father, "I'm sorry Daddy," she said apologetically.

Dr. Taylor pointed sternly to his plate, "More waffle!"

Lori tore off another small hunk and lightly tossed it onto the dish.

"Your father is right. You don't need to be in a big hurry. Hutsonville is a small school. Each grade has about forty students. If half of those are boys, that doesn't leave a large pool to pick from."

"Other girls in the school have had boyfriends. Why not me? What's wrong with me?"

"Those girls may have boyfriends, but I doubt if many of them are in love. Most of them probably change boyfriends as often as they change underwear. That's not love. That's just some sort of adolescent game."

"So, how do I find love?"

"Finding love is like finding a box turtle."

"I don't think so, Mom. I've had a few box turtles, but I've never had a boyfriend."

"Sure it is. There are box turtles around, but the woods aren't thick with them. You can spend an entire summer doing nothing but searching for box turtles, and you will probably never see one. But if you just hang around for a while, you'll eventually stumble across one. Love is the same way. You can't find it by searching for it. You just have to wait for it to appear."

"It doesn't seem to be in a big hurry to show up."

"I didn't meet your father until I was in college. He was teaching an aerobics class."

Lori turned to her father, "You were an aerobics teacher?"

"Yes, your father was an aerobics teacher," he sniped back. "I made a little money and I got a discount on tuition for being a member of the faculty. Besides, in my day, I looked pretty good in a tank top and a pair of shorts."

Coming Home

- They sent me home that same day. Home to a place I'd never been before. No yesterdays behind me, you might say I was born again. –

Gerald walked up the brick steps to the front door of the house. He ran his fingertips over the thick, white glossy paint of the wooden door and touched the gold metal knocker. He scanned the long, narrow colored glass windows that ran down each side. He tried to make it come back; to make it fit, but it was completely foreign.

"Does any of this seem familiar, Son?" John asked.

Gerald shook his head.

Christine was quiet and leaned against the car while her husband unlocked the front door and opened it for Gerald.

"Take a look inside," his dad offered. "Maybe that will help."

Gerald walked through the front door and down the long, narrow brown rug that ran down the golden oak hardwood floor. He laid a hand on the end of the banister and tilted his head to peer up the staircase. He turned around and gazed up at the crystal bejeweled light fixture hanging above the dining room table. The house seemed warm and friendly, but it was not familiar.

"I'm sorry; it's just not coming to me."

"Don't worry about it." John suggested as he stepped next to him. "Let's go up to your room."

Gerald went up the steps and through the door. He walked over to the dresser and peered into the mirror. Something about seeing his reflection in the glass made him uncomfortable.

There were pictures on the dresser. He picked up one of himself and a girl with dark hair. He was wearing a suit, and she was wearing a formal gown. Why couldn't he remember?

Gerald walked over to the bed and pressed his hand into the mattress, as if to test the springs. He went to the window and pulled the curtain aside. The view looked out over the driveway. Everything seemed to scream "normal," but somehow it just didn't fit.

He flopped down on the bed and stared up at the ceiling. He looked over at the nightstand and saw a black remote with white buttons. He pressed a button. The silver disk in the CD player began to spin and music came through the speakers. He had never heard the song before, but he liked it. Gerald listened to the lyrics to try to understand their meaning. It was something about fire in the sky and coming home to the Rocky Mountains. He closed his eyes and tried to relax.

Chapter 2

Tuesday's Phoenix

The Hallway

- Going back to school was a little weird. It was like going to a new school and not knowing anyone, but everyone else already knew me. -

Gerald stood in front of his open locker going over his schedule. His first hour class was Advanced Algebra on the second floor. Tyler walked over to him and peered over his shoulder, "You've got Mrs. Roberson for English. You'll like her. She's cool."

"You're Tyler Banks."

"You remember me?" Tyler seemed surprised.

"No, but your picture is plastered all over the hallways. You're the star of the football team."

"Well, I don't know about being a star," Tyler shrugged, "but I've had some very good games. Hey, I know you're just getting acclimated, so if you need anything, just let me know. I'll keep an eye on you till you get back on your feet."

"Were we friends before?"

"Not really, no."

"Then why would you do this?"

"It could be that I'm just a nice guy, or it could also be because I was in a car wreck two years ago and lost my memory just like you."

"So which is it?"

"It's neither," he said in a quiet voice. "The fact is that your recovery wasn't about a miracle, it was about science. There are things you're going to need to know about your new life."

"What things?"

"I can't get into it here and now. I'll tell you what. There's a pool party tonight at the LTC natatorium for the football team. It's a celebration for us making the Regional Play-offs. Each team member can invite three guests, and I'm inviting you. Show up for that, and afterward we'll go see Dr. Gauge."

"I don't know a Dr. Gauge."

21

"Dr. Gauge is sort of a local celebrity. He's a biologist with an animal show that runs on Saturday afternoons."

"I haven't seen it."

"It doesn't matter. He's a genius, and we'll go see him after the party. For now, just know that he can help you, and that I am your friend. Actually," he hesitated, "I'm really more of a brother."

"Okay," Gerald answered, unsure of what he had meant by the comment.

Tyler smiled, "I need to runs some errands in town. Could you have your folks drop you off at the Robinson Library at 7:00 so I can pick you?"

"Yeah," Gerald nodded, "I can do that."

The first bell rang through the halls, and everyone started shuffling toward their classes.

"Good deal. I'll see you tonight. Think of me as your guide. Come to the pool party tonight. You'll have some fun. Later on, the doc will explain the rest."

Advanced Algebra

- I had dreaded returning to school, because I thought the studies would be difficult. It turned out to be much easier than I anticipated. -

Carl Leslie was a tall man. He was heavy but not obese. He always wore a suit and tie to school even though it wasn't required. The thick wavy hair that was stacked on his head wobbled as he scrawled numbers on the board at a frantic pace. He loved being a mathematical speed demon and demanded no less of his students. When Mr. Leslie came to the end of the equation, he wheeled around with the point of his marker pressed to the white board. At this point, it was a horse race.

He gave a faint grin as he watched the students silently move their lips and scrawl figures in their notebooks, desperately trying to keep up. He was a teacher of the gifted. He made the quick even quicker. For anyone who wasn't up to the challenge of his advanced algebra class, there was always the option of general math. He usually tried to weed out the ones who couldn't hack it by the end of the first quarter. Time was up. "Who has the answer? Kevin?"

Kevin Baud was the quickest in the class, but he was more cautious than most. "I think . . . ." he stretched out his words to buy himself a little more time to recheck the numbers.

"I need an answer, Kevin. If you don't know, I'll have to call on someone else."

"Is it 164 point 5?"

"Correct." Leslie scrawled the answer on the board and underlined it. "Did everyone get it?" He paused for only a moment. The slower third of the class was still straining at the numbers. They'd had long enough. If they couldn't get it in class, they would have to spend their own time during study hall. It was a good lesson. People needed to learn that they must do the extra work to compensate for their weaknesses. If they couldn't accept that hard truth, then they didn't belong in his class.

Leslie was about to start writing again, when he spied Gerald sitting in the corner. Gerald was fairly smart, but he wasn't quick. He should still be struggling to find the answer. Leslie was about to single him out but hesitated at the last moment. The kid had just been through a life-threatening boating accident. Since this was his first day back, he decided to grace him this round.

Leslie started scratching another long line of calculations across the board. This one was going to be a bit harder. He never worked with notes but kept all his equations in his head. It was a way of demonstrating what a gifted person could accomplish with a little hard work. Leslie stabbed two horizontal lines on the board to form an equals sign and wheeled around to survey the class. A new race was on, and everyone was working at trying to get there first. Who would it be this time? When he glanced at Gerald in the corner, he was once again casually sitting there as if he already knew the answer.

"Gerald," he called out in a loud voice, "You seem pretty comfortable back there. What's the answer?"

Gerald shrugged, "It's fifty-seven and three quarters."

Leslie paused for a moment. He'd had a clever spiel all prepared that would teach Gerald a lesson, but by some miracle the correct answer had spontaneously come out of his mouth. "That's right," he said, writing the answer at the end of the equation. "You weren't cheating off one of the better students were you?" Leslie knew this was not the case. Even his handpicked honor students hadn't had time to work it out."

"No," Gerald explained, "the answers are just coming to me."

"Well, I suppose even a blind squirrel finds a nut every once in a while. Maybe I will drive down to the Kentucky horse races this weekend and take you with me. We'll see if you have the same luck picking winners at the track."

The class sniggered. Gerald wasn't sure if it was a gesture of recognition for getting the right answer, or a way of laughing at him. Possibly, it was both.

Leslie checked his watch and then started to machine gun the board with his marker once again. This was the one that would separate the cream from the rest of the bucket. He came to the equals sign and wheeled around. All of his prize students were working the numbers, "Who's got it? Kevin?"

Kevin held up a finger of one hand, as he scratched figures on his paper with the other.

"Sorry, Kevin, but time and algebra wait for no man." Leslie eyeballed the room. "How about you, Eugene? What's the answer?"

Eugene Crummens had short-cropped blonde hair and green eyes. He was tall and muscular. At various times, people had tried to get him to participate in sports, but Eugene wasn't interested. He was an intellectual, and scholastics was his arena. He was hunkered over his paper, as he glanced back and forth from it to the white board, struggling to produce the answer.

"Come on, Eugene." Leslie checked his watch. "The class period is almost over." Leslie smiled as he watched Eugene wrestle. "Eugene, did I tell you I had lunch with a couple of Harvard math professors last week? They asked about you, but I told them your algebra was a little sluggish." Leslie chuckled to himself, "They seemed a little disappointed." Leslie surveyed the room and saw Gerald. Once again, he appeared to be coasting. "How about you Gerald? Do you think a person can get two winning lottery tickets in a row? What's the answer?"

"Thirty-two and two-thirds."

"Sorry," Leslie answered with a smile in his voice. "That is incorrect. It appears that your mathematical epiphany didn't last very long. I hear they have some empty seats down in general math, if you're interested."

Eugene slapped his pencil down on his desk, "Got it!"

Leslie mocked a fake recoil. "Oh, my!" he said with a wry grin. "Let me not be one to stand in the way of algebraic greatness. What's the answer, Eugene?"

"Forty-nine."

"Forty-nine is correct!" Leslie exclaimed jubilantly. "It's really too bad those Harvard math professors have already headed home." Leslie smiled. "For tomorrow, do the problems at the end of the chapter. If you need my help, I will be available during fifth hour study hall. Don't bother me outside that hour. If you can't make it during that time, then you're just out of luck." Leslie clapped his hands together, "If there are no questions—."

"Excuse me." Gerald pointed to the equation on the board. "Forty-nine isn't right. It's thirty-two and two-thirds."

Lori, who always sat in the front row, was one of the smartest students in school. She whipped her head around to give Gerald a disapproving stare.

"He's wrong," Gerald answered simply.

"He's never wrong," Lori hissed in a soft voice.

Gerald leaned forward and whispered back, "When someone is never wrong, it only means that other people are too intimidated to challenge him."

Leslie smirked, pretending not to hear the exchange, "Forty-nine is right. Work on it between now and fifth hour. If you haven't got it figured out by then, come and see me, and I'll help you with it."

"No, that's not right," Gerald insisted. "You can change the numbers on both sides, or you can change the ratio and one of the numbers, but you can't change all three. Forty-nine is wrong. It's thirty-two and two-thirds."

As Leslie leaned his head to the side and prepared to let Gerald have it, Kevin lifted his head from his paper and laid down his pencil, "Gerald's right. You can't change the ratio and both sides of the equation. Thirty-two and two-thirds is the correct answer."

Leslie turned toward Kevin. Leslie initially felt betrayed, but it passed quickly. He knew Kevin was not about loyalties. For him, it was all about getting the right answer.

When Leslie turned back to the board and went over the figures again, the sound of the bell rang through the hallways.

The class started to fold up their books.

"The bell does not dismiss you!" he scolded them. "I am the one who says when the class is over! Get back in your seats!"

Leslie went over the equation another time. "No, Kevin, that's not right. You see, after you find the least common denominator," he explained, pointing out key parts of the equation, "then you have to . . . ." Leslie paused; something wasn't adding up. "No. No. Just a second. That's not right." He went over the numbers a second and third time, trying to find some hidden answer. Mathematics had always been his friend. There had to be something he was missing. Finally, he walked up to the board and wrote "32 2/3" at the end of the equation. "Class dismissed."

Fifth Hour Study Hall

- Dr. Baker had told me that with a little practice I should remember how to read. He was right. I seemed to pick it up pretty fast. -

Gerald spent the period after lunch in the library. Mr. Leslie was perched at the end of a table working his way through the queue of students who needed his help. Leslie peeked over at Gerald, and they made brief eye contact before Leslie went back to his mentoring. Gerald walked to the magazine rack and picked up a copy of Popular Science. He paged through the magazine to an article on DNA. He read the first sentence fairly slowly. He went word by word, but at least he didn't have to sound out the letters to form the words. As he read, it got a little easier. He started to read by clusters of words, taking in the phrases. Then he started taking in whole sentences, by recognizing the sentence as an assembly of phrases. Finally, he started taking visual snapshots of each paragraph, and his mind would break it into the parts and digest it.

Gerald finished the article in a few minutes. He closed the magazine. He didn't remember reading in his previous life, but he couldn't imagine that it would have been this easy. He ran over the main points of the article in his mind. All the information came easily back to him.

Gerald walked over to the rack of encyclopedias and pulled out the volume labeled "A." He ran his hand over the first page of print as he digested the material. It was coming faster for him now. His mind felt like a long-forgotten muscle that longed for exercise. Gerald shook his head in amazement. He may have lost his memory, but he was going to be catching up fast.

Leslie was helping Lori with her homework, and glanced over at Gerald scanning the pages.

"What's he doing?" Lori asked him.

Leslie shrugged, "Looks to me like he's reading encyclopedias." He tapped her paper with the tip of his pencil, "Let's get back to it."

Current Events

- Every school should have a teacher as cool as Mrs. Roberson. -

Mrs. Roberson was young, as school teachers go. She moved around a lot in front of the white board, even when it wasn't necessary to make her point. Her large, reddish brown curls bounced off her shoulders as she paced back and forth. She was poised and well spoken. Her dark eyes and apple cheeks complemented her lecture as she spoke. She had a passion for her study, that Gerald couldn't grasp.

This seemed to be a blind spot in his newly found intellectual prowess. He tried to understand the purpose of haikus and iambic pentameters, but it seemed ridiculous. So what if someone decided that a poem should be three lines and the number of syllables should be five, seven, and five? What gave them the authority to dictate poetry structure to everyone else? And what was iambic pentameter? Couldn't you read any sort of text, and pause and accentuate wherever you wanted? Despite this, Mrs. Roberson fascinated him. It was ironic that she could seem so peppy and excited about something he found so boring and useless.

Eddy Leach sat in the back row, doodling in his notebook. He was only there for one reason. His father had told him that if he dropped out before he graduated; he would fire him and kick him out of the small apartment over the auto garage. This was going to be the third repeat of his senior year. His few friends had already graduated and moved on, leaving him even more of a loner than he had been before. Another long year stuck in this deadend school in a no-name town was nearly more than he could tolerate.

Near the end of the hour, Mrs. Roberson always opened the floor for current events. Anyone could bring up something that they had heard or seen in the media, and the rest of the students could comment and discuss as they liked. Eddy never participated but sulked in the back.

When the conversation wound down, Mrs. Roberson checked her watch. Five more minutes. She gazed about the room and noticed Eddy slouched in the corner. He never joined in.

"Eddy?" she called back to him. "Do you have any current events you would like to discuss?"

Eddy lifted his head and laid down his pen, "Yes. Yes, as a matter of fact, I do."

"Well," she beamed, "please share it with the class."

"I saw something in the news the other day. It was about another lady school teacher getting in trouble for having sex with underage male students. Did you hear about that?"

"Yes," Mrs. Roberson answered, "I heard about that. It happens."

"Well, it seems to me that it happens a lot. It seems like every time you turn on the news, there's a new story about it. This one was taking them up into the score booth during baseball games. She must have been desperate. All of these repressed school teachers, so uptight and nervous, once they spot a strapping young man not quite eighteen, they just can't seem to resist the temptation. Seems like it's an epidemic, and I was just wondering what you thought should be done about it."

"Well, Eddy," she leaned back to sit on the desk, and then crossed her arms as she composed a response. "You do hear about it happening now and then, but you have to remember those are a few teachers spread clear across the entire country. When you work the numbers, it's really a very small percentage. I wouldn't exactly call it an epidemic."

"Yeah, maybe so, maybe so," Eddy answered slowly, "but you never really know who might be the next one to give in to temptation and take the plunge." Eddy leered at her in a way that made her feel naked, "Have you ever felt tempted, Mrs. Roberson?"

Mrs. Roberson leaned forward slightly and rested her palms on either side of her desk, "Not that I recall, Eddy. You've been going to this high school for more than six years, and I am quite sure that your presence helps keep that thought from ever entering our minds. So you see, you having repeated your senior year over and over actually hasn't been a waste of everyone's time. In your own way, you actually add something of value."

The classroom cackled. Eddy seethed in a quiet rage. She was always picking on him. It was bad enough that he was stuck in this school, but even the faculty was against him. How could he be expected to graduate when he was obviously at a disadvantage?

The bell rang, and the class shuffled out the door, save for two students. Gerald hung around in the doorway, and Eddy approached the front.

Mrs. Roberson had already walked around the side of her desk and started erasing the whiteboard. When she turned, she was startled to see Eddy standing so close. She let out a quiet gasp.

"You think you're so clever for embarrassing me in front of the class like that."

"Well, Eddy, you sort of started it, you know."

"You called on me!"

"I did, but you were the one who chose the subject and tried to make a confrontation out of it. Sometimes when you start a battle, you get the worst end of it," she scooted her things together on the desktop, "but I'm sorry if I embarrassed you. Will there be anything else?"

"Yeah, that's a good thought about getting the worst end of battles. You have a little dog, don't you, Mrs. Roberson? Isn't it the same kind as Toto on the Wizard of Oz?"

"His name is Charlie. He's a Cairn Terrier. Toto was black. Charlie is blonde. What's your point?"

"I just think you should be careful with him. Don't let the little guy get out. Some vandals are mean and hurt little dogs like that. Or someone could accidentally run him over. Those things happen, and he could be gone," Eddy snapped his fingers. "just like that."

"1911." Mrs. Roberson answered calmly.

"What's that? The year you were born?"

"Colt 1911. My Daddy was a veteran, and he left me his service pistol. He also taught me how to use it. I'm a very good shot. I can put seven in a two-inch-diameter group at twenty-five yards." She raised her hand to peer through a ring made with her thumb and index finger. She extended her arm to bring the circle closer to Eddy's forehead, "What do you think, Eddy? If some creep threatens you or your family, are you justified in pumping a few rounds into him? A 45 is a lot of lead. I think it might burst somebody's skull open like a watermelon."

Eddy stepped back and pushed her hand to the side, "Are you threatening me?"

"Why, no, Eddy," she smiled sweetly, "I would never threaten you, any more than you would threaten my little dog, Charlie."

Eddy scowled, then turned and strode out of the room. He brushed his shoulder against Gerald as he walked out.

Gerald made a step back to keep his footing, and then walked farther into the room.

<u>Identity Crisis</u>

- I was instantly drawn to Mrs. Roberson. She seemed so intelligent and wise in the ways of the world yet happy and perky, I liked her immediately. –

Mrs. Roberson saw Gerald entering the room, "Is there something I can help you with, Gerald?"

"Hello, Mrs. Roberson."

"Hello, Gerald," she replied as she continued to gather her things on her desk. "What can I do for you?"

"I don't remember anybody." Gerald sounded a bit lost and confused. "I'm not sure who I can talk to."

"You can talk to me. What's on your mind?"

"Tyler says he wants to be friends. He invited me to the party at the college natatorium this evening."

"That's very nice of him."

"We were never friends before the accident. Why would he approach me, now? He says it's because he had a similar accident a couple of years ago."

Mrs. Roberson nodded, "I remember that; it was a car wreck. He's telling you the truth. Still, I can see what you're saying. It does seem a little strange for him to come forward like that." She hesitated to compose her thoughts. "I think you should go. It will give you a chance to reacclimate to the other kids, in a non-school setting. Tyler is a good kid; I wouldn't think he would have any sort of ulterior motive." She gestured to the door, "That one who just walked out, though—he's dangerous. Be careful of him."

"I don't understand. If he's so dangerous, why do you confront him?"

"I have to. The only thing that works on a bully is the fear of reprisal. You can't placate them; they'll only hurt you. You can't seek human kindness where it doesn't exist."

"Were we friends, Mrs. Roberson?"

Mrs. Roberson smiled and slung her purse over her shoulder, as she sat down on her desk, "Yes, Gerald, we were friends. I'm friends with all my students." She tossed her long reddish chestnut hair behind her shoulder, and her face grew thoughtful as she considered her response. She felt ashamed of herself for giving him such a clinical, pre-packaged answer, "That's not true. They aren't all my friends. Some of them, I would like to wring their necks, but a few of them are my friends.

Most of them are just part of the herd passing by. I'm sorry. To be truthful, I liked you fine, but you were one of the herd. However, I'm always willing to make a new friend." She smiled at him, happy with her new answer. "What's bothering you, Gerald?"

Gerald pursed his lips and tipped his head to the side, "I don't know who I am."

"Losing your memory has to be very stressful. I won't pretend to know what that's like. You don't know who you can trust."

"It's not just other people. It's me. I don't know if I'm a good person or a bad person. I don't know if I'm a wise guy, or the kind of person who sits quiet in a corner and lets other people talk. I have no way of knowing who I am, or who I'm supposed to be."

"Well, those are two different questions. Let's forget about who you're supposed to be. You're starting out with a clean slate, so there is no 'supposed to be.' As far as who you are, I think you're in a uniquely gifted position to find that out."

"What do you mean?"

"Consider me. I am Amy Roberson. I know how I feel about different ideas, who I like, who I don't like, and what's my favorite restaurant."

"Yeah, so?"

"How much of that is really me? How much of that is just patterns that I have established over the years? I walk down the hall and make idle chit-chat based on past conversations. I know people who have been my friends for many years. If I met them for the first time today, would I still like them? How about people I've never gotten along with? If I were to meet them with a fresh mind, maybe I would discover that they really aren't so bad. It's all habit, really. None of us really knows who we are, because we're just going through the motions. You have a chance to be free of those preconceived notions. It may be the best thing to come out of your situation."

Gerald nodded, "I guess I never thought of it that way."

"Whoever you are," she touched his chest with the tip of finger, "should come from inside you. Consider Tammy Wells and her little entourage." She waved her hand to the side, as if gesturing toward them. "They're like a little circle of pea hens that share one brain between them. Each of them tries to be exactly what the other two expect. One day, each of them will wake up and realize that they don't have an identity, and that they have never developed a sense of individuality."

"So, what do you think I should do to find my identity?"

"Nothing," she answered flatly. "Let it find you. People who try to establish a personality end up seeming pretentious and phony. If you force it, pretty soon you'll be walking around telling people about pork chops and applesauce." She spoke the last words in an imitation of Humphrey Bogart's voice.

Gerald smiled and shook his head.

"You know, the Brady Bunch?" she smiled back. "Peter was unhappy with his personality, so Mrs. Brady told him to adopt a new one. He picked Humphrey Bogart."

"I don't remember them."

"The point is, don't try too hard to be any particular person. Don't push yourself to generate reactions to the people and the situations around you. Just pull back a little and see how you react naturally. Eventually, the real you will come out, and you will find yourself. Losing your memory could actually be a very liberating thing."

"I used to have a Grandma, but I don't remember her. I don't mourn for her, but I also can't recall the times I spent with her."

Mrs. Roberson nodded slowly, "My husband died three years ago."

"I'm sorry," Gerald answered slowly. "I didn't know that. What happened to him?"

Mrs. Roberson glanced over at Gerald, and then turned to one side, as if gazing off into the distance. "I guess you could say it was from a brain hemorrhage," she turned back at Gerald. "but how he died is not important. The question is, would we be better off without the memory of the people we lost? Does the pain balance out with the good memories?"

"Does it?" Gerald asked slowly. "If you could, would you wipe away those memories, so that you could leave the pain behind?"

Mrs. Roberson was quiet for a moment, as she considered the prospect. "No," she said with a quiet conviction. "It is true that the good memories outweigh the pain of losing him, but actually, that's not all of it." She pointed as if gesturing toward an unseen hole in the wall, "That's my pain. It's a part of me. That's my hurt that is left from someone I loved. That is the missing piece that's never going to be replaced. That's the hole that he left, and I don't want it glossed over by some sloppy patch job. For good or for bad, that's my hurt. It belongs to me, and I think I will keep it." Mrs. Roberson wiped a small tear from the corner of her eye.

"I'm sorry."

"No, no; don't be," she pressed her face into a sad smile.

Gerald stepped forward, to give her a hug, but when he came near, he paused as he started to doubt if it would be appropriate.

Mrs. Roberson seemed to read his mind. She tipped her head to the side and gave him a knowing look, "You better get going," she reached out to give him a quick double pat on the shoulder. "We'll talk again another time."

As Gerald turned to leave, she watched him pass through the door, and then listened to his footsteps echo through the hall as he went down the stairs. Finally, she heard the sound of the brass rod being pressed against the wood as he opened the door to go out.

Mrs. Roberson gathered her things together. She fished her keys out of her purse and sighed, then nodded to herself and walked out the door.

Strange Dinner

- Dinner with the parents made for awkward conversation. They seemed like nice people, but I didn't know them. I didn't even know me. What could we possibly have to talk about? -

Gerald sat at the table with his new parents. He wanted to make some sort of conversation with them but couldn't think of anything to say. He remembered his English teacher's advice and decided to wait for something to come to him naturally, rather.

"We're having meatloaf, Gerald," Christine told him, "Do you like meatloaf?"

"I don't know," he answered.

"This is good meatloaf," John sliced off a slab and put it on his plate, "but fresh fried fish is better. Hey, Son, if you're feeling better, I thought sometime we might see about putting a line in the water."

"Do you mean fishing?" Gerald asked in a surprised voice.

"Of course, I mean fishing," John responded jovially. "You've always loved to fish. It's okay if you don't remember, because the truth is, you would always catch bigger fish than me. I think it's time we started building some new memories and getting things back to normal."

Gerald knitted his brow. "I know what fishing is, but I'm not sure I understand its purpose. You tie a line to a hook, then put bait on it and throw it into the water?"

"That's right," John nodded and took a bite of meatloaf. "Then you just wait for the fish to bite and reel him in."

"Isn't that a deception? You lead the fish to believe there's something good waiting for him when in fact it's a trick. The whole purpose is to get a barbed hook stuck in its mouth, then drag it to the shore and kill it."

"You have to kill it, Son," John gave him a smile. "Otherwise, he'll flop around on you when you try to eat him."

"It seems awfully barbaric. Not only do you kill it, but you rip open the side of its body and tear out the intestines and other internal organs."

"You can't leave the guts in," John shook his head. "They would taste pretty nasty."

"Why does that bother you, Gerald?" Christine asked slowly.

"I don't know." Gerald shrugged. "It just doesn't seem like it could be fun. Why would you sit and stare at a line in the water, wait for something to bite, then drag it onto the shore and rip out its insides."

"It's a lot of fun," John said dismissively. "Trust me, you'll love it once you get out there. The fish guts won't bother you."

"Could we have less talk about fish guts at the dinner table?" Christine smiled graciously, "That's a guy thing. I find it totally repulsive."

"Me too," Gerald agreed with her. He noticed she was taken aback by the comment. "I find it repulsive, as well."

Christine didn't answer but stared silently back at him.

After a moment of quiet, John decided to change the subject, "How was school today?"

"It was okay." Gerald wiped his mouth with a napkin, "I didn't know anybody. Some of them seemed to know me."

"Did you remake any friends?" John asked.

"Not a lot. I mostly kept a low profile. I got to know Tyler Banks, even though he said we weren't really friends before the accident."

"So you're getting to be friends with Tyler Banks?" John seemed impressed. "Wow! No kidding?"

Gerald was puzzled, "Do you know Tyler?"

John huffed and jabbed at his plate, "Everybody knows about Tyler. He's the local football star. After all that anxiety about restarting the football program, they struck gold the first year. You should see that kid play." John gazed off into the distance, as if watching a game. "It is uncanny, the way he moves and twists. I've never seen agility and reflexes like that, not even at the professional level. He makes the rest of them seem like a bunch of slow-moving buffoons." John rested his elbows on the table. "Anyhow, he puts butts in seats. People have been coming from all over just to watch him play. Coach Pensyl says that every university in the country has been trying to recruit him. One day, he's headed for the big leagues."

"He introduced himself to me," Gerald continued. "He seems to want to be friends. They're having a team party at the college swimming pool tonight, and he invited me to come."

"That's great!" John reached out to pat Gerald on the shoulder. "That will give you a chance to get to know the other kids, as well. I'm very happy for you, Son."

"That's nice that he invited you." Christine frowned. "Were you planning on going?"

"Sure," Gerald answered simply, "I thought going to the pool might be fun."

"I don't know . . . ." Christine said hesitantly. "You almost died from water skiing. Haven't we had enough water sports for a while?"

"Your mother's right, Son." John held up one finger in a cautionary gesture. "If you go, you have to promise to be very careful. We don't want any more accidents."

Gerald nodded, "I'll be careful."

"Accidents can happen even when people are careful." Christine shook her head, "Maybe we shouldn't press our luck." She eyed her husband. "I don't think it would be a good idea for him to go."

"Are you forbidding me to go?" Gerald looked back and forth between the two of them.

John cleared his throat. He shifted in his chair and glanced up at his wife, then turned back to Gerald, "No, I don't think we're going to forbid you to go. It's just that you gave us a pretty good scare. If you have to go, just try to be very careful. That's all we're asking."

"I will," Gerald nodded.

Christine glanced at Gerald and smiled, then turned back to her husband, and gave him a look only he would understand.

Gerald checked his watch and feigned a shortage of time. He didn't want to create an opportunity for them to change their minds. He hopped up from the table, "I'd better go upstairs and get ready. Thanks for dinner."

John asked, "What time do you go to the pool?"

Gerald paused at the bottom step of the staircase. "Tyler is going to pick me up at the library. If you could take me there, he'll give me a ride the rest of the way, then drop me back off at home when it's over."

John nodded, "I can do that."

Christine turned in her chair, "Why are you going to the library?"

"I want to study a little bit before I have to go."

Christine smiled, "What are you studying?"

Gerald paused as if he had been caught in a lie. He didn't feel comfortable explaining that he would be speed read more encyclopedias. "I just want to do some general studying. I have a lot to catch up on."

Christine smiled again and glanced over at her husband.

John shrugged and rolled his palms up. "That sounds fine to me."

Gerald headed up the stairs, "Just let me get a few things together, and I'll be ready to go."

When Gerald had gone up the stairs and was out of hearing distance, Christine turned toward her husband, "I'm worried about him."

John shrugged, "Let him have a chance to acclimate and fit in. We can't ask him to not participate just because you're worried he'll get hurt."

"That's not what I mean. Something is wrong with him."

John smiled, "You mean something other than he's had a near-death accident and is now recovering from amnesia?"

"It's not just the amnesia. I don't remember him ever going to the library to study before the accident. I went up to clean his room earlier today, but it was already immaculate."

"That's great. You're always scolding him to clean his room."

"I didn't have to scold him. I was giving him a free pass because of the accident. He did it on his own." Christine paused. Her husband just wasn't getting it. "Did you notice the way he sat upright at the table, without slouching?"

John shrugged, "Is good posture a problem?"

"Gerald always slouched. These days, his shirt is always tucked in. His shoelaces are tied. When he finishes brushing his teeth, he puts the cap back on the tooth paste. He hangs up his jacket when he comes in. Gerald was always sloppy about those sorts of things, and now to top it off, he's going to the library to study."

"All these complaints sound like good things. Maybe his brush with death has caused him to think about being more responsible."

Christine shook her head, "I don't think so. This behavior is not like our son."

"So, what's your point?"

Christine took a quick breath, "The point is, he's not really Gerald."

The Library

- I got more than I bargained for at the library. -

Lori Taylor pushed the heavily laden book cart ahead of her slender frame. Her job at the library was working out very well for her. She made a little money and had plenty of time to do her school work and study for the Scholastic Bowl. She picked up a tattered book and studied the binder, trying to decipher the faded printing. She knew the Dewey system by heart, but some of the older books were so worn, it wasn't always easy to figure out where they went.

Examining the raised book steered her line of vision to the corner next to the encyclopedia racks. The young man sitting at the table caught her gaze. He was reading encyclopedias again? What was with this guy? What did he hope to find in those encyclopedias that he couldn't find in the ones at school? Lori thought about her first day on the job, when the head librarian told her to keep an eye out for suspicious activity. She could use that as justification to go over and find out what he was up to. She walked over to satisfy her curiosity.

Gerald was so focused on his reading that he didn't notice her approach. She leaned over the table to rest the heels of her palms on the oak surface, "Hey."

Gerald lifted his head from his reading, "Yes?"

"What are you doing?"

"Uhm," Gerald was caught off guard, "I'm reading."

"Yes," she acknowledged, "I can see that. You're reading encyclopedias. I am in charge of the library when the head librarian is away. I'm supposed to keep an eye out for suspicious activity."

"Is reading not allowed in the library?" Gerald asked. He was mocking her, but was careful not to let it show in his face.

"Don't be a wise guy," Lori countered. "You're not taking any notes or composing a report. No one just reads an encyclopedia like a book."

Gerald rolled his palms up and smiled at her. "Evidently, you're wrong, because I do."

"You embarrassed Mr. Leslie today."

"That was not my intent."

"Sure it was. You caught him in a mistake and you weren't about to let it go."

Gerald scratched his forehead. "Do you think I was out of line?"

"Nah," Lori smiled. "he's my favorite teacher, but it doesn't hurt for him to be proven wrong for once in his life. It was actually a little refreshing since he likes to give everyone else a hard time."

Gerald smiled, "Do you think he'll hold a grudge?"

"He's not like that," Lori shook her head. "So why are you reading encyclopedias?"

"Maybe I'm studying to get on the Scholastic Bowl Team."

"You're an awful liar. You should either give it up or practice in a mirror."

"What makes you so sure I'm lying?"

"In the first place, it's written all over your face."

"Maybe you're wrong."

Lori sighed and tilted her head to the side as she scrutinized him. "This is your senior year. To get on the team at this point would require that you get Mrs. Branson to give you the entrance exam, which is very difficult to pass. Before Mrs. Branson can consider you, you have to be vetted and recommended by the captain of the team."

"What makes you think I'm not already in the process of doing that?"

"I'm the captain of the Scholastic Bowl Team."

"Oh."

"People always underestimate the Scholastic Bowl and what it takes to be on the team. You can't just show up in a library for a few days and breeze through a few encyclopedias. It takes years of grueling study."

"You never know." Gerald leaned back in his chair. "I have a really good memory."

"Do you, now?" Lori reached over to the shelf and plucked the volume labeled "N," then started thumbing through the pages. "Do you know anything about Napoleon?"

"A little."

"When was he born?"

"1769."

"Month and day?"

"August 15th."

"And when did he die?"

"May 5th, 1821. Aged 51 years." Gerald smiled. "He was defeated at Waterloo, by the way."

"Yes," Lori nodded and smiled, "I think I may have heard that somewhere."

"Tell me about his first campaign."

"His first Italian campaign?"

"Yes."

"It started on March 11th, 1796, two days after he got married." Gerald leaned forward to whisper, "I'll bet that didn't set too well with Mrs. Bonaparte. I wonder if she already had the locks changed by time he got back."

Loris smiled and put her hand over her mouth to keep from giggling, then closed the book.

"Well?" Gerald asked, "Are you going to recommend me?"

"Maybe." She slid the volume back on the shelf. "It's more than just knowledge. It takes a lot of dedication."

"I think I can be dedicated."

"I need more than that if I'm going to stick my neck out for you with Mrs. Branson. I need to be sure you're totally committed."

"I'm committed."

"Someone will have to groom you. You'll need a study partner."

"Do you have a study partner?"

"No, I always study alone." She paused as if to rethink her words, "But I could always use a study partner. It would mean we would be spending a lot of time together. Possibly two or three days a week." As she slid the encyclopedia back on the shelf, she watched him from the corner of her eye for a reaction.

"That sounds fine to me."

"Okay, the first thing we have to do is get you past Mrs. Branson. She's going to quiz you verbally before she gives you the test. Fortunately, I know some of the questions she likes to ask. Can you meet me in the cafeteria tomorrow at the start of lunch break? We can to go over a few of her choice topics so you'll be ready."

Gerald nodded, "I'll be there."

"Okay." Lori got up and started pushing the book cart. "I have to get back to work. I'll see you tomorrow at the start of lunch break." As she started to walk away, her head whipped around for a last comment, "And don't be late. I hate it when people are late. It's disrespectful."

Gerald smiled. "I won't be late," he called after her. He checked his watch. He had almost forgotten about the pool party. He quickly stood up and slid the volume back on the shelf. As he walked briskly to the door, he glanced down each aisle to scan for Lori. He saw her, but she had her face down into her book sorting, so he decided not to disturb her. He pressed the vertical silver square metal bar to open the library door and walked outside.

A few minutes later, Tyler pulled up in a red car with twin black racing stripes running down the hood. As Gerald got in, he noticed the new of new leather. "What kind of car is this?"

"It's a Shelby Mustang. I got it from a university in Montana."

"You mean they gave it to you for free?"

"In a manner of speaking. They have a great football program, and they're very well-funded. They offered me a brand new Shelby Mustang, just to come visit the school. An alumnus who owns a local Ford dealership put it up."

"Isn't that against the rules?"

"I guess it probably is," Tyler shrugged. "but all I did was fly out to Montana for a weekend and visit their school."

Gerald shook his head in disbelief, "And they gave you a car just for that?

Tyler smiled, "You've got to love football."

Pool Party

- Going to the pool party was the right choice. I got reacquainted with some people, and I found out more about myself. -

Lincoln Trail College was seven miles south of Hutsonville. The natatorium was occasionally rented out for special events. When Gerald entered the pool area, he saw Mrs. Ross sitting in a chair at the doorway of the locker room, making notes in her composition book. Her gray hair offset the gold chain loops that hung from the sides of her glasses. As Gerald came through, Mrs. Ross held out her arm to stop him. She put down her pen and picked up the three sheets of stapled papers that held the guest list. "Name?" she asked in a disinterested voice, without looking up.

"Gerald. My name is Gerald."

"Last name, please."

"Gerald Camden." Gerald was puzzled. Everyone else at the school seemed to know who he was. "Don't you know me? I'm the only Gerald in this school."

Mrs. Ross lifted her glasses from her face and let them drop to her chest, "Don't you sass me, young man," she barked through her discolored teeth. "Any more of your lip and I will throw you right out of here."

Gerald silently mused how a woman of her age might forcibly throw him out of the natatorium, "I'm sorry, Ma'am. I meant no disrespect. What is your name?"

Mrs. Ross was becoming angry, "You know my name. Don't test me young man; it will go badly for you."

"No, I really don't know your name. My memory is gone."

"Yes, I heard all about it." Mrs. Ross paused and scrutinized him. "I don't think you really have amnesia. I think you're just playing some sort of little game. Sooner or later, you're going to slip up and expose yourself. When that happens, you're going to regret you ever started this little charade."

"Yes, Ma'am."

"Hah!" she exclaimed triumphantly. "You are not on the list. You're going to have to leave."

At that moment, Tyler approached, "Hi, Mrs. Ross. Gerald is a guest of mine. Are you sure he's not on the list?"

Mrs. Ross folded her hands over the set of stapled papers, "I've checked the list, and he isn't on it. If you give me any trouble, I will have you thrown out too."

Coach Pensyl walked up and rubbed his golden mustache, "Is there a problem?"

"No, Coach Pensyl," Mrs. Ross answered curtly, "there is not a problem. I have this situation well in hand, so you may go on about your business."

Tyler turned toward Coach, "She says that Gerald's not on the list."

Coach Pensyl reached back to scratch his bald spot. "That's funny, I remember typing his name." He gestured toward the stapled sheets, "Mind if I take a peek?"

Mrs. Ross sighed and leaned back, retracting her hands from atop the list of names.

Coach Pensyl picked it up and scanned the first page. "Here it is, Mrs. Ross," he pointed out a line and held the page up for her approval. "It's at the start of the C's."

Mrs. Ross didn't trouble herself to turn her head, but reached up to accept the list back. "I am familiar with the layout of the alphabet, Coach Pensyl. You'd better tell these boys to show me some respect, or I will shut down this whole thing." She picked up her pen and resumed writing in her composition book. "Proceed," she said to Gerald in an annoyed tone.

As they walked down the side of the pool, Tyler spoke under his breath, "What a witch!"

Gerald smiled, "That wasn't exactly the word I had in mind."

"Easy, boys," Pensyl interjected. "Believe me, I know what you mean." He leaned forward so as not to be overheard, "That's the thing about little old ladies. Some of them turn into sweet grandmas, and others become vicious harpies. If she gives you any more trouble, come and get me. Don't fuss with her. It will only make things worse."

"We will, Coach," Tyler answered, "and thanks."

"No problem, boys," he replied, as he walked. "Have a good time." He peeled off to go join the assistant coach Bill Wineman and the other male teachers on the far side.

When they came to the edge of the pool and hopped in, Tyler draped his arms over the concrete side and spoke to Gerald in low voice, "One thing. It's very important. Don't go under the water."

"Why not?"

"Because artificial brain waves can't pass through water. Dr. Gauge is working on a secondary band, but he hasn't got it figured it out yet."

"What do you mean by artificial brain waves?"

"Dr. Gauge will explain all of that. For now, just be careful not to let your head go under. Don't dip your head at home when you take a tub bath, either. Stick to showers in case you forget. I'm serious; it could be fatal."

"I don't have a clue what you're talking about."

"Uh, oh." Tyler suddenly changed the subject, "Guess who's here." He pointed to the doorway of the locker rooms. "The Sisters showed up."

Tammy Wells sashayed her way along the strip that ran between the dive pool and the lap pool, flanked on each side by the other two sisters. The head of every male in the place tracked her as she walked. The half-red, half-white bikini top perfectly cupped her breasts. A large chrome ring gathered the front and held the two halves together. A thin spaghetti strap went over each shoulder. The bottom was a pair of red and white triangles in front, with a reverse set of triangles on the back. The sides were fastened together by a large chrome ring on either side of her hip.

"That is some swimsuit," Gerald muttered to himself as she walked along.

"Yeah, she always looks good." Tyler tipped his head toward Gerald, "She always wears red and white, too. It's sort of her trademark."

"I guess they were on the list."

Tyler nodded and smiled, "Oh yeah, I'm sure they had no trouble getting themselves invited."

As Tammy passed, she paused to glance at Gerald in the water and smiled, then went on.

"What was that all about?" Gerald asked.

"Ohhh, that's right. You don't remember her," Tyler suddenly realized. "That's your girlfriend."

"What?"

"That's her," Tyler paused, "or at least she was your girlfriend before your accident. I'm not really sure how it stands now."

"You're kidding, right?"

"Oh, no," Tyler shook his head, "I wouldn't kid about that."

"Oh." Gerald made a face of recognition. "I found a picture of her in my bedroom."

"A picture? What sort of picture? Can I see it? Did she have clothes on?"

"Not that sort of picture," Gerald laughed, "It was a portrait of her and me. I think it may have been taken at a dance or a party or something like that."

Tammy went to the low dive and walked to the end of the board. She made a quick bounce to spring into the air. Her body made a perfect arc, and then dove headfirst through the surface of the water, making only a minimal splash.

"Every guy in the school was chasing after her," Tyler mused, "but she picked you."

Gerald paused. Something bothered him about the way Tyler had said it. "What do you mean by being 'picked'? Is that how it works around here? Suppose you don't want to be picked?"

"My friend," Tyler chuckled, "there are worse things than gettng picked by Tammy Wells."

Tammy's face broke the water, and she started to swim to the ladder on the far side of the dive pool.

"Hang on," Tyler said with anticipation, "she's going to come out of the pool. It's a shame the water's not chilly."

As if in response to his request, Tammy climbed out of the pool, went to the spigot, and turned on the hose. She tipped her head back to rinse her hair with the chilly water. A moment later, she moved the hose to her upper chest to let the cold water wash down the front of her body. The coolness made her skin draw up.

Tyler's mouth drooped open and he let out a soft moan.

Tammy shut off the spigot, and then arched her back to let her hair dangle behind her. She raked her fingers through her heavy locks to help shake some of the water loose. The fabric of her saturated swim suit clung to her body as it shifted on her skin.

"Óh my," Tyler seemed enthralled. "That is some quality stuff there." He glanced over at Gerald, but only took his eyes off Tammy for a moment. "I would ask you if you ever managed to get any of that but unfortunately for both of us, you can't remember."

"Well, if my memory ever comes back, I will let you know."

"Your memory's not coming back."

"Dr. Baker said he thought it would."

"Dr. Baker is wrong."

"How can you be so sure?"

Tyler leaned over. "Dr. Gauge can explain it much better than I can. He'll answer all your questions."

About that time, a voice spoke up behind them, "Are you girls going to actually swim or something, or just stand around talking all day?"

Tyler and Gerald turned to see some guys from the offensive line of the football team. One of them held a small inflatable ball, "Are we going to play some water ball or not?"

"Sure, sure, relax Chalon." Tyler gestured toward Gerald, "You guys already know Gerald, but he doesn't remember you, so this is going to be sort of a one-way introduction." He pointed toward the tallest guy, with auburn hair, "This is Ray; he's the center on the basketball team. In football, he plays fullback." He pointed to a slightly shorter, stockier guy with strawberry blonde hair and freckles, "This is Scott; his main sport is baseball, but he plays halfback on the football team." He motioned to the last guy, with chestnut colored hair, "And that's Randy; he's good at just about anything."

They offered for Gerald to participate, but he declined. He wanted some time to think, and he wasn't quite sure he was ready to be melded into a group. He sat on the edge of the deeper end of the lap pool and let his feet hang in the water.

Eddy Leach made his entrance at the locker room doorway and scanned the pool area. He was wearing leather sandals, ragged blue jean cutoffs, and a faded yellow tank top. Mrs. Ross stood up to intercept him, but he easily brushed past her.

Gerald was perched on the edge, and had his back to the strip between the two pools. He didn't see Eddy saunter past. Everyone else gave Eddy a wide berth. When he saw Gerald sitting along the edge, Eddy became annoyed that Gerald hadn't noticed him. He put the sole of his sandal on Gerald's back and shoved him off into the water. Gerald's head dipped under the surface, and his world went dark.

Along the opposite wall, Coach Pensyl was talking with assistant coach Bill Wineman and a couple of the other male faculty members. He spied Eddy and tapped his colleague on the shoulder with the back of his hand. They got up and walked over to meet him on the strip. "You're not invited, Eddy," Coach Pensyl spoke up, "and even if you were, you can't come in the pool area with shoes and street clothes on."

"I'm not hurting anything."

"Those are the rules, Eddy."

"Oh, yeah? And who makes up these rules? You?"

"The college. They were good enough to allow us use of the pool, and we have to respect their rules."

"I'm just here to see who showed up."

"Just members of the team and their invited guests. If you wanted to participate, then you should have tried out for the team."

"I don't want to participate."

"Then you need to leave. Go right now."

Eddy huffed and turned to go. Mrs. Ross was standing defiantly by the doorway. She had one hand cocked on her hip and the other pointed sternly to the locker room.

As Eddy passed her, he paused for a moment to smirk at her. He flicked the chain hanging from her glasses with the back of his fingernails, and then went on.

Coach Pensyl and the rest of the faculty heaved a sigh of relief.

Like everyone else, Tyler had been watching the exchange between Eddy and the faculty. Turning around, he saw a figure at the bottom of the lap pool.

"Ray!" He put a hand on his teammate's shoulder, "Gerald's at the bottom of the pool; he can't swim."

Ray shrugged and smiled, "What do you mean? The water is only five feet deep."

"I'm telling you, he's in trouble."

"He'll be fine."

"He's drowning!"

"How can he be drowning, if the water isn't even over his head? He's your friend. If you really think he's in trouble, then why don't you go fish him out?"

"I can't. Please Ray, go get him!"

Ray scowled and dove off the edge. He grabbed Gerald's limp form and pulled his head above the surface, "I don't think he's breathing." He passed a shoulder up toward the other team members, and they pulled him up onto the white concrete deck.

They circled around him, "He's not breathing. Somebody needs to give him artificial resuscitation."

The members of the football team paced nervously and began to mutter things like, "Mouth to mouth? No way," and "I'm not doing it," and "You can forget it."

Tammy pressed her way through them and knelt over Gerald. She put her mouth on his and blew air into his lungs. She lifted her face long enough for the air to come out. She blew into his mouth again. Gerald coughed and sputtered. Tammy cradled his head and gently turned his face to one side. Gerald gasped a few more times, and then started to come around.

Coach Pensyl pushed his way through the circle of standing bodies to kneel next to Gerald, "Are you okay?"

Gerald wiped some of the fluid from his face, "I think so."

Coach Pensyl took out his cell phone. "I'm going to call 911."

Gerald held up his hand. "No, I'm okay." He got to his feet. "Really, I'm fine. He just knocked the wind out of me, that's all."

Coach Pensyl held up his phone and then turned back to Gerald. "Are you sure?"

"Yes," Gerald insisted, "I'm fine."

Tyler offered his hand to help Tammy to her feet.

Gerald turned toward Tammy. "Thanks," he said quietly.

"Happy to be of service," Tammy smiled. "Call me sometime."

"Come on, I'll give you a lift home." Tyler tipped his head toward the locker room. "It's about over, anyway."

Gerald nodded and followed Tyler back to the locker room.

Mrs. Ross frowned at them disapprovingly, "I knew this was a bad idea! I told them that from the start."

Tyler's well of never-ending patience suddenly ran dry, "Then maybe you shouldn't have come, Mrs. Ross. No one asked you to guard the door; you volunteered. The one person you should have kept out, you let waltz right in."

Mrs. Ross' eyes blazed, "So insolent and so arrogant! You're just a couple years from obscurity. Once your glory days of high school sports are past, you'll be dumped into the real world. After such a cushy berth, you'll probably end up unemployed or in jail."

"Maybe so, but I think that in about that same time, you'll end up a spiteful old woman in a rest home, with no visitors because she's full of anger and bitterness."

Mrs. Ross was too taken aback to come up with a response. Tyler and Gerald left through the locker room doorway.

The Laboratory

- Tyler had mentioned that we were "brothers. "That evening, I learned the meaning behind his words. -

The Sycamore Building was a few blocks east of the courthouse. It was a tall, slender structure, twelve stories high. It loomed over the surrounding buildings of Terre Haute like a lone red brick needle pointing toward the sky. Tyler parked the car along Sixth Street, and they walked across the sidewalk to the front door.

Tyler keyed the access code into the box mounted on the column between the two sets of doors. "Dr. Gauge knows we're coming. He'll probably give you an access code, too."

"Why would I need one?"

"'Because you're going to need to come back here regularly."

Gerald decided not ask why and followed him onto the elevator. As it traveled upward, Tyler continued, "What you're going to hear may sound very strange, but just try to have an open mind."

The doors opened, and Dr. Gauge stood there to greet them. He was a slender man. He had a very round head with pointed chin and blonde wispy hair. His blue eyes peered out over his wire frame glasses, as if eyeing Gerald for some reaction. "Come in, come in," he said, as he beckoned him into the room. He reached out to shake Gerald's hand, "I am Dr. Martin Gauge."

It was a laboratory of sorts, with various pieces of electronic equipment scattered about and mounted along the walls. Running through the center of the room was a glossy black counter equipped with sinks and Bunsen burners. Dr. Gauge hooked the leg of a stool with the toe of his shoe and pulled it under himself. When Tyler took a seat on the other side of the counter, Gerald did the same.

"Gerald, you are alive today because of an experimental genetic process that was used to revive you. Unfortunately, a side effect of that process is that you have amnesia. Have you ever heard of neural oscillation?"

"I think I read something about it. Isn't that the same thing as brainwaves?"

"Yes," Dr. Gauge smiled. "Brainwaves is the more common term. A man named Hans Berger first studied alpha brainwaves in the early 1900s. Since Dr. Berger's original studies, more and more frequencies have gradually been discovered. A few years ago, we learned that the brain not only generates brainwaves, but can be affected by them as well."

Dr. Gauge pulled a white screen down in front of the blackboard and turned on an overhead projector. "It's all in the DNA. The DNA contains not only the instructions for building the body; it also contains the genetic signature for the mind. No two signatures are the same." He took out a laser pointer and highlighted areas of the screen. "This is your genetic signature, Gerald. Think of it like a setting on a radio for operating at a certain frequency."

"And my brain can only generate brainwaves for this signature?"

"Not anymore." Dr. Gauge turned away from the white screen to face Gerald. "Unfortunately, your brain is dead and can no longer generate brainwaves on its own. This type of damage can never be repaired. When this happens, a person is normally considered to be dead."

"Then how can I be standing here now?"

"Your brain can no longer generate brain waves, but it can still be influenced by them as long as they match your genetic signature. It is a bit of a paradox. Your brain will only recognize its own signature, but no other brain generates brainwaves with that same signature." Dr. Gauge placed a second transparency next to the first. "This is the natural signature of the brainwaves that are keeping you alive."

Gerald leaned forward. Dr. Gauge took the transparencies off the projector, laid one over the other, held them up to the light, and then passed them over to Gerald.

Gerald took a look then slid them apart to study them side-by-side, "They're not the same."

Dr. Gauge adjusted his wire gold rimmed glasses and continued. "Once we discovered the genetic signatures for brainwaves we began experimenting with animals."

"We?" Gerald asked. "Are there are other scientists working with you?"

"I am the only one at this location but I am in frequent contact with several of my colleagues. With the era of modern communication, many genetic scientists have gone into private study. It is often more productive for each of us to have our own facility and work remotely."

Gerald nodded. "I suppose that makes sense."

"We started by creating artificial brainwaves from scratch. When we resonated them off brain dead animals, it restored some of their synaptic activity."

"Only some?"

"Yes," Dr. Gauge confirmed. "Unfortunately there is still a great deal that we don't know about brainwaves. The ones we created were only able to trigger a low level of brain activity. Test subjects would have assorted twitches and muscles spasm but none were restored to full functioning capability. To accommodate for our lack of knowledge, we began bleeding brainwaves off of donor animals instead. With this technique we only had to remap the genetic signature of already existing brainwaves."

"And this worked?" Gerald asked.

"It worked, but there were minor complications." Dr. Gauge leaned his head to the side. "Some years ago, there was a pet store called 'Atlantis' that was a couple of miles north east of here. It was known for its exotic animals. They kept a pet lion penned in back."

"I think I've heard somebody mention it." Gerald answered. "Didn't it burn a few years ago?"

"Yes," Dr. Gauge leaned against the counter, "that's the place. A year or two before it burned, the lion got out of its pen and was hit by a car. It went into a coma for a short time. While the lion was unconscious, I got its genetic signature from a blood sample that I took from the street pavement. With it, I was able to use the lion as a host for a link with a donor animal."

"What animal?" Gerald asked, trying to digest the information.

"A hamster as a matter of fact."

"A hamster?" Gerald cocked his head skeptically.

"Yes." Dr. Gauge leaned back against the counter that ran along the wall. "A difference in species does not seem to be an inhibiting factor. There seemed to be no major side effects but there were a few peculiarities."

Tyler laughed out loud, "Tell him about the little dog, Doc." He turned back to Gerald, "You're not going to believe this."

Dr. Gauge smiled, "Let me say in my own defense that the accident came about unexpectedly, and I had to use whatever specimen that I had readily available."

"So get this," Tyler chortled as he talked. "This big, huge lion is roaming around his cage, and everyone thinks he is back to normal, except he wouldn't eat. One day, this lady comes along with this little Pekinese dog, and this huge lion freaks out and runs to the far side of the cage and tries to claw its way out."

"The lion thought the dog was a threat," Dr. Gauge shifted his glasses.

"Is it because the lion had taken on the consciousness of the hamster?" Gerald asked.

"That would imply some transfer of memories from the donor to the host. We have not seen that happen in any other cases."

"Of course the lion thought it was a hamster. The doc just doesn't want to believe it." Tyler pointed to Dr. Gauge with his thumb, "It wouldn't eat meat and why else would a lion be afraid of a small dog?"

"A newborn lion cub might have had those very same reactions," Dr. Guage shook his head dimissively.

"What happened to the lion?" Gerald asked.

"When it recovered from the coma, I terminated the artificial brainwaves and it returned to normal. This is a science that is still in its infancy. Our knowledge expands by trial and error. If you give enough chimps enough typewriters, eventually they will write you a sonnet. Progress is slow and tedious. It is impossible to get detailed feedback from an animal."

"For that, you needed a human subject."

"Yes of course," Dr. Gauge replied, "Once we found success with reviving animal hosts it was only a matter of time before we would use the process to help people as well."

"Isn't that unethical?" Gerald pointed out.

"I only use human hosts who are already brain dead. In 1982 Barney Clark was dying when he received the first artificial heart. It bought him a little more time and he was instrumental in advancing coronary science. What we are doing here is much less invasive, but it is basically the same principle. You would never do it with someone who is healthy, but what does a dying person have to lose?"

"Nothing, I suppose." Gerald answered slowly, "I was revived minutes before they shut off the machines that were keeping me alive."

"That timing was deliberate." Dr. Gauge pointed out.

"So you helped me to recover and now you have your first human subject."

"You're not the first. Two years ago, Tyler was in an auto accident, and his injuries left him brain dead. I intervened, and as a result, he is with us to this day."

Gerald turned to Tyler. "Now I understand what you meant when you said we were brothers."

Dr. Guage continued, "There are precious few opportunities to work with humans. I must seize them as they arise. With Tyler we learned that there can be a beneficial side effect to the relay. The stimulus helps the brains synapses to respond quicker, thereby improving his reflexes." Dr. Gauge bent forward anxiously, "Tell me, have you experienced any sort of advanced dexterity or agility?"

"No," Gerald answered thoughtfully, "not that I have noticed."

"Well, we can't all be the star of the local football team, driving around in new sport cars." Dr. Gauge gave a quick glance to Tyler, who shrugged and beamed at being recognized. "How about ease of learning, memory retention, that sort of thing?"

"Yes, I have." Gerald answered thoughtfully. "We were given some problems in Algebra that seemed to come very easily for me. Then later, I was speed-reading through encyclopedias in the library and my retention seemed to be greatly enhanced."

"Good, good," Dr. Guage smiled. "Your stimulated brain is functioning at a higher level than it once did. A normal brain has to do the work of generating its brainwaves, whereas yours is getting a push. Your mind has become like an overclocked computer chip. You may have noticed a slightly elevated body temperature as well, but with a few minor limitations, you should be able to function quite normally."

"What limitations?"

Dr. Gauge shrugged. "Artificial brainwaves can't penetrate water. Being caught in the rain or taking a shower is no problem, but it is important that your head never becomes submerged."

"He's already found out about that at the pool," Tyler interjected.

Dr. Gauge turned toward Tyler, "I asked you to warn him before he went in."

"I did. Someone pushed him into the water."

Dr. Gauge turned back to Gerald. "You must understand the need for caution. Your brain has become like a heart that requires a pacemaker to keep beating. For the rest of your life, your mental processes will rely on your brain resonating from artificial brainwaves that are generated from outside your body. If this stimulus is cut off, your brain will once again lose its synaptic activity."

"And you create these brainwaves?"

"I capture them, I remap the signature and send them back out through a transmitter."

"You've built a transmitter that generates artificial brainwaves?"

"It wouldn't be fair to say that I built it. There has been a large amount of brainwave detecting equipment available for many years. I just took already existing devices and modified them to fit my own needs."

"How far is the range?"

"As a matter of fact, we have yet to discover any limits to their distance."

"He's right," Tyler offered. "I went to Hawaii last year and there was a slight lag, but other than that, I didn't have any trouble."

"A lag?" Gerald asked.

"Yeah, you know a lag," Tyler explained, "There was a slight delay like a slow telephone connection going through the internet. I explained it away by telling them I was just tired."

"I told him not to go," Dr. Gauge chided, "but he didn't listen."

"It was a trip to Hawaii," Tyler countered, "and because I went, you found out that the range was unlimited."

"No," Dr. Gauge answered slowly, "I found out that it extends as far as Hawaii." Dr. Gauge sighed, "This is why I like animals better." Dr. Gauge smiled. "I think it's time we showed Gerald the mouse."

"Are you guys about to tell me that I'm hooked up to a mouse?"

"Not exactly," Dr. Gauge he went to the end of the room and lifted the shroud off a bell jar. Inside, a gray mouse was lying on its side. Wires ran to tiny electrodes mounted to its skull.

Tyler pointed at it and peered over at Gerald. "This mouse keeps me alive."

Dr. Gauge nodded to a sofa along the wall. "Tyler, if you would have a seat, please."

Tyler sat down and took a deep breath, then tipped his head back. "I'm ready."

When Dr. Gauge threw a switch on the console, Tyler gasped as his eyes rolled up and his head tipped back.

Gerald leaned over his friend and placed a hand over Tyler's mouth, "I don't think he's breathing!"

"No, he's not, but he'll be fine. It's only for a moment." Dr. Gauge motioned Gerald toward the bell jar, "Look at the mouse."

Gerald stepped up to the bell jar. The mouse inside had begun to paw the air and turn its head as if trying to right itself.

Dr. Gauge toggled the switch, and the mouse slumped. Tyler gasped a breath and sat up, "Wow, even after these last two years, that is still freaky."

Gerald leaned over his friend. "What was it like?"

"It's sort of like dropping a candle down a dark well. Only," Tyler stood up from the couch, "you're the candle."

Dr. Gauge placed the shroud back over the bell jar containing the mouse. "Gerald, I am going to give you an access code to get in this building. You can come and go as you like. Tyler has some workout clothes and weight equipment on the ninth floor. You are welcome to share that floor with him if you like. I will need for you to come back here every few days so I can get a fresh DNA sample."

"But you already have that."

"Artificial waves need occasional tuning. I need to monitor for drift. Also, I watch for genetic mutations and changes in bodily enzymes. After a month or two, the visits will become less frequent."

Gerald took a deep breath and looked at another shrouded object next to the bell jar that held the mouse. "Is that my jar?"

"Yes it is," Dr. Gauge confirmed.

"Are you sure you're ready?" Tyler asked. "That first look can be a bit of a shock."

Dr. Gauge motioned toward the end of the lab table. "Lift the cowl, if you want to see."

Gerald lifted the cover and set it aside. Under the jar was a hairless rabbit lying on its side. A feeding tube ran down its throat. Tiny wires were attached to small electrodes mounted in its skull.

"Is that a rabbit?"

"Yes," Dr. Gauge rested his hands in the pockets of his lab coat, "that's a rabbit."

"That's what keeps you alive, buddy." Tyler gave him a sidelong look.

Gerald stared down into the jar, trying to come to terms with the idea. "Why doesn't it have any fur?"

"That comes from a very simple genetic manipulation." Dr. Gauge checked some of the equipment along the wall. "The lack of fur makes the placement of the monitoring equipment easier."

"But the mouse has fur."

Tyler gave Gerald a nudge with his shoulder, "That's because mice are manlier."

"I haven't found the right genetic combination for making mice hairless. I stumbled across it early on in rabbits. Advances in genetics come slowly, and finding the genetic combination for hairlessness in mice is not a priority."

Suddenly, a different concern popped into Gerald's head, "How long do rabbits live?"

"Rabbits normally live about twelve years."

"Why couldn't you have hooked me up to something that lives longer, like a turtle or something?"

"The DNA is too different," Dr. Gauge explained,. "but don't worry. I can increase its longevity with the proper diet and a few genetic alterations. There is no reason why you shouldn't be able to enjoy a normal human life span"

Gerald turned away from the bell jar and made eye contact with Dr. Gauge, "I don't mean any disrespect. You bring me here and tell me my brain is wired to a rabbit. It's just too . . . ." Gerald paused.

"Of course," Dr. Gauge answered reassuringly, "it is important that you believe. Please have a seat on the couch."

"Now, wait just a minute."

"It's a little weird but it doesn't hurt," Tyler offered.

Gerald sat on the coach and laid his palms on the top of his thighs. He took a deep breath. "I'm ready," he said with resignation.

"Tip your head back. Your body is going to go limp and I don't want you to roll forward and spill out on the floor."

As Gerald leaned back in the sofa, Dr. Gauge threw the master switch. The room was split asunder as Gerald's mind was sucked into a vortex. His soul raced through a long worm hole and vanished into a brilliant white light.

Under the bell jar, the rabbit began to stir and try to lift its head. A moment later, Dr. Gauge threw the switch again. Gerald was yanked back through the ether and found himself sitting on the sofa, gasping for a quick breath.

"Do you remember anything?" Dr. asked anxiously. "Any sort of visions or feelings of consciousness?"

"No. There was nothing. It was as if I dissolved and reformed again."

"No matter," Dr. Gauge said, with a hint of disappointment. "This is how we learn, inch by inch." He smiled, "At least you know now that we are telling you the truth."

"Yes," Gerald nodded, "I believe it now."

The Convenience Store

- I guess I just needed some time to sort it all out. It is not an easy thing to realize that your whole existence is just the result of some genetic tinkering. -

Gerald was silent during the return trip from Terre Haute. Tyler occasionally glanced over as he drove. Perhaps it was better to let it rest and give his friend a chance to digest the news. Tyler thought back to when Dr. Gauge first showed him the mouse. It had been quite a surprise, but he didn't remember being as troubled as Gerald seemed to be.

As they crossed the bridge over the Wabash River and rolled into Hutsonville, Gerald finally spoke, "Can you just drop me by the convenience store? I'll make my way home from there."

"I can wait for you, if you need to get something."

"No," Gerald said quietly, "I just need some air."

"It's almost midnight. Tomorrow's a school day."

"I know. I just need a little time alone."

Tyler pulled the Mustang into the drive and rolled into the gas lane. The reflections from the lights overhead ran across the glossy clear coat of the red paint on the car hood. He stopped in front of the door, and Gerald stepped out.

"Thanks, Tyler."

"Hey," Tyler called out to be heard over the soft rumbling of the high-performance engine, "just take things slow. Everything will work itself out." Tyler paused. He wasn't much for gentle conversations, "Give it some time."

"I'll be fine," Gerald smiled and gave a small wave.

Tyler nodded. Gerald nodded back, and then shut the door. Tyler shifted the car into first gear and rolled away from the gas pumps.

Gerald went inside and made his way back to the magazine rack. He started thumbing through an auto magazine. It seemed like it was all photos of girls in bikinis standing in front of shiny cars. He wondered why there seemed to be such a distinct correlation between cars and sex. He tried to read the article, but he couldn't focus. His brain was spinning from the evening's revelations. He decided to just thumb through the pictures until he felt better. As he scanned the pages, the sound of the door chime signaled the arrival of another customer. Gerald didn't bother to turn his head. He heard the steps of someone walking along the next aisle, but paid no heed.

Suddenly, a familiar voice called out his name, "Gerald? Is that you?" Gerald turned from the magazine. It was Mrs. Roberson. She wore an old white t-shirt, covered by an unbuttoned blue denim jacket and a pair of red cotton shorts, "What are you doing here?" Mr. Roberson became conscious of her appearance. She hadn't planned on running into anyone she knew at this late hour. She lifted her elbows to pull her hair back behind her shoulders. Then, she remembered that she had slipped out without a bra, and hurried to close the front halves of her jacket together.

Gerald caught what she was doing. He tipped his head down and fought the impulse to smile. He liked her a lot, and didn't want to make her uncomfortable, "I'm just looking through some magazines. What are you doing out this late?"

She held up a red painted can, "Good to the last drop."

"Do you often come out this late to buy coffee?"

"Not normally," Mrs. Roberson leaned an elbow on the magazine rack, "I forgot to pick some up earlier. So there I was, lying in bed, and suddenly I realized I had no coffee for tomorrow morning. It's better to make a midnight run and lose a little sleep than to do without my morning coffee. So how about you,

Gerald? Why are you standing in a convenience store at midnight looking at a magazine full of women in bikinis? Is everything alright?"

Gerald was about to brush off the question and say "Everything is fine" but then he decided not to. He appreciated that they had maintained a certain level of stark honesty in their relationship and he didn't want to taint that by giving her a dismissive lie. "No," he shook his head, "everything is not alright."

"Do you want to talk about it?"

"What would you do," Gerald said as he struggled to form the words, "if you found out that your whole existence was completely inconsequential?" Gerald reached out to pull a paper oil funnel from the dispenser and held it up, "What if you found out this was you, and that this was all that you mattered?"

"Everyone feels worthless sometimes. Everyone feels hopeless sometimes. I've felt that way a few times."

"So what do you do?"

"I think of something good I accomplished. Something nice that I've done. It doesn't have to be something big. It could be something like buying a kid a ticket to a movie theater that he can't afford. It might be just telling someone they look nice."

Gerald thought for a moment to consider, "I can't really think of anything good I've done."

"That's even better," she piped. "If your slate is looking pretty meager, go out and do something good. Start putting some marks on your tote board. Do something you can point to, and be proud that you made a difference. It's a great feeling of satisfaction."

"I'm not sure where to start."

"Come on, Gerald!" She said in an almost scolding tone. "There's plenty of opportunity for anyone who genuinely wants to do something good for someone."

Gerald peered into her soulful blue eyes as she talked, "I will give it a try."

Mrs. Roberson dipped her chin and spoke in a strange voice, "No. Don't try. Do or do not. There is no try."

Gerald was puzzled, as he tried to understand the bizarre sentence.

"You know, that little green man that lives in the swamp. I can't think of his name just now."

Gerald was bewildered, "I don't think I know him."

"Never mind," she waved a hand off to the side. "Another thing I think about, when I'm feeling down, is the people who care about me."

Gerald started to speak, but she held up her hand to pause him.

"Don't even go there," she continued. "Everyone says the same thing. 'Boo-hoo, no one cares about me; no one loves me. The world is such a cold terrible place.' Well, here's the dark news." Mrs. Roberson face got very serious. "Most of the world *is* a cold bad place. There are a lot of people who don't care about you. Some people will go out of their way to make your life miserable, for no particular reason. That's just the way it is, and we might as well buck up and get used to it, because it's not likely to change anytime soon. But," she held up a finger, "for someone to say that no one else cares about them is bullshit. That's a lie, perpetrated by someone who wants a reason to feel bad. Some people will care a little and a few will care a lot. If you're ever really down and out and feeling you really have no one, then take a step up and become important in someone else's life. All you have to do is expend a little effort to make it happen."

"Wow," Gerald cocked his head back. "You're not that big. Who would ever have guessed you would be so tough?"

"Sometimes tough love is the best kind. Having a good self-esteem is mostly getting off your ass and making it happen. It sure beats sitting around, whining and feeling sorry for yourself."

Gerald nodded softly, "I guess I was whining a little."

Mrs. Roberson smiled, "Well, I was speaking mostly in general terms, but yes, I suppose you were a little. Don't beat yourself up over it. There's no sense in trading one bad mood for another, okay?"

"Okay."

"So, are you going to stand there and look at pictures of half-naked women all night, or do you want me to give you a ride home?"

Gerald walked with her to the counter as she paid for the coffee. A skinny bald man with a moustache and a faded black shirt took her money and made change. They walked outside to her blue Plymouth Sunbird. Gerald walked around to the passenger side. Mrs. Roberson had already begun to reach for the door handle when she paused. "Gerald, wait," she spoke over the car roof.

"What's wrong?"

She shifted the can of coffee to the crook of her arm. "I'm sorry. I don't think I can give you a ride home. I don't know what I was thinking when I made the offer. You're a student and I am your teacher. You understand, don't you?"

Gerald nodded, "It wouldn't seem proper."

"It would be very improper. I don't think it would necessarily get me fired, but it would be very embarrassing to try to explain."

Gerald nodded, "That's fine. I can walk."

As he turned to walk away, Mrs. Roberson suddenly said, "Stop!" She sighed and tipped her head to the side, "Get in the car."

"But I thought you said . . . ."

"I know, but I don't feel right about making you walk home just because some busybody might see us riding together in a car. If I get asked about it, I will just tell the truth and say that it was late, you were upset, and so I gave you a ride home."

Gerald got in on the passenger side and turned toward her as she pulled out of the gas station. "I don't think you realize how much I envy you."

"You envy me?" Mrs. Roberson gave a quick laugh, "I don't hear that one very often. Why on Earth would you envy me?"

"Because you always seem so happy and energetic."

"Don't get too carried away, my friend." She gazed wistfully forward as she drove, "I have my sad times too."

"That is hard to imagine."

"Every shiny stone has an underside that's kept hidden away from the eyes of the world."

"If it ever shows up, I hope I'm there to see it. Maybe I can dish out some tough love, too."

"Ha-ha," she laughed and patted his shoulder, "that's the spirit."

"I'm going to follow your suggestion and make an effort to do something nice for someone. I don't know how just yet, but I'll think of something."

Mrs. Roberson glanced over at him as she rounded the corner to his street, "Give a little bit of your love to me."

Gerald made a puzzled face, "What did you just say?"

"Now is the time that we need to share," she spoke slowly, "so find yourself; we're on our way back home."

"What does that mean?"

"It's the lines from one of my favorite songs." She pressed a button, ejecting a disk. "It means that you don't have to do something big. Try something small." She held up two fingers with the tips slightly apart, "Just a tiny nudge." She fished the case from the pocket built into the side of her car door. "Here, you can borrow it for a few days. It's pretty old, so if you like it you can probably find it in the bargain bin at Walmart." She pulled up to the curb in front of Gerald's house.

Gerald nodded and accepted the disk.

"I think this is your stop," she smiled. "You'd better get going. It's late and I don't want you falling asleep in my class tomorrow. We might have to get you and Eddy Leach matching pillows."

"I just wanted to . . . ." Gerald's voice trailed off as the words escaped him.

"Well, you're not getting a goodnight kiss, if that's what you're thinking. I have stuck my neck out for you enough for one night."

Gerald smiled and shook his head, "I won't tell anyone."

"Good night, Gerald. I'll see you in class."

He pulled the car handle and stepped out of the door. "Good night, Mrs. Roberson."

She gave him a smile, then shifted the car into gear and pulled away from the curb.

Chapter 3

Wednesday's Rendezvous

It's Time We Met

*- She's a craze you'd endorse, she's a powerful force
You're obliged to conform when there's no other course.
She used to look good to me, but now I find her. . . . Simply
irresistible. -*

Tammy's thick, fluffy black hair bounced on her shoulders as she strutted into the library. She plopped down in the chair across from Gerald. She wore a gathered red and white striped shirt that was cut low in the front, "Hi, there!" she said cheerfully.
"Hi."
"I'm Tammy. Her dazzling white teeth were offset by her cherry red lips. Her black eyelashes and dark blue eyes drew sharp contrast against her milky white skin. "Do you know who I am? I heard you can't remember."
"I don't remember you, but there is a picture of us on my wardrobe."
"I'm your girlfriend."
"Tyler mentioned it."
"Yeah, yeah, yeah, your good friend Tyler. The big football star. I hope you don't show him that picture. My hair is awful."
"No; he only wanted to see pictures of you if you were naked."
"If I let you take some," Tammy tipped her head to the side, "I wouldn't want to you to show them around. We could do some bikini shots. Would that be enough to impress your buddies?"
"I didn't mean that I wanted you to . . . ."
"What's the deal with you and Tyler all of a sudden?" Tammy's eyes squinted. "You never hung around with him before the accident. How's come you guys are so tight now?"
"He's my friend."
"Yeah, well, whatever," Tammy gave a bored sigh, "Don't you think it's time we talked?" Her round mouth smiled easily as she spoke.
"I wanted to thank you for helping me at the pool last night."

"You thanked me at the time. Don't you remember?"

"I remember."

"Then, why thank me again?"

Gerald didn't have a ready answer.

"If you've already thanked someone once, and that once didn't stick, then what good is it to do it a second or third time? Anyhow," she tipped her head to one side as she waved her hair back from her cheek, "that's not what I wanted to talk about." Tammy leaned a bit closer, allowing Gerald a clear line of sight at her ample cleavage.

"Okay," as he spoke, Gerald tried to keep from staring at her chest. "What did you want to talk about?"

She seemed to read his thoughts, and leaned forward a bit more, pressing her breasts onto the front of the books to make them bulge. "It's okay," she whispered to him, "you can stare. It's nothing you haven't seen before. If we weren't in the library, I'd let you reach in there. Besides," she stretched her neck to come a bit closer to whisper, "it gives me a little tingle to catch you peeking."

"I'm just trying to get back into the swing of things."

"Okay," she said, "but you still like girls, don't you?"

"Yes."

Tammy glanced down at her chest, and then peered playfully back up at Gerald, "You still like these don't you?"

Gerald smiled, "How could I not?"

"And you'd like to reach in there if you could, wouldn't you?"

Gerald glanced down, then back up at her eyes. "Probably so."

"Okay then," Tammy flopped her books down on the table, and then dug around in her brown leather purse for a white comb. She began stabbing the pick end into her hair and fluffing it out from her neck, "I know you've been through quite an ordeal." She lifted her arms then arched her back and raised her elbows as she raked her hair back with the comb. "Homecoming is in a couple of weeks. Whatever all this is," she held her hands up a moment to accentuate her frustration, "I would really appreciate it if you had it all sorted out by then. I am pretty sure I will be on the homecoming court and I will need you to by my escort."

"I don't know if I want to go to homecoming."

Tammy tipped her head and stared at him like he was crazy, "Homecoming is important!"

Gerald shook his head, "Not to me."

"Are you telling me you're not going to be my escort at homecoming? Do you know how humiliating that would be for me?" Tammy stopped combing her hair, "You're not even on a ball team. The only reason you are involved is because I'm your girlfriend and I drug you along."

"I don't know if I want drug along. I don't know what I want right now. I need some time to figure things out." Gerald explained softly, "The problem is me, not you."

"Oh, please!" Tammy stopped combing her hair. "Spare me the old 'it's me, it's not you' bit." Tammy's voice was not as self-assured as it had been earlier in the conversation, "Alright, Gerald." She dropped the comb in her purse. "One thing we are not going to do is have a meltdown in front of everyone right here in the library."

"Okay."

"I only came over here to see if we can meet sometime and talk about this in a more private place." Her voice had a faint quiver to it. Tammy took a breath to compose herself, "Don't you think I deserve that much respect?"

"Yes."

She rubbed the corner of her mouth with a fingertip, "Do you know how to get to the old gym?"

"I think I can find it."

"The old boy's locker room is under the bleachers. Now, it's become a storage room where they keep old mats, weight equipment and other stuff."

Gerald nodded his understanding.

"Alright," Tammy checked the slender, gold decorative watch on her wrist, "it will be lunch break soon. Give me a ten minute head start. Along the far end of storage room are some stairs that lead down to the old furnace room. It has a door that we can close so we won't be overheard. Can you meet me there so we can talk privately?"

"I'll be there, but please try to have an open mind. I just don't want to be making promises that—."

"Shhhhhh," she stroked the side of his cheek with her fingertips. "Enough of that." She smoothed the hair back from the side of his head. "We'll figure it all out then. Don't worry. I'm a reasonable girl." She leaned close to whisper in his ear, "I'll see you in half an hour."

The Furnace Room

*- We weren't in love, oh no, far from it. We were just
searching for some pie in the sky summit. We were just young
and restless and bored. Living by the sword . . . . -*

Gerald roamed the halls, rehearsing his lines and checking
the clock every few minutes. Everything he planned to say
seemed entirely reasonable, and she'd said that she was a
reasonable girl. He leaned over the water fountain and took a
drink. He paused for a moment to watch the water make its arc
and splash into the pan. There were two words she'd said that
kept ringing in his ears. He had no idea what "Melt down" meant,
but it didn't sound good. Was she going to cry? Was she going to
scream at him? Gerald took a drink then wiped his mouth. She
had said she didn't want a scene. Maybe she just needed to vent
a little for her injured pride. She was feeling hurt and rejected
and wanted to punish him. So, he thought, he'd allow it. How bad
could it be? The lunch period would be over in another thirty
minutes. Maybe she was entitled to that half hour. He would
allow her to vent and let the chips fall where they may.

Gerald walked over to the old gym and took the long, narrow
hallway that hooked back behind the stands. He wondered how
many layers of paint the pale blue concrete walls had seen over
the years. The storage room had a tilted ceiling, conforming to
the slope of the stands overhead. The wall on the high side had
a series of painted-over windows dotting its upper edge. The
room was stacked with rolled up canvas tumbling mats, old
weight sets, stage props for plays put on by the drama club, and
various other items that saw infrequent use. He made his way to
the far side of the room, and went down the steps without using
the two-inch piping that served as the hand rail. He turned the
door knob and found it unlocked. She must have gotten a key
somehow.

The old furnace room was as large as the room above it,
running equal length to the gymnasium. The furnace had once
been used to heat the entire school, but was now relegated to
only heating the old gymnasium. The light from the pilot came
through the heavy glass panes built into the wall of the furnace,
and bathed the room in a dim, rose-colored glow. It was hard to
see in the dim light, but it seemed to be filled with much of the
same contents as the room above. He stepped gingerly to avoid
falling over the strewn contents. As he tried to get his eyes to

adjust, he fumbled for the light switch, but a hand closed around his wrist to stop him from turning it on.

"Stop. We don't need that." He heard the sound of Tammy's voice. She gently slipped behind him, then closed and locked the door. She placed her hands on his chest and softly pressed his back against the wall. She leaned forward and pressed her forearms and breasts against his chest, and began softly kissing his neck, "I'll tell you a secret," she whispered in his ear.

"What's that?"

"I'm not wearing any panties," she whispered, caressing his neck with her lips, "but then again, I might be lying." She ran the tip of her tongue along his throat and blew a soft stream of air on his neck, then leaned into his face in the dim firelight. "Maybe you better check, just to keep me honest."

Her warm lips and hot breath on his neck made his blood stir. He reached out to touch her inner knee, and slowly ran his fingertips up the soft, smooth skin of her inner thigh.

"See, I told you," she whispered.

Gerald regained a bit of his composure and pulled his hand back, "I think we really ought to talk."

"You know, Gerald, you talk too much." She grabbed his elbow and led him sideways to sit on a big rolled up canvas mat. "Just let all that go for a while." She pressed against his chest to get him to lie down, and unbuttoned the front of his shirt. She lifted her blue jean midi up to her hips and stepped over to straddle him. "You need to take things a little easier."

She leaned over him and puckered her lips to stitch a line of soft kisses across his chest, while her hands worked the front of his jeans. She sat up to peel off the red and white striped cotton shirt, and then arched her back to unclasp her red lace bra. The skin of her upper body seemed to glow red in the soft firelight. She leaned forward again and molded her naked breasts against his bare chest, as she softly kissed his mouth, "Isn't that better?"

"Yes," he whispered through the shrouds of her fluffy black hair, "it is."

"I know you don't remember, but we've never done this before." She wiped the hair from the side of her face. "Then, when you had your accident, I decided that, if you managed to fight your way back, I would accommodate you. And here you are."

Gerald felt a little light headed, and breathlessly answered, "Here I am."

Tammy gazed into his face as she gently rocked her body. "I love you, Gerald."

Gerald didn't answer, but ran his fingers along the ravine of her spine.

"I want to hear you say it," she murmured, as she quickened her rhythm. "Tell me," she whispered.

"It's hard for me."

She put her hands on the front of his shoulders to prop herself as she rolled her hips. "Say it. Tell me now, or I'm going to get up and leave. Do you want me to leave? I'll do it. Just say the word and I'll go."

"No," he gasped, "I don't want you to leave."

Tammy began dipping her head forward, then pulling it back as her shoulders came forward, to make snakelike motions that rippled down her spine and ended at her buttocks. "Then say it." Her fingertips became talons that dug into his chest. "Say it now!" she growled between clenched teeth. "You're out of time!"

"I love you," he gasped, as he laid a weary palm across her back. "I love you."

"That's good, Gerald," she said, laying forward on his chest again and falling into a gentler rhythm. "That's what I wanted to hear."

The Cafeteria

- I was angry and frustrated with myself for forgetting to meet Lori in the cafeteria. I was also a little ashamed of the reason why. –

Gerald stepped though the double doors going into the cafeteria. It was mostly deserted. As he entered, he saw Lori checking her watch and scooping up her books. Gerald grimaced. Her face was pinched and angry. He looked down at the hardwood floor, and then peered back up. She got up and glanced over at him, then walked past him toward the door.

As she breezed by, he decided to speak, "Hi, Lori."

"So much for being dedicated. Did you forget about me?"

"I'm very sorry."

"I waited for you all lunch break."

"I know."

"Where have you been all this time?"

Gerald's mind raced to come up with a plausible answer, "I was held up."

"You were? Doing what?"

Gerald opened his mouth to answer, but no words came out.

"Never mind. It's not important." Lori shifted the backpack full of books in her arms and started to walk past.

"Are you hungry?" Gerald asked.

"Am I hungry? Are you kidding? Of course I'm hungry. I waited on you to eat, but you didn't show," Lori snapped back.

"Do you like Monical's pizza?"

"I love Monical's pizza, but . . . ."

"What do you have next hour?"

Lori paused. Her resolve was weakening, "Just fifth hour study hall."

"Now, I'm no expert," Gerald held up a finger and smiled, "but I think that if you were sitting in Monical's, stuffing pizza in your face, you wouldn't be mad anymore."

Lori bent her head to the side. "Oh, that's what you think is it? You think if you buy me some pizza, it will fix it all right up, do you?"

"I sure hope so. I'll try anything to get out of the hot seat."

"Oh, you're really suffering are you?" A faint hint of a smile crept into the corner of her mouth "The heat's pretty bad, is it?"

"Let me tell you, it's boiling."

"Do you have transportation?"

"My motorcycle is right outside. Come on." He held the door open for her.

Lori huffed. She wanted to stay mad, but it was ebbing out of her. She didn't like getting bought out so easily. "I'm only doing this because I'm really hungry and I love Monical's."

She stepped through the door and he followed her, and then motioned her over to the bike. He detached the helmet and handed it to her, "Here, put this on."

Lori took it with a hint of resentment. She didn't care for the way he casually told her what to do, "What about you?" she asked as she slid it over her head.

Gerald smiled, "Your head is prettier than mine." He swung a leg over the bike, "Besides," he pointed to the top of his skull, "it's already been established that mine is indestructible." He kicked the motor over and started the engine.

Lori tucked her hair into the sides, "Are you going to drive gently?"

"Absolutely," Gerald answered sincerely. "Only a total jerk deliberately scares a girl on the back of a bike."

"That," she slid a leg over the seat and put her arms around his waist, "or leaves her waiting all lunch hour in the cafeteria."

Gerald smiled and turned back over his shoulder, "Touché, pussycat." He gently let out the clutch and rolled down the parking lot.

Monical's Pizza

- I will never forget that first trip to Monical's with Lori. -

Gerald parked the bike and put the kickstand down. Lori slid off and took the helmet off, then handed it to Gerald. He locked it to the side of the bike, and then smiled over at her, "How much do you eat, anyway?"

"Probably more than you can afford," she quipped, as they walked up the sidewalk.

"In that case, I hope you know how to wash pizza pans."

"You know, you really are something of a smart ass."

"I guess I am," he smiled and looked down.

Lori gave him a playful swat on the shoulder. When she let her arm back down, the back of her hand touched his. Gerald turned his wrist, and their hands naturally clasped together. She glanced over at him. He made eye contact, but neither of them said anything. She was glad they had crossed that threshold, but with it had come an awkward silence. He let go of her hand to open the door and stepped through.

"I guess he never heard of opening the door for a lady," she thought to herself as she followed him inside.

Gerald stepped up to the front counter, where several paper menus were scattered on the surface. Gerald casually took her hand again, and then used his other hand to turn one of the menus and read through the selections.

Lori ignored the other menus and leaned close to Gerald to peer over his shoulder. She gently let her shoulder rest against his, and stretched her neck to read with him.

Gerald ran his finger down the page, "Does a sausage, mushroom, and pepperoni sound okay?" He turned his face toward hers.

Lori suddenly realized how close his face was to hers. Was he going to kiss her? The thought of a public display of affection terrified her. Why wasn't he saying anything? Then, she realized that he was still waiting for an answer. In her moment of panic, she hadn't noticed the question. "Yes," she answered, turning to the guy behind the counter, "sausage, mushroom, and pepperoni will be fine."

Mick, the man in the white paper hat looked up, "What size?"

"Large," Lori chirped, cocking her head toward Gerald. "He's buying."

Gerald did a single drum roll on the counter with his fingertips. "I'm buying. Could you have them bring us a pitcher of Pepsi too?"

"You got it," Mick, answered as he began punching the order into the computer.

Lori decided to take the lead for the moment, and headed for a booth in the corner, "Is this okay?"

"Sure," he said, sliding into the seat on the other side.

Lori noticed that he sat down first. He was cute, and she liked him, but his manners would need some serious adjustment. She wasn't sure if she should sit next to him or across the table. She knew some girls sat on the same side because it was more intimate. Maybe it was what guys expected. Now that she was finally on the verge of dating, she was starting to wonder if men were too complicated to be worth the trouble. She put her purse on the table and sat down on the other side of the booth.

Roma, the waitress brought a pitcher of Pepsi and two clear plastic glasses. Lori stamped the tip of her straw on the table to push the end through the wrapper, then rolled the paper up into a ball and left it on the table, while Gerald filled her glass. At least he poured her drink first. Maybe he was trainable after all.

"Do you still want to go over those questions?" Gerald asked.

"No, not really," she answered dismissively. "I don't think you really need my help."

"Really?" The comment had surprised him. "Then why did you set up that meeting in the cafeteria?"

"Because . . . ." Lori answered hesitantly as she looked off to the side, "I thought you might . . . ." she paused, nearly losing her nerve, "ask me out on a date."

"Ohhh," Gerald answered slowly, "now I get it. You women are pretty clever and sneaky."

"Yes, we are," she retorted, leaning forward to draw some Pepsi up through the straw.

"Well," Gerald watched her from across the table. "I guess your plan worked, because here we are."

"Are you serious?" She looked at him incredulously.

"What do you mean?"

"*This* is not a date!" She picked up the rolled ball of paper and threw it at his chest.

"Why is this not a date?" he asked with his arms spread, "I'm buying, aren't I?"

Lori picked up her glass and took another drink, as she rolled her eyes. "A date is not riding to a pizza place on a motorcycle over lunch."

"Okay," Gerald nodded, "so explain to me your idea of a date."

"You know what a date is. You come to the door and you meet Momma and Daddy. We go out and eat, and then we see a movie or something. You drop me off and we kiss goodnight. That's a real date. Everyone knows that."

"What makes you think I'm not going to kiss you on this outing?"

Lori put down her drink. She was suddenly at a loss for words.

Gerald leaned his forearm toward her, as if he was preparing to arm wrestle. He slowly eased it toward her as his elbow slid across the table.

"What's he doing?" she thought to herself as his extended hand came closer. "What's he reaching for?" As his fingers came near her upper body, her mind panicked. "What's he going to grab?" She instinctively thought to cover her chest, but her arms seemed frozen to the table.

Gerald's fingertips pinched the hem of her shirt and gently drew her forward.

"Easy now," she said in a choppy, uncomfortable voice, as he pulled her closer. "Don't pop the buttons."

Gerald didn't answer, but leaned forward as he gently pulled her toward the middle of the table.

"Be careful." She glanced down at the table. "You're going to spill my drink."

"Do you want me to stop?" he whispered.

"No," she whispered back, "don't stop."

Gerald lightly touched his lips on hers. She smelled nice. Her lips were warm and pleasant.

Lori put her hands on the sides of his head and pressed her lips tighter against his. For a moment, she forgot she was in a public place. Then it came back to her that she was sitting in the booth of a pizza parlor. She broke away and slid back. "That's good for now," she said and tossed her hair back behind her shoulders.

"Okay," Gerald nodded.

They were quiet for a moment. Lori tried to think of something to say. She thought about it being another threshold, followed by another awkward silence. It was getting to be a pattern. Roma, the waitress brought the pizza to the table and asked if they needed anything else.

"No, we're fine," Gerald answered.

"Saved by the pizza," Lori said as she broke off a square-shaped piece.

"Now, I'm going to find out how much you eat."

She took a bite and pulled it away, then tucked the trailing string of cheese into her mouth. "Like I said, you could never afford me." She took a sip of Pepsi and swallowed. "And it's still not a date."

Gerald and Lori quietly ate their pizza for a while, exchanging glances.

Lori finally restarted the conversation, "So, what is this? Are we seeing each other now? Is that what this is?" She never liked ambiguity.

Gerald smiled, "Well, since this isn't a real date, I guess we technically aren't dating yet. Besides, the way you put away pizza, I think you may have been right. I'm not sure I could afford you."

She grinned as she took up another piece, "Don't worry about that so much. My father is a dentist."

"Oh, really, I've heard that's a good field."

Lori smiled and shifted her eyes, "You didn't think a little crown of porcelain actually costs a thousand dollars, did you?"

"No, I guess not."

"Before we go very far down this road, there is something that we ought to talk about."

"Okay, what's on your mind?"

"Tammy Wells," she said simply.

Gerald swallowed his pizza hard. He felt like she had picked a .45 caliber pistol off the table and shot him in the chest. "As in, how do you mean?"

"She was your girlfriend before the accident."

"Yes," Gerald nodded, "Someone has mentioned that to me."

Lori smiled, "I just don't want to start any battles. I don't want to have a blood feud because I ate a pizza with someone else's boyfriend."

"She's not my girlfriend anymore."

"You say that to me, but have you told it to her? If you haven't, then you're not playing fair."

Gerald paused. His mind reeled as he tried to think of an adequate response.

"Okay, okay. Freeze. Rewind. Forget I brought it up." Lori fanned her fingers out and turned her palms toward him.

"Sounds good to me," Gerald said with relief in his voice.

"We'll leave it this way for now. The next Bowl is a week from Saturday. The topics will be released this coming Saturday. Assuming you make the team, you can come by my house Saturday morning at 9:00 and study. If you're a free man and have everything sorted out by then, we'll see where it goes. If not, then we can still study together like good, respectable teammates. Fair enough?"

"That's fair."

Lori checked her watch, "Hey, chief. We need to get out of here." She yanked the bill out from under the pizza pan, "Tell you what, since I roughed you up pretty bad, I will get this one. And," she leaned forward and whispered, "it's still not a date!"

Girl Trouble

- I occasionally wondered what the old Gerald thought of Mrs. Roberson. In the days to follow, she and I would become very close. -

Mrs. Roberson had gone down to get a cup of coffee and had just returned, when she noticed that one of her students had circled back.

Gerald stood in the doorway, "Are you busy?"

"No," she answered, "come on in. I'm just having a cup of coffee." She took a sip from the white Styrofoam cup and sat down in the chair behind her desk, "What can I do for you?"

"You're the only person that I feel comfortable talking with."

Mrs. Roberson smiled, "I'm very flattered."

"After you gave me a ride home last night, I just felt like we sort of . . . ." his voice trailed off as he searched for the right words, "like we connected on some level."

"Shhh," Mrs. Roberson smiled. "Please don't mention that to anybody. This is a small town, and things explode out of proportion pretty quickly. What's on your mind?"

"It's about Tammy Wells."

"Ahhh, girlfriend problems." She leaned her elbows forward onto her desk. "Those can be tough. Tell me about it."

"I don't remember her. She seems nice, but I'm not sure if I want to be in a committed relationship that I can't recall. It's as if the old Gerald made a bunch of promises that I'm supposed to keep on his behalf. I'm just not feeling it."

Mrs. Roberson shrugged, "It's only right that you should play the way you feel it. When the rain washes you clean you'll know."

Gerald smiled, "What does that mean?"

"Sorry," Mrs. Roberson smiled back, "it's an old Fleetwood Mac reference. So here you are, and you don't remember her. She's a nice girl but you resent the obligations of a relationship that you can't remember."

"Exactly!"

"Are you sleeping with her?"

Gerald seemed a bit surprised at her frankness.

"Gerald, if you want me to help you, you're going to have to allow me some personal information. Have you been having sex with her?"

"Yes, just once. She says it was only once. I know it was only once since the accident."

"And since you had sex with her, you now feel uncomfortable breaking up with her?"

"Am I obligated because you slept with her?"

"I don't know." Mrs. Roberson shrugged. "Is she a whore?"

Gerald shook his head, "I don't think she's been around that much."

"I didn't ask you if she was promiscuous; I asked if you thought she was a whore. A lot of women who don't make their living by working in a bordello or hanging around in a red light district are whores. If a wife sleeps with her husband so he will buy her a new dress, doesn't that make her a whore?"

"I guess I never thought of it that way before."

"It's not such a bad thing really. It's just not my style. I think love should be given, not bartered or sold. It cheapens it and makes it less special. You might as well be sliding a plastic card through an ATM machine." Mrs. Roberson paused and smiled, "If you automatically assume that you owe her something for having sex, you may be insulting her. If she's not a whore, she might not want to be regarded as one."

"So what should I do?"

"You can try the direct approach, or you can take the back door."

"What is the back door?"

"It's a little easier than being direct. All you have to do is not sleep with her anymore, and let some time go by. Make excuses for not seeing her, and try to fade out. If she feels a sense of obligation, then maybe it will eventually fade away." Mrs. Roberson lifted the steaming cup to her lips. "How long has it been since you slept with her?" she asked as she took a drink.

"It was today, over lunch break."

Mrs. Roberson coughed and covered her mouth to avoid spitting her coffee. She sat the cup down on her desk and then wiped her chin, "Well, I'd say that's pretty current." She leaned back in her chair, "Still, if you don't want to confront her, just be distant and unavailable until she drifts away." She pointed at him, "But don't sleep with her anymore. Every time you do, it's just going to restart the clock."

"There's more to the story."

"More?" Mrs. Roberson perked up, "Enlighten me."

"I met a girl at the library. I took her to eat lunch. It wasn't really a date but I think that maybe . . . ."

"Ah! The plot thickens." Mrs. Roberson puckered her lips and then grimaced a bit, "I'm afraid that changes things." She shook her head dismissively, "I don't think the back door can work for you. You're going to have to tell her. You owe her that."

"But you said . . . ."

"You don't owe her anything because you had sex with her, but it's not right for you to let her think she's in a relationship while you're out courting someone else. Not only would that make you a heel, but she will eventually find out. That would be sitting on a ticking bomb. You're going to have to face the music and tell Tammy it's over."

"Should I mention the other girl?"

"No, I wouldn't go there. That part is none of her business, but she has a right to know where she stands."

"How do you think she'll take it?"

"Badly, of course. It always ends badly, but you go through it and you move on."

"I hate delivering the bad news."

"Who knows?" She clasped her palms together, "Maybe she'll take it better than you expect."

Confession

- I didn't feel comfortable misleading the parents. It was a tough spot. I obviously couldn't tell them the whole truth, but I had to say something. It would have been wrong to let them believe in a lie. -

The dinner table was quiet at the Camden household. Gerald occasionally glanced over at Christine. Why was talking to her so awkward and difficult for him? "I'm meeting Tammy at Burger King a little later."

"That's nice, dear," Christine said politely.

"Why is it nice? Everything can't be nice." Gerald paused and looked down at his food, and then back up at Christine, "I'm going there to break up with her. Do you still think it's nice?"

Christine sat her fork down and turned toward her husband.

"Mind your tone, Son." John wiped his mouth with his napkin, "When you talk disrespectfully to someone, it only makes you sound immature."

"I'm sorry. I didn't mean to sound disrespectful. I just don't know how to respond when someone says that."

Christine eyed him from across the table. "You've seemed a little tense ever since the accident."

Gerald nodded, "I have been." He started making a stack of green beans by stabbing them with his fork.

"Why are you breaking up with her?" Christine asked.

"I don't know her. She's pretty and she seems nice, but it's like she has been preselected for me by someone I can't remember." Gerald paused. "Actually, there's something else that I wanted to talk about. It's sort of a confession, but I feel like I have to tell you."

"What's on your mind?" John asked.

"You're really nice people, and I appreciate everything you have done for me, so I don't want to be deceiving you."

"How are you deceiving us, Son?" John said.

"I'm not your son, and I can't let you go on thinking that I am."

Christine's eyes narrowed, "If you're not our son, then who are you?"

"I'm trying very hard to figure that out," Gerald answered thoughtfully, "but right now, I just don't know."

"Son, what are you talking about?" John asked.

I don't even know what I'm talking about anymore," Gerald stared down at the table and shook his head, "I'm just sorry about everything. I'd better go. I have to meet Tammy at Burger King soon."

Gerald got up from the table and went to the closet to get his denim jacket and motorcycle helmet, then headed for the door.

When Gerald had gone through the door, Christine gestured after him, "That is something that our son would not have said."

John sighed, "Give him some time to get things sorted out."

Christine leaned forward and laid her hand on her husband's. "It's not about him losing his memory and it's not about him needing time to get back on his feet. You heard him say it. He's not our son."

"He certainly looks like our son to me."

"I don't know what they did, or how they did it, but . . . ." she shook her head, "that is not our Gerald."

John leaned his head to one side, "Please don't go crazy on me. Will you listen to yourself?"

"A mother knows her own child. That's not him."

"Let's say you're right. What do you want me to do?"

"I think he should leave our house. He's old enough to survive on his own."

"We can't throw him out right after he's had a horrible accident."

"He's not pretending to be our son. Why should we keep pretending to be his parents?"

"Let's just slow down. This has been a stressful situation for all of us." John rubbed his chin while he peered over at his wife, "I think we should consider seeking professional help. I've heard good things about a psychologist named Dr. Hartman. She does counseling two days a week out of her office in Robinson."

"Send him to counseling, then, if you think it will help."

John took a deep breath, "I think you should both go."

"Both?" Christine leaned forward and her mouth came open slightly. "I'm not crazy. There's nothing wrong with me."

"I didn't say there was. We've all been through some trauma lately. There's no shame in seeking outside help. Will you go?"

Christine thought about it for a moment. "I'll go on two conditions: that *he* goes as well, and that no one else knows about this but you and me. It's nobody else's business."

John nodded, "That's fair. I'll see about making an appointment, for each of you."

The Break-Up

- I wasn't sure how Tammy was going to react. -

Gerald sat quietly at the local Burger King trying to think of a strategy, while Tammy daintily nibbled her fries and took ladylike bites out of her sandwich. She dabbed at her ruby lips with a napkin, and then took out a compact to check her makeup. She paused for a moment to notice Gerald, "You're awfully quiet over there," she commented, and then took another bite.

He gazed tiredly over at her red and white top. Its base color was red, but it was riddled with white diamond shapes, scattered about in random patterns. Tyler was right, red and white was her trademark. He tried to think of a gentle way to present it, but ultimately he just blurted it out, "I'm sorry, but I don't want to see you anymore."

Tammy stopped chewing and smiled, "Pardon me?" She put her sandwich down. A dark expression came over her face. "Are you breaking up with me?" she asked in a threatening tone.

"Yes." Gerald answered with a quiet firmness. "This is it. After tonight, it's over."

"You're such a jerk! I suppose this means you aren't even going to be my escort for homecoming?"

Gerald shook his head sadly. "I don't know if I am going, but I don't think I want to go with you. I just don't think it would be a good idea."

"How can you do this? We just had sex in the furnace room a few hours ago!"

"You're not a whore, Tammy."

Tammy recoiled at the word. "Of course I'm not a whore! Why would you even say that?"

"If I owed you something because you had sex with me, wouldn't that make you a whore?" Gerald reiterated Mrs. Roberson's words the best that he could. "I think more of you than that. We had sex, but it wasn't some sort of business transaction. I don't owe you anything."

"You don't owe me anything," Tammy repeated, with contempt in her voice. "Just like that, you're breaking up with me." Tammy's face held a mix of anger, hurt, and surprise.

"I'm sorry," Gerald said softly.

"You said you were sorry once already. You should never apologize more than once for the same thing. It makes you sound like a babbling idiot." Tammy rubbed her palms together to wipe sesame seeds from her hands. "I'm the hottest girl in this school. I could have dated anybody I wanted."

"You still can. Any guy in school would probably jump at the chance."

"Well, I didn't pick them, I picked you. You're nothing special. You don't even have a car!"

"I'm not available for the picking."

"Oh, you're not? What does that mean? Are you seeing someone else?"

"Not really." Gerald tilted his head to the side and rubbed a finger under his eye. "Not yet."

Tammy leaned back and cocked her arms on her sides. "Who is she?" Tammy demanded.

Gerald shook his head and wouldn't answer.

"Never mind. It won't take long for me to find out. By this time tomorrow, *I* will be dating someone else. Half the boys in this town are in with love me."

"I guess I'm just in that other half."

"Oh, aren't you so clever!" She got up from her side of the booth and leaned close to his face, "I promise you, you're going to regret this." As she turned to walk out, Gerald started to get up to follow her, "Stay there and finish your sandwich," she called over shoulder, "I'll find my own way home."

Chapter 4

Thursday's Challenge

The Scholastic Bowl Tryout

- I always liked Mrs. B. I would never be as close to her as Lori, but we came to have a good relationship, even though it didn't start on a warm note. -

Jamie Branson sat in her office located off the side of the library. She checked her cell phone. It was nearly 9:00 am. They weren't late yet, but it was getting close. She compared the time on her phone to the clock on the wall. Her phone was slightly faster, but it was more accurate, and that's what she was going to go by. She was a little irritated with the situation. This was a waste of her time. Gerald was an above average student at best. She'd only agreed to see him at Lori's insistence and was now wishing she had refused. At 9:01 she would be released from her agreement. There would be no rescheduling.

She saw Lori and Gerald at the window of her door, and she checked her phone again. It read 9:00 am. She waved her hand to motion them in.

Mrs. Branson noticed that Gerald went through the door without waiting for Lori to go first.

"Are we late?" Gerald asked.

"Obviously not, or we wouldn't be talking right now."

"Thanks for seeing us, Mrs. B." Lori smiled, and took a seat on the other side of her desk.

"You're welcome, Lori."

Gerald remembered Lori's coaching him that his manners were weak, "Yeah, Mrs. B. Thanks."

Mrs. Branson stiffened a little, "What is 'yeah'? Is that the lazy word for 'yes'? I don't remember asking you a question. Has 'yeah' become a catch-all word that is used for a salutation as well?"

"I don't know."

"And there's one more thing. Only my closer students call me 'Mrs. B.' "

"How does a student know?"

Mrs. Branson gave him a curt smile, "If you ever get there, I will let you know. In the meantime, 'Mrs. Branson' will be fine. Do you know how this works?"

"Sort of. There's a test or something, right?"

Mrs. Branson glanced over at Lori, and then turned back to Gerald. "Lori is the president of the Bowl. She has recommended you, and I have agreed to interview you. At the end of the interview, I may allow you to take the test, if I feel you might be a worthy candidate."

"Okay."

"Let's get started, shall we. What can you tell me about George Washington?"

Gerald shrugged, "He was the first president."

Mrs. Branson turned toward Lori, "Well, at least he's right so far." She turned back to Gerald, "Anything else? Is that it?"

"He commanded the Continental Army from 1775 to 1783. He served as president from 1789 to 1797. When he was born, his birth date was recorded as February 11, 1732; this was later corrected as February 22, 1732."

"How can they move a person's date of birth?"

"Because he was born before the British colonies switched from the Julian Calendar to the Gregorian calendar."

"What is the difference between the two calendars?"

"Julius Caesar decreed that every fourth year would be a leap year that would have an extra day. This adjustment was meant to keep the seasons in line with the calendar. It was not entirely accurate. The Gregorian calendar skips some leap years. When it was instituted, 11 days were skipped to realign the calendar with the seasons. Do you want me to tell how the skipped leap years are calculated?"

"No, but I would like to hear about Julius Caesar."

"He was born in July of 100 BC. He only reigned for 5 years, from October of 49 BC until March of 44 BC. He massively reformed Rome, until he was assassinated on March 15, of 44 BC. He was killed by—"

"He was stabbed to death by Brutus and other conspirators." Mrs. Branson handed him the test. "Go sit at the table in front of my door, facing me. Raise your hand when you're done or if you have to get out of your chair for any reason. Otherwise, I will throw your test away without grading it."

Gerald went out to start work on the test.

Lori turned to Mrs. Branson, "Thanks, Mrs. B."

Mrs. Branson shrugged, "We'll see how he does."

Making the Team

- I remember Lori coming into the cafeteria with Mrs. B. I knew by her body language that it was good news. -

Gerald sat at the table eating chicken and dumplings. The food was very good. Cafeterias often get a bum rap. It always seems to be in fashion to complain about the food, whether it's bad or not. He looked up to see Lori and Mrs. Branson entering the room. Lori was smiling, which suggested that they must have good news.

"Congratulations," Lori said in a sing-song voice.

"Did I pass?"

"Oh you definitely passed." Mrs. Branson rolled her eyes as she spoke. "I am not allowed to release scores, but you definitely passed."

"It was the highest score Hutsonville has ever had."

Mrs. Branson cleared her throat and gave Lori a piercing glare.

"What I mean is, I'll bet it was a great score," Lori said sheepishly. "The bylaws require that scores are kept confidential."

Gerald glanced back and forth between the two ladies. "So does this mean I'm on the team?"

"First, I have to be sure you're committed." Mrs. Branson held up her hand. "There is more to this than answering questions at the meet. It requires strategy and teamwork. I want to make sure you're serious about it before I start shuffling the chairs on the team. Can you meet with Lori on Saturday so she can bring you up to speed? Will you show up on time for the matches? Are you willing to rehearse one or two nights a week?"

"I can do that," Gerald nodded.

"Alright then, we'll give it a try. Remember, being smart isn't enough. You have to be responsible, as well. There is nothing more aggravating than an irresponsible young man with wasted talents."

"I will try to be responsible."

"The next meet is one week from Saturday. I want you prepped and ready by then. And another thing," Mrs. Branson touched the tip of her index finger to the table's surface, "the next time you are sitting and two ladies approach, you stand up and offer them a seat."

Gerald dropped his fork and stood up, "Would you ladies like a seat?"

"Why yes, kind sir," Lori answered, letting her pleasure in the moment show in her voice, "I believe I will."

"I can't, thank you," Mrs. Branson said. "I have to get around. Do you have any questions for me before I go?"

"Just one."

"Yes?"

"When do I get to call you Mrs. B?"

Mrs. Branson gave him a slight smile, and the faintest hint of an eye twitch suggesting a wink. "We'll see how you do at the first match."

As Mrs. Branson walked away, Lori leaned back in her chair and raised her index finger at Gerald, "You know, I think she might just make a gentleman out of you."

Gerald nodded and smiled, "She's tough."

"She takes the Scholastic Bowl very seriously." Lori leaned forward, "She grows on you. I think you're going to like her."

"I like her. She's tough, but she's not mean spirited. Everything she has asked of me is entirely reasonable."

Lori took a quick look around, "You got a 98 on the test!" she whispered excitedly. "That is phenomenal! The highest score anyone has ever gotten before this was an 87."

"I got a 98?" Gerald ran through the test in his mind, "Did I miss one?"

"Gerald. That test is not like an exam for a class. It's structured on a curve. You can't get a 100. It's impossible. To score a 98 is extraordinary. No one scores above 90; the test is designed that way."

"Okay, but still, if I got a 98 that must mean I made a mistake somewhere."

Lori sighed, "Gerald, you drive me right out of my freaking mind." She fanned her fingers on each side of her head, "Why can you not just be happy with a 98? I got an 82, and I was thrilled. You make me want to scream." She laid her hands on the table and sighed. "I'm either falling in love with you, or I'm going to kill you."

Lori paused to consider the words. The dreaded "L-word" had slipped from her lips. She noticed that Gerald wasn't reacting. Maybe he didn't notice. No. That scoundrel noticed everything. The awkward silence stretched on. Why wasn't he talking? She wanted to find a way to get the conversation going again, but she was the last one to speak.

"So . . . ." Gerald said slowly, forming his thoughts.

"Why doesn't he just spit it out?" Lori thought. She wanted to reach into his mouth and drag the words out. Her eyes narrowed. He'd better not be doing this on purpose.

"If the scores are confidential . . . ."

Lori sighed internally. He was going back to talking about the scores again. Why was he so obsessed?

"How is it that you know I got a 98?" Gerald asked with a wry smile.

"Mrs. B trusts me." She smiled and cocked her head to the side.

"She doesn't trust me?"

"No, of course not," Lori stiffened her neck and pulled back as if the idea was ridiculous. "It takes a while, but you'll get there. First, you have to get to where you can call her Mrs. B. Once she learns she can rely on you, then you can start building trust."

"Since you might be falling in love, does this mean we're dating?"

Lori eyed him suspiciously. He had circled back to the "L-word." Was he toying with her? "You haven't asked me out on a date yet."

"What if I asked you out right now?"

"Then I would ask you to wait a few days and let the dust settle. I'm going to see you this weekend to prep you for your first Bowl. Maybe you can do it then. A little patience and discretion can go a long way toward sparing other people's feelings."

"I suppose you're right."

"I'm always right. You'll learn that eventually. One day you will say to me, 'Lori, my dear, you are always right.'" She got up and stroked her fingers lightly across the back of his hand, "I have to run. I'll see you this weekend."

"Okay."

Lori walked a few steps from the table, and then spun around, "And Gerald?

"Yes?"

"You'd better eat your chicken and dumplings; they're getting cold." She grinned from ear to ear.

Gerald smiled at her quip although he didn't quite know what to make of it. The energetic way she had popped it off made him want to chuckle. He was liking her more and more. Gerald shook his head and turned back to his plate then picked up his fork.

Poking the Bear

- Mrs. Roberson had told me that the way to handle Eddy was to stand up to him. Thinking back, I may have overshot the mark. -

Gerald sat in his last hour English class. It was a strange convergence of extremes. He had become very fond of Mrs. Roberson, but sitting in her class was sheer cruelty.

Today's lesson was on free verse poetry. He thought his head would explode. If a poem doesn't rhyme and has no sort of structure, how can it be poetry? He checked the clock on the wall. Time seemed to drag.

When the bell rang, Eddy stood up and turned toward Gerald, "Still driving that motorcycle?"

"Yes, I am." Gerald wasn't sure where this was leading.

"Too bad you can't afford a car."

"Well, Eddy, most of my money comes from yard work. It's seasonal, and doesn't always pay that well. A motorcycle is cheap on gas, and it gets me around in the summer. During the winter, if I have to go somewhere, I borrow my dad's car." Gerald was bluffing. He actually had no idea what the arrangements were.

"You borrow your dad's car?" Eddy said with disgust, and then took a step toward Gerald. "That's pathetic."

"Maybe," Gerald closed his book and stood up, "but we can't all have a cushy existence working in our dad's auto shop."

"I work hard at that job. I'm a licensed mechanic. I could get a job anywhere."

"That's strange. I heard that the only reason you keep going to this school year after year is because he threatened to fire you if you don't graduate."

The class stopped filing out the door, and the room became instantly quiet. Everyone knew that Gerald was encroaching on a tender subject.

"At least I didn't get a spot on the Scholastic bowl team by sleeping with one the members," Eddy shot back.

"I'm really sorry to hear that tactic didn't work out for you, Eddy. Maybe if you'd have offered a bundle of cash instead, you could have closed the deal."

The class let out a nervous cackle.

Eddy looked around the room, and then took a couple more steps toward Gerald.

Gerald stood up from his seat. Whatever Eddy was going to do, he didn't want to be seated when it happened.

Eddy stood toe to toe with Gerald, "You and me—we're going to have a little talk later."

Gerald stared steadily back at him, but didn't respond.

"Yeah, that's right." Eddy turned and glanced to the front of the room at Mrs. Roberson, and sneered at her. If he squared with Gerald now, she would probably freak out. Maybe she would call the cops. It would be smarter to wait for a better time and place. He gave a last glance at Gerald, "I'll see you soon enough."

Demanding the Truth

- Mrs. Roberson was a good friend, but she didn't hesitate to grill me for keeping secrets from her. -

Gerald walked toward the front as the last of the other students filed out.

Mrs. Roberson glanced up to watch him approach and then turned back to her books. Gerald was puzzled. His favorite part of the day was their daily discussion at the end of school, but she seemed strangely quiet today.

"Is something wrong?" he asked as he came to her desk.

"I don't know, Gerald, why don't you tell me," she answered coolly as she started to gather up her things. "You're the one who was about to start a brawl in my class."

"I'm sorry about that. One thing led to another, and I didn't want to back down. You said that if you appear weak to a bully, you only become a target."

"That's not what I'm talking about."

"Then what is it?"

"What you did was very unlike Gerald Camden."

Gerald shrugged, "Maybe I'm finding myself, like you suggested."

"Gerald, you're a really bad liar." She eyed him closely.

"I'm not lying to you."

"No, but you're also not telling me the whole truth, are you?"

Gerald was silent for a moment, "I guess I'm not."

Mrs. Roberson put a hand on her hip and looked him squarely in the eye, "Are we friends?"

Gerald half shrugged and nodded, "Sure we're friends."

"I mean really friends, trust and confidences, and all that."

"I think we are."

"Then why don't you tell me what's going on? You're not the same as before the accident. I heard you beat Mr. Leslie in some sort of math duel. This morning, you aced the Scholastic Bowl entry exam. Mrs. Branson is dancing around on cloud nine."

"I guess if Mrs. Branson is dancing on cloud nine, that means she's probably going to let me on the team."

"Don't dodge the point. Are you going to tell me what's going on here? You know, other people are going to be asking these same questions, soon. Do you trust me or not?"

"If I told you, then you wouldn't believe me."

"Maybe you should give the chance before you prejudge me."

"It has to do with genetics."

"I can believe that. They're doing some amazing things with genetics these days."

"Have you ever heard of a man named Dr. Gauge?"

"Isn't he the biologist who has the animal show on Channel 10 on Saturday afternoons?"

"He's also a genetic scientist. I have access to his lab. If you feel up to a ride to Terre Haute, I can show you something that will help make sense of it all."

"I'd love to see it." Mrs. Roberson paused, "I can't take you in my car, and I certainly can't leave school with you. That would raise too many eyebrows."

Gerald shrugged, "Then what do we do?"

"I have a motorcycle helmet. If I wear it, nobody would recognize me from a distance. Why don't you come by my house and pick me up?"

Gerald nodded, "I can do that."

"Let's wait till later, when there aren't as many people out milling around. Go eat dinner, then meet me in back of my house around seven o'clock."

Gerald nodded. I will pick you up at seven."

The Auto Garage

- I make a rich woman beg. I'll make a good woman steal. I'll make a old woman blush and make a young girl squeal -

Tammy sat in Leach Auto Service on the little bench next to the free coffee and the ancient television. She checked her gold watch then went to the counter. An older lady with gray hair and a long face was sorting through papers. "Excuse me; I've been here over an hour. Do you know if they've started on my car yet?"

The lady peered over her glasses. "I got no idea," she answered in a bored New Jersey accent that meant, "I couldn't care less." She pointed a thumb back over her shoulder and went back to sorting her papers. "If you want, you can go back and ask the mechanics. They work on the cars, not me. All I do is sit up here and listen to people like you complain."

She walked into the shop area, where two mechanics were standing around talking. It seemed like a foreign language. She could make out words like "turbo," "horsepower," and "performance cam," but she had no idea what they meant. She waited for several moments for them to notice her, but they continued talking as if she wasn't there.

"Excuse me," she finally interrupted. "Which of you is supposed to be working on the silver Celica?"

The two mechanics stopped talking and turned to her. One of them shrugged. The other one gestured toward the front parking lot. "Oh, yeah, the Celica. New shocks. That's Eddy's. He hasn't started on it yet. He's out back."

"Well, what's he doing out back? It's been over an hour, and I need to get the car back. Can one of you work on it?"

"Sorry lady, Eddy is the boss' kid. Besides, I got my own cars to work on. You drew Eddy and that's how it is. Better luck next time."

Tammy walked around to the back of the shop.

Eddy had parked his 1961 sky blue Cadillac convertible under a shade tree. The top was down. Eddy had the driver's door cocked open, with the glass rolled down, and one leg sprawled across the top. His head was leaned back, as he listened to the music on the car stereo.

Tammy watched him moving the toe of his foot with the music, and became instantly furious. "Hey!" she called.

"Hey, yourself," he answered without lifting his head.

"I've been sitting on that bench, waiting for you to work on my car for over an hour."

Eddy looked up to dust a fly off his arm, and then turned down the radio. "I'm real sorry about that," he said with sarcasm, "but work's been real hectic today."

"So, are you going to work on my car or not?"

"All in good time," Eddy leaned his head back again.

"You've had enough time. It's been over an hour."

"You said that already. When a person starts repeating themselves, it's time to quit talking."

"What do you expect me to tell my mother when she asks why her car didn't get done? Huh? Tell me that. What am I supposed to say?"

Eddy lifted his head up and shifted his glasses back. "Just tell her the truth, that I was out back having a beer." Eddy took a drink from his can of Miller beer. "I'd offer you one, but that was the last can."

"I know who you are. You're Eddy Leach."

"The one and only." He raised the beer to toast himself, and then took a last long drink to finish off the can. "I know you, too. You're the chick who goes with the guy who had the boating accident. I beat him up in the fifth grade. He's going to get it again pretty soon if he doesn't learn to shut his mouth."

"Don't expect me to warn him for you," Tammy shrugged. "He doesn't matter to me. We split up."

"I'll try real hard not to get too emotional about it."

"You must think that you have to talk tough all the time because you're the school hoodlum."

"A renaissance man, born in the wrong era. I should be wearing armor, riding a horse, and running a lance through someone." Eddy sat up,

"All I see is a guy who is too lazy to do his job, and engaged in illegal drinking."

"Then why don't you go call a cop!" he said, as he threw the empty beer can at her.

"Hey!" she said, raising her hands to deflect the empty container off her forearms. "Watch it!"

"I think that you'd better watch it," he said with a growl in his voice.

"Alright, alright; I'm sorry I said that, but my mom really needs this car back."

Eddy made a sarcastic grin and peeked at her through the corner of his eye. "So Mama sent you out to get the shocks replaced?"

Tammy shrugged her shoulders. "It's not like there's much else to do in this boring town."

"Too many people say this town is boring, but they don't want to do anything to liven it up."

"Oh, yeah?" She put a hand on her waist and cocked her hips to the side. "And what would you suggest?"

Eddy sighed, "Maybe you should indulge in your appetite for bad boys. I'll pick you up Saturday at 6:00."

"You mean like a date? What makes you think I want to go out with you?"

"Because you're still hanging around here, pestering me."

"You assume a lot."

"I like the shirt, but get rid of the blue jean dress thing. I hate those. Wear some cut offs, if you like jeans so much."

"I don't have any."

"Well, I suppose you better get some before Saturday."

"I guess I have some jeans that I could cut off."

"Cut them short. I like to see a lot of leg. Make sure they're not too tight. I hate it when a girl's thighs bulge out like marshmallows. And wash them a few times to fray the edges."

"I can do that. But I haven't actually agreed to this yet."

"At 6:00, I'm going to pull up and honk the horn once. If you're not out in two minutes, I will roll on, and I will never ask you out again. If you don't want to go, all you have to do is not come out. Just don't come back here, whining to me about how your life is boring."

Tammy nodded, "So, are you going to fix the car?"

"I'll do it at the end of this next song. Will that make you happy?" He turned up the radio a notch, and then leaned back, "You people are so selfish."

Tammy stood there for a moment, not really sure what to say next. "Well, that's good, because my mom really needs her car back."

"You're repeating, again," he called out over the music. "Now stop bothering me. I have to prepare myself mentally before I go back to work."

"I guess I will see you Saturday."

If Eddy heard the response, he didn't acknowledge it. He laid his head back and listened to the music, while she walked back to the front of the shop.

Pork Chops and Applesauce

- I just didn't know how to connect with the Camdens. -

Gerald sat quietly at the dinner table, staring down at the food. Christine and John exchanged a glance.

"Do you want some pork chops, Gerald?" Christine asked as she eyed him closely.

Gerald didn't answer, but kept looking down. He began to feel uncomfortable and wasn't sure what he should say.

"Gerald?" Christine repeated. "I asked if you wanted some pork chops. They're stuffed with sausage and barbequed, from Siever's meat market. You like them, don't you?"

Gerald continued staring down at his plate.

"Son, your mother's speaking to you." John touched the side of Gerald's upper arm. "I'll trouble you to be respectful and answer her."

Gerald looked up and stared into his face with a puzzled expression. He turned toward Christine and pulled back the side of one cheek as he spoke out of the corner of his mouth "Pork chops and applesauce."

Christine's lips drew slightly tighter. She delicately poked her food with the end of her fork, and then peered back across the table. "That doesn't make any sense," she said curtly. "We're not having applesauce."

Gerald didn't answer right away. He lifted a piece of broccoli from his plate. Turning it slowly in the air, he took bites out of it as he spoke. "That's what Peter Brady said, when he was trying to find his personality."

"Do you need help finding your personality?" John asked.

"No, I think I can manage."

John rested his elbows on the table, "Are you having problems at school?"

Gerald shrugged and picked up another piece of broccoli. "I provoked the school bully today. I think he's gunning for me now."

"If you *are* having trouble, I would like to try to help."

"You can't help," Gerald shook his head. "High school is full of troubles. That's what high school is. It's this crazy game where the moves don't make any sense, but you don't dare break the rules. All you can really do is try to catch on, play the best that you can, and hope that you aren't the one who loses."

John nodded, "Just remember that there's help, if you ever feel like you're in over your head."

Gerald nodded, "Thanks, Dad." The dad was cool. He was a good guy. He turned toward Christine. He wished he could find a way to break the ice with her. Maybe, if he could start up a conversation, things would become less tense. He studied the heavy makeup on her face. He hesitated for a moment, and then blurted out, "Why do you always wear so much makeup?"

Christine cocked her head back and raised a hand to her cheek, "I always touch up my makeup before I come to the dinner table."

"I know you do, but why?"

Christine smiled politely, "When you get to be my age, you need a little help to keep yourself looking young." There was a cool reserve to her answer.

"Why is that important? What's wrong with looking your real age? Isn't wearing a lot of makeup a form of lying? It seems like you're hiding your true self away from the real world. Why do you do it?"

Christine laid down her fork and turned toward her husband, "Why is he asking me this? What does he expect of me?"

"I don't know," John looked over at Gerald. "What are you getting at, Son?"

"It just seems to me that she always hides her face behind a lot of cosmetics. It occurred to me that I don't know what she really looks like. Just once, I would like to see my mother's real face."

John was about to respond, but his wife put her hand on his arm to quiet him. Something about hearing the word "mother" pass through Gerald's lips softened her demeanor, "That's okay, John. I don't think what he's asking is so bad." She sighed and turned to Gerald, "I'm not going to get up and wash off my makeup in the middle of dinner, but if you like, I will come to dinner tomorrow with no makeup. Now that we have that settled, can we have a pleasant dinner?"

John was quiet for a moment, and then spoke with some reluctance, "Gerald, we'd like you to see a Dr. Hartman. We've already made you an appointment for tomorrow afternoon. We also spoke with Mr. Hawk to arrange for you to have an early dismissal."

"Have you grown dissatisfied with Dr. Baker?"

"She's not a medical doctor."

"Then what is she?"

John leaned his elbows on the table and wove his fingers together as he peered across the table. "She's a psychologist. I think she could help. We're hoping you'll cooperate and go willingly."

Gerald nodded, and then slowly tipped his chin high as his teeth snapped off the end of a carrot stick. It was a way to stall the conversation so he could have a chance to digest the information. He peeked at John from the corner of his eye. "Do you think I'm crazy?" He asked with an awkward grin.

"No, we don't think you're crazy." John shook his head as he poked at the food on his plate, and then glanced back up. "We think you're going through a difficult adjustment, and it might help if you have someone to talk to."

"It sounds to me like you already have it all planned out for me."

John spread his hands, "Your mother and I aren't qualified for this. We're in over our heads. You've been through a horrible ordeal and we're not equipped to shepherd you through it."

Gerald nodded slowly, "You really think this psychologist is going to help?"

"She might. Try not to think of her as a psychologist. Just think of her as a very intelligent woman, which is exactly what she is."

Gerald nodded, "I'll go."

"Really?" John seemed surprised, "That was easier than I thought it would be."

"Sure," Gerald snapped off another chunk of the carrot stick with his teeth, and then stuck the rest in his mouth, "I'll go." He picked up his knife and fork and began whittling off a piece of pork chop. He stuck the bit of meat in his mouth and ground it with his molars. He turned to Christine, "The pork chops are great, Mom. Thanks."

The Storm

- It was a little strange giving Mrs. Roberson a ride on my motorcycle. With her body pressed against my back and her arms around my waist, it seemed to melt away the student/teacher barrier. -

Gerald glanced down at Mrs. Roberson's hands clasped together in front of his stomach. Showing her the lab seemed like a good strategy. He had been too careless about allowing his new abilities to be visible. It was only a matter of time before people started to ask questions. If he brought her into his confidence, she would be a good ally.

As Gerald slowed the bike to accommodate the lower speed limit of Prairie Creek, he noticed heavy purple clouds gathering. They were already more than halfway to Terre Haute. He decided to press on and hope to get lucky. Gerald glanced back over his shoulder and then pointed to the line of clouds forming. Mrs. Roberson nodded her understanding.

When he went opened the throttle and bent low into the curve, he felt Mrs. Roberson's body tense. It was strange to feel her body hugged tightly against his back. He kept reminding himself that she was his teacher. He slalomed his way through the many curves of Route 63, and occasionally glanced up at the sky. It was going to be hard to beat the storm.

When he entered the Terre Haute city limits, he slowed to 30 mph. The clouds opened up and drenched them in a massive downpour. Gerald negotiated his way down Third Street, trying to get to the Sycamore Building. With the water splattering his face shield, he could barely see.

He pulled into a gas station and took off his helmet. Mrs. Roberson took off her helmet as well. Her long, reddish brown hair whipped around in the wind. She pulled it back from her face and pressed it flat against the back of her neck as she leaned toward Gerald, "How much farther?" She spoke close to his ear to be heard over the wind and rain.

"It's a few blocks east of the courthouse."

Mrs. Roberson motioned him over to an oak tree. They leaned against the trunk to take shelter from the gusting wind. Mrs. Roberson shielded the side of her face with one hand, "I hope this is worth it."

"Me too."

With the next gust of wind, they leaned harder to brace themselves against the tree. Gerald's hand shifted on the bark and his fingertips accidentally grazed the side of her hand. She glanced down, then back up at him.

When the wind stopped gusting, she stood up from the trunk and placed her hands into the pockets of her gray hooded sweatshirt. The rain lulled to a heavy drizzle. "This may be as good as we get," she said, brushing back strands of hair that clung to her cheek.

"I can't see anything with the water coming off the visor," Gerald said.

"I'll hold your helmet. If a cop stops us, we'll just tell them the truth, that we unexpectedly got caught in the storm." She took a beaded tie from her pocket and then pulled her hair back to bind it into a pony tail. She turned back toward Gerald, "I'm ready."

Gerald kicked the bike, and Mrs. Roberson molded on behind him. She held one hand flat against his stomach to hold on. She slung her other arm over the top of his shoulder, holding the straps high enough so that his helmet wouldn't rattle on the gas tank. When they made the turn at the courthouse, the downpour resumed.

Gerald pulled the motorcycle up onto the sidewalk in front of the building, and Mrs. Roberson slid off. He put the kickstand down, and then went to the column between the sets of doors and started punching the access code into the keypad. With all the rain, he miskeyed the code on the first try. He glanced over at Mrs. Roberson, who had made a hood over her eyes with her hands. He peered up the side of the building. The rain deflecting off the brick facing made the water seem to come from every direction. Why was there no awning? He entered the code a second time and the doors unlocked.

Gerald went back to wheel the bike inside, as Mrs. Roberson held the door open.

She watched him as he put the kickstand down and leaned the bike onto it. "Is this okay?" she asked him. "Are you allowed to be in here?"

"Sure. Dr. Gauge lets us come here whenever we want." Gerald walked over to press the button next to the elevator door. "It works," he explained, "but the button doesn't light up anymore. You can tell what floor it's on by the needle on the brass dial over the top." The needle on the half-circle began to move off the twelfth floor, and rotated counter-clockwise until it ultimately pointed directly to the left.

"What is this place?" she asked.

"It used to be office space that was rented out to the local banks."

"And Dr. Gauge owns it?"

"He owns the entire thing, all twelve stories. Most of the lower floors are empty. He lives at the top."

The painted three-panel door of the elevator shuddered and opened. The elevator had a musty smell, and some of the loose tiles of linoleum were strewn about the floor.

"How old is this elevator?" she asked as she stepped inside.

The lift squeaked and groaned as it started upward. "I don't know." Gerald braced a hand against one of the side walls. "Pretty old, I think. There's a column of stairs on the back side that zig-zags its way to the top."

"That's not going to do us much good, if we get stuck in here."

"Dr. Gauge isn't the tidiest person," he explained, "and he's not much for maintenance."

"I'm freezing. Are there any dry clothes in here?"

"I can't get into Dr. Gauge's apartment, but Tyler has some workout equipment on the floor below the lab. I think he may have some t-shirts up there."

"Anything," she said shivering. "I had pneumonia a few years ago, and I can't afford to get that sick again."

The doors opened, and Gerald led her inside. There was an old padded mat spread across the floor, along with assorted barbells and other weight equipment scattered around. On a far wall, he found a shelf with some folded t-shirts. "Here you go," he said, handing her one.

"Thank goodness!" Mrs. Roberson pulled open the buttons on the front of her red cotton blouse, and then slid up it up over her head. Underneath, she wore a red bra with ruffles.

Gerald was struck speechless at seeing her state of partial undress.

"Yes," she said, as she quickly pulled the T-Shirt over her head to cover herself, "it's red and it has ruffles. I was wearing a red top, and white shows through." She lifted her hair out of the shirt collar, and then arched her back and crooked one arm up under the back of her shirt to pull the snap on her bra. She pulled one strap through a sleeve and took her arm out of the loop. She then threaded the entire bra through the opposite sleeve and dropped it on the weight rack. She hesitated for a moment, took a quick glance at Gerald, then opened her pants and slid them off. She smoothed out the side of her shirt, which had bunched up on the side of her hip.

Gerald stared at her, dumfounded.

Mrs. Roberson snapped her fingers in front of his face a couple of times. "Settle down, Beavis." She lifted his chin to make his eyes meet hers. "This isn't some peep show."

"I'm sorry," he said as he averted his eyes. "I didn't mean to stare."

"Up, up," she lifted his chin again. "Just keep your eyes up, and we won't have a problem. Don't apologize. You're hard-wired. You can't help it. Just don't get confused as to why we're here."

"Who's Beavis?"

"He's a typical male, just like you. How far did you say it was to get up to the lab?"

"Up one floor," Gerald pointed at the ceiling. "The research lab is two floors up, but what I came to show you is on the next floor."

Rabbit in a Bottle

"Where are those stairs you told me about? I'm not climbing back in that clunky elevator for just one floor."

They made their way up the back staircase. Gerald led the way, squishing water out of his track shoes with every step. Mrs. Roberson scampered nimbly behind him in her bare feet. She was so silent, he had to occasionally glance back to be sure she was still there.

Gerald threw the switch to bring on the lights in the main laboratory, and stepped inside. He placed a hand on the counter and pulled off his sneakers and socks. Mrs. Roberson stepped around him in her bare feet. He tried not to stare at her legs or gawk at her breasts jiggling about in the t-shirt as she walked by.

Mrs. Roberson scanned the massive control bank of switches, lights, needle gauges, and circuits. "What is all this?"

"I don't have any idea how any of it works. All I know is that this is what keeps me alive." Gerald walked over to the shroud covering the bell jar and pulled it off, then pointed to the hairless rabbit lying inside.

Mrs. Roberson stepped forward and peered through the glass, then turned back to Gerald. "What is that?"

"It's a rabbit," Gerald paused. "Somehow, Dr. Gauge uses its brainwaves to keep me awake. I don't expect you to believe me."

No," she patted him reassuringly on his chest. "I believe you. It's a fantastic story, but it all fits. An incredible event often has an incredible explanation."

"The stimulation makes my brain more active and increases things like reasoning, learning, and memory retention."

"Which is how you became a math whiz and are now poised to become the next star of the Scholastic Bowl?" She pointed to a second shroud next to the rabbit in the bottle, "What's under that one?"

Gerald hesitated. He didn't feel right about exposing Tyler's part in the secret, but he didn't want to lie.

Mrs. Roberson sensed that the question had put him in a difficult position. "Never mind, I'm sorry I asked." She had it mostly figured anyway. He had inadvertently mentioned that the weights on the lower floor belonged to Tyler. They both had survived similar near-death accidents. It wasn't hard to piece the rest of the story together. She decided to change the subject, "So now you're back, and you're the smartest student at school." She slid her arms naturally up onto his shoulders.

She had made the transition in such a supple, discreet way, he only partially noticed at first.

"I made a mistake. I should have kept a lower profile. Now I'm vulnerable."

"Don't worry." She peered up into his eyes. "I am your friend. The one great human quality is being able to be a good friend to someone. I'm smart, and I'm on the faculty. I'll protect you."

Gerald gazed down into her eyes, and then became conscious of her arms over his shoulders. Her moist, disheveled hair made her seem very appealing. "Mrs. Roberson," he fumbled for the right words, "what are you doing?"

"I don't know, Gerald." Mrs. Roberson sighed and laid her forehead against his chest, Her breath felt warm against his chest. "I just really don't know." She lifted her head to peer back into his eyes. "I guess I'm trying to seduce you."

"You are?" Gerald wasn't sure what she expected him to do.

"We're thinkers, you and me. I guess that's why I like you so much." She paused. "But sometimes we think too much, and we're better off putting it all aside for a moment."

Gerald's mind was racing, "I think too much," he repeated.

"Gerald, when a girl puts her arms around your neck, you're supposed to put your hands on her waist."

As Gerald put his hands on her waist his fingertips grazed the sides of her panties. He immediately pulled his hands higher to avoid them, and then laid them over the outside of her shirt.

Mrs. Roberson smiled at his reaction. "It's okay. You can put your hands on my sides. Go under the shirt. I promise you I don't have a bear trap hidden in there anywhere."

Gerald used his thumbs to lift the sides of her shirt over his hands, then nestled his palms against the sides of her torso in the recessed curves just above her waist.

Mrs. Roberson gently fondled the locks of hair on the back of his head, "I'm really flattered that you trust me enough to bring me here. She stepped up and kissed him lightly on the lips. She moved her face forward to put her cheek next to his, "I guess I trust you, too."

"Mrs. Roberson," he stammered, "I told Lori . . . ."

"Shhhhh; Lori gave you a day or two to straighten out other relationships, before anything would start up with her; isn't that right?"

"Yeah," Gerald's mind was in too much of a disarray to remember clearly.

"Then you need to consider this a part of that in between phase." Mrs. Roberson whispered in his ear. "You can reach under there now."

Gerald slid his hands from her sides to rest on her firm stomach. Her skin felt unbelievably smooth.

"Go ahead," she coaxed him, "do it now, before I lose my nerve."

He slid his hands up her toned bare abdomen until his fingertips gently touched the bottoms of her breasts. Mrs. Roberson kept her cheek pressed tight against the side of his face. He could tell she had closed her eyes, by feeling her muscles move in her face.

She made small gasp and tensed. "Do it," she whispered, with a sense of urgency.

He tucked his elbows low then slid his forearms up her stomach, as he reached higher to cup her breasts in each hand.

Mrs. Roberson took a deep breath, then opened her mouth as if to speak, but didn't say anything.

Gerald rubbed his thumbs sideways across the tips of her breasts.

"Easy, easy," she winced. "You can squeeze as much as you like, but don't tweak my nipples too hard. They're tender."

Gerald nodded and molded her breasts with his hands.

Mrs. Roberson dipped her head slightly and breathed a bit harder, as she seemed to stare through his chest, "Now," she swallowed hard, "grab the bottom edges of my shirt and gently pull it up over my head."

Gerald slowly pulled the bottom of her shirt up, peeling it from her body. She raised her arms to accommodate him, and her breasts spilled out.

"Up. Try to look up." She raised his chin with the backside of her red painted fingernails. "When you stare at the other person too much, it makes them feel naked. You look into my eyes," she pointed toward her eyes with her two forefingers, "and I look back into yours," she said, pointing toward his.

She embraced him for a moment, and then pulled back slightly, "Now it's your turn. Lift your arms." Gerald raised his arms over his head as she lifted the sides of his shirt and pulled it over his head. She slid her arms around his sides, and then stepped closer to press her naked breasts against his chest. She reached up to put her arms against his back to hug him close. "Let's just pause here for a second. There's no need to get in a rush." She leaned her shoulders back a bit to gaze into his face, "Are you okay?"

Gerald nodded, "I'm okay."

"That's it," she coaxed him slowly, "just relax and look into my eyes."

He felt her fingers at his waistband, and then heard the unmistakable sound of his zipper.

"Easy. Nice and slow." She peeled the soggy jeans down off his body.

When Gerald stepped out of his wet pants, Mrs. Roberson stood up and grabbed his waist, and pressed her breasts into his chest again. "Are you ready to go over to the couch?"

"Yes," Gerald nodded, "the back lets down to make a bed."

"You get one side, and I'll get the other."

Gerald worked the latch on the left side of the sofa, and gazed across at her. It was a surreal moment, watching her naked except for her panties. She was beautiful. Her body was toned and well proportioned. Her brow was knitted in concentration, as she tried to work the latch on the back of the couch. When the latch gave way, she eased it down, and then glanced over at him.

She realized he was gawking at her again."Eyes," she reminded him as she pointed toward her own face with two fingers. "Remember the eyes."

Gerald smiled, "I'm trying; I really am."

Mrs. Roberson stood up and put her hands on her hips. "Why don't you lie down on the bed, and I'll get on top of you."

Gerald was slightly taken aback by her frankness. Somehow, actually hearing her verbalize it made the moment seem more real.

"Don't worry about your underwear," she went on. "I'll work around that."

Mrs. Roberson paused for a moment and took a breath to compose herself mentally, then quickly bent to shove the sides of her panties down to the floor. She stepped out and flicked them to the side with the toes of one foot. She placed one knee next to his hip, then swung the other knee over him and gently sat down. "That's good," she nodded and cooed softly, "that's good."

Dr. Gauge awoke to the red flash of a warning light. He sat up in bed and checked the console. Someone was in the lab. He punched up some numbers on the screen. Someone had come in the front door, but it wasn't a forced entry. Whoever it was, they had used an access code. He flipped a switch to bring the laboratory camera on line. The image of the upper profile of a naked woman came on the screen. He stared at the monitor for a moment, and then rechecked his equipment. He turned back to the screen to notice the figure on the monitor was swaying. What was she doing? Dancing? He worked the lever to pull back the zoom on the camera. There was Gerald, lying on the couch with a naked woman on top of him. Dr. Gauge scowled, "That damn kid." He slapped the power switch to shut off the monitor, and then rolled back over in his bed.

The Morning After

- Maybe the sun's light will be dim and it won't matter anyhow. If morning's echo says we've sinned, well, it was what I wanted now. -

Mrs. Roberson slid off the couch and folded her arms across her naked breasts as she walked to the window. She gazed down the ten stories and watched the tail lights of a lone car go up the street. Her line of sight shifted to a lighted sign in front of a bank that alternated between displaying the time and temperature. The digits changed from "74°" to "2:17am." It was a lucky break. For the time of year, the temperature could easily have been in the 50's.

She turned back to Gerald to watch him sleep for a while. He had a look of innocence about him. Her mind drifted back to her job as school teacher. A feeling of dread swept over her as she considered that her career had been tarnished. She shook her head with a bitter sweet smile. It was what she had wanted at the time and it was too late for second guessing. Gerald rolled to his side as he slept.

She walked over to pat his chest and wake him, "Gerald, you need to get up."

Gerald squinted his eyes. "What time is it?"

"It's two in the morning. I need you to take me home."

Gerald rubbed his eyes. He gazed at her nude form sitting on the side of the bed. The situation seemed both wonderful and surreal. "Are we—?" He wasn't sure where to start.

"Hey," she gave the side of his chin a light pat. "You have to keep it together."

Gerald propped himself up on his elbows, "So what happens now?"

"What happens now is you take me home." Mrs. Roberson paused. "It's still warm out, but the temperature could start to drop. She paused as she realized that he wasn't absorbing any of her words. "First thing, I can't have this conversation with you sitting there staring at my tits." She bent over him to grab her t-shirt from the far side of the bed, and then pulled it over her head. She rolled the front of the shirt up around her thumbs, exposing her breasts, "Here you go. Take a good long look. It's the last one you'll ever get."

"So we're not going to . . . ?"

"No," she said as she rolled the front of her shirt down, "we're not going to be sleeping together on a regular basis." She stepped into her panties, and then grabbed the sides to pull them up and over her butt.

"Then why did . . . . ?"

"I don't know." She knitted her brows and stared off in the distance as if looking for some hidden answer. "It's just . . . . things are a little jumbled right now. I can't really explain why, but it's done now and we just have to think of it as our secret bond."

Gerald nodded.

"You have to accept that was a one-time thing. I care about you, Gerald." She paused, trying to find the right words. "I want to say that I love you, but it's not the 'let's go crazy and just run off and get married' sort of love. The word love means so many different things; it's become sort of a catch-all." She lifted his pants from the back of a chair. They were still slightly damp, "Here, you'd better put these on so we can go. I'll turn my head in case you're shy."

Gerald slid out of bed and pulled the pants on. He stood up and fastened the buckle. Everything she had said made sense, but he felt sad that it had passed so quickly and was now over.

Gerald reached out to grab her around the rib cage, and pulled her toward him, pressing her breasts against his chest. He ran a hand through the back of her hair and pressed his lips hard on hers. He took his time. If this was the end of their one night of intimacy, he was going to bring it to a satisfying conclusion.

She seemed to understand his thinking and was willing to give the fullness of the moment. She gently put a hand on his cheek as she kissed him back. After a few moments, she broke away and rubbed the side of her finger across her lower lip, "Are we okay?"

He nodded and smiled. "We're good."

Rabbit in a Bottle

Chapter 5

<u>Friday's Tempest</u>

<u>Taking Physics</u>

- I couldn't tell if Mr. Leslie despised me or sort of liked me. He normally let everyone know right where they stood with him. With me, however, he seemed to amuse himself by keeping me guessing. -

Gerald struggled to stay awake in his first hour Algebra class. Occasionally, his head would dip, and he would start to drift off. Leslie was loving it. Whenever he saw Gerald's eyelids drooping, he would stop talking and call in a loud voice, "Gerald, are you with us over there?" When he was at the white board, he would occasionally call on Gerald to give the answer, but those tactics proved not to be fruitful. Somehow, even being groggy, Gerald still seemed to come up with the right answers.

Leslie went back to his desk. He had originally planned to spend the rest of the period at the board writing up problems but for today, lecturing was more fun. He read from the book in a deliberately long-winded discussion. As Leslie read, the rest of the class followed along. He discreetly watched Gerald from the corner of his eye. When the time came to turn to the next page, Gerald failed to turn his.

Leslie stopped lecturing, "Gerald?"

"Yes?"

"We're on the next page now."

"Oh," Gerald reached down and turned the page. "Sorry, Mr. Leslie."

Gerald put his elbow on the table and propped his head on his arm, as he followed the lines along with Leslie's voice. Gerald had already read through the entire book a few days earlier. Going over the same material made it hard for him to stay focused. Eventually, his tiredness caught up with him. When the time came to turn the page again, he had already zoned out.

Leslie was quietly exuberant. This was too good. "Gerald," he called out. "It's time to turn the page again."

Gerald reasoned that Leslie couldn't keep track of the pages of everyone's books. He shrugged as if not understanding, "Okay." It was a bluff to make Leslie think he'd already turned the page when he wasn't watching.

The bluff didn't fly. Leslie relished in the moment. It was like manna from heaven. "Gerald, you need to turn to the next page."

Gerald shrugged again.

"You're on page 57, Gerald. We're all on page 58. You need to turn your page, so you will be up with the rest of us. We're waiting on you."

A moment later, the bell rang. Leslie shook his head. It was a shame. Leslie wished he could have had another twenty minutes to torment him. "Class dismissed. Except for you, Gerald. Come up to the front, if you don't mind."

Gerald walked up to his desk, "I only have two minutes to go to my locker and get to my next class."

Leslie shook his head, "Don't worry about that. I'll give you a hall pass."

"I'm sorry I wasn't more alert in your class today, Mr. Leslie."

Leslie ignored the apology. "I think you should take my physics class."

The request caught Gerald off guard, "I can't; the semester has already started."

"Yes, you can, if I give you special permission. You'll have some catch-up work to do, but if you have trouble with that, I will help you."

Gerlad was caught offguard by the request. "Why would you want me to take physics? I didn't think you liked me that well."

"That's true, I don't" Leslie's lip curled as if he silently enjoyed his response. He knitted his fingers and rested them on his desk. "Lately you have developed an exceptional talent. I have tried to motivate you for the last few years and you have finally started showing some promise." Leslie adjusted his black tie. "You need to take my class so that your talents are not wasted. Everyone in this school knows that I teach only the smartest students. I am the best, and I teach only the best. Please don't quote me, so no feelings are hurt, but everyone knows it's the truth."

"That doesn't make any sense to me. Why would the best teach only the best?"

Leslie grimaced, "What don't you understand about it? It's completely logical."

Gerald shrugged, "It seems to me that the best students are preordained to excel. Teaching them is like teaching a bird to fly or a fish to swim. I can't see how it would be much of a challenge."

Leslie leaned back in his chair. He was liking this kid less and less.

"If you take a mediocre kid, or a below-average student," Gerald cupped his hands, as if gathering water, then lifted them up, "if you could do something with them, and bring them up and teach them something, now that would be a wonderful thing. That would seem like more of a challenge than tossing a few text books at the honor students, then letting them chew through the material and churn out some good grades."

The bell for the next period started to ring. Leslie took a pad of hall passes from his desk drawer and scratched a large "L" across the top slip. He ripped it from the pad and lifted it near his shoulder without looking up.

Gerald took the slip and started to leave.

"I want an answer by Monday, or the offer is closed."

"I'll think about it."

Leslie huffed and pulled out his text book to go over the problems for his next class.

The Confrontation

- Hell hath no fury . . . . -

Tammy strutted through the hallway like she was on a victory march. About halfway down, she spotted Gerald turning the combination to his locker. Her eyes locked on him like a laser zeroing in on a target. She moved in and flipped her head back to toss her hair as she leaned a shoulder on a locker. She gave him a warm smile, "Hi, there."

"Oh, hi, Tammy." He gazed warily off to one side, wondering what she was up to.

"I just wanted you to know that I'm okay. I'm not mad anymore."

"I'm glad," he answered in a relieved voice. "After the other day, I was afraid that . . . ."

"I'm seeing someone," she interjected, with a hint of dark sinister in her voice.

"That's great! I'm happy for you. Anyone I know?" He patted her on the shoulder.

Tammy yanked her shoulder back indignantly, "Oh? Curious are we?"

"Well, no, I just . . . ."

"It's Eddy Leach. I'm sure you must remember him. He beat the crap out of you in the fifth grade."

"I don't remember that, but it doesn't surprise me much. He seems like something of a bully. I've heard he works in his dad's shop and drives that old Cadillac."

"Yes, he does," she said triumphantly. "It's a classic, and the seats are reeeeeeaaaaallll comfortable."

"Are they?"

"Yes, they are. I should know." She spoke slowly, accentuating every word, "I've been *fucking* him in them every night." She leaned forward and let her lower lip flip off the edge of her teeth as she venomously spat the words into his face. "Ah; what's the matter?" She drew her head back slightly, as her face took on an expression of fake concern, "Does that bother you, Gerald?"

"Not at all," he shook his head and closed his locker. "It's none of my business. I don't care what you do." Gerald turned to walk away.

"Maybe *that's* your problem, Gerald; you don't care. Maybe you should start to care." Tammy put her hand on his shoulder to stop him. "You'd better start showing me a little more respect. Otherwise, I think I might have Eddy beat the crap out of you again. How would you like that?"

Gerald brushed her arm away, "Like I said, it's none of my business. I don't care." He started walking down the hall.

"Yeah, well; you're repeating yourself." She called after him, "When you start repeating yourself, it's time to leave the conversation."

Gerald spun around and smiled, "I'm leaving," then turned and went on down the hall.

The Water Fountain

- I should have known it was coming. Maybe I shouldn't have provoked Eddy, but somehow I think it was going to happen either way. -

As Gerald walked down the hallway, two hands came from behind and shoved him forward. Gerald took a quick step forward to catch himself, and flopped up against Tyler. He turned around to see Eddy.

"Come on," Eddy motioned him forward, "you like to run that big mouth and make fun of me in front of the class. Let's see if you can back it up." Eddy pointed at Tyler, "This doesn't concern you! Stay out of it. It's not your business."

Tyler helped Gerald back up to his feet, "Did you make fun of him in front of the class?"

Gerald nodded, "Yes, I did."

Tyler sighed, then put an arm on Gerald's shoulder to move him off to the side. "Listen," Tyler glanced back, then spoke to Gerald in a low voice. "He seems intimidating, but he's really not that tough. It's just some theatrics. Don't let him spook you. He fights like a gorilla. Keep your fists up, your elbows tucked in, and your head back. Try to block his line of fire with your forearms. Don't block too wide or you'll leave a hole. Just block enough to deflect him, then get right back in position. Don't try for the haymaker. Wait for openings and take little jabs. Be patient."

Gerald stepped up as the gathering students made a circle around them. Eddy made a big swing with his right arm. Gerald pulled his head back and deflected the blow with his forearms. It hurt and would leave a bruise, but it was better than getting punched in the face. As Eddy got back in position, Gerald realized he'd squandered a chance to counter. Eddy made another swing. He deflected with his forearms again. He glanced over at Tyler. This was starting to get painful.

With the second swing, Eddy had left himself open. Not getting a response from the first blow had given him a false sense of security. Gerald seized the opportunity and turned his fist up to punch him in the lower ribcage as hard he could.

Eddy coughed, and paused a moment. He stood up and threw another swing. This one was sloppier than the first two, and Gerald was able to sidestep it completely. He punched Eddy in the side of the face as he came past. The blow was only of moderate strength, but it grazed the side of Eddy's cheek and slammed solidly into Eddy's nose. Blood immediately started to stream from his nostrils.

Eddy wiped the red from his upper lip and stared at the back of his hand, then glared at Gerald, "I'm going to kill you, you son of a bitch."

Eddy stepped up and brought a punch down the centerline of Gerald's body. Gerald turned to pull his shoulder back in an attempt to let it roll past him. Eddy's knuckles scraped his chest, stinging his flesh, but it was only a glancing blow. Gerald turned forward again and put his weight behind a punch to Eddy's face. It landed solidly, striking him just under the nose.

Eddy's head rocked back, as stars burst through his skull. He staggered dizzily to the side, and flopped over the water fountain. "Enough!" he gasped, as he held out a hand to stop Gerald. Eddy held the other hand under his dripping face. "I'm bleeding badly here." He bent over the water fountain and turned the white plastic lever to let the icy water run over his face. He ran some into his mouth to rinse the blood, and then let it dribble into the stainless steel pan. When he had caught his breath, he bent to take a long drink.

Gerald stood waiting for him to finish. "I'm sorry I teased you, Eddy. You seemed like you were out to get me, and I figured it would only be worse if I backed down."

Eddy turned his face toward him. He opened his mouth as if to speak, but instead, blew a geyser of water into Gerald's face. Gerald made a step back, trying to get his vision. Eddy stepped around the water fountain, locked a hand around his fist, reared back, and drove the point of his elbow deep into the middle of Gerald's chest.

Gerald gasped and slouched, trying to breathe. He put an arm out to try to steady himself from falling down.

Eddy walked around to his side. "You're not very smart," he taunted him. He put the edge of his shoe into the back of Gerald's knee and shoved it downward, slamming his kneecap into the aged hardwood floor. Eddy grabbed Gerald's hair and yanked his head up with one hand, and reached into his pocket with the other. He flicked open his switchblade and put it to Gerald's throat, "Do you know why you lose, Camden? It's because I'm smarter than you are. I know how to play the game, and you don't. I think I might slit your throat right now. Consider it a penalty for being stupid. I might go to jail for it, or I might get off with a self-defense plea. Maybe they'll consider it a mercy killing. Either way, you'll still be dead."

Tyler's oversized fist closed around Eddy's wrist. He slowly and gently torqued Eddy's forearm upward, making him loosen his hold on the knife.

"I told you to stay out of this," Eddy growled at Tyler.

"Hey," Tyler shrugged, "You have a knife and he doesn't. In my book, that makes you a chicken shit." Tyler slid his other hand under the blade and held open his palm. "Let it go."

"No way," Eddy growled back.

"I'm not getting stuck with a blade today," Tyler assured him as he raised Eddy's forearm a little more. "If you don't drop it, I'm going to have break your arm." Eventually, the pain became too great, and Eddy's hand cocked open, letting the knife slid out of and drop into Tyler's palm. Tyler tucked it in the side of his belt then used his other hand to straighten Eddy's arm and press his face against the row of gray metal lockers, "Now, there's just one more thing, and I'll let you go. I want you to explain something to me."

"You're going to regret this!"

"You might be right, Eddy," Tyler nodded, "but we can stand here all day making threats back and forth with you in this uncomfortable position, or you can answer just one question and we'll quit for now."

"What is it?"

"What's wrong with you, Eddy? Most people are born with the same basic parts to their character. What's missing from yoiur soul that makes you a bully? Why is it that you can't feel good about yourself unless you're hurting someone else? Why can you not be happy unless you're making someone else miserable? If you don't like someone, why don't you just stay away from them?"

"Are we done yet?" Eddy watched Tyler through the corner of his eye. "Have you finished your little sermon?"

"Sure, Eddy, I'm finished." Tyler let go of his arm. As Eddy rubbed his shoulder, Tyler drew the knife out of his belt and offered it to Eddy, handle first. Eddy glanced down at the knife handle as if it were a trick. Tyler shook his head, "Take it, Eddy. I'm not a thief, and I'm not a bully. You should give it a try. It's a happier existence, I promise you."

Eddy grabbed the handle of the knife. Once it was back in his fist, he eyed the blade for a moment, then glared back up into Tyler's face.

"You go right on ahead, if you still have an itch," Tyler said softly. "I promise you, though; this time I will absolutely break your arm. Maybe you should quit before it gets any worse."

Eddy glared back as he folded the blade and tucked it into his back pocket, "You're going to regret this."

"You said that already, Eddy."

Eddy didn't answer, but turned on his heel and waded through the crowd. He would bide his time for now. He needed a chance to think and regroup.

Get Charlie

- It was the first time I'd seen Mrs. Roberson since the night at the laboratory. -

Gerald watched Mrs. Roberson dance around in front of the white board, making marks with her pen. He was very tired, and could barely stay awake. If she was tired, she didn't show it. She had the same perky exuberance for her English class as normal. She glanced his way a few times, but there was no sort of special recognition, no hidden meanings behind her eyes.

Gerald glanced over at Eddy. He was sulking in his corner, immersed in his own world, doodling in his spiral notebook.

When the class was over Gerald walked up to the front of the class. Mrs. Roberson lifted her head to greet him.

"Hi, Gerald, how's it going?"

"I was wondering if we should stop talking after class."

"No," she said in a low voice. "Just keep everything normal. We have to be careful. I could lose my job, or even go to jail."

"That's ridiculous."

"Maybe, but according to the law, a high school boy and his teacher are in the same bag as a pervert who hangs around a playground and molests little girls." Mrs. Roberson sighed and leaned back. "I heard you got in a scuffle with Eddy this morning. Do you want to talk about it?"

"What did you hear?"

"You were getting the better of him, but he took a cheap shot and then pulled a knife on you. After that, Tyler stepped in."

"That's about it," Gerald shrugged. "He threatened Tyler. Do you think he'll actually do something?"

"It's hard to say. Eddy's threatened about half the people in this school. If he went around making good on all his threats, that would be all he ever got done. He even threatened my little dog. It was subtle, but it was still a threat."

"I remember that. You mentioned that he was the same breed as Toto, and Eddy insinuated that he might hurt him."

"Charlie," she nodded. "My dog's name is Charlie."

"Is Charlie okay?"

"He's had no trouble from Eddy so far, but he's been a little sick. I've had a problem with moles tearing up my yard, so I bought some of those poison peanuts that you drop down into the hole. Charlie chewed open the pouch and ate them all."

"What did you do?"

"It was after-hours, so I couldn't take him to the vet. I went to the drugstore and bought some ipecac syrup."

"Is that the stuff that makes you throw up? Did it work?"

"Oh, yeah," Mrs. Roberson smiled. "It worked all too well. After I gave it to him, I took him into the back yard." She shook her head, "Poor little guy, he really wretched up hard. I felt sorry for him, but it was necessary to keep him alive."

"So he's going to be okay?"

"Pretty much. He's been a little sick. It took me a while to get the ipecac syrup from the drugstore, so I think some of the poison got into his system. Which reminds me," she said quietly, "I have a favor to ask of you."

"What's that?"

"Can you can come by my house tomorrow and pick Charlie up and take him to Mrs. Branson's house on the other side of town?"

"What time? I was going to study for the Scholastic Bowl with Lori, but we should be done by mid afternoon."

Mrs. Roberson nodded. "That works out fine. Can you be sure to pick him up if I leave him on the front pourch? I will have him in the carrier on my front porch. Mrs. Branson has to go to Terre Haute tomorrow, and won't be back till around 7:00. I need you to watch him for a few hours, and then drop him off at her house after she gets back."

Gerald nodded, "I can do that."

"I need you to be sure and get him so he's not sitting in the carrier all evening."

"I can't take him on the motorcycle, but I can go home and get the folks' car."

Mrs. Roberson seemed satisfied, "Okay. I will lay his leash out for you so you can walk him."

"That sounds like it will work." Gerald checked his watch, "I'd better roll."

As he went to the door, she called out to him, "Gerald."

"Yes?" he spun around in the doorway.

"I just wanted to say thanks." She paused and gazed off to the side, then back at him, "Thanks . . . ." the words trailed off, "for everything."

Gerald smiled and pointed at her, "Keep it normal, Mrs. Roberson," then turned and walked down the hall.

"Keep it normal," she repeated quietly, and then started gathering up her things to go home for the day.

The Psychologist

- I was a bit apprehensive about seeing a psychologist. I wasn't sure what to expect. -

Gerald walked down the hall until he came to a heavy door made of blond wood with a window of marbled glass. The black lettering read "#107 – Dr. Karen Hartman." He turned the round silver door knob and opened the door. Inside, a dark haired receptionist looked up as he approached, "May I help you?"

"I'm Gerald Camden. I have a 2:00 appointment with Dr. Hartman."

The receptionist checked her watch, "One moment, I will see if the doctor is ready to see you." She picked the receiver up from the phone on her desk and pressed one of the clear buttons on the base, "Gerald Camden is here for his 2:00 appointment." She nodded and cradled the phone receiver, then gestured toward the door. "You can go on back. The doctor will see you now."

Gerald walked through the door. In the center of the room, a large rug stretched across the hardwood floor. At each end of the rug was a large, brown leather overstuffed chair accented with gold rivets. The back wall was shelved from top to bottom with books.

Dr. Hartman stood in the middle of the room. She was nothing like what Gerald had expected. She was as tall as he was, and in her early fifties. She wore a white shirt and a dark blue pants suit. Her long, dark brown hair was pulled back into a pony tail. As she approached, there was something about her body language that conveyed a sharp intellect. Perhaps it was the elegant precision with which she approached him. A powerhouse brain peered out from behind her large brown eyes. As she surveyed him, it seemed that she was already studying and reverse-engineering him, "Hello, Gerald, I'm Dr. Hartman," she said as she extended her hand.

Gerald shook her hand, and then nodded toward the expansive library case covering the back wall. "Have you read all those books?"

"No," she shook her head and smiled, "All this," she waved her hand, "is just there for decoration. It's supposed to provide a homey atmosphere so you feel comfortable. Are you ready to get started?"

"Do I sit in a chair or lay on the couch?"

"That depends on you," she answered, picking up a spiral notebook and a pen. "Are you more comfortable or honest?"

"I don't understand."

"If you are feeling nervous or inhibited, then you should use the couch, to help you relax. If you feel like you're going to have trouble opening up, then you should sit in the chair. It allows me to make eye contact, and steer the conversation if you start to hedge."

Gerald was feeling outgunned intellectually, but he wasn't ready to run up the white flag just yet. He moved to sit in one of the chairs. "This is fine for me; I'm not afraid to make eye contact."

Dr. Hartman sat in the other chair. "This will work better if you try not to take an adversarial position when we talk. Keep in mind that I am here to help you. That's what I'm paid to do."

Gerald eyed her inquisitively. It almost seemed like she was reading his mind. "You seem very perceptive."

Dr. Hartman smiled and nodded, "That's my job, but we're not here to talk about me. We're here to talk about you."

Gerald waited for her to speak again, but she sat quietly in her chair, gazing back at him. It made him think of a staring contest. He thought about staying quiet, and just letting the clock run, but then he remembered what she'd said about not being adversarial. He pressed the heels of his palms into the arms of the chair and leaned back, "I'm not sure what I'm supposed to do or say."

"Why don't you start with telling me why you're here?" She spoke in a low, welcoming tone.

Gerald turned up his hands, "I'm here because my parents asked me to come."

"I see," Dr. Hartman made a few scribbles in her notebook. "Why do you suppose they asked you to do that?"

Gerald felt like he was on the end of a string, being gently led in. He fought back the instinct to resist her and close down, "I had an accident a couple of weeks ago and I can't remember anything before that."

"Would you say that it was only due to your lack of memory, or are there other reasons that brought you here?"

"I suppose it was because of our awkward dinner situations."

"Why are they awkward?"

"Because I don't know them. I know they're supposed to be my parents, but they're strangers to me."

"So, you feel emotional obligations that are unable fulfill and therein lies the conflict?"

"Yes," Gerald nodded in surprise. "That's it." The answer seemed so simple and easy. How had it eluded him? "That's exactly it." He eyed Dr. Hartman. The lady knew her craft. "The same thing happened with my old girlfriend."

"What did you do?"

"I broke it off. I guess you can't do that with parents."

"Yes, you can," Dr. Hartman scribbled in her pad, "but there are a lot of legalities involved. Since you are approaching your eighteenth birthday there wouldn't be much point, but it's an option."

"No, they're nice people," Gerald shook his head, "I just want to make it better."

"Okay," Dr. Hartman gave an approving nod, "What's preventing that from happening?"

"It's very awkward."

"Why?"

"I guess I've been acting a little weird."

"Does that seem to be productive?"

"No." Gerald shook his head. "It's definitely not productive."

"Then why do you do it?"

Gerald was quiet for a moment as he tried to determine the answer. "I think sometimes when I'm very uncomfortable; my natural reaction is to want to speak. When that happens, if I don't have anything prepared to say, something meaningless or weird sort of pops out in its place."

"Can you see how that would make your parents uncomfortable?"

"Yes I do, and that's not fair to them. I will try not to do it in the future."

"I think that's a good plan. On your next visit, please let me know how that works out."

"I'll do that."

"I would like to hear more about this old girlfriend. Did you handle that conflict in the same way?"

"No, we had sex in the furnace room at the high school."

"I see."

"It was her idea. I think she sensed that I was going to break up with her. I went there to talk to her, but she wanted to have sex, instead. I think she was hoping it would help preserve the situation and delay my breaking up with her."

"But it didn't it help?"

"No, I broke up with her that same evening."

"Were you not attracted to her?"

"Oh no, she's the prettiest girl in school."

"Yet you broke up with her, anyway. Was all of this due to the feeling of obligation that came with the relationship?"

"It was, initially, but then I met another girl. Most people think Tammy is prettier, but I like Lori better."

"Why is it that you prefer Lori over Tammy?"

"We just seem to click. When we're together, I feel really happy and comfortable."

"Is Tammy unhappy with the change?"

"She seems pretty angry. I guess no one likes to get dumped. She's started dating an older guy named Eddy."

"Do you think this is going to be a source of conflict between you and Eddy?"

"He picked a fight with me earlier today, but it wasn't over Tammy. I teased him in class and it made him angry. He pulled a knife on me, and my friend Tyler intervened and twisted his arm to make him let it go."

"It sounds to me like being teased didn't sit well with Eddy."

"Eddy's just sort of . . . ." Gerald was quite for a second as he searched for the right adjective, "he's mean."

"Why is he mean?"

Gerald shook his head. "I don't really know."

"Do you think he's dangerous?"

Gerald shrugged. "He might be, but right now it seems like he's more upset with Tyler than he is with me."

The Stadium

- Unfortunately, Eddy wasn't a stereotypical thug. He was bold, clever, and devious. That's what made him so dangerous. -

The office for Wabash Valley Heat & Gas was just west of the school. Eddy picked his way through the woods that ran between the gas office and the football stadium. Encircling the stadium was a strip of grass that the groundskeeper kept mowed through the summer. As he walked along the perimeter, he scanned the area for any weaknesses in his plan. The canopy from the trees met with the back of the scoreboard overhead, forming something of a tunnel. Everything seemed to be within acceptable risk.

As Eddy made his way to the first gate, he brushed aside the hair of the long black wig. Some years earlier, he had bought it at a garage sale for just such a purpose. With the air-filled, gallon-sized Ziploc bags tucked under his oversized shirt, anyone who happened to see him from a distance would describe him as a paunchy dark haired fellow. He figured it was unlikely anyone would see him, but he took pride in his prudence and careful planning.

When he came to the first of two small gates on opposite ends of the backside, he found it locked by a padlock that was old and weathered from hanging outside for several years. It was doubtful that anyone would still have a key, but he couldn't take the chance.

He opened the side of his jacket and untied the foot-long section of rope looped over his shoulder. There was no way he was going to carry a set of bolt cutters the entire distance. Tying a rope to the ends made the cutters easier to carry and less likely to be seen. The black metal handles slid down his side as he caught the jaws with the toe of his boot. The handles had been red at one time, but he had painted them flat black to make them less noticeable. Details were key to the success of an operation like this, and Eddy considered himself the master of details.

Eddy turned his body to hide the gate. The padlock connected the two ends of the rusty chain that made a loop, connecting the pipe that made up the edge of the gate, with the pipe of the surrounding frame. He slid the mouth of the bolt cutters around the end link of the chain, and pulled his elbows. With a snap, the metal gave way as the jaws of pinched shut.

Eddy reached out quickly to catch the old lock and pocketed it in his jacket, then brought out the replacement and snapped it in its place. He gave it a quick yank to make sure it was secure. One down; one to go. All too easy.

As he walked around the west end toward the second gate, he surveyed the back end of the stadium. Two tiers of metal stairs wove their way up the rear to the backside of the score board. Between the two tiers was a catwalk running midway across the back. The metal backing would keep him from being seen. Everything was in order.

He replaced the other lock in the same manner as the first. He surveyed the area one last time; to make sure he hadn't missed anything. The stage was set. He had done his due diligence. Everything should go according to plan.

Trip to the Drugstore

- Mrs. Camden was actually a very nice lady. She knew me for a fraud. I was a fraud, and there was really no way of getting around it. -

Christine had spontaneously asked Gerald to accompany her to the drugstore. Gerald knew it would be so that she could talk to him alone for a while.

Christine put the car in reverse and backed out of the drive. "Your father loves you, you know."

"He's a nice man," he acknowledged.

"When you had your accident and it appeared that you were gone for good, it broke his heart. It broke mine, too. Now that you're back, he thinks everything is right with the world again."

"What do you think?" Gerald asked

"I think that there are things that you're not telling us."

Gerald was slow to answer.

"I told him I wanted you to move out of our house. I can't live like this. Something has to give. If we can't fix this, if we can't come to an understanding, then I will get a divorce and leave the house."

"I don't want to see that happen."

"Then just be honest with me. If you can do that we'll call a truce. I have to know that I am not crazy."

"What would you like to know?"

"You said the other night that you weren't our son. What did you mean by that?"

"I just say things sometimes. I'm not sure why."

"Are you my son or not? Is it really just amnesia, or is there something else going on here?"

"I don't think I am your son. It's true that I have no memories, but it's not just amnesia."

"At least I'm not crazy. There's more to a person than just a bunch of memories. It's not like spinning up a disk on the computer." Christine paused, "If you're not him, then who are you? Are you going to tell me what's going on?"

Gerald sighed, "Do you want the complete truth?"

"Yes, of course." she answered with conviction. "You live in my house. I wash your clothes and I cook your meals. You owe me that much."

Gerald nodded, "That's fair." He puffed his lips slightly and slowly exhaled a stream of air through his lips. "I can only tell you what I know, which isn't much. There is a new process that is used to bring back someone who is brain dead or comatose. It involves genetics and brainwaves, and has only been attempted a couple of times. I have no recollection of anything prior to the last week. I really don't know who I am. No one knows. I could be your son and have just lost my memory, or I might be a new person entirely."

"You're not my son," Christine smiled a sad sort of smile. "Let me put your mind at ease about that."

"No, I don't think that I am."

"Of course, if you're not him, that would mean that my son, my real son . . . ." Christine's voice trailed off.

"I think he's dead. I'm very sorry."

Christine's eyes welled up. She blinked out a tiny ball of salt water that slid over her makeup and came about halfway down her cheek. "He was a good person. You would have liked him. He had a very simple view of the world. He floated along at the top," she lifted her hand and moved it side to side, "just like his father. Most people only acknowledge what they can feel, touch, and see. Gerald was like that. He was smart, but he had innocence about him."

"I would have liked to have known him, somehow."

"He smiled more than you do, and he had an easy laugh that put people at ease." Christine stared far down the road. "He was just like his father in every way, very easy going. He was a more likeable person than you are." Christine glanced over at him. "No offense."

Gerald smiled and shook his head. "None taken."

"As strange as it sounds, you're actually more like me than he was. He didn't need to sort everything out and tuck it into place like you and me."

"I'm not him; I can't be him," Gerald said slowly, "but maybe you could think of me as a new son." Gerald touched his chest. "These are still the genes that came from your body. In a way, I'm like your newborn son. I'm a week old. It's just a little awkward, because I'm in an older body. Maybe if we try to think of it that way, it could work for both of us. Neither of us asked for this. It was visited on us by circumstances outside our control."

For the first time, Christine felt a comfort with his presence. He wasn't her son, but he didn't claim to be, and he seemed to be a decent person. He still had her eyes, regardless if someone else was looking out from behind them. She held out her hand, "I'm pleased to meet you. My name is Christine."

Gerald shook her hand. "Pleased to meet you, as well. I'm the imposter pretending to be your son."

Christine nodded and smiled, "Welcome to the family." She gently reached out with her arm; at the halfway point, she paused for a second with hesitation, then she softly laid her hand on the top of his head and gently stroked back his hair. She laid her palm across the side of his cheek for a moment, and then slid her hand down to caress the top of his shoulder. The turn for the drugstore was coming up. She put her hand back on the wheel, flicked on the turn signal, and then pressed the brake.

Rabbit in a Bottle

Chapter 6

Saturday's Festival

Meeting the Parents

- I was a little nervous about meeting Lori's parents. -

Gerald stood on the front steps. He checked his watch. It was just a couple of minutes before 9:00 am. He wasn't sure if her parents were sticklers about time like Lori. Gerald took a deep breath before he rang the bell. There were so many variables. Should he offer to shake the father's hand first, or wait for him? Should he call him "Sir"? "Dr. Taylor" sounded too cold and distant. He didn't know the first name, and even if he did, using it could seem disrespectful. How do you refer to a girlfriend's father?

Gerald pressed the doorbell and heard the chime inside the house. The point of no return. He wondered how the introduction to her parents would be configured. Would Lori open the door, with them standing behind her? Probably not. More than likely, the man of the house would be the one to let him in. Gerald knew he was about to be closely scrutinized. He wondered if Dr. Taylor would turn out to be one of those, "No boy is good enough for my little girl!" types, and conduct a full interrogation as to his intentions. That would be a nightmare.

He heard the unmistakable thumping sound of someone coming down a staircase. What was taking so long for them to get in formation and open the door? Gerald prepped himself. He would look them squarely in the eyes; he wanted to show confidence in a non-aggressive manner. He saw Lori's face appear in the small diamond shaped door window. The latch turned. It was show time.

Lori pulled the heavy, reddish brown wood door back, and then popped the latch of the white aluminum storm door with the heel of her palm. He looked past her but didn't see the parents. That was good. Maybe they were going to play it low key.

Lori smiled her warm smile, "Hey, Gerald. Come on in."

Gerald stepped in through the door.

Lori leaned close to him and whispered, "Don't be so nervous." She gently touched the side of his arm. "It will be fine."

Gerald followed Lori as she walked back into the house. In the kitchen, a lady who had to be the mother was leaning over the green granite surface of a kitchen island, going over her notes in a tiny spiral pocket notebook.

"Mom, this is Gerald, we're going to go upstairs to study and go over the Scholastic Bowl rules."

"That's fine, honey," she said, glancing up from her grocery list, then back down. "Lori, do you still drink those specialty teas? You know—cinnamon, jasmine, vanilla, and green tea, all of those? Should we get more?"

"I can always drink regular tea but if they are there, I will drink them. Except for the jasmine; that stuff is nasty."

"We still have almost a full box of jasmine that isn't going to be used." She turned to Gerald, "Gerald, do you like jasmine tea?"

Gerald shrugged, "I don't know if I've ever had it." He peered into the living room where a television was playing with the volume turned low. On the couch sat a pudgy man in his late forties. He had dark brown hair and a square face. On his lumpy, oversized nose, he wore a pair of half-moon reading glasses. His dark brown eyes tracked back and forth over the lines of the morning newspaper.

"That's Daddy."

Dr. Taylor didn't trouble himself to look up from his paper.

Gerald cleared his throat, "Lori tells me you're a dentist."

Dr. Taylor flipped the page of his newspaper. "The most beloved profession in the world," he called out, without making eye contact. He held up one hand, as if holding a small invisible device between his fingertips, then made a whirring sound through his teeth, imitating the sound of a drill.

"Come on," Lori gave Gerald a light slap on the chest, "let's go upstairs and get cracking." She snagged his elbow and led him up the stairs.

Gerald followed her down a long hall through the second floor. "This is a pretty big house."

"It's ridiculously big, about eight thousand square feet. It's too much space for just the three of us. That's because of Daddy. He tends to overdo everything. It is a nightmare to keep it clean. When we got it, Mama threatened to leave him unless he hired a maid service." Lori pointed to a door, "That's the bathroom." She stopped at the next door, "This is my room." She opened the door and let him walk in first.

Gerald stepped inside and scanned the room. It seemed like everything in it was white. The centerpiece of the room was a huge canopy bed, with white ruffles and white lace swelling from every part of it. The wardrobe and dresser were a glossy white with gold accents. "This looks like a princess's room," he said, speaking aloud.

Lori closed the door behind him. "That's good, because I am a princess." She walked around to his front and draped her arms over his shoulders, "I'm glad you came."

"Thanks for having me." Gerald remembered what Mrs. Roberson had told him and slid his arms around her waist. He worked his hands just under the bottom of her shirt and caressed the sides of her torso.

"Easy there, chief." Lori pulled back for a moment and smiled. "The folks are right downstairs." Lori chided him, "Don't think that just because you manage to work a foot into a girl's bedroom, you can start getting all frisky. Keep it over the shirt, mister."

Lori hesitated for a second, and then realized he wasn't going to take the hint and kiss her. How could he be so gifted in some areas, and such a clueless idiot in others? She gave him a pat on his shoulder. "Okay, let's go get on the bed." Lori bounded across the room, and then jumped high as she turned in the air and let her butt bounce on the mattress. She flopped back against the pile of white fringe pillows heaped at the top of the bed. She scooted them around as she moved to the far side of the bed. "Come on," she said, as she patted the mattress beside her and looked up at Gerald, standing awkwardly in the middle of the room.

Gerald came over sat on the edge, then glanced over at her, "What now?" He felt a little strange being on the bed with her.

"Kick your shoes off and lay back. You can use my belly for a pillow."

Gerald slid his sneakers off and leaned back. Lori put her hands on the side of his head to tip him back. Lori laid her hand across his forehead. "You seem a little warm. Are you running a fever?"

"Maybe slightly; I've been that way ever since the accident."

"As long as you're sure you're okay. She ran her fingers over his scalp and toyed with the locks of his hair, as he studied the underside of the canopy. It was a massive creation of white satin. Seams, gathers, and ruffles were everywhere.

"What sort of bed is this?"

"It's a Queen Anne. Daddy bought it when he went on a trip to Boston to attend a dental conference."

"He goes all out, doesn't he?" Gerald answered as he studied the massive web of stitched fabric.

She nodded, "That's Daddy, he's OCD."

"OCD?"

"Obsessive compulsive disorder. Everything he does is extreme. Sometimes Mama wants to kill him."

Gerald was still feeling a bit confused about how casually she had invited him onto the bed. "Have you brought a lot of guys up here?"

Lori gave a short laugh. "What kind of question is that?"

"No, I didn't mean it that way. It's just that, I don't know. You just seemed so comfortable with the whole idea of . . . ."

"With you climbing in bed with me?"

"Yeah."

"Well, we're not going to be breaking out the scarves and the baby oil just yet." She patted his cheek as she spoke. "But to answer your other question, no; you're the first guy I've ever had up here."

"Okay." Gerald felt awkward for having asked the question.

"Are you ready to get down to business?"

"What sort of business did you have in mind?"

"Do you know anything about scholastic bowls?"

"Not a thing."

"We go by standard NAQT rules. A topic is chosen one week in advance to give everyone the same amount of time to prepare. At the actual meet, there are three types of questions: toss-ups, bonuses, and a lightning round. In the toss-ups, anyone can buzz in. The moment someone does, the host stops reading the question and the person who buzzed has to answer, with no help from the rest of the team. If they answer correctly the team gets to collectively answer a bonus question. If the toss-up is missed, the moderator reads the rest of the question, and the opposing team confers and tries to come up with the answer. That's called a pick-up. Make sense so far?"

"I think so. Is there a bonus question after a pick-up?"

"No; there is only a bonus question if the toss-up is answered correctly. Toss-up questions are worth 30 points; bonuses and pick-ups are worth 15. There are 4 packets in a meet. Each packet consists of 12 toss-up questions and their follow-ups. Got it?"

"Yes, I've got it."

"There is a lightning round after each set of 12 packets. In a lightning round, each team gets to answer as many questions as they can, at 5 points each."

"That all sounds easy enough."

"I know what you're thinking," she said mischievously.

"Oh you do?" He tipped his head up to peer into her face, "And what do you suppose I'm thinking?"

She ran the tip of her finger over the upper curve of his ear. "You think that you're going to answer all the questions by yourself and impress me," she said flippantly, "but it doesn't work that way. You're not allowed to buzz in on two toss-ups in a row, and the same person can't answer two questions consecutively in the lightning round. It's set up that way, so the most any one person can individually answer is half the questions."

"So what's the topic?"

"Mrs. B called me this morning. It's US presidents, from Washington through the Civil War."

At that moment, there was a knock at the bedroom. Gerald tensed and quickly started to sit up. Lori grabbed a handful of his hair and pulled him back, to keep his head lying on her stomach. "Will you calm down?" she hissed. "You're going to freak my parents out."

Lori turned her head to call out to the door, "Come on in."

The door opened, and Mrs. Taylor stood in the doorway. She saw Gerald, lying back with his head on her daughter's stomach, "Well, now," she said to him, "you certainly seem comfortable."

Gerald was dumbfounded, and fumbled for something to say.

Lori gave him a light swat on his cheek, "Answer Mama."

Gerald nodded, "This bed is great." As soon as he said it, he winced at the suggestiveness of his answer.

"Now, Lori, please don't do strike him like that. He's not a dog, you know."

"Oh I know, Mama," she ruffled the top of his head with the tips of her knuckles. "I think a dog would be easier to train."

"I'm sorry to interrupt, but I'm going to start lunch soon. Are the two of you going to be eating here or going out?"

"Out." Lori laid her palm across the top of Gerald's forehead. "I owe Gerald a trip to Monical's." She swatted his shoulder. "Get up. I'm starting to get hungry. We'll be down in a minute, Mama."

When Lori and Gerald came down the steps, Dr. Taylor was lying on the couch watching an episode of "Columbo." Lori walked over and thumped the couch with her knee, "Hey, fat man. I need some money. We're heading for Monical's and it's my turn to buy the pizza."

Dr. Taylor lifted one side of his body and reached into his back pocket to pull out his billfold. He pulled it open and took out three $100 dollar bills and offered them to her.

Lori shook her head. "I don't need that much, Daddy; we're only going out to eat pizza."

"Oh, for crying out loud, take it, already! The next thing, you'll need some shoes or some jeans or something, so use it for that. Go on and take it, so you quit disturbing my show. Dick Van Dyke is the killer, and Columbo is about to catch him."

Lori turned back toward Gerald, "Do you see what I mean about obsessive compulsive?"

"I'm not digging around in my wallet again," Dr. Taylor huffed at his daughter. "If you don't want it, I'll give it to . . . . uhm," Dr. Taylor' voice trailed off as he fumbled for the name.

"Gerald," Lori prompted him. "His name is Gerald."

"Yeah, right. Whatever. Will you just take it and quit fussing at me, so I can finish watching this show? You're making me miss the best part."

Lori took the bills and stuffed them into the pocket of her fuzzy yellow shorts, "Thanks, Daddy."

"Yeah, yeah, welcome, welcome, go, go, bye, bye." He waved his hand with one arm, and then lifted the remote with the other to turn up the volume a few steps.

Mrs. Taylor stepped up to speak, "How are you going to get to the pizza parlor, Lori?"

"On Gerald's bike," she answered.

"But, Lori, you don't have a helmet!"

"She can wear mine," Gerald offered.

"Okay, but if you're going to let her use your helmet, what helmet are you going to wear? Did you bring an extra helmet?"

"No, I only have the one."

"Well, that won't do," Mrs. Taylor shook her head. "That simply won't do at all."

Lori sighed in frustration. She knew this was an area in which her mother wasn't going to budge.

"Let's do this," Mrs. Taylor offered. "If you two are going to be using his motorcycle with any regularity, you're going to need to get a helmet. Why don't I drive Lori into town, we can go by

Walmart and pick up a helmet, then I will drop her off at Monical's."

Gerald nodded to Lori, "Sounds reasonable to me." Then he glanced over at Mrs. Taylor, "Actually, you're welcome to stay and have pizza with us, if you like."

Lori turned to glare at him.

Mrs. Taylor knew her daughter well enough to know that Gerald's idea would not be well received, "Oh no, thank you," she said with a chuckle in her voice. "I will drop Lori off, and you kids have a nice time. Just please be careful with Lori on the bike."

"Yes, Ma'am, I sure will."

Lori felt a little frustrated. She would have preferred to ride over on the back of Gerald's motorcycle, but she didn't see any way for that to happen. "Okay. Give me an extra hour." Lori checked her watch, "I'll meet you at Monical's around 12:30." Lori turned toward the living room couch, "See you later, Daddy."

Dr. Taylor kept his eyes locked on the television, but reached out a hand to wave goodbye.

The Bathtub

- She would never say where she came from. Yesterday don't matter if it's gone. While the sun is bright or in the darkest night, no one knows. She comes and goes. -

Gerald had a little extra time to kill, so on a lark he drove down the street that went past Mrs. Roberson's house. It was hours early, but as he passed by he thought he saw the dog carrier on her front porch. He put on the brakes and turned around, then came back and pulled into her driveway. There was the dog carrier, in front of the aluminum storm door. Gerald climbed the three unpainted concrete steps and knelt next to the box, "Hey, Charlie. What are you doing out here this early?" He slid his fingers through the square holes in the chrome wire door of the carrier. "I wasn't supposed to pick you up for another four hours or so. Good thing I happened to come by. I guess I'd better go get the car and come back and get you."

Gerald noticed an envelope stuck in the carrier handle. When he bent closer, he saw his name was on it. When he opened it, the inscription read, "Gerald, thanks for everything. You're one of the best friends I have ever had."

Gerald stood up and slid the card back in the envelope. He glanced from side to side, whacking the side of the envelope against his clenched fist as he paced around. Something just didn't feel right. He slid the dog carrier to one side, then opened the storm door and tried the door knob. It was locked. He studied the window sill. There were no signs of forcible entry.

He hopped down the steps and walked over to the garage. He cupped his hands against the long, horizontal oval window to make a shadow for his eyes, as he peered inside. Her car was still in the garage. He pulled his head back. Someone could have picked her up, but somehow he didn't think so.

Gerald walked around the corner of the house. He wasn't familiar with the internal layout, so he started going from window to window. He peered into the kitchen from a window on the back side of the house. It was empty, but everything appeared to be normal.

He circled around to the far side of the house. The side windows were shrouded by heavy bushes. He pressed his way through the branches to get a closer view. He squatted down to try to peer through the one-inch gap under the venetian blind. The ends of the branches bunched up around his face, as he cupped his hands around his eyes to get a look. He could see the top of a nightstand and an open bottle lying on its side. He couldn't read the label but a few of the pills were strewn around next to the bottle on a doily.

Gerald shifted sideways, trying to see through the glass at an angle. He saw an arm wrapped in the sleeve of a bathrobe, draped across the edge of a bed. Puzzled, he pulled back from the window. As a realization dawned on him, he ripped his way out of the bushes and ran around the side of the house. He bounded up the front stairs and pulled open the storm door. He kicked the wooden door with the heel of his foot. His sneaker left a foot print on the white paint, next to the door knob, but it didn't budge. He kicked it again, and the molding around the door jamb started to crack. With another kick, a quarter-inch gap appeared between the door and the frame. Gerald worked his fingers into the gap and pressed his shoulder against the side of the door. With a crackling of splintered wood, the door lurched open.

Gerald ran to the back bedroom and found Amy slumped across the bed. He picked up the bottle to take a quick look. "Oh, you bitch!" He threw down the open bottle, letting the capsules scatter across the carpet. "You stupid, stupid bitch!"

128

As he tugged at her sleeves to sit up, her bathrobe gaped open to reveal her nakedness. When he tied the sash to close up the front, he noticed that something was crooked in her arm. He slid it out. It was a studio portrait of her and a man. Probably her dead husband, he thought. He put his arm around her waist and tried to lift her out of the bed. She was too limp and slipped from his grasp. Gerald put his arm back around her waist, and grabbed a fist full of hair with his other hand. He draped her across his knee and shuffled her into the bathroom. He let her slump over the edge of the tub, then grabbed her hair and lifted her head up. With his other hand, he started quickly tapping the front of her chin, until her mouth gaped open. Gerald slid his hand into her mouth and crammed his two fingers in as deep as he could then tickled the back of her throat. "Come on, come on," he urged.

Amy gagged, and started to heave. Gerald let her slump forward, as she wretched and started to vomit into the tub. He remembered what she had said about the dog. Gerald went to the medicine cabinet over the sink. She had mentioned that the dog had eaten something poisonous and she had given him ipecac syrup to make him vomit. He yanked open the mirrored door and scanned the bottles on the frosted glass shelf, then began to knock them off one by one. It had only been a couple of days. It had to be here somewhere. He picked up a bottle to read the label as he went back to the tub.

Amy groggily up at him as a ribbon of drool streamed from her mouth. Gerald grabbed a handful of hair and lifted her to her knees. He stuck the end of the bottle in his mouth, and twisted the cap off with his teeth. He spit the cap off to the side, and then braced her head against the side of his body, as he worked the neck of the bottle into her mouth. He simultaneously tilted her head back and lifted the bottle to run the syrup down her throat. "Come on, you have to drink it." He massaged her throat to make her swallow. Just as she started to heave, he let her back down to belch up another cup full of gastric contents. Gerald grabbed her hair again and pulled her up once more. "One more round. You can do it!" He let her down to heave into the tub again. Amy put a hand on the wall to brace herself, as she coughed and spit some of the residual fluids from her mouth.

"Where are your keys? I'm taking you to the hospital."

"No," Amy wiped the front of her mouth, then reached back to tap the front of his shin. "I think I'm okay. There's no need for the hospital. Just make me some coffee."

Gerald put the lid down on the toilet, and then lifted her with his arms under her shoulders to help her sit down. He put a hand on her shoulder to steady her. "Are you sure you're okay?"

"Yes," she wiped her mouth with the sleeve of her bath robe. "Just give me a second, and I'll be fine."

"Alright," Gerald snugged the loosened sash on her bathrobe. "Coffee, right?"

"Yes," she said, wiping her face, "strong and black, please."

Pleasant Coffee

- It was a little sad to see Amy so disheveled, but at least she was alive. –

"Gerald?" Amy pressed her palms against the ceramic sides of the warm mug with the large red apple on the side. "Did you call me a bitch?"

"I don't know," Gerald shrugged, "I might have. Probably once or twice. I didn't really keep count. I was a little upset at the time."

"It's okay." She smiled then took a sip.

"Are you going to tell me what this is all about? Remember, you said that we were friends and that there shouldn't be any secrets that we can't share."

Amy smiled, "Touché." She peered down into her mug. "It's Denny," she answered quietly.

"Your husband?"

"He died three years ago today. I guess I was just feeling worn out and ready to quit the game."

"So you decide to kill yourself? Why would you do that? Killing yourself only punishes the people who care about you. It's certainly not going to bother people who don't like you."

Amy shook her head and peered into her mug. "It just got to be too many problems."

"I never would have guessed that you would do that."

Amy took another drink from her mug, and then glanced back over at him. "Have you ever thought about it?"

"Do you mean killing myself?"

"Yes," Amy nodded. Did the thought ever cross your mind?""

"Not really," he answered thoughtfully. "I wouldn't want people to wonder why I wasn't strong enough to finish the game. I don't want to cash in my chips before I finished playing my hand." Gerald paused a moment, "I didn't mean to sound judgmental. It's just how I feel."

"It's okay," she answered softly. "While we're airing our souls, I suppose I ought to tell you that I wasn't completely truthful about how my husband died."

"You said it was brain hemorrhage."

"It was a brain hemorrhage, alright," she gently nodded her head and gazed off in the distance. "One day he came home from work, stuck my Daddy's 45 in his mouth, and shot a bullet through the top of his head."

"I can't imagine what that was like."

"It was horrible," she said as she gazed aimlessly forward. "The cops and the ambulance just haul away the body and you clean up the mess. It's not a job you can hire a maid to take care of. I had to mop his blood from the floor and wipe his brain matter off the walls. Months later, I was still finding little bits of his skull lying around."

"I'm very sorry."

"It is a strange feeling to be furiously angry at someone and desperately miss them at the same time. At the funeral, part of me wanted to yank him up out of that coffin and slap his face. And do you know what was the cherry on top?"

"What?"

"It's that he did it just a week after our anniversary, and that he did it with Daddy's service pistol. To me, that was a sacred artifact. If he had to kill himself, why did he have to do it right after our anniversary, and why did he do it with Daddy's gun? I used to hold it and have warm thoughts about Daddy. Now, it's tainted, and it always reminds me that my husband used it to commit suicide."

"I don't know. Maybe he didn't think about it that much. He saw the pistol and he did something stupid."

"That happens, I guess," she said thoughtfully, as she ran her finger around the upper edge of the steaming coffee mug. "People you care about will do stupid things that hurt you, but it doesn't mean that they don't love you." Amy heard a dog bark and turned to the open door. "Can you let Charlie in? He's been out there a while. I'd do it, but my legs are still a little wobbly.

"Sure," Gerald got up and opened the front door. He plucked off a piece of the splintered wood, then knelt down and opened the wire mesh door. The little dog came bounding out, and ran across the kitchen floor to paw at Amy's calves.

She reached down to pet him, and then looked back up at Gerald. "Dogs are wonderful. No matter what you've done, they will always love you and greet you warmly."

Gerald sat back in his chair. He glanced down at the Charlie and then back at her. "He's a cute dog."

Amy sat back and sighed. Her face took on a faraway look. "You were the only man I ever slept with, other than my husband."

"So, did you plan all this?" Gerald asked, "Did you know all along that you were going to sleep with me, and then try to kill yourself?"

"Every year when this week rolls around, I give serious thought to checking out. This time, I was just feeling worn out and ready to quit. As for our night in the laboratory, it was a spur of the moment thing."

She turned up one hand from her mug; "Actually," she took a drink and sat the mug down, "at the start, I was pretty uncomfortable with the way you kept leering at me when I was changing my clothes. Then . . . ," she trailed off, "I don't know. Something happened, and the moment seemed to take control. I had never considered having sex again. Then I realized I wanted to feel that warmth one last time. It seemed like a closure. Like the last chapter to a book."

"You're not going to try this again, are you?"

"No." She took his hand and kissed the back, then pressed it against her cheek. "I promise you, as my special friend, that this is the only time. I will never do this again."

"Sort of like our one night together."

Mrs. Roberson nodded and rotated the bottom of her cup on the surface of the table. "Exactly like that."

Gerald checked his watch. It was ten minutes past noon. He stood up, "I have to go!"

Mrs. Roberson glanced up from her coffee, "What's wrong?"

"I'm supposed to meet Lori at Monical's in 20 minutes."

Mrs. Roberson waved him off. "I guess you'd better get going."

The Pick-Up

- I was a little late meeting Lori at Monical's. Somehow, I thought it was best not to tell her that I had spent the time pouring ipecac syrup down our English teacher's throat. -

Gerald walked into Monical's and scanned the dining area. Lori was sitting in the same booth they had used the last time. She spotted him and waved him back.

"Sorry I'm late." Gerald scooted in across from her.

"No problem. I went ahead and ordered. Sausage, Mushroom, and Pepperoni and . . ." she lifted the plastic jug off the table, "a pitcher of Pepsi, right?"

Gerald smiled, "I guess this makes our second non-date?"

Lori raised an eyebrow as she filled his glass. "Are you going to drag me across the table again?"

"Well, I don't know," he answered casually."I don't like to repeat already used material and besides, you might get spoiled and start expecting that all the time."

"Listen to you talk," Lori laughed. "Okay, big stud man, we still have one last thing to go over strategy."

"Strategy?"

"Yes," Lori leaned forward slightly. "The scholastic bowl is mmore than memorizing encyclopedias and flirting with the girls."

"Okay, hit me with it."

"Only four members of a team can participate at a time." Lori tucked in her thumb and fanned out her other four fingers.

"Got it." Gerald raised his glass to take a drink.

"There are three main chairs and a pick-up. Each one studies a third of the material."

"What about the fourth person?"

"The pick-up is usually the strongest team member and studies the whole thing."

"Which chair am I?"

"You're the pick-up. There are six on the team. At half time, Mrs. Branson switches out two people so everyone participates."

Gerald was quiet for a moment.

"What's wrong?" Lori leaned back as the pizza arrived.

Gerald gazed down at the steaming pie, "Nothing. Why?"

"Oh, for Pete's sake. Your face looks like a little lost puppy that didn't get his doggy treat."

Gerald immediately shifted his face into a pressed smile.

Lori broke off a square of pizza. "I'll tell you what, big boy. While you wallow in the depths of your despair, I'm going to stuff my face and watch my ass get fat."

"You don't have a fat ass."

"Well played, sir." She pointed at him, as she lifted her chin to adjust the steaming bite of pizza in her mouth. "A lesser opponent would become totally distracted, and start obsessing about whether or not her ass was fat. Unfortunately for you, I already know I don't have a fat ass. As a matter of fact, I have one of the nicest asses in the whole school." Lori wiped her lips with her napkin. She liked this new Lori that he brought out. She felt tough and sassy. "So are you going to tell me what's bugging you freely, or am I going to have beat it out of you?"

Gerald reached for a square of pizza, "There are six people on the team."

"And . . . . ?" Lori had no idea what he was getting at.

"Before I came on board there were only five."

"That's correct. Your reputation as a math whiz is secure."

"Now that I have joined, someone else is going to have miss an extra half. It's my first Bowl and I'm going to be the pick-up. How is the person who got bumped out of that position going to feel?"

"Well, you can put your mind at ease," Lori broke off another square of pizza, "because I was the pick-up before you came along."

"So how do you feel about me taking your seat as pick-up?"

Lori up a finger to pause him as she chewed her mouthful of pizza. She swallowed her food then continued. "What I'm about to say may crush you a little."

"Crush away, kiddo." Gerald took a square of pizza and bit off a corner. "I'm tough. I can take it."

"You've over-estimated your own importance."

"Oooh!" Gerald mocked a recoil, "That is harsh. You're brutal, but I must admit that I'm intrigued. Please continue."

"I'm conceited enough to think I am pretty smart," Lori pointed back toward her chest.

"You're extremely smart," Gerald concurred.

"After all, I got an 82 on the Scholastic Bowl test. At the time, that was a record at Hutsonville."

"You sure seem to know an awful lot about those secret test scores."

"I'm on a roll; don't distract me."

"Sorry. Please continue."

"Gerald, I never, ever thought I was the smartest person in the world. Now, you came along with your hyper cross-wired brain. That doesn't make me any less smart than I was before. If I'm going to have someone in my life who is smarter than me, I'm happy that it's at least someone I like." Lori dabbed her hands with a napkin. "Comparing yourself to others only leads to frustration. There's always going to be a bigger fish. Make your own mark and be happy with it."

Gerald tipped his head to the side, "Wow, that is pretty insightful. I think you're wrong about me being smarter than you."

"There are all kinds of smart. I was talking about book smart. And yes, you are smarter than me in that arena. There's also people smart. That's where I have you outgunned."

"I bow to your greater expertise."

"That brings us to another question." Lori pointed to the last piece of pizza on the plate, "Are you going to eat that?"

Gerald smiled and waved it away with his hand. "Was that the question or is there some other nefarious subject we're encroaching on?"

"You really don't know?"

"Nooooo," Gerald answered slowly. "Is it something I should know already?"

"Yes it is. Here's your chance to prove me wrong about you being a social buffoon." Lori pursed her lips and waited. She wanted him to come up with the answer on his own, but he was obviously clueless. She decided to drop a subtle hint. "Like you said earlier, this is our second non-date."

"Yes," Gerald strained his brain trying to understand.

"And you came by the house and studied with me today."

"That's true. What's your point?""

"I also know that you broke up with Tammy Wells."

Gerald made a face like a deer in the headlights. "Uhm-hum," he said softly.

Lori picked her fork up from the table. She gripped it in the heel of her fist and raised like it was a weapon. "If you don't ask me out, right now, on a real bona fide date, I'm going to stab you right in the chest with this fork!"

"Well," Gerald cleared his throat. "Under threat of being impaled by an eating utensil, I'd like to ask you out on a real date."

Lori sat down the fork and smiled sweetly as if he had just given her a dozen roses. "That would be wonderful. I would be delighted to go out on a real date with you."

"Is that it?"

"When and where?" Lori prompted him, "You need to tell me when and where."

"When and where?"

"Yes, tonight at the big game."

"I don't have tickets," Gerald answered aimlessly.

"Yes, you do." Lori insisted.

"I do?"

Lori nodded "All members of the Scholastic Bowl Team get complimentary tickets on the fifty-yard line. Mrs. Branson brought me my ticket and yours yesterday afternoon."

"I guess we're all set."

Lori lightly tapped the table top with the palm of her hand, "You still have to tell me what time."

"What time?"

"The game starts at 7:00, so you need to pick me up around 6:00."

"Got it. I will pick you up at 6:00."

"Great!" Lori scooped up her helmet and checked her watch. "Are you ready to head back? I'd invite you to hang out at the house, but . . ." Lori jerked the ticket out from under the stainless-steel pizza pan, "I have to get ready for my real date."

"That works out fine." Gerald got up from his seat. "Tyler asked me to stop by his house around 3:00 so we could visit before the game."

"Really?" Lori pulled the gold Visa out of her purse as they walked to the counter. "It sounds like you and Tyler are getting to be pretty good friends. This isn't any sort of pre-game orgy like they used to give for Roman gladiators, is it?" Lori bit her lower lip as she passed the ticket and her card to the man behind the cash register. She wondered if she had pushed the envelope too far with the "orgy" quip.

The man behind the counter grinned as he swiped her card through the machine.

"Oh, great!" she thought to herself as she realized that he'd heard her quip. She felt the blood rush to her face.

Gerald grinned at her moment of discomfort. "Well, you know, I enjoy a good orgy as much as the next fellow, but I think it was just going to be some sort of pre-game pep talk."

Lori scratched her name on the visa slip and went through the door, then held it open for him to follow. She didn't want to risk waiting for mannerless-boy to open the door for her. "Okay, please be be back at my house by 6:00."

Girl Talk

- One thing that struck me about Lori's family was how at ease they were. They always seemed to be laid back and having fun. -

When Lori came in the front door, she breezed into the kitchen. She laid her helmet on the polished green granite surface of the kitchen island and folded her hands on top of it, then rested her chin on her hands, "I'm home, Mama."

Mrs. Taylor raised an eyebrow as she studied her daughter. "And how was your date with Gerald?"

"It wasn't really a date." She whispered as she glanced over into the living where she saw her father sleeping on the sofa.

"Hmmm." Mrs. Taylor leaned forward to rested an elbow on the other side of the counter. "Well whatever it was, it seems like you had fun."

"Yes, it was fun. He's sort of a smart aleck but I always give it right back to him."

"Sounds like you're getting pretty attached."

Lori raised her head to peek into the living room to verify that her father was still napping, and then turned back to her mother, "Mama, I think I'm in love."

"Oh my," Mrs. Taylor sighed. "How much in love are we talking here? Is this the 'hey, this is fun' type of love, or the really, really in love?"

Lori hunched up her shoulders and smiled, "I think this is getting close to really, really."

"So . . . ." Mrs. Taylor paused to ready herself, "should we be talking about birth control?"

"No!" Lori recoiled, "For Pete's sake, Mama, he has only kissed me once, the other day when we were at Monical's."

"Well, you know how it goes." Mrs. Taylor took out a plate and a vegetable peeler, and then pulled a couple of cucumbers from the refrigerator. "Teenage sex is a little like pushing a car off of a cliff. It starts out pretty slow, but once it gets rolling, it's not easy to get it stopped."

"You can relax, Mama, because I'm not headed over any cliff."

Mrs. Taylor took a peeler from a drawer then started shaving the skin off of a cucmber. "I just thought I would mention it, in case the time comes when it's getting close you would know what to do. There's a public clinic in the Commercium Building just south of the courthouse in Robinson, where you can get a prescription. You don't need parental permission or notification."

Lori's mouth fell open, "I can't believe you are saying this to me, Mama! What do you think I am?"

"I think you're a responsible young woman who has just acquired her first boyfriend. That's a very exciting time for a girl your age. I just don't want you to get all giddy and become careless. A single lapse in judgment can end up being a life-changing event. I don't want you to make the same mistake that many girls your age end up making."

Lori stared off to the side. She felt like she was being persecuted for a crime she hadn't committed. She went out for an innocent pizza and suddenly, her mother thinks she's a harlot. "Duly noted, Mama. Is there anything else or can we move on now?"

"Sorry, honey. I know that was hard to hear, but I had to get it out there. I need to tell you just one last thing, and then I'm done."

"Fine!" Lori's voice took on a sharp tone as she flipped her hand in the air. "Let's put it all out there and get it over with, so we can move on."

Mrs. Taylor leaned her forearms on the granite surface and spoke in a serious voice, "If the time comes that you decide to go to the clinic, please don't tell me about it."

"You don't want to know?"

"That's right." Mrs. Taylor began raking the peelings off of the cucumber again. "I don't want to know."

Lori was puzzled, "Why wouldn't you want to know?"

"Because if you tell me, I'm pretty sure you wouldn't want me to tell him." Mrs. Taylor pointed to the living room with the tip of the peeler. "If I keep it from him, he's still going to find out sooner or later. When he does, the first thing he is going to ask me is if I already knew. I would just as soon you didn't put me in that position."

Lori nodded, "I guess that's fair."

Mrs. Taylor reached for another cucumber. "So he only kissed you once?"

Lori took out a knife and a second plate. "Yes, it was the other day."

When Lori reached for a cucumber, Mrs. Taylor nudged her away with the side of her arm. "Stop! Wash your hands first."

Lori sighed and put her hands in the sink to run water over them.

"The other day?" Mrs. Taylor scraped the last few shavings from the side of the last cucumber. "Was this another date that wasn't a date?"

"Yes. He kissed me in the booth at Monical's. Can you imagine that? He leaned over right there in the restaurant!"

"That does seem a little strange."

"I really like him, but he is such a social klutz." Lori began slicing up the cucumber.

"Since that was the only kiss, I suppose that means you didn't get one today."

Lori had started to bring a slice of cucumber to her lips and paused. "No, he didn't kiss me today, but he certainly had the opportunity."

Mrs. Taylor shifted he head to one side. "You gave him the chance but he didn't take it? Sounds to me like, for all this worry, he's heading the other way."

"He's a social klutz, Mama; he'll figure it out."

"So, you've had two non-dates; is there a real date in the future?"

"He's picking me up at 6:00 tonight. That's our first real date."

"Well at least he was interested enough to ask you out."

Lori grimaced, "He only asked me out because I threatened to stab him with my fork."

"I suppose that's one way to get a boy to ask you out." Mrs. Taylor scraped the peels off her plate into the trash, then went to the sink and started rinsing off the plate and the peeler. "Are you sure he's not gay?" she asked over her shoulder.

In the living room, Dr. Taylor grunted and rubbed his face as he started to sit up. "Who left the TV on?"

"That was you, dear." Mrs. Taylor called from the kitchen. "You fell asleep during Columbo and left it on."

Dr. Taylor pressed the button on the remote to shut off the television, and then staggered toward the kitchen. "That was the one where Dick Van Dyke played a photographer. I have never gotten to see the end of it."

"That's because you always fall asleep, Daddy." Lori turned back to her mother and hissed sharply, "He's not gay!"

"What asre you two about?"

"Just a little girl talk, Daddy," Lori answered sweetly. "Nothing for you to worry about."

"Nothing for you to worry about," Dr. Taylor repeated, mocking the tone of her voice. "That's how they tell you 'none of your business' around here. So who's gay? That boy you brought here this morning?"

"His name is Gerald."

"I'm not surprised he turned out gay. He seemed a little anxious to me."

Lori dropped her hand to the counter. "He's not gay."

Dr. Taylor held up his hands. "Hey, I have no problem with him being gay. If he's going to be chasing around with my daughter, the gayer the better."

"I told you he's not gay!" She put her hands on her hips. "And we're not 'chasing around.' "

"No need to get hostile," He said as he reached down toward the plate of cucumber slices.

"Stop eating up all the slices." Lori scolded him. "You didn't help."

"Listen to you sassing your Dad." Dr. Taylor leaned to toward his wife, "This is your fault you know. You raised her up to be this way."

"You were there, too," Mrs. Taylor quipped back, "It's half your fault."

Dr. Taylor waved one hand in the air as he ambled back toward the living room with his stack of cucumber slices. "Oh no. That was you,." He pointed a thumb back over his shoulder as he walked away. "This was all your doing."

Mrs. Taylor gathered up the plates and glanced over at her daughter. "I'll clean up. You go on and get ready for your date."

"Thanks, Mama." Lori grabbed her helmet, ran through the kitchen, and bounded up the stairs.

Dr. Taylor saw her go up the steps, and wandered back into the kitchen. "What was that all about?"

Mrs. Taylor sighed, "Your daughter is in love." She sprayed the last bits of cucumber peels into the garbage disposal.

"Really?" He looked over at the stairs. "That kid on the motorcycle?"

"Yes, dear." She put the dishes in the strainer basket and dried her hands on a kitchen towel. "Our little girl is growing up."

Dr. Taylor nodded, "A little too quickly for my taste."

Secretariat

- I think Tyler was a better person than me. Having an advantage in sports really disturbed him. I never gave being in the Scholastic Bowl team a second thought. -

Gerald drove to the North side of town and pulled into the circle drive. He went to Tyler's front door and rang the bell. Tyler opened the door and waved him inside. As Gerald stepped through the door, Tyler flopped down on the couch. "Come on in; make yourself at home."

"Where are the folks?" Gerald sat down in a gold cloth easy chair across from Tyler.

"They went out to the grocery store."

"Are you ready for the big game?"

"No, not really." Tyler answered hesitantly. "I wanted to get your thoughts on something I've sort of been wrestling with. You're the only one I can ask, since you're the only one who knows the truth about my situation."

"Sure. What's on your mind?"

"I'm considering throwing the game."

"What? The Regional Championship game tonight?"

"Yes."

Gerald scanned his face for some sign that he was kidding. "Are you crazy?"

"Maybe," Tyler nodded.

"Why would you do that after all your hard work? You know you can win it."

"I know," Tyler answered softly. "That's not the point."

"Then what?"

"Because it's not fair."

"Because you're hooked up to a mouse?"

"Yes. The relay improves the speed of my neural synapses, giving me enhanced reflexes. It's the same thing as taking steroids."

"It's not the same thing at all. You worked hard to get this far. Who's to say how much of that is you and how much of it is caused by the relay?"

"People who use steroids make the same argument."

"People who use steroids had a choice. You didn't."

"It doesn't matter."

"So you're going to disappoint everyone—the school, the other players, all the people in the stands."

"At the risk of sounding self-centered, I'm not doing it for them." Tyler sighed, "I have to live with myself."

"It's not like you're committing some sort of crime. We're talking about a ball game here."

"I know, but I have to make my choices, and I just don't know if I want to play. Maybe it would be better to sit out the game than to accept some phony laurels that I don't deserve."

"What about the rest of the team? What about their laurels?"

"I would feel bad about that. I thought I would bring the game to a tie score at the end of the third quarter, and then pretend to be injured and let them finish the game without me."

"You know they can't win without you."

"I've been lying to them. I've been lying to everyone. Maybe I didn't start the lie, but I've been going along with it all this time. The thing about a web of lies is, sooner or later the truth has to come out."

"Have you ever heard of a horse called Secretariat?"

Tyler shrugged, "I think so. That was some race horse, wasn't it?"

"Secretariat is a horse that won the Triple Crown and set many track records that still stand to this day. No other horse has even come close. There was never one like him before, or any like him since. Do you know what made him so different?"

"I have no idea."

"Secretariat came from a blood line that has a genetic defect. Every few generations, it would crop up and a horse would be born with an enlarged heart. Normally, with an enlarged heart, it is malformed and weak, and the horse can't perform well. Secretariat was the only known exception. His heart was over twice the size of a normal horse's heart, but it was perfect. Years after he quit racing, Secretariat died of a hoof infection. They did an autopsy, and his heart is estimated to have weighed twenty-two pounds. The physician just stood there in stunned silence. He couldn't believe it. The heart was perfect. There were no problems with it. It was just this huge engine."

"What does that have to with playing football?"

"Secretariat didn't buy that heart. He didn't go out and earn it in some way. It was a gift, and he took that gift and he went out and did something extraordinary with it. He didn't worry about whether or not it was fair to the other horses. He just did what he was capable of doing. We're just dropped here with whatever gifts we have. We have to seize those gifts and make the most of them before they start to fade away."

"So you think I should play?"

"Absolutely, I think you should play, but only if you give them your best game. Don't do it halfway. Don't hold back because you feel guilty, or because you feel sorry for the other team."

"I don't like to embarrass anyone. I always win. Isn't that enough?"

"No. It's not enough. If you're going to hedge, then don't even bother putting on your jersey. You're not saving the other team embarrassment; you're insulting them. Be like Secretariat. Go out there and show them what someone with extreme talents can accomplish. The extraordinary is too rare to be wasted. The people deserve the chance to see it."

Tyler nodded, "Okay, I'll do it," he shrugged, "and I promise I will play this one full-out."

"Good. I think you're doing the right thing."

Tyler sighed, "There's something else."

Gerald judged from his demeanor that it was not good news, "Something bad?"

"Yes."

Gerald shook his head. "I can't really imagine anything worse than you thinking about throwing the Championship game."

"I have . . . ." Tyler's breath caught in his throat. He swallowed hard, "I have cancer," his voice cracked as he said the dreaded word.

Gerald was stunned, "Cancer? Are you sure?"

"Yes, I'm very sure."

"Well," Gerald fumbled to grasp the new information, "how bad is it?"

"It's very advanced. I don't have long left."

"But," you don't seem sick"

"No, not this me. The mouse in Dr. Gauge's laboratory. That me. I'm eaten up with cancer, and I'm going to die soon."

"How?" Gerald had trouble finishing the question. "How did you get cancer?"

"It was deliberate. I was injected with it." Tyler's voice quivered as he spoke. He stood up and turned toward the wall. In case he cried, he didn't want his friend to see it. "When I had my accident, Dr. Gauge used what he had on hand, which was a lab mouse from a cancer research facility. They were testing vaccines to make people cancer resistant. Dr. Gauge has been trying to find a cure. He keeps fiddling with it, trying to prolong my life, but he's running out of time."

"Tyler, I don't know what to say."

"You don't have to say anything."

"I do, Tyler. I really do." Gerald swallowed. "I have to thank you for helping me through this and looking out for me."

Tyler smiled and nodded. "You're gonna have to start looking out for yourself, soon."

"Yeah," Gerald answered softly.

"Alright, enough of this moping around." Tyler flashed his wide smile. "Are you coming to the game tonight? If I can get you a ticket, will you show?"

"I'll be there. I already have a ticket."

"Really?" Tyler seemed surprised. "It's been sold out for over a week. How did you manage to get a ticket?"

"I'm going with Lori Taylor. Members of the Scholastic Bowl Team get free tickets."

"Wow, aren't you the big stud. From Tammy Walters to Lori Taylor in one week. You are making the rounds. Is that it, or are there any other women that you wedged in-between that you're not telling me about?"

Gerald froze for second as he thought of the night he spent with Mrs. Roberson. "None that I am allowed to talk about," he answered coyly. "A gentleman never tells." Gerald silently replayed the moment in his mind, trying to measure the gap between Tyler's question and his response.

"Lori's a nice girl. She's cute. In my opinion, she's not as hot as Tammy, but to each his own."

"Tammy's seeing Eddy now. She's not being real discreet about it, from what I hear." Gerald checked his watch, "I have to run home and catch a shower before I pick up Lori."

Tyler smiled, "Mustn't keep the lady waiting."

"So we have this all settled, right? You're going to play it full-out."

"Yep. Full-out. Secretariat is going to run the Triple Crown tonight. It will be a show that no one will ever forget."

Questionable Intentions

- I will never forget picking Lori up for the game. Visiting Lori's house never seemed to go quite the way I expected. -

Gerald rang the doorbell and watched the small square of glass, waiting to see Lori appear. A face showed up on the other side, but it wasn't Lori's. Dr. Taylor peered through the glass for a moment, and then his face was gone. Gerald heard the bolt turn. The door opened, and Dr. Taylor leaned his body through the opening and pushed open the white storm door, "Yes?"

"I'm Gerald. You met me earlier today."

"What can I do for you, Gerald?"

"Hi, Mr. Taylor . . . ."

"I'm a dentist. It's proper to call me Dr. Taylor."

"I'm sorry, Dr. Taylor."

Dr. Taylor's face seemed to be getting impatient. "Are you going to tell me why you're here?"

"I'm here to pick up Lori. Didn't she tell you?"

"Hey, kid," Dr. Taylor held up a finger. "This is my house. People don't 'tell' me around here, they 'ask' me. I don't remember you asking me if you could invite my daughter out on a date."

Gerald swallowed hard. Things had gone so easily earlier that day; he hadn't expected to be grilled. He cleared his throat, "Dr. Taylor, may I have your permission to take Lori to the game tonight?"

"Maybe," Dr. Taylor rubbed his chin as he looked Gerald over. "I might have a few questions first. I figure a boy starts showing up at a man's house and his daughter starts getting all doe-eyed, then he's got a right to ask a few questions. Wouldn't you say that's fair?"

"Yes, that's fair." Gerald was little surprised to hear that Lori was getting "doe-eyed."

"Maybe you should start by telling me your intentions. You seem to me like someone who might have questionable intentions." As Gerald fumbled for an answer, Dr. Taylor's cheeks billowed out. His eyes started to bulge. He bent over and burst into wild spasms of laughter. "Ah crap, kid. You should see the look on your face!" He sputtered between gasps for air, "I just couldn't keep it going any longer. I'm sorry about all that, but you looked so sheepish when I opened the door, I started to pull a gag, and it just sort of took on a life of its own."

Gerald breathed a sigh of relief, "Is Lori here?"

"Sure, kid, sure. Come on inside." Dr. Taylor stepped inside and motioned for Gerald to follow him. He closed the door, then put a hand on Gerald's shoulder and called up the stairs, "Lori! Are you ready yet? Your date is here."

Gerald watched her bounce lightly down the steps, with one hand on the cherry wood banister. Her hair was perfectly styled. Her only makeup was a slight touch of blue eye shadow. Her shirt had a shallow vee that showed a slight hint of cleavage. The fabric was a woven series of one-inch horizontal blue stripes separated by thin white stripes. A gold heart locket dangled from a necklace, and bobbed lightly against her chest as she trotted down the steps. Her jeans looked soft and supple, and were only slightly faded. On her feet, she wore a pair of spotless white sneakers. She stopped on the landing and leaned on the banister. She beamed as she saw Gerald. "Hi. I guess you made it."

Gerald was mesmerized, "You look beautiful."

Lori stepped one foot back and bowed to a curtsy, as she spread her imaginary skirt. "Why thank you, sir."

Dr. Taylor quietly sighed and nodded slowly. He felt a bit sad. He had given her the golden necklace for her birthday.

Lori glanced over at her father. "Is everything okay, Daddy?"

Dr. Taylor snapped out of it, "Everything's fine," he answered, as if the question were ridiculous.

Lori smiled. "For a second, I thought your eyes were getting moist like you were about to tear up."

"Heck, no." Dr. Taylor waved the notion away as if he was swatting at a fly. "Let him feed you for a change." Dr. Taylor turned to Gerald, "Have you seen how much she eats?"

"I have," answered Gerald. "How do you manage?"

Dr. Taylor leaned over to Gerald as if conveying a dark secret, "Are you kidding?" He held up his thumb and index finger as if holding something small. "You don't really think a little piece of steel and porcelain costs a thousand bucks, do you?"

"So, what were you and Gerald talking about on the front porch for so long? You weren't giving him a rough time were you?"

"Nah. Well maybe just a little. Just some guy talk. Nothing for you to worry about."

Lori came down the last tier of stairs and picked up her helmet from the antique cherry credenza. "Are you ready to go?"

"Hey, uhm . . . ." Dr. Taylor held out a set of keys. "Your mother and I were talking, and you guys can take the car if you want."

Mrs. Taylor came over from the kitchen. "Yes, Lori, you worked so long on your hair. Are you sure you want to smash it down with that helmet?"

"Well, I didn't work on it *that* long. Careful now." She spoke out of the side of her mouth to her mother, "You're going to give him a swelled head. He's already a wise-ass, anyway."

"Hear now. Language!" Dr. Taylor barked.

"Oh, Daddy, I've heard you say worse."

"Yes, but I am still the Dad in this house and you are a seventeen-year-old girl. I don't want your date to be getting the wrong impression about you."

"Don't worry, Daddy. I have this one right where I want him. He never even knew what hit him. Thanks for the offer," Lori waved away the keys, "but if this is going to be my guy and he has a motorcycle, then that is what we need to be taking. Besides," she held the helmet up over her head, "I just bought this brand new helmet. There's no point in letting it sit around and collect dust." She pulled the helmet down over her head, then turned toward her mother and turned her palms up. "See, Mama? No problem."

Mrs. Taylor stepped up and tucked Lori's hair under the sides of the helmet. "You kids be careful out there."

"We will, Mama." As Lori started to walk to the door she looked over at her father. "Love you, Daddy."

"I love you too, baby."

Lori gave Gerald a swat on the chest as she passed. "Let's go, before Daddy embarrasses himself and starts blubbering." She opened the door and stepped out.

Mrs. Taylor smiled at Gerald. "We're still working on her ladylike behavior."

"I hope you make some progress soon." Gerald smiled as he pulled his helmet over his head. "Today at pizza, I narrowly escaped being stabbed by a fork."

Dr. Taylor closed the door and stepped up to the glass. He watched as Gerald kicked the bike over to start it, and Lori climbed on the back. The motorcycle went up the street and disappeared from sight. Dr. Taylor turned from the door. "I think you were right."

"What's that, dear?"

"I think our daughter is in love."

The Cut Offs

- I've heard about him, but I never dreamed, he'd have blue eyes and blue jeans. –

Eddy did exactly as he said he would. He pulled up in front of Tammy's house and honked the horn once. Eddy checked the second hand on his watch, to count off two minutes. He reasoned that it was wise to establish dominance early in the relationship. Less than a minute later, Tammy bustled out the front door. She had on a pair of frayed blue jean cutoffs, and the red and white cotton top. Eddy nodded to himself with satisfaction.

She climbed into the car. "Hi, Eddy."

"You look nice." Eddy knew how to mind the carrot and the stick. She had done as he'd asked, so he complimented her. Feedback was important.

"Thank you, Eddy," she smiled over her shoulder. Tammy pulled a brush out of her purse and started stroking back her hair.

"Don't do that," Eddy stopped her.

"Don't brush my hair?" She seemed a bit surprised by his request.

"I don't want you dropping any loose hair strands on my seats and carpet."

"Okay," she answered quietly, and dropped the brush back into her purse.

"Besides," he reached over and stroked her bare shoulder lightly, "You don't need to change anything. You look great."

"I do?" Tammy beamed.

"Sure, you do." Eddy put his hand back on the wheel. He smiled inwardly. There would be a break-in phase, but the girl was going to work out fine.

Day of Reckoning

- Tyler was true to his promise. He played the last game full-out. –

On the night of the Regional Championships, the small, sleepy town of Hutsonville, Illinois, was buzzing. The town had swelled well beyond its normal capacity. Cars jammed the streets. Police directed traffic at every intersection.

Gerald picked his way through the crowded streets and came to the east side of the school. He pulled into a narrow space, and then slipped off the bike. "At least driving a motorcycle gives you more places to park."

As Gerald locked down their helmets, Lori stepped up to him. As he stood back up straight, Lori took his face in her hands and kissed him. "Gerald, I have to ask you a favor."

Gerald smiled. "Well, that is certainly a nicer bribe than the threat of being stabbed with a dinner fork."

"Once we get in the stadium, I really don't want any PDA's."

"PDA's?"

"I hate public displays of affection. I like kissing you, but I don't want to be making out along the side of the fifty-yard line."

"Okay."

Lori glanced over at the packed stadium then back at Gerald and took a deep cleansing breath. "Are you ready?"

"I'm ready." Gerald took Lori's hand and they made their way through the sea of people moving toward the stadium entrances. Lori reached over to hug the side of his arm. She was a little anxious. This was the first time she had publicly appeared with a male escort.

The stadium was packed. The gridiron was bathed in artificial light. The cheerleading squad was out on the field, going through their routine, as the high school band performed the school song, which was a variant of the Notre Dame Fight Song. Student council members made their way through the crowds selling popcorn, drinks, and hotdogs.

It seemed like everyone who knew Gerald or Lori called out to them and acknowledged them. Across the way, Lori saw a couple of girls she knew. One nudged the other and pointed at them. Lori smiled and waved. As she walked, Lori leaned over to speak in his ear, "I've never felt so visible in all my life."

"Ah, you'll live." Gerald patted the back of her hand. "Just pretend you're up for an Oscar and you're walking the red carpet."

They waded through the crowd to make their way to the sideline seats for the Scholastic Bowl members. The faculty was sitting in the next set of seats. Mr. Leslie stood up and shook Gerald's hand. "Hi, Gerald, good to see you. I'm expecting your answer on the physics class on Monday."

"Thanks, Mr. Leslie. I haven't really decided just yet."

Mr. Leslie gave him a wry smile, "I can see you've had some distractions." He gestured toward Lori, "She's in my physics class. Ask her, she'll tell you it's a great class."

"It is but," Lori nodded and smiled sheepishly, "I like all your classes, Mr. Leslie."

Mr. Leslie beamed and nodded. "That's a great answer, Lori." He turned toward Gerald. "You just follow her example and you'll be fine."

Next to Mr. Leslie was Mr. Hawk. Mr. Hawk was an ex-marine. He was fairly short in stature but had a massive build. He was all muscle and seemed to be chiseled out of stone. He was often an intimidating presence. When he spoke, he had a squeaky, nasally voice, and was sometimes hard to understand, but his demeanor was always unmistakable.

Mr. Hawk smiled warmly, and his eyes sparkled as he held his hand out to Gerald. "I'm happy to see you here supporting the team. Mrs. Branson tells me you joined the Scholastic Bowl Team. It's good to see you getting so involved in the school."

Gerald shook his hand. Mr. Hawk's grip felt like the jaws of a hydraulic clamp that could crush his fingers. "Yes, well, I have my first meet a week from today, so we'll see how it goes."

"Ahhh, Mrs. Branson seems to think you'll do fine." He patted Gerald on the shoulder. "You listen to Lori, here," he gestured in her direction. "She knows the game. She's been on the team since she was a freshman."

The next seat held Mrs. Roberson. She turned around to greet them, "Hello, Gerald."

"Hello, Mrs. Roberson."

Mrs. Roberson gave him a faint, "Don't act so guilty" look with her eyes. She turned to Lori. "Hi, Lori," she smiled warmly. "You look beautiful."

"Thank you, Mrs. Roberson."

Ultimately, they came to Mrs. Branson, "Well, Camden, it's about time you got around to this."

Gerald smiled and glanced over at Lori, "I guess you could say that I was strongly motivated."

Lori gave him a sidelong glance.

Mrs. Branson put her hands on Lori's shoulders and smiled. "The two of you make a very nice looking couple."

Lori gave her chin a quick dip, "Thanks, Mrs. B"

"Yes," Gerald agreed, "Thanks for everything, Mrs. B."

Mrs. Branson raised her finger, "I'll grace you that one until Saturday. I have been saying some very good things about you, so you'd better show, and you'd better not make me out to be a liar."

"Oh, no, I wouldn't do that to you. I'll be there."

"Here," Mrs. Branson motioned to the seats next to her. "You two are next to me. They're just getting ready for the kick-off."

When the game started, Tyler Banks began composing his ninth symphony. Every time Hutsonville had the ball, he fired off a pass with laser beam precision. Nearly all of them were caught, and with each play they stitched their way down the field for one first down after another.

During the first half, Hutsonville acquired a healthy lead, but it wasn't a blowout. Each time the Marshall team got the ball, it was hard for the Hutsonville defensive line to stop them. As the game rolled on, Hutsonville gradually widened the spread.

When there were nine seconds left in the first half, the Marshall coach called for a timeout and pulled his team into a huddle. "Listen fellas," he said to the team, "you guys are playing a great game, so I'm not going to criticize you on that. We are seventeen points down, and I'm not going to start blowing smoke about our chances of winning and going to the state playoffs, but I do want to accomplish one thing. We have one goal for this game, and it is right now. We're going to sack the quarterback. Joe, I want you and Bob to go deep. I want the rest of you to rush him the second the ball is snapped."

One of the Marshall players objected, "But that's suicide. He'll have his choice of receivers."

"No it's not." The Marshall coach shook his head. "He's not going to pass. He's going to run the ball. I have watched every game he's played. He always runs the ball at the end of a half. It's a pride thing. He thinks he's unstoppable, because he's never been sacked. He's wrong. This is his day of reckoning. Today, we show him that he's not invincible. If we can do that," the coach held up a finger, "if we can sack him for the first time ever, then it might throw him off balance. His confidence is his weakness. If we can mess with him psychologically, maybe we can turn this around and win the game. Even if we don't win, we'll at least have this moment. This is our time now. This is what we have worked for all season. We're going to hit him hard and we're going to put him on the turf."

Tyler took his position and got ready for the snap. He scanned the faces of the Marshall defensive line. Something was up. For most of the game, whenever they faced off at the line of scrimmage, he could see frustration in their faces. This time they were eyeing him expectantly, as if they had shared some nefarious secret that they had saved back for a key moment.

Tyler called for the snap. As the ball left the turf, an ominous red dot appeared on his left knee. He looked down, puzzled. The distraction nearly caused him to fumble the ball, but he glanced up just in time to snatch it out of the air. Tyler saw that nearly the entire defensive line was rushing toward him from all sides. He was tempted to pass, but he thought he could still slip through. A second later, there was strange sound from the far end of the stadium. It sounded like someone had whacked a stick on the side of a pipe. As it was an intense moment of the game, the people who heard it gave it no notice. Tyler's knee cap burst. The Marshall defensive line slammed into him from all sides, driving him hard into the ground. Tyler's streak of having never been sacked had come to an abrupt end.

Every fan in the stadium came out of their seats when Tyler went down. A moan wound through the stands. As the Marshall defensive line gradually peeled off Tyler, there was a moment before anyone realized he wasn't getting up. Coach Pensyl glanced up from his clipboard when he heard someone shout. He jogged out to the field to where Tyler was lying.

"Tyler, what is it? Are you hurt?"

Tyler's face was flush and he was gasping air as he started to drift into hyperventilation. "Slow down, Tyler." He took Tyler's head in his hands, "Try to breathe normal."

Tyler's face was bathed in sweat, and his eyes seemed to glaze over. Coach Pensyl felt along his rib cage, but there was no sign that anything was broken. Then he saw that the left pant leg of Tyler's uniform was becoming blood-soaked around the knee. He bent over for a closer view. On the side of the pant leg, he saw a small hole about the diameter of a pencil. He worked his fingers into the hole, and then pulled them apart to tear open the fabric. In the side of Tyler's knee was a gaping black hole that oozed blood. Inside the pant leg were loose hunks of bone, flesh, and gristle. Coach Pensyl stared at the wound in disbelief. This wasn't like any injury he had ever seen in football. It had to be a bullet. He looked up and surveyed the stadium. Bill Wineman, the assistant coach ran to Coach Pensyl's side.

"Call an ambulance," Coach Pensyl said to him, "and call the police. Tyler's been shot."

The River

- Eddy was one of the most despicable people I ever met, but he was crafty and thorough. –

No one saw the lone figure with a knit cap and long black hair as it walked briskly across the thin strip between the edge of the fence and the woods. With a bedroll tucked under one arm, the figure melted into the trees and was gone.

Eddy came out of the woods and jogged back to the car. He handed the rifle and blanket to Tammy.

"What am I supposed to do with this?" she asked, as she took it from him.

"Keep the blanket around it and lay it in the back. I need to go inside."

As Tammy did what she was told, Eddy grabbed a video tape from under the front seat. He reached into his pocket for the key, as he hurried to the back door of the gas office. He worked the lock and went inside. A few moments later, he emerged with a tape in his hand.

"How did you do that?" Tammy asked.

"A couple of summers ago, I worked here painting LP tanks. One day I was going to be getting back late, so they let me borrow a key. I made a copy of it in case I ever needed to get back in." He slid the tape under the front seat and started the car. "I switched out the tape in the recorder for the security camera."

"Won't they know?"

"They rotate the tapes and copy over them once a week or so. Nothing was stolen. With no sign of forcible entry, they have no reason to check it. Even if they did, all they would have is a blank tape and think it was some sort of mix-up." Eddy put the car in gear. He pulled out from in back of the gas office and onto the highway.

"Why did you bring a rifle?"

"It's an old bolt-action Remington. The chamber doesn't fly open when you shoot it. If you tape a soda bottle over the end, it makes the shot very quiet."

"What did you shoot?"

"I just shot Tyler Banks."

"You shot Tyler?"

"Damn right, I did. Serves the son of a bitch right."

"You killed him?"

"No." Eddy tossed the black wig and knit cap out the window as he turned onto Main Street, "but I don't think that football scholarship is going to work out for him." He turned to glance over at her. "I shot him in the knee."

"Why would you do that?"

Eddy pulled onto the blacktop leading to Shaw Butte. "Because he twisted my arm and he embarrassed me." He made the turn and then glanced over at Tammy. "I'm not the kind of guy you can disrespect and then just walk away. You need to remember that."

"Okay."

Eddy slowed the car as he wove through the trees along Shaw Butte Lane. "He was going to be heading off to some big college to play ball, where he can enjoy all the women and crazy parties. Meanwhile, I've spent three years repeating my senior year at this backwater school. Is that fair? Sometimes you just have to reach in and level the playing field." He rolled the car close to the edge of the bluff, then shut down the lights and turned off the car.

"Stay here," he told Tammy, then pulled the rifle from the blanket and walked to the edge of the bluff. He gazed over the Wabash River and took in the town lights that reflected off the still waters. It was a nice spot. Many times, couples came here to park, but not tonight. They were all at the big game. He looked down at his Grandpa's Remington. It was a sad sacrifice, but if it were ever found and matched to the bullet, it could be traced back to him. He turned it in his hands to take one last look then lifted it over his head to sling it over the edge. It made a splash far below. It was a good throw. Far enough that it would sink into deep water and never be found in the mud. He stood for a moment with his hands on his hips, watching the water ripples dissipate until the surface was calm again. "Well, that's that," he sighed to himself. The only thing left was to take care of the girl.

Eddy walked back to the car, and then glanced over at Tammy, "Take your clothes off."

Tammy was a bit upset by the evening's events, "Look Eddy, this is not what I had in mind, and right now I think I just want to go home."

"I think you'd better do what I told you."

"Come on, Eddy," she gestured toward the night air, "it's chilly out."

"I'm not telling you again," he said in a menacing tone.

Tammy peeled off her shirt and started to fold it up.

Eddy yanked it away from her and threw it in the back. "Stop stalling. This is a heavy night, and you don't want to make me angry."

Tammy unhooked her bra and slipped it off, then dropped it in the back. She unbuttoned her cut-offs and lifted herself to slide out of them. She looked back over at Eddy.

"All of it."

Tammy slid her black cotton panties off and let them rest on the floorboard next to her cut-offs.

"In the back." Eddy tipped his head toward the rear of the car. "Put that with the rest of it."

Tammy's heart pounded in her chest as she lifted the shorts and underwear over the seat and let them drop in the back.

Eddy reached into the back and brought out a Polaroid camera. He pressed the "On" button and then held it up, "Smile now."

Tammy looked up and gave a half-hearted smile.

"Come on, you can do better than that. Look sexy for me."

Tammy tipped her head back to let her hair fall over her shoulder, and then tipped her lower lip down with her fingertip.

"That's it," Eddy flashed the camera. "Give me just a couple more."

Tammy lifted her elbows high and ran her fingers back through the sides of her head, then arched her back to raise her naked breasts into the air.

"Excellent," Eddy remarked, as he flashed the camera and it spit out another picture. "One more and then we're done."

Tammy put her hands on the sides of her breasts and pressed them together, then tipped her head back and closed her eyes.

"Very good." Eddy pulled the three photos from the front of the camera and laid them on the dash. He tossed the camera onto the back seat and then turned toward Tammy. "Now," Eddy leered at her for a moment, "open your mouth."

Tammy was confused by the request, but she opened her mouth to accommodate.

"Hold still." Eddy leaned forward and gently placed his palm against the side of her face. He slid his fingers just under her hairline to hook the tips behind her neck. As he went, he drug his thumb into the corner of her mouth and pushed the flesh of her cheek back between her teeth. He paused for a moment to observe her, and then pressed his thumb a bit harder to wedge the inside of her cheek back into her molars.

Tammy stiffened in the seat, but didn't cry out. The back corner of her mouth had a faint taste of blood.

"Yes," he smiled, "that hurts doesn't it? But look at you, not a peep. That's good. Too many girls whine and fuss and are too caught up in themselves to be worthwhile. I think you will work out just fine." He ran the tips of his fingers from his free hand along the top of her thigh. He loosened his grip slightly to let off some of the pressure. "Now open the glove box and hand me what you find there."

Tammy shifted her eyes toward the dash and started to reach her arm.

"Hey," he tightened his grip slightly, "you know where the glove box is. Look at me."

Tammy focused on watching Eddy's face as she felt along the dash. Her hand found the latch of the glove box. When she worked the latch, it flopped open.

"Take it out."

Tammy reached into the glove box and felt something cool. It was metal and uneven to the touch. She lifted it out and handed it to him. She was careful not to turn away from Eddy, but with her peripheral vision she could tell it was black.

Eddy lifted the pistol up by his face with the barrel pointed up. "Okay," he said as he moved the tip of the barrel toward her mouth, "and here we go." He brought the gun level and slid the barrel between her teeth.

Tammy's breaths came quick. A tear rolled down her cheek. She started to lift her hand to wipe it away.

"Don't take your hands off the seat!" Eddy snarled.

Tammy laid her palms flat on the seat cushion.

Eddy slowly let go of her cheek, "Now close your lips around the end."

Terrified, Tammy did as she was told. It tasted of metal and gun oil. She struggled not to gag.

Eddy slowly brought his thumb up and cocked the hammer back, "Now, this is very dangerous. This gun has an easy pull, and I'm already squeezing just a little. I wanted to impress upon you that what we did tonight is not like soaping windows. Shooting someone in the knee cap is assault with a deadly weapon. That's serious prison time for both of us. As my accessory, you would be in almost as much trouble as me. You need to try real hard to keep me convinced that you can keep your mouth shut. That rifle belonged to my Grandpa. He was a mean old man and I don't miss him. I loved that gun, though; I really did. But it could have tied the shooting back to me, so I tossed it in the Wabash River without a second thought. As for you," Eddy shrugged, "I barely even know you, so you can think about what will happen to you the day I decide I can't trust you anymore." Eddy put his thumb on her chin to open her mouth, and slid the gun out. He pointed it to the sky and put a thumb on the hammer then gently eased it back into place. He dropped it heavily into her lap. "Put the gun back in the dash, and get your clothes back on. I'm going to put the top up."

She stared at him, upset and bewildered.

"Yeah, yeah, I know. Don't take it personal; I'll romp on you some other time. It's been a very intense night, and I've had enough excitement for one evening. Now hurry up and get your clothes on. I want to get home to catch a movie that's going to be on the late show."

The car was mostly quiet for the ride home. When they pulled up in front of Tammy's house, Eddy put a hand on her shoulder. "You did good. I'm pleased. You just need to know not to cross me, that's all. I'm actually a very kind and gentle person. I get my feelings hurt easily. If you can adjust yourself to that, we'll be fine. I'll call you in a few days."

Tammy nodded and gave him a half-hearted smile.

"Now go on. I need to roll. My movie's going to start soon."

Tammy tried not to seem too rushed as she opened the door and walked quickly across the front lawn and up the front step. She went into the house and walked through the front room to go to her bedroom.

Her mother was lying on the couch watching television. "How was your date, sweetie?" she called to Tammy, without taking her eyes off the screen. "There's a good movie coming on, if you want to come and watch."

Tammy didn't answer. She went down the hall to her room, closed the door behind her, and then flopped down on her bed. She buried her face in her pillow and cried.

The Broadcast

- Somehow, Eddy seemed to make sense to himself. He had a bizarre kind of pride in the terrible things that he did. –

Eddy opened the door leading to the stairs of his apartment over the auto garage. He went in, locked the door, and then jogged up the stairs. Eddy always kept his apartment very tidy. Discipline is the key to success. He flipped on the television and then sat down on the couch. He slid open the drawer on the coffee table then dropped the security tape and the photos inside. Eddy put his feet up and turned on the television to wait for his movie to start.

The local news came on. Eddy sat up and took notice. It was the Hutsonville football stadium. The Marshall coach was speaking into a microphone, addressing the crowd, " . . . . has already been rampant speculation that someone from Marshall or someone wanting Marshall to win might have committed this atrocious act."

Eddy shook his head and rolled his eyes. He was surrounded by clueless idiots. He had just completed one of the most daring acts of his life, and they were already writing it off as an attempt to alter the outcome of a football game.

". . . I hope that everyone will be patient and wait until the facts come out. Allow me to say this. If helping us win was indeed the intent of the culprit, I say to him and everyone else, that we do not want to win this way. Whoever has done this terrible thing has done a disservice to our town, our school, and our team—."

"Oh, shut up, already, and take the trophy."

". . . I have consulted with the players and the coach. Speaking on their behalf, we would like to forfeit the game to Hutsonville, thereby defaulting to them the Regional Championships . . . ."

Eddy jumped up off of the couch. "You have got to be kidding!" He talked back to the face on the screen, "I gave you a Regional Championship! I delivered it to you on a silver platter, and then you piss it away, and for what? A little grand standing for the cameras and the microphone?"

Eddy turned off the television. He no longer felt like watching the late movie. He shut off the lights and went to bed.

Chapter 7

The Sunday After

Deep Trouble

- I had never seen Tammy so downtrodden. -

Gerald had just come down from bed on Sunday morning. He checked his watch. It was already 9:00. He had intended to get an early start to drive up to Terre Haute to see Tyler at the hospital.

The phone rang and Christine picked it up. "Hello?" Christine glanced over at her son, "Yes, he's here. Do you mind if I ask who's calling?" Christine made an expression of surprise when she heard the answer. "Hello Tammy!" she said happily. "I didn't recognize your voice. You should come by and see us."

There was a pause as Christine listened to the receiver.

"That doesn't matter. You are still our friend. Please come by and visit now and then." Christine nodded as she listened. "Okay. Yes that's fine. He's right here." She held the phone out to Gerald, "It's Tammy Wells."

Gerald thought about refusing to take the call, but he didn't want to set off a series of questions from his mother. He sighed and took the phone, "Hello, Tammy."

"Gerald, I need to see you."

"I can't this morning, Tammy. I'm going to Terre Haute to see Tyler."

"Gerald, I'm in real trouble. I'm at work. Can you meet me at the Coffee House in fifteen minutes?"

Gerald heart leapt into his throat. The words "Real trouble" from a female sexual partner generally always meant the same thing. He swallowed hard. "Okay, Tammy. I'll be there soon."

"Thanks Gerald."

When the phone clicked he handed the receiver back to his mother.

"Is something wrong?" Christine asked, as she hung the receiver back on the hook.

"Yes. Tyler got shot last night."

"Oh my. I heard about that. It was terrible. Such a tragedy, just to win a football game."

"Tammy seems upset, so I'm going stop by and talk to her at the Coffee House before I drive on to Terre Haute and visit Tyler at the hospital."

The Coffee House was owned by a retired senator named Chuck Evans. It was a quaint little place at the foot of the Hutsonville Bridge that lead into Indiana. It offered a repertoire of different flavors of coffee, as well as a small menu.

Gerald went into the Coffee House and sat at a table. He started cracking peanuts from the small complimentary buckets that were kept on the tables. He glanced up to see Tammy come out from the back. She was different, somehow. Something was strange about her.

Tammy slid into a chair on the other side of the table and leaned forward across the table top. "Gerald, I'm in real trouble."

Gerald felt ice water ran through his veins. "Are you pregnant?"

"No," she whispered, "it's worse than that."

Gerald thought for a moment, "I really can't think of anything worse than that."

"It's Eddy."

"What about Eddy?"

"I can't get free of him."

"I didn't really see what you saw in Eddy, but then again," Gerald paused, "I suppose a lot of people probably wondered what you saw in me. Anyway, just break up with him."

"I can't," Tammy hissed. She bit her lip for a moment. "I think he's going to kill me."

Gerald shook his head. "He's not going to kill you. Why would even you say that?"

"Because he shot Tyler."

Gerald crushed a peanut shell in his fist, as a slow rage boiled over him. He dropped the crumbs in the bucket, and then took in a deep breath though his nostrils. "Please continue."

"I had no idea what he was planning. He parked behind the office of the propane company and went through the woods. When he came back, he handed me a rifle and told me to put it in back."

Gerald took a moment to relax. He had to put aside his anger for the moment, so he could reason clearly. "If what you're saying is true, then you should go to the police."

"I can't. He has a video tape of me taking the rifle from him and stashing it in the back. He has a key to the gas office. After the shooting, he went inside and swapped out the security tape. If he gets caught, he's going to use it to incriminate me as an accomplice."

Gerald nodded slowly, trying to reason out the situation. "What did he do with the tape?"

"I don't know. He had it with him when he dropped me off."

Gerald nodded, "It must be in his apartment over the auto repair garage. Does he ever take you up there?"

"No, never. Last night was the first time I ever went anywhere with him."

Gerald eyed her suspiciously, "But you told me . . . ."

"I know, I know," Tammy said softly. "I told you we'd been having sex. That was a lie. I was hurt, and I wanted to hurt you back. It was stupid and childish. When I agreed to go out with him, I had no idea how crazy he is, or that he would do such a horrible thing."

Gerald nodded his understanding.

"There's more."

"What?" Gerald asked.

Tammy took a deep breath, "He knows about you."

"He knows what about me?"

"Eddy knows about your trips to Terre Haute. He saw you riding your motorcycle one day followed you from a distance."

Gerald paused. "Where did he say I went?"

"It was some tall brick building uptown. He pulled up the address on the county registry website. It belongs to the doctor who has the animal show on Channel 10."

"His name is Dr. Gauge. He's a biologist," Gerald answered simply, as if the information was of no great consequence. "He's just a friend"

"Eddy did a profile search on him. He used to be a doctor at some cancer research hospital in Denver. Before that, he worked for some huge genetics research company in Los Angeles."

Gerald tried not to seem excited, though his heart was racing. "Sounds like Eddy's done his homework."

"You've been different ever since the accident. Your personality has changed. Suddenly you're really smart. You've been making trips to see some rogue genetic scientist. Are you part of some weird DNA experiment?"

Gerald smiled, "I think you've been watching too many late night movies."

"It doesn't matter." She stopped for a moment to compose her thoughts. "The thing is, I need your help. I'm scared, Gerald. I'm really, really scared. I don't want to go to jail and I don't want to be found dead in a ditch somewhere. You've got to help me."

Gerald leaned forward, "Okay, first thing. Don't tell anyone any of the things you just told me. Lock it down tight. If someone blabs, or if you subconsciously let something slip, or even if you act a little funny, Eddy may get nervous and it could escalate the situation."

Tammy nodded.

"In the mean time you need to make sure Eddy thinks you're head over heels in love with him."

"I hate him."

"Maybe so, but if you can pretend that you love him, it will buy us more time."

"I'll try," she nodded. "To pull that off, I might have to sleep with him." Tammy watched him closely for a reaction.

"I can't advise you to do that," Gerald shook his head. "That has to be your call."

Tammy nodded slowly.

"One last thing," Gerald continued, "keep your eyes open for that tape. If you get a chance to go up to his apartment, discreetly look around. Don't ask him to let you go up there. Wait for it to be his idea. Once you're inside, don't go nosing around. Just wait for him to go to the bathroom and study the room with your eyes. Don't even leave your seat. The least little thing could get him suspicious and that could be dangerous."

"I will. Thank you, Gerald."

The Mustang

- Masquerading as a man with a reason. My charade is the event of the season. And if I claim to be a wise man, it surely means that I don't know. -

When Gerald walked into the room, Tyler's parents were sitting by his bed. Tyler looked up and smiled, "Well, it's about time you showed up."

"I figured I'd wait till some of the herd thinned out a bit."

The couple stood up to greet him. "I'm Jenna Banks," the lady shook his hand and then gestured to the man next to her, "and this is my husband, Robert."

"Hello," Gerald shook his hand. "It's very nice to meet you."

Robert nodded, "I wish the circumstances were better."

"We've heard so much about you," Mrs. Banks spoke up. "Tyler tells me you're on the Scholastic Bowl Team, and that you're a genius."

"You'll have to take that with a grain of salt." Gerald turned toward Tyler, "How's the hospital treating you?"

"Pretty good. I've been grabbing a few of the nurse's asses, but not too many. I try to restrain myself so they don't fall in love."

"That's probably a good idea," Gerald agreed. "We can't have them all upset and crying their eyes out when it comes time for you to go home."

"My left knee cap is gone. I will have to walk with a knee brace for at least a year, until it heals. Then, I will need an artificial knee replacement and have to start my recovery all over again."

"I'm really sorry."

"It won't be so bad. I'll be getting around like Mad Max, and all the girls were crazy over him. What do you think, Mom? Do you think I would make a good Road Warrior?"

Jenna Banks smiled. Even in this hard time, he still tried to be cheerful and funny to put everyone at ease.

"I have something for you." Tyler dug around in the drawer of the cabinet by his hospital bed and pulled out a set of keys. "Hey Dad, do you have that paper I asked you to get?"

Robert took a document and a slip of paper out of a large envelope laying off to the side. "Are you sure about this, Son?"

"Oh, I'm sure." Tyler answered casually, as he signed the back of the document and the slip of paper. He handed them with the keys to Gerald, "Here, take this."

Gerald looked down puzzled. "What is this?"

"I'm giving you the Mustang."

Gerald pushed it back toward Tyler. "I can't take your car."

Jenna Banks tried to reason with her son, "Maybe you should wait a while and think it over for a couple of days."

Tyler smiled up at her, "I've already thought it over. In the first place, it's a stick shift. Without a left knee cap, I'm not going to be working a clutch anytime soon. Second, it didn't cost me anything. All I had to do was take a joy ride out to Montana for a couple of days." Tyler leaned forward and grabbed Gerald's wrist, and stuffed the keys into his hand. "I want you to take it. Here are the keys; there's the title, and a bill of sale."

Gerald nodded and accepted them, "Okay, Tyler."

"Just don't turn it into some sort of shrine. It's a car, so use it like a car."

Gerald nodded, "I will, Tyler, I promise."

"You can come by the house and pick it up anytime. It will be waiting for you in the front drive. The other set of keys will be locked in the dash." Tyler turned toward his mother and father. "Would you guys mind getting me a Pepsi?"

Tyler's mom smiled and nodded, "You mean you want the old folks to clear out for a while so you and your buddy can talk about girls."

Tyler smiled, "We just need a moment."

Mrs. Banks turned to her husband, "Come on, dear, the boys want their private time."

Tyler waited until his parents left the room and were out of ear shot, then turned toward Gerald. "Are you headed over to Dr. Gauge's lab after this?"

"I am," he nodded. "He wants another DNA sample. I'm getting pretty tired of getting poked."

"That's Dr. Gauge. He's not content with getting a swab of saliva or plucking a hair. He has to poke the end of that finger every single time. I think he's a sadist," he joked. "He was the same way with me at first. He wanted a new sample every two or three days. It levels off, though, once he gets everything fine-tuned. Eventually, you'll only need to go in once a month or so."

"I was worried that it might seem conspicuous, running to Terre Haute all the time." Gerald deliberately omitted the fact that Eddy had followed him, or that Eddy had been the one who had pulled the trigger.

Tyler spoke with some hesitation, "I'm going to go back soon."

"You're going back where?"

"Back to wherever I came from. Maybe it's back into Tyler-mouse. Who knows? I'm going to have Dr. Gauge shut down the relay."

"Why would you do that?"

"My knee hurts. I will need about a year of difficult recovery. By then, Tyler-mouse will be long dead from the cancer. There's no point in suffering through a painful recovery, when I will never see the other side."

Gerald was both surprised and very sad. "Are you sure that's what you want? Is there anything I can do for you?"

"Yes, there is. I would like you to bring me some sunflower seeds once in a while—the kind that are already shelled. Also, let him out of the cage now and then, so he can run up your arm and sit on your shoulder. I think a mouse would like that."

"I'll do it, but you don't even know if any part of you will go back into the mouse."

"I think it will."

"Dr. Gauge doesn't think so."

"He's just guessing." Tyler smiled.

"Is there anything else?"

"One more thing. Since Tyler-mouse has cancer, when it gets close to the end, Dr. Gauge is going to give him a shot to put me to sleep."

"Is that what you want?"

"I know what I don't want. Whether I'm in there or not, I don't want him to die gasping for air with cancer-ridden lungs. One nice thing about being a mouse is that there are no laws against being euthanized."

"I guess not," Gerald grimaced at not coming up with a more consoling answer.

"I'd like you to be there when it happens."

Gerald nodded gently, "I'll be there. I promise."

"You are the only one who will remember me." Tyler said quietly.

"People will never forget you, Tyler."

"People don't even know I exist. I'm not Tyler Banks. He died two years ago." He put his hand on his chest, "I just borrowed his body for a while. I'm an impostor, walking down the street on Halloween wearing a rubber mask on your face."

"Me, too." Gerald shrugged. "I'm a part of that same hypocrisy."

"You are my one true friend. It's up to you, buddy. Except for Dr. Gauge, you're the only one who will know that I ever existed. You're the only one who will be grieving for the real me, the imposter. Dr. Gauge is detached from all this. To him, we're just specimens in an experiment." Tyler leaned forward a bit and rubbed his chin. "You know one thing I think I've learned from this secret experiment that has broadened the scope of genetic science?"

"What's that?"

"Maybe just being a plain old mouse was better."

Playing God

- There are times when all the world's asleep. Tthe questions run to deep for such a simple man. Won't you please, please tell me what we've learned. I know it sounds absurd. Please tell me who I am. -

Gerald watched as Dr. Gauge pricked his finger, and then smeared a drop of blood across a small, rectangular glass microscope slide. He slid it into the slot of a square black box and then pressed a button on the side. The edges became illuminated and gibberish of graphs, columns of numbers, and other data began flashing on his screen. Gerald felt like he had spent enough time with Dr. Gauge that he should start to get to know him better.

"Dr. Gauge," Gerald felt odd about interrupting his work, "I was curious about something."

Dr. Gauge glanced over at him and smiled, "Curiosity is the precursor to discovery. What can I help you with?"

"All these incredible things you're able to do. It just seems like you're not getting that much credit, and that you should have your face on the front of magazines, and should be appearing on television."

"Well I am on television." Dr. Gauge retorted as he peered through the dual lenses of a microscope.

"I'm not talking about a local Saturday afternoon animal show. I mean like being interviewed for your major advances in science. With the things you're doing, you deserve to be famous."

Dr. Gauge paused and turned toward him, "Genetics isn't like other sciences. In our field, it's wiser to keep your advances quiet."

"What about that sheep they cloned? Or that mouse with a human ear growing on its back."

"Yes," Dr. Gauge, "and how long has that been?"

"I'm not sure. I overheard some people talking about in the library. I'm guessing it has been a while."

"Dr. Charles Vacanti is an old colleague of mine, and we still keep in touch occasionally. Vacanti's mouse was news in 1995. Dolly the sheep was in 1996. She was cloned by Dr. Ian Wilmu and Dr. Keith Campbell at the Roslin Institute. I haven't met them personally, but I have studied their work. They took an adult somatic cell and created a clone using a nuclear transfer.

Unfortunately, she died six years later of progressive lung disease. The science of genetics has increased exponentially since the mid-90s, but how many breakthroughs have you recemtly seen raised to the public consciousness?"

"None," Gerald shook his head. "Why is that? Why is it kept secret?"

"A sheep is a mammal. So is a human. What we can do with one, we can do with the other. Advances in genetics are not always well received. People start to think we are playing God."

Gerald was quiet for a moment. "Are you playing God?" he asked gently.

Dr. Gauge became very serious as he composed an answer, "Maybe." He nodded to himself as he considered the question. "But if I am, I think it is with permission."

Gerald smiled, "So how did you get permission? Did God send you an email and tell you it was okay?"

Dr. Gauge smiled back, "Well, I haven't checked my inbox for a while. Do you think I should?"

Gerald chuckled and shrugged. It was the first time he had ever heard Dr. Gauge make a joke.

"No," Dr. Gauge continued, "I reason that someone doesn't pose a riddle unless it is intended to be solved. You don't make a jigsaw puzzle unless you want someone to put it together. If God has left us a trail of bread crumbs and given us the means to follow it, then he must have intended for us to do so."

"Do you believe in God?"

"Oh absolutely. I don't claim to know what he is, exactly, but the evidence that he exists is all around us. A creation implies a creator."

"What about people who say it happened all on its own?"

Dr. Gauge shook his head, "That doesn't seem feasible. There is too much design. If a chimp grabs a felt marker and scribbles marks on a paper, that's one thing. If he starts making letters to form words and writing sentences, that is another thing. There is too much intelligent design in our world to dismiss it all as happenstance."

Gerald was delighted that Dr. Gauge had opened up to him, "So you're on board with God and Heaven—the whole bit?"

"I said I believed; that doesn't mean I understand it all."

"Do you believe in Heaven?"

"I think there has to be another stop. It seems to be the nature of things to grow, evolve, expand, and get better. It makes sense that the same pattern would apply to Heaven and, whatever it is, it will be an upgrade over what we have now. I doubt that it's all white clouds and angels with golden harps, like the preachers say."

"You sound a little cynical."

"A little, I suppose." Dr. Gauge adjusted his glasses. "Too many preachers like to talk about Heaven as if it's a place they visit for a few weeks every summer. There is no shame in being ignorant of something, so long as you don't make a pretense of knowledge that you don't posses. By the way, most preachers also say that animals have no souls and don't go to Heaven."

Gerald's face became grim. "What do you say about that?"

Dr. Gauge tipped his head to the side, "You only have to pet a dog once and watch him wag his tail to know that he has a soul. That is more compelling evidence than what some preacher has to say."

"So if God exists, why isn't He seen?"

Dr. Gauge smiled, "You're asking me questions in a realm where I don't have solid answers."

Gerald shrugged, "So tell me your guesses."

"I think God stays mostly hidden, for the same reason you don't stick your finger into a Petri dish. We are sentient beings and are able to make our own choices. If we weren't, studying our personalities and movements would make about as much sense as you studying your right hand. It does whatever you tell it. There would be no science in observing it. I think God has to remain mostly hidden, so he can discover our true nature. How many people take their foot off the gas pedal when they see a squad car? A behavioral test is contaminated by the presence of an obvious authority figure."

"So you think we're being studied?"

"Of course. You don't create something without observing the results. If you rebuild an engine in shop class, don't you want to see how it runs?"

"Sort of like you're studying me?"

"I didn't create you, Gerald. I'm a doctor and I do what doctors do. I use my skills to manipulate the circumstances toward a more favorable result. Doctors aren't God. They just stir the pie a little." Dr. Gauge checked his watch. "That's enough talk about God for one evening. I need you to get out of here so I can I do my job. I'll finish analyzing this and adjust the signal if necessary."

The Colt .45

- In my own way, I loved Mrs. Roberson. Our one night together seemed to fade into a distant dream. Other than Tyler, she was the best friend I had ever had. -

Gerald drove his motorcycle toward Mrs. Roberson's house. His mind was spinning and he felt the need to talk to someone. As he pulled up to the rear of the house, he saw a van in the driveway.

The door was off the hinges and leaning against the wrought iron railing of the back porch and two men were working on the busted door frame. The carpenters turned and stepped aside to let him pass, then went back to their work.

Gerald stepped inside. To announce his presence, he knocked on the inner door jamb that separated the living room and kitchen. "Mrs. Roberson, are you here?"

Mrs. Roberson glanced up from her cup of coffee. "Hi, Gerald, come on in. I wasn't expecting you today."

"I really need to talk to you." Gerald gestured toward the workmen. "Could we go someplace more private?"

"It's a small house, and I can't really leave while the workers are here. I suppose that we can go back to my bedroom." Mrs. Roberson waved him back. Once they were inside, she closed the door and rested her red apple coffee cup on the nightstand.

Mrs. Roberson smiled, "So, tell me what's so important that it couldn't wait until tomorrow?"

"Eddy Leach shot Tyler."

Mrs. Roberson was taken aback, but not altogether surprised. "How do you know this?"

"Tammy was with him. She didn't know what he was going to do until it was over. They parked behind the gas office and he stole the security tape that shows him handing her the rifle. He told her that if he goes to jail, he will implicate her as well. He said he would kill her when he starts to think he can't trust her anymore."

Mrs. Roberson nodded, "As paranoid as he is, that's only a matter of time."

"Do you think he'd actually do it?"

"Eddy Leach? Oh, yes, I'm quite sure he would." She gave him a quick glance. "If he thought she might put him in jail, he would kill her. What's more, he's cunning enough to do it in such a way that he won't get caught."

Gerald shook his head, "I can't let that happen."

Mrs. Roberson studied him. "What are you prepared to do?"

"I was thinking that the world might be a better place without Eddy Leach."

Mrs. Roberson nodded her agreement. "That's a pretty big step, Gerald. Are you sure you're ready for it?"

"I don't know." Gerald shook his head then took a deep breath through his nostrils, "Do you still have that Colt 45 your father had when he was in the military?"

"Yes," Mrs. Roberson nodded, "do you want to borrow it?"

"I don't want to borrow it," Gerald answered, "but I was thinking that if it got stolen a while, and then it was brought back, no one would ever know."

Gerald looked down and knodded slowly.

Mrs. Roberson pointed to the nightstand. "I keep it in the top drawer, in case someone tries to break in and rape me. The clip is loaded, but there isn't a round in the chamber. All you have to do is pull back the slide, and then drop the safety, and you're ready to go. You only have to cock it on the first round. After that, you just keep squeezing the trigger. Also, there's an extra box of shells next to it

If someone were to steal the gun, they might want to practice with it for a while, to get accustomed to it. Going to the store to buy bullets for practice would be stupid. It would leave a trail of paperwork. Also, the gun is very loud, so they would need to go pretty far out into the country to practice."

Gerald nodded, "Thanks, Amy. Thanks for everything."

"In the crotch of the little maple tree in the back yard, there's a blue birdhouse. The birds won't use it because it's too close to the ground. Inside is a small bird's nest that has been sprayed with polyurethane. Underneath the nest is a key that opens the back door of my house."

Mrs. Roberson rose from the bed. "I'm going to take a shower. While I'm in there, you can do whatever you need to do and then slip out."

Gerald stood up and glanced down at the nightstand drawer, then back up at her.

"Be careful, Gerald. Think it out first." Mrs. Roberson gave him a long hug, then walked into the bathroom and closed the door behind her.

Chapter 8

Monday's Remorse

The Plan

- I never realized how important Tyler was to the school, until he got hurt. Everyone seemed to love him. -

Gerald saw Tammy walking down the hallway before first hour. They made eye contact and Gerald shifted his eyes to the water fountain next to his locker. As Tammy bent to drink, Gerald made sure no one was in ear shot, "I need you to be near Eddy when he opens his locker."

Tammy lifted her chin to answer but was careful to continue to stare straight forward and pretend to be drinking, "I'll see what I can do."

"Try to get the combination to his locker. Notice if he keeps his keys with him or leaves them in his locker. If you can get me the combination before lunch, I will get his keys and make a copy of the key to his apartment. Once I have that, you can tip me off to when he'll be gone, so I can search through his apartment and try to find the tape."

Tammy nodded, and then glanced at him to make brief eye contact. "Thank you, Gerald." She turned away and headed down the hall.

The Newspaper

- Sometimes, you just feel like taking it easy. -

During fifth hour study hall, Gerald walked to the media area in the corner of the library. He plucked a newspaper out of the rack and then sat down in one of the large, wood-framed chairs with cream-colored cushions. He thumbed through the pages until he came to the comics page. As he read through the panels looking at the artwork and captions, he noticed that his new-found intellect did not seem to help digest the material any faster. It was another blind spot, like Mrs. Roberson's English class. Gerald became aware of someone standing over him and looked up to see who it was.

Mr. Leslie peered down at Gerald. "I know you must be checking up on stock quotes for your portfolio," he said with a wry grin. "I'm quite sure that a man of your prestige wouldn't be spending his time reading the funny pages."

Gerald glanced at the newspaper in his hands and realized that the stock market quotes were on the adjoining page. He looked back up at Leslie, trying to understand the intent behind the words. Was it playful camaraderie or a veiled expression of angst? "Well, I don't really have a portfolio and I suspect that I am equally lacking in prestige."

"It's Monday. You didn't give me an answer on the Physics class."

"The class sounds interesting and I appreciate the invitation, but I'm already taking Mrs. Roberson's English class last hour, and I'm getting a lot out of it."

"Of course, it is very important to your future that you have a sound understanding of haikus and iambic pentameter," Leslie quipped.

"She's a very nice lady. I wouldn't want her to feel slighted because I left her class for yours."

"Yes, yes, I can see how your absence from her class would be a terrific blow." Leslie adjusted his black plastic glasses. "It could take years of costly therapy before she managed to recover from the disappointment."

"I'm really enjoying her class."

"I'm sure you are, just like you're enjoying reading the comics section of the newspaper."

"They can be enlightening. I think I'm starting to find myself."

Leslie nodded, "I'm sure the funny pages is a very good place for you to look." Leslie rubbed his chin, "Lori Taylor is taking my Physics class."

"Why, Mr. Leslie, surely you're not suggesting that I make my academic selections based on the girls who are already taking a class."

"Oh no," Mr. Leslie waved away the idea. "That would make you a young hormonal spastic." Leslie gave a brief pause before delivering the sting. "You're not that young anymore, are you?"

"No I guess I'm not," Gerald smiled. "I suppose hormonal and spastic are all I have left." Gerald shrugged his shoulders. "I think I'd like to just leave things as they are."

Mr. Leslie nodded his head, and then turned aside. "Suit yourself. If that's your answer we'll consider the matter closed."

"Yes, I'm sorry but I think that's my answer."

Leslie didn't respond, but walked toward his favorite table on the other side of the library, where his students were waiting for his help.

The Brawl

- Thinking back, it was stupid, but the moment seized me. -

When the last period came, Gerald saw Eddy walk through the door and flop into his chair in the corner. It was the first time Gerald had seen him since the shooting. He wanted to pounce on Eddy and strangle him. He looked to the front of the class at Mrs. Roberson. She had seen Eddy come in, but hadn't shown any reaction. It occurred to Gerald that she was just better at keeping a poker face.

Mrs. Roberson tried to teach her class as normal, but even she had lost some of her zeal. When it came close to the end of the hour, Mrs. Roberson sat at her desk and addressed the class, "I know we normally have current events at this time, but I thought that we would use these moments to reflect on Tyler a little bit."

One of the students raised her hand, "Does anyone know what happened?"

"They have come to the conclusion that he was shot, but they are not sure from where or by whom. No one seems to know who might want to hurt Tyler. Some people are suggesting it might have been a radical from Marshall who wanted their team to win at any cost, but that is only speculation. It is important that we put that aside until there is more information available."

Another hand went up, "How's he doing? Will he recover?"

"He will never fully recover. Tyler is missing most of his left knee cap. He may eventually be able to walk, but things like running and playing sports are over for him. As far as how he is doing," Mrs. Roberson took a deep breath, "Marjorie, the school secretary, called the hospital today at lunch. Tyler has developed an infection. With a wound of this severity, that can be serious thing. If they don't manage to get it under control soon, it could even be life threatening."

Eddy tilted his face down toward the books on his desk and made a slight noise. It lasted only a half second but everyone in the room heard it. It was a quiet snort, as if he were suppressing a laugh. Everyone was irritated by it, but for Gerald something snapped. Blood rushed into his skull and his hands became knotted into tight fists as a slow, seething rage washed over him.

Gerald stood up and walked slowly toward Eddy's desk. The room seemed to be bathed in red light. In a foggy corner of his mind, he could hear Mrs. Roberson telling him to return to his seat. He stood over Eddy's desk with his fingernails digging into the palms of his clenched fists.

Eddy looked up at him and smirked. "What?" he asked in a defiant tone.

Gerald punched him across the side of his face. Eddy rolled out of his chair and sprawled onto the floor. As he started to right himself, Gerald stepped up and punched down into his face again. Blood oozed from Eddy's lower lip. Convinced that he was still smirking, Gerald hit him again. This blow caught him square under the nose, knocking his head back. As Eddy slumped back, Gerald lifted Eddy's upper body and punched down into his face a fourth time. He had to get the smirk off that face, once and for all.

Gerald was about to punch him again when something from behind hooked his arm. Gerald glanced up to see his elbow locked with Ray's, "You're Tyler's friend," Gerald scowled in an accusing tone.

"I *am* Tyler's friend," Ray grabbed the back collar of Gerald's jacket and pulled him back, "but this isn't helping him."

Mrs. Roberson knelt over Eddy and tipped his limp head up. "Scott, go get the nurse right away. Hurry. I don't know how badly he's hurt." Mrs. Roberson glanced back over her shoulder. "Gerald, go to the office. Ray, go with him to make sure he gets there."

"Come on," Ray patted Gerald on the back. "Let's go."

Gerald stood up and stared at Mrs. Roberson in disbelief. He felt confused and betrayed. He stepped over Eddy's limp form and followed Ray down to the office.

The Advocate

- There was nothing as intimidating as being sent to the office to meet with Mr. Hawk. It was like knocking on the gates of hell. -

Gerald sat waiting in the office. Occasionally, he glanced over at Marjorie McCain. She sat at her desk with excellent posture. Her makeup was perfect and her black hair was immaculately groomed. She was a very proper lady with a friendly nature. She allowed the students to call her "Marj," and everyone seemed to like her. She was usually a cheerful, talkative person, but today she was darkly quiet when Gerald entered the office. She turned to him with a grim expression and motioned to a seat along the wall. "Mr. Hawk will be with you in a moment." The pronouncement had the ring of an executioner calling out a two-minute warning to a condemned man.

Gerald sat numbly awaiting his fate. When the final bell rang, he wasn't sure how much time had passed. He could have checked the clock on the wall but didn't trouble himself to turn his head. Eventually, the door to the hall opened and Lori came in. She sat down next to him and leaned over to rub the back of his shoulder. "Hi," she said softly, and gave his cheek a quick stroke with the side of her finger.

"Hi," he answered weakly. It was good to see a friendly face.

"Do you know how this works?"

"No, I have no idea."

"It's sort of like a trial," Lori shrugged. "Mr. Hawk likes to pattern everything after the way the outside world works. It's his way of preparing us for going out into the world after we graduate." Lori leaned toward the side and shifted her hair away from the back of her neck, "You're allowed to have two people go in with you when you talk to Mr. Hawk. One is a member of the faculty who acts as an advocate and may speak on your behalf. The other is a fellow student who acts as a character reference."

Gerald nodded and patted her on the knee, "Well, of course I want you as the character reference. I assume I need to pick a member of the faculty as my advocate?"

"Not in this case, "Lori shook her head. "Mrs. Branson has already volunteered to be your advocate. I suggest you ride with that. I wouldn't recommend trying to switch to someone else."

"Mrs. Branson," Gerald repeated. "Is that good or bad?"

Lori laid a hand across his fist, "Normally, that would be good, but you have to understand something. This whole incident is very embarrassing for her, since you're on the Scholastic Bowl Team. I have to tell you, she is pissed. I mean, she is really, really pissed. I've known her for three years now, and I've never seen her this mad. You've blown this one right off the scale."

Mrs. Branson came through the office door. Her face was pinched and angry. As she approached, Gerald started to speak, but Mrs. Branson waved him back with a finger. "Don't even open your mouth. You're in enough trouble already. You've embarrassed me today, and one thing I simply will not tolerate is someone embarrassing me. Are you hearing me?"

"Yes, Ma'am."

Mrs. Branson sighed, glanced over at Lori and gave her a weak smile, then turned her focus back toward Gerald. "Did she tell you not to speak unless Mr. Hawk asks you a direct question? If he asks you a yes or no question, make sure you only answer 'yes' or 'no.' Don't start rambling and trying to explain what happened. Eventually, he will allow you to speak freely and tell your side of the story."

Mrs. Branson went up to Marjorie's desk. Marj waved her forward. "Hello, Mrs. Branson. Mr. Hawk is expecting you; please go on back." Mrs. Branson went to the door and gave a quick knock, then went inside. Ten minutes later, Mrs. Branson reappeared and waved for Gerald and Lori to enter.

Gerald and Lori stepped into Mr. Hawk's office. The chair behind his desk was empty. On the opposite end of the office, a second door led to the detention room. The detention room was Mr. Hawk's personal creation. At one time, it had been a closet. It was just large enough to accommodate a laminated table and a few gray folding metal chairs. An eight-foot fluorescent light fixture ran along the ceiling. There was a single window, made from mortared tiles of heavy wavy glass that allowed light to enter. The pale blue walls were completely barren. A spiral notebook and a few pens were neatly laid out on the table.

Mr. Hawk stood in front of the center chair situated in front of the window. Mr. Hawk glared over at Gerald and pointed to the seat directly across from himself. "That's your chair in the middle." His voice held a sharp restraint, as if it took every ounce of his willpower to keep from shouting.

Mr. Hawk's eyes were blazing. His face was flushed red and contorted in anger. His head seemed ready to explode at any moment. Gerald could not believe this was the same friendly man who had greeted him at the stadium just two days earlier.

"Lori, would you close the door, please?" Mr. Hawk asked quietly.

Gerald took a seat in the chair across from Mr. Hawk. The moment the back of his pants touched the metal of the seat, the small giant reached across the table with both hands and grabbed two fistfuls of his denim jacket. With no visible effort, the two short, muscular arms yanked him into the air as if he were light as a feather, "The ladies haven't been seated yet."

Lori and Mrs. Branson took a seat on either side of Gerald's chair. Gerald glanced from side to side, to make sure they were seated, and was about to sit, when Mr. Hawk held up a finger to pause him. Mr. Hawk waited a couple of seconds, and then took his seat. He scooted the chair a bit to adjust his distance to the table, and then gestured for Gerald to be seated. Gerald sat down and glanced quickly over at Lori.

Mr. Hawk slammed his fist down on the table, making the pens bounce. Gerald wasn't sure if it was a reprimand for looking away, or just for the general purpose of getting his attention.

"In all my years of being principal at this school," Mr. Hawk blared at him in his nasal, squeaky voice, "I have never seen such a flagrant act of unwarranted violence. I want to make sure that I have my facts straight, before we proceed, so I will ask you a few questions. I expect to receive only yes or no answers. This is not an open discussion where you can add any explanation or excuse that you see fit. Do you understand?"

"Yes."

"Did you hit Eddy Leach?"

Gerald cleared his throat, "Yes."

"And was it in response to him hitting you?"

"No."

"Did he throw something at you, spit at you, kick your chair, write on your book, or anything like that?"

"No."

"Did he call you a name, insult your mother, challenge you, or otherwise verbally assault you?"

"No."

"And yet you got up out of your chair, walked across the room, and struck him in the face."

"Yes."

"After you hit him, did he hit you back?"

"No."

"And yet, you hit him again."

"Yes."

"Then, after you hit him a second time, did he hit you back?"

"No."

"Did he strike you at any time during this entire incident?"

"No.

"But you kept hitting him, even after he appeared to be unconscious."

"Yes."

"And the only reason you stopped hitting him after he was unconscious was because Ray Thompson stepped in and grabbed your arm."

"Yes."

Mr. Hawk opened the spiral notebook and scribbled a few notes. He turned to Mrs. Branson, "I am going to have Mrs. McCain draw up a note of student commendation to go out to the Thompsons."

Mrs. Branson nodded.

Mr. Hawk turned back toward Gerald and glared at him, "This is not a case for a principal. This is a case for the police. There's really only one reason they haven't already been called." Mr. Hawk paused for a moment, to see if Gerald was going to take the bait and ask what the reason was.

Gerald gazed silently back at Mr. Hawk, waiting for him to continue.

"Mrs. Branson has asked me to be lenient with you, and take into consideration your recent accident and the residual trauma, and the fact that you're good friends with Tyler, and you are upset because of his injury on the field." Mr. Hawk leaned his face closer to Gerald. "Leniency is not in my nature. This school functions on structure and discipline. If you excuse today's problems without reprimand, you extend an open invitation for larger ones tomorrow. What's more, I think this school has already gone the extra distance for you. Mr. Leslie has requested that you be allowed to join his Physics class. Mrs. Branson has allowed you to join the Scholastic Bowl Team. Can you understand how this horrible incident you have perpetrated has been a slap in the face to our kindness?"

'Yes, sir, and I am sorry."

"If I'd had any previous troubles out of you, this incident would have gotten you permanently expelled. Even for a first offense, this warrants a minimum of a three-day suspension. If I were to let you off with just detention, that would be inconsistent with punishments I have administered in the past. Do you understand that to give the students structure, I have to follow my own precedents?"

"I do, sir."

Mr. Hawk nodded. He was impressed that Gerald had managed to keep his head while under fire. "I'm going to offer you a chance to speak and tell your side of the story, while I consider what the appropriate punishment might be."

"Mrs. Roberson was telling the class about Tyler getting an infection, and Eddy was making fun of him."

"How did Eddy make fun of him? Did he make a comment? Did he laugh? What did he do?"

"He made a noise as if he were about to laugh."

"Eddy makes a noise, and you think that justifies walking over in the middle of class to start hitting him?"

"I was wrong, and it wasn't justified, but it was the noise that made me upset. It sounded as if he was about to laugh, and something snapped."

"You think Eddy shot Tyler at the football game."

Gerald's mouth dropped open. He was speechless.

"That's right, isn't it?" Mr. Hawk continued, "Isn't that what this is really all about?"

"Yes," Gerald cleared his throat. "Eddy shot Tyler."

"Did you see him shoot Tyler?"

"No."

"Did you hear him brag about shooting Tyler?"

"No."

"Did someone else tell you that Eddy shot Tyler?"

Gerald looked down, "I'm not at liberty to say."

"It doesn't matter. I can't roam the hallways trying to chase down idle gossip. I suspect this stemmed from an incident in which Tyler twisted Eddy's arm, after he pulled a knife on you." Mr. Hawk kept a serious face, but he was secretly amused by Gerald's blank expression of surprise. "Yes, I knew about that," Mr. Hawk continued, "but I let it go because there was no faculty present, and there were no direct complaints made. I know everything that goes on in this school, from the Chemistry lab on the top floor, down to what goes on in the furnace room under the old gymnasium."

Gerald's blood ran cold at the mention of the furnace room. Had he found out, somehow?

Mr. Hawk leaned forward as he spoke, "Just because I don't act on everything I hear, doesn't mean that I'm unaware of what goes on." Mr. Hawk rubbed the close-cut stubble on top of his head, as his angry demeanor began to soften. "Eddy Leach has been a thorn in my side for the last several years. If his grades don't improve, he is likely to be here another year. If this situation had been reversed, and he was the one in trouble, this matter would have been resolved very easily. I would have called the police and had him permanently expelled." Mr. Hawk paused, "I'm very disappointed in you. I don't expect these sorts of situations to arise from our better students. Do you have anything else you want to add, before I decide on your punishment?"

"No, sir."

"Unfortunately, even if I scale back your punishment to detention, the school bylaws won't allow you to participate in the Bowl this coming Saturday. Therefore, I will do something for you this once." Mr. Hawk raised his index finger to underscore his commitment. "This one time only, instead of detention, I will let you write a thirty-page term paper. Mrs. Branson will select the subject, and when it is complete you will give it to her for her review. If she informs me that she is dissatisfied with it in any way, you will have to start over with a new subject. If you don't get it right on the second try, you can make your third attempt right here in this room, during a week's detention. Do you understand me?"

"Yes. Thank you, Mr. Hawk."

"Don't thank me just yet. You're going to have to do something for me. You stay away from Eddy Leach. Don't talk to him. Don't try to apologize. Just leave him completely alone. If you see him come down one end of the hall, then you turn around and head in the other direction. You totally screwed up today, and you can't afford to have this situation continue in any shape or form."

"I will do as you ask, sir."

"Do you have any other classes with Eddy, besides Mrs. Roberson's ninth hour English class?"

"No, sir."

Mr. Hawk scribbled more notes on his pad. "That makes this part of it easy. Starting tomorrow, you will be taking Mr. Leslie's physics class, instead. I will have Mrs. McCain change your schedule, and notify Mrs. Roberson that you're no longer enrolled in her class."

"Yes, sir."

Mr. Hawk sighed, "That's all I have, as far as school matters on this subject. I do have some unofficial advice for you, if you want to hear it."

"I do, sir."

"Go see Eddy's father."

"How do you mean, sir?"

"Go see him tonight and apologize, and try to deescalate this whole thing between you and Eddy. If he decides to call the police, he's got you dead to rights for battery or aggravated assault. If that happens, you could very well be spending this evening in jail. You need to get over there before he makes that phone call and convince him otherwise. He's a local businessman and you may be able to reason with him. Stay away from Eddy, but talking to his father might help."

"I will do that, sir."

"If you like, I will have Mrs. McCain call him and tell him you're coming. That will make a better impression than you calling yourself, or showing up unannounced."

"That would be great if you could do that for me, sir."

Mr. Hawk took his pen and jotted more notes into his spiral notebook.

Lori raised her hand, "Mr. Hawk, is it okay if I go . . . ?"

"No, you can't accompany him. He should go alone. I'm afraid you missed the bus, though." He turned to Mrs. Branson, "Would you mind giving Lori a ride home?"

"I'd be happy to, Mr. Hawk."

Mr. Hawk checked his watch, "It's 5:30 now. I will have Mrs. McCain tell him you're going to be there at 7:00. Can you be there on time? I know Frank. He hates tardiness."

Gerald nodded. "I'll be there on time."

Mr. Hawk stood up and rubbed his palms together. "Mrs. McCain will get you the address. Lori, thank you for coming. I need a moment to finish up with Mrs. Branson. She'll meet you in the hall in just a few minutes."

Mrs. Branson watched Gerald and Lori leave the room and close the door, and then walked over to Mr. Hawk, "Tell me the truth."

"What's that?"

"Did you let him off the hook to accommodate me, or was it because you would have loved to have beaten the crap out of Eddy Leach yourself?"

"Ehhhh," Mr. Hawk gave a slight smile and peered off into space. "I suppose it was a little of both."

Breaking the Dinner Plate

- I didn't know what to expect in meeting Eddy's father. I wasn't sure how much good the visit would do, but I was willing to give it a try. -

Gerald checked his watch. It was three minutes before 7:00. He rang the doorbell and waited. A short time later, Mr. Leach came to the door. He was of average height and build, with conservatively short cropped ash gray hair. His perfect white teeth could fold easily into a smile when dealing with customers.

"Hi, my name is Gerald Camden."

"I know who you are. The school called and told me you were coming. Do me a favor." He pointed off to the side toward what had once been the garage. "Meet me at the other door. It's sort of a secondary office at home. I'll be there in a couple of minutes."

Gerald walked along the front of the house and waited on the other side. Mr. Leach came to the door and let him in. Mr. Leach sat down behind a desk while Gerald took a seat on the other side.

Mr. Leach studied him for a moment. "So, you're here because you beat up on Eddy for little or no reason, and you want to try to influence me not to call the police."

Gerald nodded, "That's mostly why I'm here. I would also like to apologize."

Mr. Leach gave him a strange smile. In a way, it looked like he was baring his teeth. "First off, let's forget about the apology. I don't think you're sorry. There is nothing more insulting than an insincere apology."

Gerald nodded, but didn't reply verbally.

"As far as the police, they haven't been called, nor do we intend to call them."

"Thank you."

"Don't thank me. The police are the least of your worries." Mr. Leach leaned back in his chair and pointed at Gerald, "Why do people like you find Eddy so hard to understand? Eddy doesn't have a problem. You're the one with the problem."

Gerald didn't understand, "What makes you think I have a problem? You don't know me."

"I don't know you specifically, but I know your type." Mr. Leach paused to take a breath. "Let me try this from a different angle, and maybe you will understand a little more about Eddy and the way he was raised. When Eddy was ten, a couple of older boys beat him up and took his lunch money. What do you suppose I did?"

"You called their parents and met with them."

"No, no, no." Mr. Leach rocked back and gave a small laugh. "I'm sure that's what *your* parents might have done, but not me. I beat his ass with a belt. I told him if it ever happened again, he'd just as well not even come home."

"That's terrible."

"This is the real world. There is always going to be a bigger fish. No one cares if you are at a disadvantage. What matters is how you deal with a situation when the odds are stacked against you. You have to be able to stand on your own two legs. Do you want to know what happened?"

Gerald shrugged.

"The next day, Eddy went up to them and punched the bigger one as hard as he could, square in the nose."

"And what did they do?"

"They beat the shit out of him." Mr. Leach gave a short laugh. "Eddy could barely walk the next few days."

"I guess it wasn't such a good strategy."

"You are totally clueless," Mr. Leach said with contempt in his voice. "It was an excellent strategy. There's a reason that you don't swat a bee that lands on your arm. You respect that, even though you can kill it, it can still hurt you. Eddy may have taken another ass whopping, but it was the last one. He'd hurt them. The ring leader spent the rest of the day with a throbbing nose. After that, they decided picking on Eddy wasn't much fun and left him alone. You don't get through life by registering complaints. It takes focus and direction. That's something Eddy understands, but you haven't figured out."

"You're creating a criminal."

"Thanks for sharing your vast parental expertise with me. It is duly noted. I'm creating a survivor. Here you are at my house, pleading your case. I can assure you that you won't see Eddy come whining to your parents' house. Eddy is a businessman in the purest form. Everything he does is to help promote himself in some fashion, or better his situation. Eddy doesn't hate you. Eddy doesn't care anything about you. He's like a shark. If you're in the water and he's hungry, he's going to have you for lunch." Mr. Leach opened a drawer. "Here, let me show you something." He brought out a wedge-shaped piece of white ceramic and handed it to Gerald. "Have a look at this."

Gerald took it and turned it in his hand. "What's this?"

"It's a shard from Eddy's dinner plate."

"I don't understand." Gerald handed it back to Mr. Leach.

"We have a family tradition." Mr. Leach put the piece back into his drawer. "It's a ritual that has been practiced for generations. On your sixteenth birthday, you select a dinner plate from the cupboard and hand it to your parents. The family gathers on the front step, and they throw it to the ground and break it in front of you. Do you know what that signifies?"

"No."

"It means that you make your own way from that moment forward, and that your free plate at the table has come to an end. In strict practice, you leave and don't make contact again until after you have become self-sufficient.

I hedged a little. I gave Eddy a job working in the shop and let him use the empty space on the upper level. There wasn't any heat, running water, or even a bed to sleep in. All he had were some clothes and a sleeping bag." Mr. Leach cracked a smile. "He froze his ass off that first winter.

He turned it into an apartment without any help, and paid for the materials with his own money. Today, it's climate controlled with inner walls, plumbing, carpeting, and furniture. I've never been up there, but I suspect it's quite nice."

Gerald was spellbound. "He did all the work and paid for it, but you'll kick him out if he doesn't finish school."

"What?" Mr. Leach seemed confused. "Are you feeling sorry for Eddy, now? It's still my building. I'm a businessman too. I'll kick him out sooner or later. If he quits school, it's definitely going to be sooner, but he has no promises, either way."

"That's pretty cold."

"The world is pretty cold, and we're living in it. Eddy's not the problem. Eddy can take care of himself. He knows how to make money, and he knows how to save it. When the day comes that I kick him out of that apartment, I'm sure he has enough salted back to get re-established somewhere else." Mr. Leach paused. "Enough worrying about how Eddy is going to survive in the cold, harsh world. Eddy's going to be fine. We're here to talk about how you're going to survive."

"How can I avoid any further conflicts with Eddy?"

Mr. Leach huffed, "I'm not sure you can. If you've embarrassed him, Eddy's going to feel the need to get even in some way. He's not going to be satisfied until he's had his revenge. My advice to you is to become small in Eddy's eyes, and stay on the back burner. Avoid him and stay toward the bottom of his to do list. If he has a free evening and it's a choice between squaring things with you and making some money, you're going to lose out. If you can manage to be a low priority, he might eventually write you off."

"I will give that a try."

"You lit the fuse, now you're trying to juggle the dynamite."

"Eddy's not totally innocent in all this."

"I know that. Eddy has barely spoken to me in the last five years, but I hear things around the shop. Eddy started seeing your old girlfriend so you and a friend on the football team decided to get even. The two of you ganged up on Eddy in a hallway, but that wasn't enough for you. So later, you decided to give it another whirl on your own. You managed to get the drop on Eddy and gave him a few sucker punches. Now you're afraid that he will get revenge, and you're here to ask me for help. Is that pretty close?"

"That's not exactly the way it happened."

"Whatever. If you want to stay out of Eddy's sights, just avoid him until things cool off." Mr. Leach checked his watch. "That's the best I can do for you. If you want any more of my time, then you're going to need to make out a check."

Gerald stood up. "Thanks for seeing me. I will give it some thought." He turned to go through the door.

"You do that," Mr. Leach answered as he stood up and followed Gerald to the door. After Gerald went out, Mr. Leach closed and locked the door from the inside.

The Photo Album

- I was late for dinner. -

When Gerald home, the kitchen table had already been cleared and Christine was sitting in a large, red, heavily cushioned leather chair. Behind her, two tall cherry bookcases met at the corner of the room. She glanced up from the photo album opened across her lap. "Hi, honey."

"Hello, Mom. Where's Dad?"

"He went bowling. You missed dinner but there's a plate for you in the fridge."

"What are you doing?"

Just thumbing through some old pictures of you," she glanced down at her lap, then back up. "Actually, they're pictures of the old you." She smiled a bittersweet smile, and then motioned him forward. "Do you want to see?"

"Sure, Mom," Gerald walked over to kneel by the arm of her chair. "Is 'Mom' what he used to call you?"

Christine gently lifted a hand to the side of his face and peered into his eyes. "It doesn't matter what he called me. You can call me whatever feels natural for you." She ran the fingertips over a large school photo. "Look," she said softly, "this is your brother."

Gerald tilted his head as he studied the face. "The brother I will never know."

"He was a good boy. He was always happy and in a good mood. I wish he was still here."

"I'm sorry," Gerald mumbled softly.

"Don't be sorry." Christine put a hand up to quiet him.. "Don't ever think that I am wishing I could trade you off for him."

"Wouldn't you?" Gerald seemed confused. "I mean, isn't that what you would want?"

"What I want—what I really want," she answered thoughtfully, "is for both of my sons to somehow be magically sitting next to each other at my dinner table, like a couple of identical twins." She stood up and slid the photo album back onto the shelf, then patted him on the shoulder. "Come on; I'll heat up your plate."

Gerald rose to his feet, "I'll take care of it."

"No," she countered as she walked toward the kitchen. "You go sit at the table. I'm going to feed my son." She paused to turn and look at him. "I need to feel like I'm still a mother."

When the microwave dinged and Christine was taking out the steaming plate, John came through the door, carrying a bowling bag.

Gerald glanced up. "I didn't know you were a bowler, Dad."

"I'm not on a league. I get together with some friends for an occasional game," John opened the closet door and put the ball away. "We haven't been seeing much of you lately."

"I've been spending a lot of time with Lori Taylor."

"The dentist's daughter?"

"Yes," Gerald confirmed. "Do you know her?"

"I know her dad. He crowned a tooth for me six months ago. How can a little piece of porcelain cost a thousand bucks?"

"Is she your girlfriend now?" Christine crossed her arms. "Is that why you broke up with Tammy?"

"I don't know if you could call her a girlfriend just yet."

"You should invite her to dinner." Christine suggested. "Find out when she's free this week and we can have her over. If you've already met her parents, then it's time you returned the favor."

"Your mother's right," John concurred. "A girl could take that the wrong way, as if you didn't want her to meet your parents."

"Next week would be better. It would give her more notice."

"That would be fine," Christine nodded. "Let us know which day and we'll get dressed up for a nice dinner."

Gerald couldn't envision Lori wanting to dress up. "How formal of a dinner are we talking about?"

Christine shrugged, "I thought I might wear a dress. You two don't have to wear ties, but a nice long-sleeved button-up shirt would be nice."

"What if we did something more casual," Gerald answered evasively, "like a taco night or something?"

"Oh, I don't think that's a good idea," Christine rebuffed the notion. "We want to make a good first impression."

"I have to agree with your mother," John interjected. "A formal dinner is better for the first time we meet her."

Gerald nodded. "I'll see what I can do."

Rabbit in a Bottle

Chapter 9

Tuesday's Games

Musical Chairs

- I grew a little more attached to Lori every day. I think I had to be in love with her, because her stubbornness made me want to scream. –

Lori came down the hallway and leaned on a locker close to Gerald's. "Are you okay?"

Gerald glanced up and smiled, "I'm fine." He ran his eyes down her slender figure. She was wearing jeans with a gingham shirt and blue cotton vest. "You look very pretty."

"Why thank you, kind sir," Lori smiled. "I'm glad you're switching to Physics."

"I can't believe I am going to be in two of Mr. Leslie's classes."

"Is that so bad? Kevin, Eugene, and I are all in both classes." Lori smiled, "and we get to spend more time together." Lori seemed a little insecure about bringing up the next subject, "I wondered if we might start sitting together in algebra."

Gerald nodded. "That's fine."

"So, you would be willing to move up to the front row?"

"I suppose I could do that," The corner of his mouth bent into a wry grin, "or you could move back to the middle row."

"I can't move back to the middle row!" Lori quickly objected.

"It was your idea," Gerald grinned, "Why can't you be the one to move?"

"You know why. Mr. Leslie expects all of his students to sit in the front row."

"Everyone in the class is his student. They can't all sit up front."

"That's not it. He has sort of an unofficial group that he considers 'his students.' He likes them to sit up front in his classes."

"Maybe I want you to sit in the middle row with me. Why is what I want less important than what he wants?"

Lori smiled, "He wants me to sit up front, because that is his preference. You only want me to sit in the middle to aggravate him. Why do you keep provoking him? I think you're starting to gain his favor."

Gerald smiled, "I always thought gaining someone's favor would seem a little more . . . ." he paused, trying to find the correct word, "favorable."

"He's started to recognize that you have some talent. That's first step toward him liking you."

"I don't want to like me just because I am good at math. How is that any different from being liked for having big muscles, or a lot of money?"

"Gerald, you drive me absolutely crazy. Being on his front row is a place or honor."

"Maybe the reason everyone thinks being on his front row is so wonderful is because everyone else is anxious to get there. If you move back to the second row, that could introduce a new mind-set. If you do something to break people out of a mindless habit, you have done a service to the rest of the race."

"Why don't we just switch for a while?" Lori's eyes lit up as a new idea popped into her head. "You move up to the front row, and I'll go back to the second row. We'll each try out the other side of the fence, to see what it's like, and then we can decide from there."

Gerald didn't speak but eyed her suspiciously.

"It's a good compromise," Lori pointed out. "A compromise means that both sides sacrifice something, so they can meet in the middle."

"You know he's going to blame me for this."

"Yes, I know that," Lori smiled innocently.

Mr. Leslie was running a little late. He wasn't late for the class, but it was late for him. He walked in the door just a few seconds before the morning bell. Gerald kept his face tilted down toward his desk, as if he was reading. Leslie gave a quick glance through the room as he entered, then walked to the front desk and laid down his books.

Leslie sighed, and put his fists on his hips then walked around the front of his desk to loom over Gerald. Gerald felt his presence, and raised his head up to peek at him through one eye. Mr. Leslie made a troubled face and turned back to the second row.

Lori was caught in the beam of his gaze. She pulled her neck down and hunched up her shoulders, as she smiled back at him and gave him an abbreviated side-to-side wave of her hand.

Leslie didn't respond, but stared down at Gerald again. "Well, it can only be one of two things," Mr. Leslie finally said. "Either the seating arrangement has become confused, or Lori needs to spend a lot more time and money on her makeup." He gave Gerald's desk a nudge with his toe. "So you think you've graduated up to Lori's seat in the front row do you?"

"I'm giving it a try, sir," Gerald answered innocently. "It's really quite comfortable."

Leslie popped the top of an erasable marker, and then walked up to the white board to start hammering out an equation. "Let's see if you can take the heat."

The Dinner Invitation

- Lori was like a house with many rooms. Just when you thought you had explored them all, you would come across a door you hadn't opened yet. –

Gerald sat quietly at the lunch table, occasionally making eye contact with Lori. She cocked her head and smiled. Each time, he smiled back.

"I need to ask you something," he finally blurted out.

"Is this a marriage proposal? If so, you're supposed to get down on one knee first."

"How would you like to come over to our house for dinner next week?"

"Oh my," she fluttered her hand in front of her neck as if to fan herself, "a dinner invitation from a handsome young gentleman."

"The whole thing is my parents' idea. They forced me into it."

"What's so bad about me coming over for dinner?"

"Do you ever wear dresses?"

"A dress?" she cackled sarcastically. "Are you kidding?" She drew her head back as if trying to determine if he were making a joke. "I don't even own a dress. We don't do dinners in our family."

"You don't eat dinner?"

"Of course we eat dinner, but it's not an organized event." Lori smiled, "Daddy usually nukes a burrito in the microwave or something like that, and Momma and I will make a big salad and split it, but we never all sit down to a formal dinner. We don't do the 'sit around the table and pass the potatoes' thing; it's just not how we operate."

"Really? We sit down to dinner every night. When do you ever talk to each other?"

"Mamma and I talk all the time."

"What about you and your dad?"

Lori paused. "I guess we don't talk that much. He played with me all the time when I was little, but when I got bigger it tapered off. Somehow we just forgot how. It seems like after you turn fourteen it gets awkward."

"I didn't mean to pry."

"No, I'm glad you did. I guess it's just like anything else. If you don't make the effort, it just doesn't happen."

First Physics

- Every time I had an encounter with Mr. Leslie, it seemed like I was fencing. Physics turned out to be no different. –

Gerald walked into the science lab on the top floor. He deliberately came in just before the bell, so that most of the class would already be seated, and he would be able to find a chair that wasn't occupied. All the lab tables had a black glossy finish. Built into each end was a sink, a gas jet, and an electrical outlet. He noticed that the top of one of the faceplates was welded, as if from an arc of electricity. Mr. Leslie was already seated at his desk in the front.

"Gerald! Welcome to our physics class." Mr. Leslie made a sweeping motion with his arm. "I knew that eventually, Mr. Hawk would come to your senses."

"There's not much victory in catching a rabbit when its foot is tied to a tree," Gerald quipped back.

Mr. Leslie smiled. Gerald couldn't tell if it was an expression of welcome or triumph. "Do you know how this works, Gerald?"

"Not really."

"We do labs, and we study the results. Everyone has a lab partner."

"Okay."

"Do you have a preference of who you would like for a lab partner?"

"Well, I was thinking that . . . ."

"The rest of the class has already been assigned partners. There were an odd number of students when we paired up. Lori is the only one without a partner."

"That's fine," Gerald started to move toward the empty seat at Lori's table.

"I normally partner with Lori, so you'll have to trio with Eugene and Kevin."

"That will be fine." Gerald walked back to one of the two empty seats at the lab table where Eugene and Kevin were sitting.

"Welcome to Physics," Mr. Leslie called out.

A Plague on the World

- Talking with Mrs. Roberson always helped me to gain a perspective. -

At the end of the day, Gerald slipped out the back of the lab. He would have liked to have walked with Lori, but he didn't feel like sparring with Mr. Leslie. He walked to the end of the third floor hallway, and peered down the stairwell to watch Mrs. Roberson's last period English class file down the steps then went into the classroom.

When he walked into the room, Mrs. Roberson looked up and smiled, "If it isn't Mike Tyson!" She held up her fists, as if readying herself for a fight. "Sorry I had to send you to the office, but I really didn't have much choice. Was Mr. Hawk pretty hard on you?"

"He grilled me for a while. I took it and stayed respectful, so he let me off easy. He suggested that I meet with Eddy's father, so I went to his house to visit him."

"Really?" Mrs. Roberson leaned closer. "What was that like?"

Gerald shrugged, "It wasn't what I expected. He explained why Eddy behaves the way he does. It actually seemed to make sense. Eddy is like a shark . . . ."

"Stop. I'm sorry I asked."

"What do you mean?" Gerald asked.

"I really don't want to hear the justifications from his father. He can stuff it. The world doesn't owe him an audience. I don't want to hear about his rough childhood and all the other reasons. Everyone has horrible events in their life, and that's no excuse for going around hurting people.

My husband used my father's Colt pistol to blow his brains out just one week after our anniversary. That didn't turn me into some vile monster. When someone does something completely wicked, it doesn't matter what they've been through and I don't want their excuses. It's adding insult to injury."

"I wish I had said something like that to Eddy's father."

"Eddy can't be fixed. Neither can his father. You can't help someone who thinks they don't have a problem."

"So what do you do with people like Eddy?"

"You just try to avoid them. The more you try to handle a turd, the more crap you get on your fingers."

"Eddy's father said the same sort of thing—that I should avoid him—but he didn't think it would stop Eddy."

"I think he's right," Mrs. Roberson nodded her head, "He's already shot Tyler. Eventually, he's going to hurt you or Tammy, then maybe someone else." She sighed. "What are you going to do?"

Gerald's lips pulled tight and his eyes narrowed. "Don't make me say it."

Mrs. Roberson shook her head. "You don't have to say it."

An Empty Shell

- I went to the hospital to see Tyler, but he had already left. -

Gerald walked into the hospital room to see Mr. and Mrs. Banks sitting on each side of their son, holding his hands. Tyler seemed to be sleeping. Gerald glanced over at the parents, "How's he doing?"

Mrs. Banks shook her head and looked down.

Robert Banks cleared his throat, "The infection is worse. A few hours ago, he slipped into a coma. The doctors don't understand why."

"Maybe it's for the best," Mrs. Banks said quietly. "He was in so much pain."

"I'm so sorry." Gerald knew immediately that the coma was caused by Dr. Gauge shutting down the relay with Tyler-mouse.

"His breathing is becoming labored. The doctors say that they may have to put him on a ventilator soon. It's a tough spot, but we've been through this before. When Tyler had a car wreck a couple of years ago, things looked pretty bleak, but he fought his way back."

Gerald felt guilty for allowing them to cling to false hope. By the time Tyler's human body would recover, Tyler-mouse would already be dead. "He won't recover this time," Gerald said quietly.

"How can you know this?" Mrs. Banks lifted her head angrily. "You're not a doctor."

"I'm sorry." Gerald's heart felt heavy in his chest. He walked to the head of the hospital bed and gently laid his hand across Tyler's forehead. Gerald took a deep breath. "Goodbye, Tyler," he said softly.

Gerald took a last look, and then slowly walked out of the room. He left without giving the Banks a farewell greeting. He just didn't feel like it, and if he didn't feel like it, he wasn't going to force himself. He hoped they'd understand.

Gerald took the elevator to the first floor and made his way down the hall toward the entrance. As he neared the lobby, he came to the glass door of a gift shop. A small cellophane bag on the counter caught his eye. He lifted it up to take a closer look. It was a bag of sunflower seeds, the kind that had already been shelled from the hull. Gerald dug a couple of dollars from his pocket.

Out of the Cage

- I knew there was only one thing that would make me feel better, and I knew where to find it. -

Gerald parked the Mustang along Sixth Street. He saw that the tenth floor lights of the Sycamore building were on. Dr. Gauge must still be working in the lab. He keyed the access code into the front door and went inside.

When Gerald got off the elevator on the tenth floor, he saw Dr. Gauge bent over the lab table, peering into a microscope and making notes on a scratch pad, "Ah, Gerald." Dr. Gauge looked up from work. "I thought you might show up this evening."

"Is Tyler here?"

Dr. Gauge smiled, "Tyler-mouse is here, if that's what you mean."

Gerald pulled the shroud off of Tyler-mouse's bell jar, but found it empty except for some loose strands of wire. "Where is he?"

"Over there." Dr. Gauge pointed to a small cage on a table off to the side, "He doesn't need to be in the bell jar anymore."

Gerald walked over to the table and peered inside the cage. Tyler-mouse came to the door and fastened his paws around two of the bars of the door, like a prisoner at the door of a jail cell. "Do you mind if I let him out?"

"Sure, that's fine."

Gerald opened the cage door, and Tyler-mouse scampered out. He stood on the table in front of the cage, and sat on his hind legs. His black eyes stared at Gerald without blinking. Gerald reached out to stroke the top of his head between the tiny nodules mounted in the skull. "You left the electrodes in."

"Yes. They don't really hurt anything. There's no point in taking them out."

Gerald took out the bag of sunflower seeds. "Do you think he remembers me?" He tore open the cellophane and fed a kernel to Tyler-mouse.

"Oh, I doubt that." Dr. Gauge adjusted his glasses on his nose. "It's a whimsical notion but I suspect that there isn't anything of your friend in there."

Gerald offered another kernel and then ate one himself. "Why did you pull him back so soon? I thought the plan was to wait a while."

"It was," Dr. Gauge nodded, "but then Tyler developed an infection, he became very uncomfortable, and asked that the link be dissolved."

"Tyler was breathing without a respirator."

"That happens with a controlled shut-down, as opposed to a quick blip like you saw the other day. I suspect the body will breathe on its own for a few hours as it slips back into a coma."

Gerald let his hand down next to Tyler-mouse. He scampered up Gerald's arm and sat on his shoulder. Gerald cocked his head to get a look, and offered him another seed. "He seems pretty spry for a sick mouse."

Dr. Gauge shook his head slowly. "Don't be fooled by his liveliness. He is in the advanced stages of cancer. I have been searching feverishly for a cure but it continues to elude me."

"Are you getting close?"

Dr. Gauge shook his head. "Cancer is very tricky. A cure for this particular strain could be just around the corner, or it might be years away."

"I sure hope you find that cure, Doc."

"I wouldn't get my hopes up. He'll likely expire before I stumble across it."

Chapter 10

Wednesday's Gambit

The Attempt

- There was more to Tammy than I initially realized. As I got to know her better, I came to like her. I sometimes wonder if things could have worked out between us, had I not become involved with Lori. –

Tammy walked to the end of the hall on first floor. She made a few quick steps when she spotted Eddy approaching his locker. She peered over his shoulder to watch him turn the dial but as he worked the knob, he shielded the numbers with his other hand. Eddy yanked the lock open and glanced over to notice her. "Well look at you."

"Hi, Eddy," she smiled sweetly as she silently wished she could claw the eyes out of his head.

"I was thinking of coming by to get you tonight." Eddy pulled open his locker and began digging out some textbooks and a spiral notebook.

Tammy peered over his shoulder. She had expected his locker to be a mess of rumpled papers, but it was neat and orderly. "I thought I might bring you a picture of me."

"I already have some pictures," Eddy smiled.

"I talking about one you could hang in your locker, Silly. I hope you aren't showing those other pictures around."

"Those pictures are secure," Eddy shrugged, "but you can give me one for my locker. I'll put it up."

Tammy squeezed in close and put her palms on the front of his thighs. Through the denim, she could feel the lump of his keys, "What time are you coming by?"

"I'll pick you up at 6:30."

Tammy peered into his eyes with her chin only a few inches from his. She gently slid her fingers over the hems at the top of his pockets, and curled the tips inside. "I'll be ready," she said in a deep voice that was nearly a whisper. The keys were too deep. It was going to be hard to get them out without being detected, "Are you going to tell me where we're going?"

"You'll find out soon enough. I think I've reconsidered on those blue jean skirts you're so fond of. You can wear one tonight."

"I'll wear anything you want," she whispered as she stuck her hands deeper into his pockets and discreetly rubbed the sides of his penis through the pocket canvas.

"Alright; well, wear a tube top along with it. I like tube tops."

"I want a kiss," she whispered. She brought her right hand up to slide under his shirt and lightly drag her nails over the skin of his torso to distract him. The pinky of her left hand deftly hooked the ring of his keys and gently drew it upward, as she pressed her lips on his.

Eddy kissed her back a few times. When the keys came past the hem of his pocket, Eddy felt the clump rub against the front of his hip. He glanced down, "What are you doing?"

Tammy cursed silently, but didn't let it show in her face. She lifted his keys up and slid them around on the front of his chest, "I want to know when I get to drive the Cadillac." Tammy let her mouth gape open and rolled her tongue across her lower lip to wet it. "I want to know when you're going to let me come up to your apartment over the shop." She waggled the key in front of his face, "One day, I even expect to get a key of my own."

Eddy gently reached out to take the keys from her grasp, "You have to prove yourself first."

"Haven't I proven myself, Eddy? I didn't freak out on you the other night, did I?"

Eddy slipped his keys back into his pocket and nodded. "You've got a start, but you're not there yet."

"I'll do anything you want, Eddy." She leaned close to whisper in his ear. "Anything," she repeated softly.

Brothers in Arms

- Tammy was a good ally. She was smart and she was tough. A romantic relationship just wasn't in the cards for us, but she was becoming a very good friend. -

Gerald was headed over to meet Lori for lunch in the school cafeteria when he became aware of Tammy walking next to him.

"I couldn't get the combination," she spoke softly as they walked. "He covers the dial when he twists in the numbers."

Gerald grimaced, "That's not good. That means he doesn't trust you."

"No," Tammy answered, "I don't think that's it. It seemed like it was just habit. He's so meticulous about everything; I think he's grown accustomed to being overly cautious."

"That's what makes this so risky."

"The locker combination doesn't matter. He always carries his keys with him. I tried to slip them out of his pocket, but he caught me."

"He caught you?"

"Sort of, but it's okay. I covered for it pretty well. I told him I wanted a key to his apartment and to drive his car."

"Did he buy it?"

"I think so, but he won't trust me until I sleep with him. I think that's what he's expecting this evening."

Gerald shook his head, "I hate for you to have to do that."

"It's only sex. It's not like he's going to break my arm or punch me in the mouth. If I could only have gotten those keys, you would have known the coast was clear, and you could have gone after the tape while he was with me."

Gerald nodded and looked down at the concrete sidewalk as he walked, "That would have worked out great."

"At least, he's going to be taking his pants off, so maybe I'll have a better chance at getting the keys." Tammy paused. "You know, even if we get the tape, that still won't be the end of it. When he finds it missing he'll want revenge."

"I've been giving that some thought." Gerald dipped his head and rubbed his chin as he walked.

"You know what I think," Tammy stared straight ahead. "Someone ought to shoot the son of a bitch."

"That's pretty extreme," Gerald eyed her closely, "Are you serious or is that just angry talk?"

Tammy stared off in the distance. "When he stuck that revolver in my mouth and pulled back the hammer, I really thought I was going to die. Do you want to know the strange part? I handed him the gun. All I could think about was how stupid I was, and how I should have taken the gun and shot him when I still had the chance.

He's taking me for a drive tonight. I think he's expecting sex. Maybe he'll take me somewhere remote. Once we're alone, I'll look for an opportunity to get the revolver out of the dash and kill him." Tammy began to veer off in another direction. "Brothers in arms, right?"

"Yeah, Tammy," Gerald concurred, "that's us, brothers in arms."

The Cure

- Only missed by a fraction, slipped a little off your pace. -

Gerald entered the lab on the tenth floor of the Sycamore building and stopped at Tyler's cage. He unlatched the door and let it tilt open, then shook some sunflower seeds out of the bag into his hand. Gerald held them up one by one for the mouse to take. He glanced over at Dr. Gauge, working in the corner of the lab. "I think you're wrong, Doc," he gestured toward the gray mouse. "He acts like he remembers me."

Dr. Gauge looked up and smiled, but did not answer verbally.

"He's moving around better," Gerald added.

"Yes, of course he is. His cancer has been cured."

"He's been cured of cancer? Are you sure?"

"I was poking around this morning when I discovered a cure. I had been searching for the last two years and it was right in front of me the whole time."

"You've cured cancer? Doc, you're going to be famous."

"Oh no, not really. Cures have been found for other types of cancer, and this is an uncommon strain. Still, this will help some people. I'm planning to clean up my notes and pass my findings on to other scientists in the field. With the right care, Tyler-mouse will live to a ripe old age."

"This is great! When are you going to hook him back up to Tyler?"

"I wasn't planning on doing that," Dr. Gauge shifted his glasses. "Remember that Tyler himself asked that the link be dissolved."

"He might not have, if he had known there was a cure."

"Yes, yes; that is entirely possible, but we can't know that."

"Why don't you hook him up long enough to ask him?"

"I'm afraid I can't do that."

"Why not? Is there some sort of scientific reason?"

"Well, there's a reason but it's not very scientific." Dr. Gauge paused to straighten his sleeve. "I'm sorry, Gerald. I thought you would have already known. The Tyler Banks that you knew died from an infection this afternoon."

Gerald was stunned. "I told his parents," he said slowly, his breath catching in his throat, "that he wasn't coming back this time."

"You were correct."

Gerald lowered his arm and the gray mouse crawled onto his palm. He swallowed hard. He didn't want to cry in front of Dr. Gauge. He stroked the top of the mouse's forehead with a finger. Gerald sighed, "Tyler was my friend."

"He may have been your friend, but he wasn't Tyler." Dr. Gauge pointed out. "Tyler died a couple of years ago. The person you knew was created when I hooked him up to a mouse."

"What if you hooked him up to another body?"

"Use the same mouse up to a new human host?" Dr. Gauge paused, "That's not likely. I would need a human subject who was near death. I'm afraid that the right circumstances don't occur very often." Dr. Gauge rubbed his cheek. "Even if that were to happen, it would be better to use a fresh specimen."

"A fresh specimen?" Gerald was becoming angry. "That's Tyler in that cage!"

"No, it is not Tyler. It's a mouse. That's all he is; that's all he ever was. Even if we established a link with a new host, there is no reason to expect that any of Tyler's personality would be salvaged. I'm sorry, but the Tyler you knew has had his day, and it has passed."

"I can't believe you could be this cold," Gerald said bitterly. "What kind person are you?"

"I am a scientist and a doctor," Dr. Gauge had a seldom-heard sharpness to his voice. "I don't engage in whimsy. I take an objective, scientific view and that is how I base my decisions."

Gerald grabbed his jacket and started to leave, "You do whatever you want, but I am not coming back here anymore. If you don't care about Tyler, then you certainly don't care about me."

"You're in an emotional state." Dr. Gauge suggested. "You're not being logical."

"Maybe there comes a time when you have to abandon logic and start dealing with people." Gerald gently cradled the small gray rodent to his body as he turned to leave. "I am taking Tyler with me."

"Gerald, wait." Dr. Gauge got out of his chair and put up his hand to stop him. "You may be right. I have a tendency to get caught up in the science." He paused to compose his thoughts. "You have to understand what it is like; watching people slowly wither and die. Doctors have to distance themselves in order to survive the job."

Gerald was starting to cool down a little, "I'm sorry, Doc. This has been an emotional day."

Dr. Gauge sat his work aside and clasped his hands on the table. "I will tell you something that I never told Tyler. It may help you to gain perspective." Dr. Gauge stopped and took a deep breath. "It was me."

"What was you?"

"His cancer was my doing. I was the one who gave Tyler the shot."

"You injected Tyler with cancer?"

"Yes, of course I injected him with cancer. During my tenure at the cancer research center, I injected many mice with cancer. I remember the day I injected Tyler. In those days, injecting the mice had become routine, but something about this one gave me pause. He was an unusual specimen. He was more tame than the others. I hesitated before injecting him, and considered sparing him, but I had a busy schedule that morning, so I injected him and moved on. When I left the institute, I took him with me, and tried to find a cure. Sadly, I found it a day too late."

Gerald nodded, "That's why you don't want to believe that some of Tyler's memories could transfer. As long as it's just an ordinary mouse, you didn't inject him with cancer."

"You may be right," Dr. Gauge said slowly, "Guilt, may have biased my objectivity. I can't afford to become friends with my patients, but I liked him and as his doctor, his well-being was my responsibility."

"You didn't do anything wrong, Doc."

"Maybe, but there's a body lying in Goodwine Funeral Home that would not be there if I had acted differently."

"You gave him time that he wouldn't have had. You gave me time, as well."

"I will do this for you and for Tyler, wherever he may be. If a suitable human host becomes available while Tyler-mouse is still with us, I will use him for the new relay. Even if that happens, there is no reason to think you will ever talk to your friend again."

"If you could just give him a chance; just a sliver of hope."

"I'll give him that chance," Dr. Gauge nodded, "I promise."

The Coal Dock

- Beelzebub has a devil put aside for me. -

Eddy pulled his powder blue Cadillac up in front of Tammy's house, and gave the horn a quick beep. Tammy emerged just a few seconds later. When he saw her, Eddy nodded his head with satisfaction. She was wearing a red and white striped tube top and a denim skirt, as he had requested.

"Hi, Eddy," she said as she got in the car. "Where are we going?"

Eddy checked his watch, "It's still daylight for another hour or so. I thought we might drive into Robinson and get a bite to eat, then after it gets dark, head out in the country. Does that sound okay to you?"

"Sure, Eddy, that sounds fine." Tammy reasoned that if Eddy was taking her on a drive, with the expectation of sex, he was probably planning to take her to a secluded place away from town. It could turn out to be her opportunity.

Eddy pulled into the Dog-N-Suds on the east side of Robinson. It was an old-style burger drive-up, where waitresses brought the orders out to the car. At one time it had been a fairly large chain of six hundred restaurants throughout the Midwest, but in recent years it had dwindled to fewer than twenty locations. It was Eddy's favorite place to eat. The food was good; he could listen to the radio as he ate; and owning a convertible made it easy for him to take the tray of food from the carhop. He ordered a "Texas Burger" for himself; Tammy said she would be content with an order of fries.

Tammy was thankful for the radio. It gave her excuse not to talk as she quietly nibbled on her fries. She discreetly peeked over at the door of the glove compartment. Was the revolver still inside?

Eventually, the sun set and the food was gone. Eddy wiped his hands on a napkin and then dusted his palms together. He started the motor and glanced over at Tammy, "Are you ready?"

"Yes."

Eddy drove north on Route 1 but rolled past the Hutsonville spur. A few miles down, he turned right onto a small road that ran east of the Annapolis junction. A looming wall of corn ran along each side of the road.

A half-mile down the narrow country road, he turned onto a small, grassy lane that ran down the middle of a cornfield. As they threaded their way through, the tips of the corn leaves licked the windshield on both sides of the car, Eddy looked over at her, "I hope you're not allergic to corn."

"Not as far as I know."

Eventually the strip widened into a small clearing. Eddy pulled close on one side, then steered the car around in a U-turn to face back the way they had come. He parked the car and shut off the motor. Tammy scanned the area and could see scattered broken timbers, piles of white rock, and broken pieces of concrete lying about, "What is this place?"

Eddy clutched the steering wheel and stood up to see over the windshield. "This used to be the old Penn Central Railroad that ran up to Chicago. They took up the rails some years back." He made a sweeping with his hand. "This wider part was a coal dock that they used in the old days when the locomotives ran on steam. It was torn down when they were switched to diesel." Eddy rested his elbow on the chrome upper edge of the windshield. "It's actually quite nice in the daytime. It gets a little creepy after dark." He slid back down in his seat and turned toward Tammy. "Do you know why I brought you here?"

"I think I have a pretty good idea." Tammy realized her voice held a hint of resentment.

"Maybe you do; maybe you don't," Eddy said in a leading way. "Do you know how long it takes me to make a thousand dollars?"

"No, Eddy, I don't know." Tammy's pulse quickened as she tried to formulate a strategy. If she rushed to open the dash and get the pistol, things could go bad. She might be the one getting shot instead of Eddy.

"I make thirty-five dollars an hour working in my dad's shop."

"That's good pay." Tammy tried to act natural as her heart thundered in her chest. She needed enough time to get the pistol and shoot it before he could wrestle it away from her.

"I work about twenty-five hours a week." Eddy continued. "By the time the government takes their cut, it takes me a few weeks to make a thousand dollars."

"I don't care about money." Tammy looked around. "Are you sure we're not going to get stranded here? I think the car smells a little hot."

Eddy glanced at the hood then went on. "Everyone cares about money. It's the difference between eating and not eating, or having and not having. That skirt, your tube top, this car, the sandwiches we ate, it's all about money. Everything else revolves around it."

Tammy stretched in her seat and peered through the windshield toward the front of the car. "Do you smell antifreeze?"

Eddy seemed to not notice the question but kept rambling. "We all barter our lives to get money. I dig through grease and oil to get mine. Let me tell you, if it wasn't for the money, I wouldn't be doing it."

Tammy tilted her head as if trying to get a better vantage to see the front of the car. "I think I see steam coming out." She rehearsed the scenario in her mind. When Eddy got out, she would time the opening to the glove compartment with the closing of the driver door. When Eddy raised the hood, she would get the revolver then stand up and cock the hammer as she rested her arm on the upper frame of the windshield. "Could you please check the motor, Eddy? I really don't want to be walking home."

"I will in a minute," Eddy eyed her expectantly. "First, I need to know that you're firmly committed to this relationship."

"Yes, Eddy," she answered quietly, "of course I am." She silently wondered if her anxiousness had made Eddy suspicious.

Eddy reached over and slowly pulled her tube top down until her naked breasts hopped out. "Are you okay with that?"

Tammy nodded. "Yes, Eddy," she swallowed, "do whatever you need to do."

Eddy checked the clock in the dash. It was a few minutes till eight. He needed to move things along. "Hold still," he told her. He slowly reached his hand under her denim skirt and grabbed the crotch of her underwear. The backs of his fingernails lightly brushed against her nether region, as he pulled them across her thighs and then down over the curve of her knees. "Get those off."

Tammy's hands trembled a little as she slid her panties down to her ankles and stepped out of them. She dreaded the thought of having sex with him but she kept telling herself not to be scared. If she could relax, it would pass easier. She considered making a last gambit to get the revolver. If Eddy could be distracted and she was quick, maybe she could get it and shoot him before he could think to react. She turned her upper body toward him as her right hand casually drifted over to rest on the door of the glove compartment. She took a deep breath then arched her back. She ran the tips of her fingers over her abdomen while her other hand discreetly felt for the glove compartment latch. "Would you like to touch my breasts, Eddy?"

Eddy paused to study her. "In a second. Right now I need to see your hands."

Tammy's heart skipped a beat. She cleared her throat. "My hands?"

"Yes," Eddy answered firmly. "Let me see them."

Tammy lifted her arms and held up her hands, with her palms spread toward him.

"Not like that, I need to see your wrists. Point your hands toward me."

Tammy tipped her forearms forward and made her hands horizontal. Eddy took a white plastic Walmart bag from the back seat and removed a pair of dish towels, then started wrapping one around each of her wrists.

Tammy watched as he worked the wraps of terry cloth to be sure they were snug. "What are you doing, Eddy?"

"I don't want the rope to chaff your skin." He took out a spool of blue painter's tape and meticulously wrapped it around the cloth covering each of her wrists.

"Why are you going to tie my hands?"

"You said you would do whatever I wanted, right? Did you mean that or not?" He took a spool of rope out of the back and used an end to tie her wrists together

"Yes, I meant it," her lower lip got tight, "but you don't need to tie me up. I'll do anything you like."

A pair of headlights appeared at the far end of the grassy lane. Eddy checked his watch. It was 8:00 on the dot. He glanced back over at Tammy. "Here comes anything," Eddy said with a dark resignation. He opened the glove compartment to talke out the pistol, then reached into the back seat to gather up the blanket he had used to conceal the rifle the other night.

Eddy opened the door and stepped out of the Cadillac. "Let's go," he said, giving the rope a tug. Tammy stepped out of the car. Eddy waited for her to get her footing, and then led her around to the front of the Cadillac. He spread the blanket across the hood, and then put his hands on her hips to position her in the middle of the hood, facing away from the car. "Lie back," he told her. As Tammy let her back rest against the blanket covering the nose of the car, Eddy ran the rope over the middle of the windshield frame and brought the loose end down to tie it off on the tee-shaped aluminum gearshift handle.

He came around the front of the car to give her a last check, and tested the tension on the rope. "Can you rest your heels on the ground?"

"Yes I can, Eddy, but please let me go."

Eddy leaned next her as the headlights from the other car came closer and lit up the car. "It's a thousand dollars," he said slowly, accentuating the amount. "You couldn't make that much waitressing tables for a month."

As the headlights slowly approached, Tammy started to twist around on the hood and tug at the rope.

Eddy bent next to her over the hood and laid a hand on the side of her cheek. "Hey, hey, calm down. Try to relax and this will go easier."

Tammy turned her face toward him. "Are you going to kill me when this is over? Are you going to put the gun in my mouth again—only this time, blow my brains out?"

"No, Tammy," he said in a soothing voice. "I'm not going to kill you. Why would I do that?"

"You killed Tyler."

"I only shot Tyler," he answered simply; "it was the infection that killed him. It's not my fault they couldn't keep his wound sterile."

"You said you would kill me if you ever decided that you didn't trust me."

"That's not going to happen," he said smoothly. "I am trusting you more all the time. After tonight, if you just go along with what I ask, I'll never have another doubt."

"What do I have to do?"

"There are a couple of guys in that car. I want you to let them have a good time. I promise it will go quickly. Then I will set you loose and we'll go home."

"I can't do that!"

"Yes you can!" Eddy growled, then checked himself and began speaking in a soft tone once more. "It's not going to be that bad. In half an hour, it will all be over, and I'll have a thousand dollars in my hand. I'll give you some of the money, but I need you to cooperate."

"I'll try," she said in an unsteady voice.

"That's my girl." Eddy got up from the hood as the second car stopped ten to twelve feet from the front of the Cadillac. The beams from the headlights lit up Tammy's body, and made her eyes squint.

Two men got out of the car. The driver was taller. His orange-red hair was combed straight back over his head, with a small swath of gray that ran back through the middle. The skin on his face was rough and had a ruddy hue to it that seemed to offset the yellowish-green pupils of his eyes. He wore a red cotton shirt a pair of faded jeans.

The shorter man had long, bushy brown hair and a thick, heavy beard. He was much fatter and very hairy. He wore black jeans and a faded blue denim shirt with the sleeves torn away. Scattered curly hairs ran down the length of each arm. He looked sweaty and oily.

Vic, the taller one, spoke first, "Why is she tied up? I thought you said she would be doing this of her own free will. I don't need some sheriff knocking on my door over all this."

"She's just a little kinky, that's all. This is my girlfriend, and she'll do anything to please me."

"What about next week, after the two of you have split up?" Earl, the shorter, fatter one spoke up in his squeaky voice, "What then?"

"Don't worry. I have a videotape of her committing a felony. As long as I have that, she'll do anything I say. This is perfectly safe, and she is perfectly willing." Eddy turned back toward the Cadillac, "Isn't that right, honey? Are you willing to go along with this? Can you show these gentlemen a good time?"

Tammy stared up at the stars and caught her breath. She wished she could somehow be whisked away to somewhere safe.

"Speak up, honey; they can't hear you."

"Yes," Tammy coughed out.

"And so you see, I am a man of my word. You have to admit she's pretty hot. It's the same girl as in the pictures, just like I promised." Eddy pause briefly, and then continued, "Alright," he rubbed his hands together, "money first, just like we talked about. I need five one-hundred-dollar bills from each of you." Eddy collected a clump of bills from each man, and then pulled a small marker from the front pocket of his jeans jacket. He leafed through the bills and made a small mark on each one. "The money's good," he announced, as he tucked the bills into the front pocket of his jeans. Eddy took out a quarter and positioned it over the tip of his cocked thumb, "Vic, do you want to call it in the air?"

Eddy flicked the quarter and it spun into the air, flickering in the headlights. "Heads," Vic called as it reached its apex.

Eddy slapped the coin on his wrist, and then took his hand away, "Heads, it is."

"Remember, no marks of any kind. You can pull her hair a little, so long as you don't yank out a clump. You can slap her ass if you want, but no scratches or bruises."

"A man pays five hundred dollars; he ought to be able to get a little rough if he wants."

"Sorry," Eddy shook his head. "That's not part of the deal. One last thing, don't blow inside her unless you want to risk a paternity suit."

"Bullshit!"

"Hey, I didn't make any promises on that angle. I have some condoms in the glove box if you want to go that route. Or, you can roll the dice and take your chances. Makes no difference to me."

Vic stepped up to the front and moved his large, heavy body over to Tammy. "Come 'ere, Bitch!" She grimaced, and her eyes closed, as he heaved his mass onto her. She thought she might asphyxiate from his crushing weight. With each rhythm, the small of her back was pressed hard against the curve of the car hood. After a few minutes he broke away, and then flopped his weight back on top of her as he gasped for air. Tammy could feel warm fluid pool up on her lower belly. She gagged and twisted to the side. She instinctively wanted to reach down and wipe herself clean, but the rope kept her arms stretched out over the windshield. Vic stood up and glared down at her with contempt, then spat on her breasts.

"Your ride's over," Eddy came around to the side of the car and tossed Vic a new dish towel. "Clean her up, so Earl can have his turn. He paid the same price as you did."

Vic wiped the spittle off her breast and toweled down her lower stomach.

Eddy held open an empty white plastic bag, "In here. We don't want to leave anything lying around when we go."

Vic grunted and tossed the towel in the bag, then ambled to the side as Earl eagerly stepped up to take his turn. Earl was heavier, but the weight from his soft fat tissue was more evenly distributed. Tammy recoiled from his horrible body odor. Earl tried to kiss her on the lips, but she turned her head away. His mouth reeked of stale tobacco and beer. Earl firmly put his hands on each side of her face to hold her chin high, and then pressed his lips down on hers. A moment later he abruptly jumped back, then flopped forward much as Vic had done. Once again she felt a tiny warm circle on her stomach.

Tammy tried to catch her breath under the weight. Earl was gasping for air. His body glistened with sweat. Tammy could feel his heart thundering against her chest. It was over; why couldn't he just get off of her?

Eventually, Earl slid off of Tammy, and Eddy threw him a dish towel. Earl caught the cloth against his chest and began wiping her down her stomach area. He glanced up at Tammy's face, and grunted a quiet "Thank you."

Earl noticed he had left sweat drippings on her upper body, and started to wipe her down with the same cloth, but Tammy stopped him, "No; I'm fine; just put it in the bag."

Earl dropped the soiled towel into the plastic bag that Eddy held open for him. Eddy dropped it into the back seat of the Cadillac, then brought out his denim jacket and draped it over one hand, as he crossed his arms. "Thank you for coming, gentlemen. If you wouldn't mind being on your way, the night is growing cool, and I need to get the lady home."

"Just a second!" Vic put a hand on one hip, and leaned toward Eddy. "I don't think that was worth five hundred bucks."

Eddy leaned back against the front of the Cadillac. "I am sorry you feel that way, but our business here is concluded."

Vic ran his fingers back through the gray streak in his hair. "I think I want my money back."

Earl put a hand on Vic's shoulder. "Come on Vic, we got what we came for. Let's just get out of here."

Vic brushed Earl's arm aside. "Shut up! You may have an extra five hundred dollars to throw away on this little skank, but I don't." Vic turned back toward Eddy. "Kid, you've got two choices. You can give us our money back or we can kick your scrawny ass, take our money back, and then slap your little bitch around for good measure. Now, what's it going to be?"

Eddy slipped the denim jacket off his arm to show the revolver in his hand. He tossed the jacket over Tammy's trussed-out arms. A corner pocket, heavier than the rest, gently thudded against the glass.

Eddy was focused on his customers. "I think," he said slowly, "that it would be wise for everyone to think over this situation." Eddy let the end of the barrel droop lazily at a downward angle, but cocked the hammer back with an audible click. "I have DNA evidence on the both of you in the back of my car. What do you supposed would happen if she testified that the two of you raped her?"

"You wouldn't dare go to the cops."

"I wouldn't need to. They would come to her after she put a couple of bullets in each of you. Now that," Eddy spoke slowly and deliberately, "is a very strong case for self-defense."

Vic looked at Eddy and down at the revolver, then gauged the distance between them. It was too far. To try to jump him would be risky.

"This doesn't have to end badly," Eddy offered. "I've got my money; you guys got laid; and she got a little excitement. Everybody's happy. Everybody wins. Just ride out and call it a night."

Vic paused for a moment to consider the situation, then turned around and walked back to his car. Earl climbed in the passenger side. The car backed up to turn around and then spun out over the dew laden grass.

Eddy walked over to Tammy stretched across his car hood.

Tammy glared back up at him, "Are you going to take your turn now?"

Eddy shook his head, "No, I was thinking about it for a moment but I'm not going to take seconds after those two. I'll wait until tomorrow, after you've had a hot bath."

"Can I be cut loose now? It's getting cold."

"Sure," Eddy lifted his denim jacket off her wrists and laid it across her body, then began untying the knots. "Now, that may have seemed pretty bad at the time, but it really didn't last all that long. By tomorrow, you'll probably have forgotten all about it." Once the rope was loose, Eddy stepped back to pull his jacket on.

Tammy sat up and stuffed her hands in the pockets of her denim skirt. She adjusted her tube top to cover her breasts, and then begin peeling the blue painter's tape off her wrists.

"Hey," Eddy called out as he untied the rope from the Hurst gearshift, "do that inside the car. I don't want to leave anything behind. Come on, let's get out of here."

Tammy walked around to the side of the car and got in, then continued plucking the tape from her wrists. Eddy felt around in his denim jacket. He took a flashlight from the backseat and got out to shine the beam around the car.

Tammy leaned up to the door, "What are you doing?"

"I can't find my car keys. I'm pretty sure that they were in my denim jacket."

"I hope you're not going to tell me that we're stranded here."

"No, I've got a spare set tucked away under the dash. I just want to see if I can find them first."

"Do you think those guys might have taken them?"

"No," Eddy answered thoughtfully, "they were never close enough. I think they may have fallen out while I was using my jacket to hide the revolver." Eddy walked around the car a few more minutes and then switched off the light. He opened the car door and squatted down to reach up under the dash for his spare keys. "I'll come back tomorrow and look for them in the daylight."

Eddy sat in the driver's seat and started the motor, then worked the controls to raise the convertible top. As the white canvas bonnet rose from the back and started to stretch out overhead, Eddy fished the money out of his pocket. He peeled off two of the one-hundred-dollar bills and tucked the rest away. "Here," he held out the money to her, "this is your share, two hundred bucks."

"I don't want the money, Eddy," she said, waving it away with her left hand. "You keep it." She kept her right hand tucked in the pocket of her denim skirt.

"No, take it." Eddy lifted her hand and put the bills in it. "You earned it. Go into town tomorrow and buy yourself something nice. Pretty soon this will all seem like a distant dream."

"If I take that, then it makes me a whore. I don't want to trade sex for money."

"If you don't take it, it makes you stupid. Being stupid is worse than being a whore."

"Okay, Eddy," she grudgingly took the bills and tucked them into her pocket, "if you say so."

Eddy locked down the front of the canvas top to the upper rim of the windshield, and then put the car in drive to take off. "I'll tell you what I'm going to do. I'm going to pick you up after school tomorrow and take you up to my apartment. Not many people get to see my apartment. You'll be one of the few."

"That'll be great, Eddy."

"Who knows, maybe I'll even let you drive the Cadillac."

Lying Close

- As I listened through the cemetery trees, I saw the sun coming up at the funeral at dawn, the long broken arm of human law. -

Lori heard something ping at her window pane. She slid out of bed and crept across the room in her nightshirt and panties. She lifted the sill, "Gerald?"

"Hi, Lori."

"How did you get here?" She peered over his shoulder toward the street, "I didn't hear your motorcycle."

"I shut the motor off a block away, and then coasted in so I wouldn't wake anyone."

She looked past his head through the window, "How did you get on top of the porch?"

"I climbed up the lattice work." His voice sounded weak and sad, "Can I come in?"

"Yes, of course." She backed away and held his hand to help him crawl in through the window.

"Tyler's gone," he said sadly.

"I know." She gave him a hug, and then kissed his cheek. "I heard. I'm so sorry."

"I just don't want to be alone tonight. Can I come in and just lie next to you for a while?"

Lori paused for a moment. "I think that will be okay," she whispered. "Just try not to make too much noise." She walked back to the bed and pulled the covers up to the pillow, then laid down on top. She wasn't sure if she was comfortable with lying underneath the blankets with him. "Get your shoes off. I don't want tracks on my blankets."

He took off his shoes and slid next to her. He moved the hair back from her cheek. "What are you going to do if your dad comes in and catches us?" he whispered.

"Me? What about you? What are you going to do?"

"I don't know." He smiled at her in the darkness. "The big question is, what is your dad going to do?"

"He would lose his mind," she lifted her chin to whisper, "You can bet he would be pretty mad."

"Mad at *me* or mad at *you*?"

"He would be pretty mad at both of us, but I'm not the one he would be throwing out the window."

"Surely, you don't mean *moi*!"

"Oh, yes, I mean *moi*. Let's just say that *moi* would be helped to exit the window very quickly. He might not be as gentle helping you out as I was helping you in."

"That sounds painful."

"He's a dentist so he's used to giving people pain."

"What's he going to do after we get married?"

"He'll make you sleep in the other room."

"That doesn't sound like any fun. Maybe I would sneak down the hallway and have my way with you."

"What is all this talk of marriage? You haven't even officially declared me as your girlfriend."

"It was on my 'to do' list." Gerald answered thoughtfully

"It's not very close to the top or you'd have gotten it done."

"How's to work?" Gerald asked. "Do I need to sign a contract in blood or something like that? Do you have something I can use to prick my finger?"

"For tonight, I will accept a verbal."

"You're not going to threaten me with a dinner fork are you?"

"Stop stalling. You're starting to hurt my feelings."

"Lori," he said sincerely, "I love you and I would like for you to be my girlfriend."

Lori bent toward him to give him a soft kiss, "I would be honored." Lori gazed up at the ceiling and then spoke again, "Gerald," she paused to work up the nerve to say the words that were on her mind, "you know, I'll do whatever you want me to do."

"I know."

She rolled her head over to peer into his face. "I mean, I will have sex with you if you want."

He stroked the hair back from the side of her face and kissed her softly. "You are so sweet," he whispered, "I want to sleep with you, I really do, but the first time that happens I want it to be a really special moment, and tonight has been tainted with too much sadness. I don't want you to look back at our first night and remember that it was the same day that Tyler died."

"Alrigh," she gave him a bittersweet smile.

"Thanks for making me feel better. I'd better go and let you get some sleep," he whispered as he slid out of bed. "I'll see you in the morning."

Lori hopped out of bed and went to embrace him in front of the window. "I love you, Gerald."

"I love you, too," he answered, then slipped out of the window.

214

Chapter 11

Thursday's Burden

The Key

- It was beginning to seem like every time I saw Tammy, she looked a little worse, as if she had taken another step deeper into the abyss. -

Tammy walked into the library toward the table in the corner where Gerald was scribbling mathematical equations on a pad of paper. She tossed the set of keys onto the wooden surface. "You were wrong, Gerald, I am a whore. At least I'm a high-priced whore. The going rate is five hundred dollars."

Gerald looked up at her in confusion. "I don't understand."

Tammy peered off in the distance and shook her head. "It doesn't matter. He's taking me up to his apartment tonight. I'm sure he's planning on hiding the tape before then. He's very meticulous. If you're going to try something, you're going to have to do it today."

"I'll have to do it while he's still in school. I have to find a way to get out, while he's still in."

"You know, even if you get the tape, we're still not going to be free of him."

"At least, he won't be able to put you in jail," Gerald offered.

"No, but when he finds out the tape is gone, he's going to be plotting his revenge on me. Just like he's plotting his revenge on you for beating up on him the other day."

"You're right," Gerald leaned back and stretched his arms. "You're absolutely right. It's like his father said, he's not really that hard to figure out."

"Yeah, well, there's really only one solution to the problem."

"What's that?"

"Somebody has to kill the son of a bitch."

Early Dismissal

- If there was one person in this school who could touch Mr. Hawk's softer side, it was Lori. -

Lori walked down the hallway prior to first hour. A wild jumble of thoughts was running through her head. She was haunted by her own words echoing in her ears. "I'd have sex with you, Gerald." She remembered that she had been very offended when her mother mentioned birth control. "He's only kissed me once." She'd said with righteous indignation. The statement had been true, at the time. She remembered her mother's analogy of pushing a car of the cliff. Mama had been right—she'd went right over the edge without a second thought. Lori counted back to the start of her last period. Yesterday was day fourteen. The ovulation day. Her traitorous ovaries had spit an egg right on schedule, and the only reason she wasn't pregnant right now was because her boyfriend was depressed.

Lori felt frustrated that her mother had been right and she'd been irresponsible. She thought back to a saying she'd heard somewhere, "Acknowledging a problem exists is always the first step in fixing the problem." She had been irresponsible, but fate had granted her a reprieve, and now was the time to put her house in order. She would take her mother's suggestion and get a prescription at the public clinic. The next step was working up the nerve to ask Mr. Hawk for an early dismissal slip.

Lori paused at the door of the principal's office. A wave of dread swept over her. What if Mr. Hawk asked her where she was going? Maybe she should just keep going down the hall. Lori peered through the glass and made eye contact with Marj. It was too late. Lori opened the door and stepped through.

Marj was behind her desk, and lifted her head and smiled, "Hi Lori, how are you today?"

Lori heard the copier running and glanced over toward the far wall. Mr. Leslie was running the photocopy machine. Her visit to the office was not starting out well. She silently wished that it was noisier, so Mr. Leslie would be less likely to overhear her conversation. She bent over Marj's desk. "I'd like to see Mr. Hawk, please," she said in a quiet voice.

"Sure; let me see if he is available." Marj slipped on her headset and then pressed the button on the earpiece, "Mr. Hawk? Lori Taylor is here and wondered if you could come out and speak with her for a moment."

"No! That's not what I meant," Lori said quickly. Mr. Leslie turned to peer over his shoulder.

"One second, Mr. Hawk," Marj looked up at her with a puzzled face.

"I would like to see him in his office, if that is okay." Lori felt her face start to flush.

Marj nodded and smiled, "Yes. Mr. Hawk? Lori would like to come back to see you in your office." Marj was quiet for a moment, "One moment; I'll ask." Marj looked back up at Lori, "Mr. Hawk would like to know if this regarding the altercation between Gerald and Eddy. If so, he says it is inappropriate for him to discuss it without Mrs. Branson and Gerald present."

"No, it's about something else. It's about me."

Marj smiled and held up one finger, while she worked the com with the other. "Mr. Hawk, Lori tells me it is about something else."

Mr. Leslie took his copies from the photocopier, and bumped the edge of the stack on the plastic surface to align them. He walked back toward Lori and checked his watch. "Hi Lori. Algebra is going to start in a few minutes." Mr. Leslie bunched up his nose to bring his black plastic glasses higher on his face, without having to adjust them with his hand. "I am curious to see which chairs you and Gerald are going to be sitting in today."

Marj spoke into her microphone, "Okay, Mr. Hawk. I will send her back." Marj looked up at Lori, "Mr. Hawk will see you now."

Mr. Leslie smiled, "You're not in trouble with the principal again, are you Lori?"

"No, it's nothing like that; I was just going to . . . ." Lori swirled her hand in the air as she tried to compose her thoughts into coherent sentences. "Me and Mr. Hawk, I mean, Mr. Hawk and I, we were just going to talk about some things that we were going to discuss, so I was going to go in and talk to him about those sorts of things. Just some general things, really, simple sort of regular things that we were going to talk about, him and I, so we were going to talk." Lori felt the blood rise heavily in her face as her mind replayed the gibberish that had just come out of her mouth.

Mr. Leslie smiled, "Well, there's one thing that has certainly come out of this."

Lori took a deep breath, "What's that, Mr. Leslie?"

"The scholastic excellence that I have observed in my Algebra class does not seem to extend into the realm of English skills."

217

Marj reached out to touch Lori's arm, "Mr. Hawk is waiting for you."

"Oh," she turned back to Mr. Leslie, "I have to go." Lori walked briskly to the office door and gave a quick knock. She heard Mr. Hawk's voice on the other side asking her to enter.

When Lori walked in, Mr. Hawk was standing behind his desk. "Welcome; come on in." He gestured to a chair on the other side of his desk, "Please have a seat and make yourself comfortable." He smiled warmly, "I promise I won't make you sit in the detention room today."

"Thank you for seeing me, Mr. Hawk." Lori sat in the chair.

Once she was seated, Mr. Hawk sat down behind his desk. "What's on your mind, Lori?"

Lori took a deep breath and combed her hair back from her forehead with her fingers. She made eye contact with M. Hawk, and then quickly looked away again. The words seemed to catch in her throat. She felt moisture welling up in her eyes. A lone tear slid down one cheek.

"Slow down, slow down. There's plenty of time." Mr. Hawk held up his hand. "First thing, let's get organized here." He opened a drawer and took out a box of tissues, then plopped them on the desk. "There are those, in case you need them. Whatever it is that has you upset, I'm sure we can figure it out; but take your time. Don't rush to get it out." Mr. Hawk leaned his back in his chair and smiled. "Maybe we can do charades until I guess what it is. I'm pretty good at charades, you know."

Lori smiled and let out a small chuckle, "It's not that bad, I guess."

"Are you in some kind of trouble? Do you have a problem you need help with?"

"No, not really." Lori pulled a tissue from the box as she dabbed at the corner of her eye.

"That's a pleasant change. I have to deal with problems every day," he said with a smile in his voice. "Whatever it is, just let it come out. When you've been a principal as long as I have, you've heard all. There's nothing new under the sun. So let me have it. See if you can throw me a curve ball."

Lori balled the tissue up in her hand, and stared down at the surface of the desk for a moment to get her nerve, and then looked up into Mr. Hawk's eyes, "I need to ask you for an early dismissal."

Mr. Hawk nodded, "I'm sure that won't be a problem. Do you mind if I ask why you need it? Do you need to rush out and buy a new pair of shoes that are on sale?"

"No," Lori smiled and shook her head, "I don't need shoes. I have plenty of those. My father's very obsessive. Every time I buy a new pair, my Dad sees what kind I'm getting, and buys me a few more of the same style."

Mr. Hawk smiled, "He does? Now, why does he do something like that?"

"He's crazy." Lori tipped her head to the side and smiled. "He says that if I like one pair, it will eventually wear out; so when it does, I can keep wearing the same style of shoe, in case the stores quit stocking them." Lori gave a small chuckle. "Really though, I think it's to feed his own compulsive disorders."

"Try not to be too hard on him." Mr. Hawk answered slowly, as he gently rocked his chair back. "Having your nose in people's mouths and breathing their bad breath all day would make anyone a little flighty."

Lori nodded her agreement, "It has. It certainly has. No," Lori paused for only a split second, and then pressed forward to keep her momentum, "I need to see a doctor."

"A doctor? Do you have a health problem that the school should be aware of?"

"I need to go to the clinic." Lori paused again but struggled to trek on, "I need to go to the public clinic to get a prescription for birth control pills."

When Mr. Hawk's warm smile dropped from his face, Lori's heart skipped a beat. A wave of sadness came across his face, as he looked down at his desk.

"I'm sorry, Mr. Hawk."

When he looked up and realized she was studying him, his expression quickly molded back into his standard poker face, "No, no. There's no need to apologize. I told you to throw me a curve ball and . . . ." his face turned back into a warm smile, "I guess you did. It's a responsible thing that you're doing. I'm sorry if my first reaction wasn't receptive." Mr. Hawk held up a finger. "I don't normally ever put myself in a position where I end up apologizing to a student, so please don't go running up and down the halls telling everyone. People will start to think I'm getting soft."

"I won't, Mr. Hawk. Your secret is safe with me."

Mr. Hawk rested his forearms on the edge of his desk, and then began gently tapping the tips of his fingers together. "Lori, I just want a chance to say how important you are to this school, and how much you mean to the morale of the teachers."

"How do you mean, sir?"

"Students don't often realize what it's like on the other side of the desk. For the better teachers, the job is a lot more than getting a paycheck at the end of the week. It's about devoting your life to a cause, and trying to make a difference in the lives of young people. That's often a disheartening thing, because most student's problems are brought about from total stupidity." Mr. Hawk held up a single finger. "Every year, though, there are one or two students that the faculty can point to and say, 'There— that one is on the right track. All our efforts weren't in vain.'" Mr. Hawk sighed. "It's students like you that inspire us and give us hope."

Lori spoke back in a calm voice, "I'm trying to be responsible."

"I appreciate that," Mr. Hawk nodded, and then slid open the shallow middle drawer, pulled out a yellow pad and a pen, and put them on his desk. "If more of my students did the same thing, we'd have a lot fewer young girls becoming mothers and dropping out of school to raise babies." Mr. Hawk made out the slip. "I'm putting my home number on here. If you are ever in trouble, I want you to call the house, and Mrs. Hawk will come and get you. Don't be reluctant to call anytime, day or night." Mr. Hawk peeled off the slip and handed it over to Lori.

Lori accepted the slip and tucked into her bag, "I need a second slip."

"For?"

"It's for Gerald Camden, so he can drive me to the clinic."

Mr. Hawk nodded, then made out the second slip and slid it across the table, "Be careful, Lori."

"I will, Mr. Hawk."

Finding a Ride

- Lori seemed like a soft, gentle person, but she was stronger than most people realized. -

Gerald glanced up as Lori entered the cafeteria.

"I need a favor."

"Certainly, madam. I am at your service."

Lori sat down and slid the early dismissal slip across the table.

Gerald picked it up to study it. "What's this?"

"It's an early dismissal slip."

"I see that. It's got my name on it." Gerald glanced back across the table. "Why am I getting an early dismissal?"

Lori took a deep breath, "I need you to give me a ride to the public clinic so I can get a prescription for birth control pills."

Gerald made a confused face. "But we haven't even . . . ."

"Yes," she answered slowly. Why was he so dense sometimes? "I know that we haven't . . . ." Lori cleared her throat, "been together in that way, but we came close last night, and I can't afford to be stupid and irresponsible."

"So, does this mean we're going to . . . ?"

Lori smiled, "Just don't read too much into this, big guy. Don't expect that I'm going to get one of those big triangular dinner chimes that they used to have at farmhouses, and that I'm going to hike my legs up in the air and ring it over my butt until you come running."

Gerald smiled back. It was nice to see a small break in the seriousness of her demeanor. "Well, I will keep my ears perked for that dinner triangle, just in case it starts ringing sometime." Gerald folded the slip and tucked it in his pocket, then reached out to put his hand on hers. "I will be happy to take you and come along for moral support."

"No," Lori said, "you're not coming along. You're going to drop me off and then go get lost for a while. I will give you my cell phone, and then call you from the office when it's time for you to pick me up."

Gerald was a little bothered by her response. "You don't even want me to sit in the waiting room with you?"

"No." Lori put her hands around Gerald's. "I would enjoy having your company, but everyone knows why a girl my age goes to that clinic. I don't want people staring at us and assuming that you must be the boy I'm sleeping with. It is already going to be awkward and uncomfortable. I just want to go in, get it over with, and leave."

"Okay." Gerald was quiet for a moment. "I have some errands I can run while you're at the clinic."

The Teachers' Lounge

- Never underestimate Mrs. B. -

Gerald knocked on the door of the teachers' lounge. Mrs. Branson opened the door. She eyed him with a bit of reservation when she saw who it was. "If it isn't Gerald, my new star of our Scholastic Bowl Team. Did you come to apologize for dragging me into an embarrassing situation the other day?"

"No," Gerald stammered. "I mean yes, I want to apologize, and I want to thank you, but that's not why I stopped by."

"What can I do for you?"

"Is Mrs. Roberson in there?" he asked as he peered past her shoulder.

"Yes," Mrs. Branson answered as she stepped back to partially close the door and block his line of sight. "She's in here. Can I tell her what this is about?"

"It's about her English class."

"You're not in her English class anymore. Did you forget that I was in the room when Mr. Hawk changed your schedule?"

"No, that's right, I'm not in the class anymore, but I wanted to ask her something." Gerald's mind raced to come up with a quick answer. "I have a question about iambic pentameter."

"Oh, well, I am an English teacher, too. What's your question? I am sure I can help you."

Gerald realized that she knew he wasn't being honest. "I'm sorry, Mrs. Branson. This has nothing to do with school work. Mrs. Roberson and I have become friends, and I really need to talk to her about something."

"I would like to be your friend too, Gerald, if you give me the chance."

"You are my friend, Mrs. Branson. Please understand that this is very personal, and I have known Mrs. Roberson a little longer, so I . . . ."

"It's okay. All you have to do is tell the truth." She gave him a reassuring smile. "You might as well stick to that. You're not a very good liar."

Gerald smiled, "I think I may have heard that before."

Mrs. Branson held up one finger. "Wait right here. I can't let you come inside, but I'll send Mrs. Roberson right out."

A moment later, Mrs. Roberson appeared at the door, "What is it?"

"I need to talk to you. Can you come out and walk with me awhile?"

Mrs. Roberson stepped out of the door and pointed toward the stairs that led down to the east door, "Let's take a walk in the east courtyard."

When they were outside, Mrs. Roberson glanced quickly around, and then walked with him along the east lane. "Gerald, I asked you to be more discreet."

"I know, but this is an emergency."

The sound of the bell rang throughout the school yard. "Well, there's the bell. Okay, Gerald. What is so urgent that it couldn't wait till after school?"

"I need you to do something for me."

"What?"

"I'm going to be away from school during last period. I need you to make sure that Eddy is still here."

"What's going on, Gerald?"

"I'm going to break into Eddy's apartment. He has something in there he's using to blackmail . . . ."

"Stop. I'm sorry I asked." Mrs. Roberson nodded, "What do you want me to do if he's not there?"

"Just call me on Lori's cell phone and warn me. The number is 618-555-5599."

Mrs. Roberson reached over and pulled the pen out of Gerald's shirt pocket, then wrote the number across the palm of her hand. "I hate it when people write on their skin." She glanced back up at Gerald, "Be careful, Gerald."

"I will. Thanks, Amy. Thanks for everything."

Then she smiled, "And one more thing."

"Yeah?"

"My name is Mrs. Roberson. Not Amy."

"Sorry about that, Mrs. Roberson."

She gave him a smile, "Come back inside, and I'll make out a hall pass for you."

The Clinic

- I hated Lori going alone, but it was what she wanted. -

The Crawford County Commercium Building was two blocks south of the Robinson Courthouse. Gerald pulled his motorcycle into a parking space along the curb and put down the kickstand. He switched off the motor as Lori slid off the back and lifted off her helmet. Gerald pulled his helmet off, as well. "I really don't want you to have to walk in there alone," he said sadly.

"Ahhh, look at the lower lip stick-out," Lori reached out with the tip of her finger to press his lip down. "Better be careful. Pigeons might come along and shit on it."

Gerald sighed and looked up at her.

Lori laid her hand on his shoulder and ran her fingers along his hairline. "I have a favor I want to ask."

"What is that?"

"I want us to sit in the front row together in Algebra."

"I didn't realize it really was that important to you."

"I figure I've got you on the ropes, so it's a good time to ask."

"I suppose I can do that."

"Come here, you." Lori grabbed the front of Gerald's denim jacket, then pulled him close and began to kiss him lightly on the lips and pulled back.

Gerald smiled. "What happened to all that talk about public displays of affection?"

"Hush up, wise guy." Lori pulled him close and gave him a few more quick kisses, then pulled back to rub her lower lip. "I'm a virgin. I'm about to walk into that building to get a birth control prescription." Lori pointed back over her shoulder with her thumb. "By the time I come out of the clinic, the gossip mill is going to have half the county convinced that I'm some sort of harlot. So I figure I've earned the right to kiss my boyfriend if I want to."

Gerald smiled and nodded, "Well, I was planning to do a nice little write-up about the harlot business on the bathroom wall at school. I thought stall number three might be nice."

Lori smiled and shook her head.

"I'm sorry, Lori." Gerald suddenly felt as if he had crossed a line. "When I get nervous and don't know what to say, I crack a joke."

"Tsst, Tsst," Lori hissed between her teeth. "It's fine. Relax." Lori peered into his eyes and smiled. "You think I haven't figured out you're a smart aleck by now?" She gave him another light kiss. "You better get going. I need to get in there. I'll call you when it's over."

Lori stayed and watched him put on the helmet, then start the motorcycle and go down the street.

When Gerald was gone, she turned her gaze to the four-story, light gray building. The Commercium Building was covered with riveted gray metal panels. All the corners and edges were rounded. As she walked across the sidewalk Lori wondered if, forty years ago, it was meant to look modern and futuristic. She approached the double glass doors. The aluminum frame on one door was either warped or misaligned. It wedged against the grooved steel threshold, leaving a one-inch gap. Cool, musty-smelling air streamed out.

Lori pressed the opposite door open and made her way down a short hallway. The walls were covered with faded, almond colored fabric. There were nail holes, scuffs, and scattered graffiti speckled everywhere. She walked across the ash gray linoleum floor. The decorative pattern had long been worn away, except for the edge running along the wall.

Lori stepped up to the directory. The glass front was cracked in one corner. Inside the aluminum housing was a faded black felt board with yellowed plastic letters. She read the wording aloud, hoping the sound of her voice would make her feel more comfortable. "First floor: Garage; Second Floor: Food Stamps and Welfare; Third Floor: Women, Infants, and Children; Fourth Floor: Family Planning Clinic." Lori sighed and pressed the elevator button. "All wayward schoolgirls contemplating a sexual encounter, please report to the fourth floor."

When the doors opened, she stepped inside the elevator and pressed the translucent #4 button. As the doors closed, she realized the lighting was weak. She looked overhead and saw that one of the fluorescent tubes was dim, and the other was completely dark. She braced one hand against the wall and stood on her tip toes. She reached into a triangular hole in the corner of the faded plastic cover and tapped the dark bulb with her fingers, until it flickered on. With the new light Lori could see the same style of worn linoleum as what had been in the hall. The tiles were marked with streaks of brown clay, as if something heavy and dirty had been dragged off the elevator.

The elevator opened on the second floor, revealing a tall, disheveled looking older man. His eyes were bloodshot and had a slightly yellowish glaze. His reddish, acne-scarred cheeks were ringed with a ragged, copper colored beard and moustache. His long, dark blonde hair hung down and disappeared under the collar of his worn brown leather overcoat. Upon seeing Lori, he smiled with his worn dingy teeth, "Going down?" he asked.

Lori smiled and pointed toward the ceiling, "Sorry, headed up."

The blonde man stepped inside, "I'll come along for the ride. I've got nothing better to do."

Lori shifted to one side to give him plenty of room, and then stared straight ahead.

The blonde man noticed the lone button that had been pressed on the console. "Are you headed up to the Clinic?"

"Yes," Lori gave him a quick glance and then turned back to the door. "I'm picking up a friend."

"My name's Arnie."

"Hi, Arnie," she gave him a quick smile.

"Are you going to tell me your name?" Arnie asked.

"Susie," Lori's pulse quickened a bit. "My name is Susie Walters."

Arnie smiled and extended an arm to put his hand out. "I'm pleased to meet you, Susie."

Lori glanced down at the rough, calloused palm, "I'm sorry, but I don't like to shake hands."

"Suit yourself." Arnie retracted his arm, and then reached out and pressed the #3 button on the console.

"Are you going to the third floor?"

"No, but I like to stop on every floor. It's just a superstition I have."

When the doors opened on the third floor, Lori was tempted to run out but she knew that if he followed her, she could be cornered at the end of a hall. A moment later, the doors closed again and the elevator resumed its ascent.

Arnie turned and faced Lori, "You got any money, Susie?"

Lori cleared her throat, "Not much. Maybe ten or twelve dollars. I was going to pay with a credit card."

Arnie cocked his head to one side, "What would you be paying for, if you're only picking up a friend?"

The elevator door opened to the fourth floor, and Lori hurried out. "Oh! Here we are. It was very nice talking to you, Arnie." She went out into the hallway, and then turned around to make sure she wasn't being followed. Arnie was watching, and smiled with his yellowed teeth just as the door closed.

Lori walked up to the heavy wooden door. She peered through the wire-interlaced glass, and pressed on the round brass hand bar. The mechanism in the turn box retracted the vertical posts, and the door swung open. She walked into the waiting room. Padded chairs with chrome and wooden frames were scattered about. She passed an end table that held a few issues of National Geographic. She looked at one of the yellow trimmed magazine covers. It was two years old. About six or eight young adult females were dispersed throughout the room..

None of them seemed to be talking to each other or sitting together. Each was waiting alone, biding their time.

Lori made her way to the far end of the waiting room, where a heavy blonde lady in a white smock was sitting at a desk behind the partition window.

"Can I help you?" the blonde receptionist asked.

"Hi," Lori said resting her arms on the counter, "I'm here to see a doctor."

"What would you like to see the doctor about?"

Lori cleared her throat, "I need to get a prescription for birth control pills."

"Do you have a card?"

"What card?"

"A state medical card."

Lori propped an elbow and stroked the hair back from the side of her face, "No, I don't have one. Do I need one?"

"You do if you want the state to pay for it."

"No; that's fine."

"Are you on Welfare or WIC?"

"What is WIC?"

"Women Infants and Children. It's a state program."

"No; I don't have any of that. I don't want the state to pay for it"

"Do you have health insurance?"

"Yes."

"Let me see your card."

"No." Lori paused, "I mean, I don't want to use an insurance card. Can I just pay for it myself?"

"Sure," Amanda shrugged. "Makes no difference to me. That will be $275 plus tax, which will come to just under $300."

Lori took out her Gold Visa and slid it across the counter, "Do you take plastic?"

"Oh, yeah," Amanda reached for the card, but Lori scooped it back up.

"I just remembered, I don't want to use my card. I think I'd like to pay cash, instead." Lori stuffed the credit card back into her pocket purse, and pulled out three crisp one-hundred-dollar bills. She paused a second, remembering that her father had handed them to her just a few days earlier. How could her life have changed so much in such a short time? She handed Amanda the money.

Amanda printed out a receipt and passed it over, along with a clipboard and a clear plastic Bic ink pen. "Fill this out and bring it back, then wait till they call your name."

Lori filled out her paperwork and dropped it back at the window, then returned to her seat. As she leafed through an old National Geographic magazine, her resolve weakened. She hadn't needed pills before now. Why couldn't she just get by for another year or two? More than likely, she wouldn't be able to get her $300 back. Screw it. She would have them take her name off the list, and come back one day when she really needed the pills. As she stood up, the door in the corner opened, and a girl in her twenties emerged, wearing a green smock. She had glasses and a brunette pony tail. She called her name, "Lori Taylor?"

Lori walked down to the door, "I'm Lori."

"Hi, I'm Sheila," the girl said, giving her clipboard a quick look. "Just follow me." She led Lori down a narrow hallway with equally spaced doors on each side. "They've got you in number seven." Sheila opened the door and stepped inside.

Lori sheepishly entered behind her. "I'm a little nervous."

"Don't be nervous. Nobody is judging you. We have girls come in and out of here all day long." The small room held a sink and a padded examining table with a dark green vinyl covering. Sheila opened a cabinet, took out a stack of folded paper linens, and placed them on the corner of the examining table. "These are your clothes." She held up the first piece, "This is the top. You put it on like a shirt and make sure it opens in front." She handed it to Lori and then picked up the other piece. It was shaped like a long rectangle. "This is sort of like a skirt. You wrap it around your waist and tie it off on the side. This stuff only comes in one size, so it's not going to fit perfectly. Any questions so far?"

Lori shook her head.

"I need you to take off everything." Sheila made a sweep with her hand, "Shoes, socks, the whole bit. Stuff like earrings, jewelry, and hair ties can stay, but everything else goes. You can put your things in the big chair in the corner. Dr. Elliot will be in to see you in a moment. He's very nice and he's very gentle."

Lori took off her clothes. She laid her sneakers in the chair, and then laid her socks on top. She put her bra and panties on the next layer, then neatly folded her clothes and laid them on top, to conceal her underwear. The paper garments were similar to a paper towel, but thicker and heavier. They felt rough on her skin, and tended to buckle whenever she moved. She pressed the heel of her hand down into the green cushion of the examining table, and then watched the handprint rise. There was a large roll of white paper at the head of the table. A strip of the paper ran down the middle of the cushion and folded around the bottom of the end, to the jagged tear-off strip on the underside. On each of the lower corners stood two metal posts. Atop each of them was a large, aluminum spoon made of thick metal. She ran her finger along the edge of the flat part that ran around the inner oval. "I wonder whose heels are going in here?" she mused sarcastically to herself.

Lori walked slowly around the room. Next to the sink was a roll of paper towels mounted on the wall. Just below the mirror was a stainless steel shelf with a box of tissues and a box of blue plastic gloves. Along the walls were various medical pictures. There were instructions for a breast self-exam, and everything you would ever want to know about yeast infections and menopause.

There was a knock on the door. Lori ran back over to the examining table and hopped onto it. The door opened and a short, sandy haired man with a beard came in. "Hello, I am Dr. Elliot." He motioned to a slender lady with short cropped blonde hair coming in behind him. "This is my nurse, Jennifer Foster. She will be present at all times, as required by state law." He looked down at the chart, "You're Lori, right?"

"Yes, I'm Lori."

"Okay, Lori, please lay back and rest your arms over your head. Today, you'll be getting a breast exam and a pelvic, which will include a Pap smear."

Lori shuffled back on the examining table and then laid down.

Dr. Elliot took her forearm and draped it over her head, then reached into the front of her smock and start pressing his fingertips along her breasts. "How long have you been sexually active, Lori?"

"I'm not. At least, not yet. I'm not really planning on necessarily doing anything, but I just got my first boyfriend . . . ."

"And you want to be safe, in case things get carried away."

"Yes."

"Smart girl," he smiled reassuringly. "We need a lot more girls being responsible. We would have a lot fewer unwanted pregnancies." Dr. Elliot took his hand out of her smock and reached over to her wrist, "Give me your hand. You're going to help me do the other one." He took her fingers and pressed them gently into her other breast. "You need to be doing this on your own, at least once a week. Look for any sort of little lump or hard spot. It could be the size of a peanut, or a kernel of unpopped popcorn. If you find anything like that, you let us know right away, okay?"

Lori nodded.

"I'll give you a chance to go ahead and close up your top. When you're ready, I need you to put your heels in the big spoons."

Lori pulled the front of her smock together and lifted her heels into the stirrups.

Dr. Elliot used the tips of two fingers to press down hard on Lori's lower stomach. It didn't hurt, but it was uncomfortable. He glanced up at Lori and smiled, "Just making sure that all the parts are normal size and that they are where they're supposed to be."

Nurse Foster bent the flexible neck of a stainless steel lamp, and pointed the round hood under the paper skirt. When the light came on, Lori could feel the warmth against her skin. Nurse Foster took a stainless-steel tool out of a canister of fluid, and handed it to the doctor.

Dr. Elliot held it up for Lori to see, "Look, but don't touch. It's been sterilized. This is a speculum but a lot of people call it a duck bill. It looks sort of like a duck bill, doesn't it?"

"Yes."

"This is what I'm going to use to take a peek at your cervix. Do you know where your cervix is?"

"I think so."

Nurse Foster opened a tube and squirted a line of clear jelly along the end of the speculum.

Dr. Elliot moved the speculum under the paper skirt. "We keep this warm so it won't be as uncomfortable. I'm going to touch the side of the handle to your leg first, so you don't jump off the table."

"Okay." Lori felt part of the metal handle touch the skin of her inner thigh, and her breath came a little quicker.

"Try to relax," Nurse Foster spoke in a soothing voice. "It's going to feel tight, but try not to tense up."

Lori closed her eyes, and her mouth opened as it slid inside her.

"Almost done," the doctor said gently. "Mrs. Foster, if you would hand me a swab."

Lori flinched when she felt the end of the swab tickle inside her.

"Easy," Dr. Elliot glanced over the top of the paper skirt draped over her knees. "We'll be done in a moment."

Dr. Elliot slid the instrument out and turned off the light. "You're all done." He handed the speculum to Nurse Foster. "We'll step out and let you get dressed. There are tissues by the sink if you need them. You can pick up your prescription at the front desk and then you're free to go. If we find anything abnormal, we'll call you back in; otherwise, I'd like to see you back for a follow-up in three months."

When the nurse and the doctor had left the room, Lori took off the paper smock and skirt and gathered up her clothes. She breathed a sigh of relief that it was over.

The English Student

- Mrs. Roberson was a friend; she'd briefly been a lover. She was a mother figure; and my big sister. Above all else, she was my best ally. -

Mrs. Roberson watched the students file into her last hour English class. She held her breath, waiting for a certain face to appear. Finally, Eddy strolled into class and plopped into his usual seat in the back by the door. She breathed a sigh of relief and started counting heads. As the class settled she scribbled "OK" on the attendance slip, and put it in the clip outside the classroom door.

When she walked back up to the front, Eddy leered at her as she passed by him. She was pretty hot for a teacher. Why did she have to be so cold? "Where's your favorite student?" he asked in a mocking tone, "Doesn't he take this class anymore?"

Mrs. Roberson knew that "favorite student" was bait, but she wanted to speak up quickly, lest anyone in the room mention his early dismissal, "Gerald isn't in this class any more. He has switched to the physics class, at Mr. Leslie's request."

"It's just as well," Eddy leaned back and crossed his legs. "If he was here I might have to put his lights out." Eddy leered at Mrs. Robinson again. "Still, I'm sure he's going to miss you dancing around in front of the white board in your short skirts. I know I would."

"Eddy, I'm very sorry about what happened the other day and any bruises you may have. But if you continue to disrespect me in my class, you're going to end up spending the period with Mr. Hawk."

Mrs. Roberson went to the front and began writing out the first three stanzas of "The Raven" on the white board. When she had finished, she stepped back to a rear corner of the room and gestured to the board, "Who wants to interpret the first line on the board?"

Mrs. Roberson leaned against the back wall and called on a student who raised her hand. She worked her way through the board, line by line, allowing the students to offer their interpretations before putting out her own. "Okay, who's next?" She called out to the class, "Everyone has to interpret at least one line, or I will just keep putting up stanzas until we have full participation." Mrs. Roberson called out to the opposite rear corner, "Eddy, I don't think we have heard from you. Would you like to take the next line?" When he didn't answer, she took a few steps forward to look in the far back corner. "Eddy?"

Mrs. Roberson's breath caught in her throat when she saw the empty chair. "Where's Eddy?"

Ray spoke up, "I think he slipped out when you first started writing. I turned around and he was already gone."

Mrs. Roberson quickly walked to the front and opened the lower drawer on the desk. "Everyone go ahead and read 'The Raven.' I have to step out for just a couple of minutes." She bent low to pull her cell phone out of her purse, and discreetly shielded it with her hand as she walked to the door. "Please don't cause any trouble. I'll be right back."

She stepped into the hall and went around a corner. As she brought up her cell phone to punch in the number, she suddenly realized the paper with the phone number was still in her purse. She had transcribed the phone number from her hand to the piece of paper, and then washed off the ink. She glanced back over her shoulder. She didn't want to have to walk back into the classroom just to leave again. She studied the remaining shadow of ink on her hand in an effort to read the digits. All of them were still readable except for the last two. They appeared to be the same but she couldn't tell if they were sevens or nines. She searched her mind, trying to remember, but couldn't bring it back. No problem. She would try it first with the nines, and if Gerald didn't answer she would just hang up and try again using sevens. As she started keying in the number, she became aware of someone standing in front of her. She looked up to see Mr.

Hawk. "Oh. Hi, Mr. Hawk. I just need a moment to make a quick call."

"Who's tending your class while you're out here in the hallway?"

"I gave them a reading assignment. I will only be a gone for a moment. I just need to make this call and I will get right back to them."

"The last time you left a class alone was around Christmas, when you let them have a party with snacks. As soon as you left the room, they threw finger Jell-O at the ceiling. The janitor had to get a stepladder and clean it off with a putty knife."

"I remember that, Mr. Hawk."

"You promised me it would never happen again."

"This is really important."

"Can't it wait until the end of the period?"

"No, Mr. Hawk; it really can't."

"Do you want to give me the number, and I will make the call for you?"

"No. I'm sorry, but it is very personal and I really need to make it right now. Please, Mr. Hawk, you have to cut me a break on this one."

Mr. Hawk nodded. Her impassioned plea seemed to soften his demeanor, "Go make your call. I will watch your class until you get back."

"Thank you, Mr. Hawk."

Mr. Hawk walked down the hallway toward the noise of cackling students. A couple of moments after he went around the corner, the noise abruptly became silence.

Mrs. Roberson started punching numbers into her cell phone.

The Apartment

- Eddy didn't fit the hoodlum stereotype. I had imagined that his apartment would have been messy, and strewn with empty beer cans and pornographic magazines. -

Gerald drove his motorcycle past the front of the auto shop. The big garage doors were open, flooding the air with the sounds of impact wrenches, hammers, air compressors, and hydraulic lifts. As long as he was quiet, he shouldn't have to worry about someone hearing him in the apartment. He drove around to the opposite side of the block and parked the bike in front of a couple of abandoned buildings.

Gerald took a quick glance around and then lifted the motorcycle seat to open the compartment underneath. He lifted out Mrs. Roberson's Colt pistol and stuffed it into the pocket of his denim jacket, then walked down the narrow space between the two closed-up buildings.

When he got to the opposite end of the walkway, he stopped to survey the area and consider his strategy. In the middle of the block was a huge oak tree with a graveled circle drive around it. He could see the door to Eddy's apartment on the back side of the auto shop. It would be a thirty-yard walk across an open area in broad daylight, but it was an unavoidable risk.

Gerald strode quickly toward the door. As he went, he took Eddy's keys from his pocket and sorted through them. Three of them were house keys. He had no idea which one he should use. When he got to the door he inserted the first key. The lock turned easily and he opened the door. It was a lucky break. He stepped inside, locked the door behind himself, and then gingerly walked up the staircase.

At the top of the stairs he turned left through an archway and stepped into a small, immaculately kept living room. A large flat-screen Sony television was on the wall that separated the room from the stairs. Gerald glanced quickly around. There was a tall video disk storage cabinet on each side of the television. Beyond that, on each side, was a tall Pioneer speaker case. Gerald opened the video cabinet on the left and scanned each shelf. It held nothing but blue-ray disks. He stepped over to the other case and opened it. This one was about half blue-ray, and most of the rest were DVD's. On the top shelf were a dozen video cassettes. He put his hands on each side to press them together, and then brought them all out as a unit. He gently turned the stack and laid them on the coffee table, with the spines turned up. Tammy had said it was a Maxell tape, with glue left from where the label had been peeled away. Gerald slowly ran a finger across the stack. All of the tapes had labels and they were all in cardboard TDK slips. He took a moment to slip each tape out in the off-chance there would be a Maxell tape inside a TDK slip, but there was none. He gently pressed the stack together and lifted them back onto the shelf, then closed the cabinet door. It had to be somewhere else.

He scanned the room again. In the far right corner was a half-sized door, probably a small closet over the stairs. Maybe

Eddy had left the tape in his jacket. He opened the door to reveal a rack of coats, jackets, and other outer wear. A rapid search of the pockets found each one empty. As his eyes examined the closet floor, which was at knee level, he noticed that the carpet along the back wall was slightly curled. He pinched the edge of the carpet and rolled it back, exposing a two-foot-square piece of plywood with two hinges mounted on the far side. The closer edge had a recessed metal ring. Gerald reached down and pulled the ring to lift the trap door. This had to be it. He tipped the lid against the back wall, unveiling two small compartments. One side held clumps of one-hundred dollar bills, neatly bound in stacks. He figured there must be eighteen or twenty bundles. Gerald lifted one of them to flip his thumb along the edges. Every bill was crisp and faced in the same direction. On the other side was a small chrome pistol with pearl handles, a black velvet pouch, and assorted jewelry. Gerald opened the tie on the pouch and peered inside. He tilted the bag and spilled a few sparkling stones into his palm, then rolled them around with the tip of his finger. They were diamonds that varied in size. The larger ones were about the size of peas. He dumped them back in and pulled the drawstring to close the pouch and put it back into the compartment. Gerald sifted through the jewelry, which mostly consisted of diamond rings and bracelets. He sighed in frustration. He would have to search elsewhere to find the tape.

Gerald lowered the trap door then rolled the carpet back in place and pressed it down with his hand. He closed the closet door and tried to think. There wasn't enough time to comb the entire apartment. He needed to be smarter instead of searching in frantic desperation. He walked back over to the couch and sat down for a moment, trying to think as if he were Eddy. Where would he put it? Where would it be?

Lori's cell phone vibrated in his pants pocket. Gerald wasn't accustomed to carrying a cell phone. He'd put the ringer on silent to avoid being overheard. When it suddenly began to vibrate he jumped up from the couch and grabbed his crotch. His knee cracked against the coffee table, making it lurch forward. He rubbed his aching knee with one hand, as he used the other to pull the phone from his pocket. He pressed the button on the front and brought it to his face, "Lori, is that you?"

"No!" the voice on other end of the line whispered urgently. "He's gone! Eddy slipped out when I wasn't watching. It's been about fifteen minutes. Get out of there, Gerald! Get out of there now!"

Gerald scanned the room to see if anything was disturbed. Everything seemed to be the same as when he had entered, except for the coffee table. Bumping it with his knee had moved it out of line with the couch, and the drawer had slid open about an inch. He slid the drawer shut and was about to move the coffee table back into place when, on a hunch, he pulled the drawer back open. Inside was a black plastic videocassette. He pulled it out and checked the spine. There was the residual glue from the label. He slid it out of the case and read "Maxell" molded on the plastic in raised letters. He drew the replacement Maxell tape out of his jacket and switched it for the one in the drawer.

As Gerald put the dummy tape in the drawer, he spied three Polaroid photos. He pushed the tape aside and picked them up. They were shots of Tammy, nude from the waist up. As he tried to decide whether or not to take them, he heard the lock turn in the door at the bottom of the steps. He stuffed the photos and the tape into his jacket pocket, then closed the drawer and adjusted its position to align with the couch.

Gerald walked to the archway. He glanced anxiously around as he heard Eddy's footsteps come up the stairs. There was no place to hide and no other way out. He was going to have to confront him. He reached into his denim jacket and grasped the handle of Mrs. Roberson's Colt pistol, then stepped through the archway to the landing at the top of the stairs.

Eddy glanced up and recoiled from the surprise.

"Hello, Eddy," Gerald said slowly, coming down a few steps. If he could somehow get around him, Gerald figured he could bolt for the door.

"How did you get in my place?"

"Relax, Eddy, I just want to talk to you." Gerald's mind raced, trying to produce a legitimate reason for his presence.

"Talk about what?"

"About Tammy. She's feeling trapped, and I want you to let her go."

Eddy's eyes made a slight squint as he cocked his head. The story didn't add up, "What do you care about Tammy? You're seeing someone else."

"Tammy and I are still friends."

"I'll tell you what." Eddy brought out a switchblade and flicked open the blade. "You can talk all you want. You're in my place uninvited, and I'm going to slash you to ribbons."

Gerald pulled the Colt .45 from the pocket of his denim jacket, "I'm going to blow your ass back to hell."

Eddy froze and eyed the end of the barrel.

"Ahhh, Eddy," Gerald mocked him, "so clever. Always the master of circumstances. Now, you've gone and brought a knife to a gun fight."

Eddy gazed calmly down the barrel and then smirked, "I don't think you have the balls."

"Oh, I think you're wrong about that, Eddy. You see, I know things. I know that you shot Tyler in the knee."

"Don't look for me at the funeral." Eddy was quiet for a moment, and his demeanor started to change, "Let's just relax for a moment." Eddy lightly tapped the dull edge of the knife against the frame of the Colt .45. "I'm sorry about your friend but I had nothing to do with it. Why don't you just put the gun away?"

"You put the knife down first."

"Alright, I'm going to get rid of the knife. Just relax, and don't do anything rash." Eddy turned and stabbed the tip of the blade into the wall. "I'm going to have to spackle that hole, you know."

"Step to the side and let me get past." Gerald motioned him to the side with the tip of the pistol. "I think I will be on my way."

Eddy held up his open palms and stepped close to the wall to let him by. "I put the knife down. Do you mind lowering your gun?"

Gerald walked carefully around Eddy, keeping the pistol between them. "I'll be out of here in a second." As he stepped backwards down the stairs, he missed his footing and glanced down.

Eddy quickly slid his hand beneath his jacket and brought out his revolver, "What were you saying about bringing a knife to a gun fight?"

"I just want to leave, Eddy."

"In a minute. Put your gun down and we'll talk. Isn't that why you said you came here?"

Gerald was at an impasse. He knew there would be no way of getting Eddy to lay down his gun. Gerald also knew that if he put his own gun down, Eddy would probably shoot him and claim self-defense. "I'll tell you what, Eddy," Gerald said, lowering the barrel of the Colt slightly, "why don't you just go ahead and shoot me."

"Don't think I won't do it." Eddy brought the end of the muzzle close to Gerald's forehead.

"I know, Eddy," Gerald said slowly, pointing the Colt to Eddy's leg, "but whether you shoot me or not, it doesn't matter. I think I'm going to blow off your knee cap either way. Tyler's dead and I just really don't care anymore. What do you think, Eddy? A knee for a knee? Isn't that fair? Maybe you'll give everyone a present and die from an infection."

Eddy moved the end of the revolver closer to Gerald's head. "You don't want to play this game with me. You're going to lose."

"I know that, Eddy," Gerald answered with resignation. "You win again. You always were the clever one. I should have known you were too clever for any of us to ever beat you." Gerald cocked the hammer back on the Colt. "You may have won this one, Eddy, but I'm damn sure going to take out your knee cap."

"Stop, stop!" Eddy took a second to think. He couldn't see any outcome to the situation that didn't include him writhing on the floor in pain. If there was going to be a shootout, it would be better to wait for a time when the odds were more in his favor. Eddy pointed the gun to the ceiling and gently let the hammer back down, "Get out of here."

Gerald paused for a moment. He had been so intent on shooting Eddy's knee; he was tempted to pull the trigger anyway.

"Well what are you waiting for?" Eddy grumbled. "Go on before I change my mind."

Gerald turned to go down the stairs.

Eddy would've liked to have shot him as he left, but an entry wound in the back would have been difficult to explain. When Gerald disappeared though the door, Eddy pulled his knife free of the wall and slogged his way up the stairs.

The Favor

- I had come to like Tammy, but there would always be awkwardness between us. Sometimes, there has just been too much water that has passed under the bridge. -

Gerald drove his motorcycle to Tammy's house. It was a medium-size cottage, with white aluminum siding. The front yard had a few trees and two large flower beds. Gerald pulled his motorcycle up on the concrete drive that ran in front of the detached two-car garage. He parked the bike next to Tammy's mother's silver Toyota Celica, and walked down the "L" shaped sidewalk to ring the front doorbell.

A lady with very tan skin and long brown hair came to the door. She wore sunglasses with thick plastic frames. She appeared to be in her late 30's. "Gerald!" she exclaimed as she pushed open the white, wooden-framed screen door and stepped through. "Oh my goodness. It is so nice to see you!" She gave him a gentle hug.

"Hello," Gerald answered softly.

She stepped back. "Oh that's right. I'm so sorry. Tammy told me that you don't remember anyone. Well let me help you out. My name is Sandy Logan and I'm Tammy's mom." Sandy held her arm up and slid the sleeve of her training suit back. "I was just getting ready to head out to the YMCA. Feel that!" she said, as she flexed her bicep.

Gerald dutifully reached out to gently squeeze her muscle, "It's very firm."

"Hard as a rock," Sandy dropped her arm and shook her sleeve down. "I've been pumping iron for eight weeks. Check this out," she turned from side to side, to show off her physique. "How many of your friends' moms are this trim?"

"None, that I can recall," Gerald said with a smile.

"When did you become such a diplomat?" She smiled and shook her head. "Listen, Gerald," she leaned close as she spoke in a hushed voice. "What is the deal with this Eddy guy?"

"How do you mean?"

"He's a real jerk. He pulls up in front of the house and honks the horn as if we're running some sort of car-hop service. Every time he does, Tammy obediently runs out the door and gets in his car. I hope this winds down soon."

"Don't worry; I think it's on the decline."

"I sure hope so." She stepped back inside the house for a moment and called to the back of the house, "Tammy, you have company."

"Who is it?" a voice wafted through the door.

"It's some good-looking young feller. You better get out here before your cougar of a mother whisks him away." Sandy stepped back out. "I've got to run." She gave Gerald a hug, then leaned back to peer in his eyes. "I always liked you." She patted his shoulder, and then walked toward the Celica.

Tammy appeared at the front of the house and propped open the wooden screen door with her hand. "Hi, Gerald, come on in."

Gerald stepped through the doorway as the silver Celica pulled out of the drive. He smiled and handed Tammy the tape, "I brought you a present."

Tammy's eyes got big, "Wow! You pulled it off!" She plopped into a large easy chair and opened her purse to put it in, and then she motioned for Gerald to sit on the couch. "I can't wait to tell that creep to get lost! He's coming by here in a few hours. Maybe I'll let my mom do it. She can't stand him, anyway. We ran into him at Walmart the other day. He was buying a crowbar and some duct tape. It's hard telling what he was going to do with it."

Gerald sat on the end of the couch. "It's hard telling," he repeated back to her. "Even though you have the video tape, be careful breaking it off with Eddy."

"You know what's strange about all this?" Tammy sighed.

Gerald shook his head, "What's that?"

"When we started going together last year, you were just something to have on my arm. I was riding high in those days, and I picked you out. It was like giving you a winning lottery ticket, or a queen selecting a commoner for marriage. Back then, I thought I was doing something nice." Tammy held out her hand to explain, "Now I realize it was sort of condescending."

"It's okay, Tammy."

"The real irony is that when I had you, there was no . . ." Tammy paused for a moment to think of the right words, ". . . emotional content. And now that I don't have you . . . ." Tammy's words trailed off. "But you're with Lori, now."

"That's right," Gerald nodded in confirmation, "I'm with Lori."

"Are you having sex with her?"

"That's really not your business, Tammy."

"I know. I'm sorry. I shouldn't have asked. I was just thinking that Lori is a nice girl and . . . ." Tammy hesitated, and then blurted out, "I just thought that, since she's a nice girl you're probably not having sex with her. So maybe you would want to have sex with me. I'm not trying to cause problems with you and Lori. You could still date her but come by and see me now and then. I'm okay with playing second fiddle. We could go back to my room, right now." Tammy shrugged. "If you get tired of the arrangement, we could just stop."

"Why would you want to do something like that?"

"You told me one time that if you barter sex, it makes you a whore. At least what I'm offering has no strings attached."

Tammy's voice got quiet, "I guess I still want to feel like I'm desirable."

"You're desirable, Tammy. You're the hottest girl in the school. Everyone knows that. And . . . ," Gerald was slow to continue, "Even though I would love to have sex with you. It's just . . . ."

"Just what?"

"I don't want to see you degraded like that."

"It's just sex," Tammy shrugged. "It doesn't have to mean anything."

"It always means something. It might be good or bad, but there is always something going on. You can try to disassociate yourself from it, and try to pretend that it's the same thing as sticking a quarter in a Pepsi machine, but it's not. Whenever you find yourself thinking that way, it's probably the first sign that something is wrong."

"You really aren't the same as before," Tammy smiled sweetly at him, "It's like you're an entirely different person."

Gerald shrugged, "This is the only me that's left." Gerald's pocket suddenly began to vibrate. Gerald bolted up straight and grabbed his crotch.

Tammy giggled, "Looks like someone's not used to carrying a cell phone."

Gerald pulled the phone from his pocket and pressed a button, then put it to his face. "Hello? Yes, I'm just hanging out, waiting for you to call. Sure, I will be there in ten or fifteen minutes." Gerald shut off the phone and stood up.

"Was that Lori?" Tammy stood up from the easy chair.

"Yes." Gerald tucked the phone back into his pocket. "I have to go."

Tammy walked over to give him a hug. "Thanks Gerald," then slid her hands down to the sides of his waist. "I'm in your debt, and I won't forget it. If you ever need a favor—any kind of favor, just let me know."

"You're welcome, Tammy." He smiled at her. "I really have to go. I'll see you at school." He opened the door and stepped through.

"Bye, Gerald." She walked to the door and peered through to watch him kick the bike and leave.

As he pulled away from the curb he remembered the partially nude Polaroid photos in his pocket. It was just as well he had forgotten them. The visit had already been awkward.

When Gerald got home, he went up to his room and slid open the underwear drawer on his dresser. He pulled out the photos and took a long last look, then pushed the pile of briefs away from the corner and laid the pictures face down on the bottom. He took Eddy's keys from his pocket and dropped them in on top then shifted the stack of underwear back over to cover them up. He closed the drawer and went downstairs.

Chapter 12

Friday's Memorium

The Request

- It had been a bizarre week. Sometimes, everything seemed normal, and Tyler's death would slip my mind for a while. At other times, it was like a lead weight in the pit of my stomach. -

Lori and Gerald sat in the front row of the advanced algebra class, waiting for Mr. Leslie to come in. Lori was anticipating his reaction with a mixture of glee and a little nervousness. Mr. Leslie walked in and glanced their way, "Lori, it's good to see you back on the front row where you belong. Gerald, go to the office."

"What for?"

"I don't respond to questions that are not formed in proper English."

"Why am I going to the office?"

"Because I told you to go there." Mr. Leslie scribbled "OK" on an attendance slip, peeled it from the pad, then held it out. "Please post this outside the door on your way out."

Gerald gathered his books and got up. He took the slip from Mr. Leslie and walked out the door, putting the slip in the clip as he went.

When Gerald walked into the office, Marj glanced up from her keyboard, "Hi, Gerald, Mr. Hawk is expecting you."

"What's this all about?"

Marj smiled, "You're not in any trouble."

Gerald went to the door of Mr. Hawk's office and knocked.

Mr. Hawk opened the door, then stepped back and motioned him in.

As Gerald entered, he saw Tyler's parents standing on the other side of the room. Across the top of Mr. Hawk's desk was an orange football jersey. Gerald winced when he saw the black "20" lettered across the front.

"Gerald, these are Tyler's parents." Mr. Hawk shifted over to stand behind his desk. "They tell me that you have met them before."

Gerald nodded slowly. "We met at the hospital."

"Mr. and Mrs. Banks have brought in Tyler's football jersey. It is going to be permanently displayed in the school trophy case. We're retiring his number."

Gerald cleared his throat, "I think that's great."

"Since you were his friend," Mr. Hawk gestured to the Banks, "they wanted you to be the first to know."

Gerald dipped his head, then nodded and turned toward the Banks, "Thank you; I am very honored."

Mr. Hawk stared down at the jersey and was quiet for a moment, "Also, the Banks would like to make a request of you."

"What request?"

"I will let the Banks' speak to that."

Mrs. Banks leaned forward, "We would like you to speak at Tyler's funeral."

"What would you like me to say?"

"Anything," Mr. Banks offered. "We're going to have our minister speak, as well, so if it's not that long, it doesn't matter. If you could speak even for a few minutes as a tribute, we would appreciate it."

Mr. Hawk looked over at Gerald, "If you're not feeling up to it, it's okay."

"No, I'll do it." Gerald reached out to run his fingertips across the fabric of Tyler's jersey. "I'll come up with something."

Parting Company

- When I was a child, I spoke as a child, I understood as a child, I thought as a child; but when I became an adult, I put away childish things. -

Most students took their free periods in the study hall room downstairs. It was a more permissive environment than the library. Students were allowed to talk quietly, as well as have reasonable movement through the room. They used the opportunity to study together, quiz each other, or play chess, which was the only game permitted. Tammy Wells sat in a corner reading her history assignment, but she wasn't really reading. Her eyes tracked over the sentences but none of the information was soaking in.

Violet and Jean came through the door, and saw her sitting alone in the corner. "Sister!" Violet said, "Where have you been?"

"I was just reading my history assignment."

Jean leaned forward, "We hear you've taken up a taste for bad boys, lately."

"That's over," Tammy answered flatly. "I learned my lesson about bad boys. They only treat you bad. It's like eating poison, then wondering why you got sick. Anyone who is fascinated with bad boys has self-esteem issues. I'm trying to work on mine."

"I think it's exciting!" Violet said, with a hint of admiration. "At least, he's more interesting than that nerd you were seeing. It's about time you came to your senses and broke up with him."

"Gerald may have saved my life."

"Sister!" Jean exclaimed. "So dramatic."

"Please don't call me that anymore."

Violet and Jean were taken aback for a moment. "But we're sisters," Jean answered slowly, "We've been sisters for years!"

"We have different mothers. We're not really sisters. We never have been. It's just sort of a game we've been playing. It was a way of having fun, back in the days when we were innocent. Well," Tammy closed her history book and stared at the cover, "I'm not innocent anymore."

Violet leaned over the table. "What is going on with you? Why are you being like this?"

Tammy scooped up her book and got up to leave. "We can still be friends. I would just like to retire the whole 'sister' thing and move on."

Violet and Jean looked at each other for a moment, and then left up the stairs leading out of the study hall to the hallway.

The Kiss-Off

- I wished I could have remembered Sandy from the days before the accident. She seemed pretty fun. -

Eddy pulled up outside Tammy's house and gave the horn a quick beep. The screen door opened and a figure came out, but it wasn't Tammy. Sandy Logan walked over to the powder blue Cadillac and bent over the window. "Hello, Eddy."

"Where's Tammy?"

"I guess you'll have to go honk youir horn somewhere else from now on." Sandy said cheerfuly. "She's not coming."

"Why not?"

"She doesn't want to see you anymore."

"Did she actually say that?"

Mrs. Logan leaned an elbow on the upper rim of the windshield. "That was pretty much the gist of it. She said something like, 'Tell that jerk to kiss off'. Actually, she used the f-word, but I'm too much of a lady to say it that way."

Eddy nodded. For a moment he felt angry and considered peeling out to move the car from beneath her arm, to make her lose her balance. Then the cold, calculating side of Eddy rose up to take control. "Tell her I'm sorry to hear that and I hope she reconsiders." Eddy put his hand out to shake her hand. "It was a pleasure talking to you, Mrs. Wells."

Sandy shook his hand. "Actually, my name is Logan, and it has been a pleasure talking to you as well, but I wouldn't get my hopes up on any sort of reconsideration."

Eddy nodded and shifted the transmission into drive. He waited for her to step back from the car, and then gently pulled away.

When Sandy walked back into the house, Tammy was waiting, "How did it go? Was he mad?"

"No," Sandy shrugged, "he didn't seem mad at all. He was actually quite nice about it. It sort of took the fun out of it. Maybe I was wrong about him."

"Oh, no, you weren't wrong. There's a lot about him that you don't know. I only went out with him because I felt like I couldn't get out of it."

"Then you should have just called me and told me. I'd have gotten you out of it."

"Well, you know Mom, that can be pretty hard to do when he's sitting right there."

"Oh for Pete's sake, Tammy, don't you know how to be a cat like your mother? If someone is listening in, you just mix it up a little. Say something like, 'I can't come home early because I can't get out of school,' or 'I'm going to be late, because I can't get out of work.' When I hear that phrase, I'm smart enough to pluck it out and figure out what's really going on."

The Tribute

- Shadows are fallin' and I'm runnin' out of breath. Keep me in your heart for a while. If I leave you, it doesn't mean I love you any less. Keep me in your heart for a while. -

Gerald stepped up to the podium. He looked over to make eye contact with Lori. She gave him a faint smile and tilted her chin. Gerald scanned the crowd of people. Every seat was taken and many people were standing along the walls and in the doorways. In one corner was a sea of orange uniforms. Tyler's teammates had all shown up wearing their football jerseys. Gerald pursed his lips and blinked a couple of times to clear the moisture welling up in his eye. He cleared his throat and leaned close to the microphone, to speak.

"We're here to say goodbye to Tyler. He was my friend. He was the best friend I ever had." Gerald took a breath, and struggled to control the tone of his voice. "Everybody liked Tyler. He was always happy, always friendly. I think of Tyler and I know the type of person I wish I was," Gerald looked across the room, "but know that I can never be. Tyler had a rare gift that most of us will never have.

Tyler brought something good to this town, with his extraordinary football talents. He could have left at any time. People were pounding down his door with offers. That red Mustang out in the parking lot," Gerald pointed back over his shoulder with his thumb, "some university in Montana gave him that just for coming to visit." Gerald paused, "Officially, it came from a third party not involved with the university." Some of football players in orange jerseys smiled. "When he couldn't use the car anymore, he gave it to me. He could have sold it for a lot of money but that thought didn't even enter his mind. Tyler got it free so he passed it on the same way.

Tyler got his satisfaction by playing here in Hutsonville, the small town that spawned him. For him, here and now was good enough and really, here and now is the only promise that we can really count on.

Now Tyler's gone, and we're the less for it. But we were enriched for the time that we had with him. Every life that touched his seemed to benefit from him in some way and mine was one of them. You always felt like Tyler wanted the best for you. He seemed to get satisfaction from helping to make your life good in some way. So on behalf of myself and all those people who knew him, I would like to say, 'Thank you, Tyler. You were the best amongst us, and we will never forget you.' "

Gerald took a deep breath, then walked back to his seat and sat down. He reached down to take Lori's hand and then stared forward as the minister came to podium to speak.

Rabbit in a Bottle

Chapter 13

Saturday Bowl

The Hostage

- Eddy seemed to plan everything he did. He had an eye for detail. -

Eddy watched Tammy come out of the house. He waited until she had walked about a block before he eased the Cadillac up behind her. He leaned his elbow on the door, and kept the pistol down at his side.

Tammy heard him roll up behind her and turned around. "What do you want?"

Eddy lifted the pistol just above the profile of the door, "I thought I would give you a ride."

Tammy glanced at the pistol, "That doesn't really scare me anymore, Eddy. I've had that gun in my mouth before, remember? If you're going to shoot me go ahead and do it right now."

"I'm not going to shoot you, Tammy, but you should know that your mother's in danger."

"How is she in danger? From you?"

"I'm a disciplined man. If you know nothing else about me, you know I'm a man of principle. I give you my word that if you come with me today I will never trouble you again. You know I always honor my promises. If you refuse . . .," Eddy grimaced, "whatever would end up happening to your mother, you would have to remember that I gave you a choice. I keep those sorts of promises, as well."

"What do you want from me, Eddy?"

"I know you have the tape. I also know you won't go to the cops. I just need to make sure we part company in the right way."

"Are you going to kill me?"

"Oh course not!" Eddy seemed surpised at the suggestion. "Why would I do that? I just want you to take one last ride with me, then we're done and I will leave you alone. You have my word."

Tammy turned and glared into his face, "This one ride and then we're done, right?"

"That's right. I'm a businessman, Tammy. If I make a contract, I honor it. Come on, get in the car. Do this last thing for me and we're quits."

"How long will this take?"

"It shouldn't be more than a few hours. I will have you back by this afternoon."

Tammy paused, and then grabbed the door handle on the side of the car, "If I go with you I have to call the Coffee House, so I can tell them I won't be in."

Eddy nodded, "That will be alright, but make the call from in the car so I can listen in."

Tammy opened the door to get in, and then settled into the seat. Eddy turned the car to go over the bridge into Indiana. Tammy dialed the number of the coffee house.

Chuck Evans, the owner, answered, "Hutsonville Coffee House."

"Hi, Chuck. This is Tammy. I'm not going to be able to come in to work this morning."

Chuck dipped his head and sighed, "Tammy, you can't do this. We're doing biscuits and gravy this morning, and we're expecting a large turnout."

"I'm sorry Chuck, but it's something I just can't get out of."

"I'm not happy about this."

"Please call my mom and tell her I won't be home for lunch."

"Are you kidding? Do you want me to pick up your laundry for you, too? You have a phone; call her yourself."

"Thank you, Chuck. I have to go. Good-bye."

"I said 'no.' " Chuck raised his voice slightly.

Eddy laid a hand over the phone to end the call and glared at her, "What was all that?"

"Mother was going to fix lunch. If I don't show she might get suspicious."

Chuck slowly put the receiver back on the hook.

Chuck's wife stepped up behind him, "What is it?'

"Tammy called to tell me she's not coming in."

"You have got to be kidding! She can't just ditch us like that on a Saturday morning! I've had enough of this. You have to fire her and get someone else."

Chuck didn't answer, but made a troubled face as he replayed the phone conversation in his mind.

"What is it?" she asked him.

"Tammy asked me to call her mother and tell her she wouldn't be having lunch with her. Since I was feeling irritated with her, I told her 'no.' "

"So?"

"She thanked me and said 'Goodbye.' Why would she thank me, if I had refused?"

"Maybe she misunderstood."

Chuck shook his head, "I don't know." He picked up the phone and dialed Tammy's house.

Sandy heard the phone ring and groaned. She rolled over and looked at the clock. She draped her forearm over her eyes, silently wishing it would not ring again. With the second ring, she grumbled, "Alright, alright, I'm coming." She flopped an arm over the nightstand then clumsily lifted the phone off the receiver, and brought it to the side of her face. "Please tell me you have a good reason for calling me this early on a Saturday," she groaned into the phone.

"Sandy, this is Chuck. Tammy is not going to be in today. She asked me to call you and tell you she won't be home for lunch."

"Chuck, you were in my graduating class. We go all the way back to the first grade, and you know I love you. That's why it's going to pain me greatly to have to come down there and stuff your face into the fryer. I don't know if I will even be home when she takes lunch. Most of the time, she just walks down to the gas station and gets a sandwich or something, so why on earth would you need to call me to tell me she won't be here?"

Chuck sighed, "Because she asked me to. It seemed a little weird."

Sandy sat up in bed, "What did she say? Tell me her exact words."

"I don't know what her exact words were. She said that she wouldn't be in, and then asked me to call you to let you know she wouldn't be home for lunch."

"Did she use the phrase, 'Can't get out of it'?"

"Yes!" Chuck answered excitedly, "I can't remember how she said it, but she used almost those exact words."

"I have to go, Chuck. I think that Tammy has been kidnapped."

Sandy clicked the receiver to get a dial tone, and then dialed 911.

North of the Border

- There seemed to be only one constant in my life. The more exposure I had to women, the less I understood them. -

Gerald pulled the Mustang up to the curb, then got out and walked up to ring the bell on Lori's front door. Two seconds later Lori opened the door. "Hey," she gave him a quick kiss on the lips. She was dressed in hemmed denim shorts and a long-sleeved, dark blue shirt that had pearl embossed snaps up the front. "Mama and Daddy wanted us to ride up with them."

Gerald shrugged, "That's fine."

"No it is not fine," she shook her head. "I already told them that you wanted us to drive separately. Let's get going. I want to be far enough ahead of them that they're not following right behind us." She walked down to the curb.

"Okay," he answered as he opened the door and slid in to start the car.

"Do you know how to get there?" she asked.

Gerald pulled away from the curb. "Just cruise up Route 1 until you hit Marshall."

"Yes, but do you know how to get to the high school once we get to town?"

"I have no idea."

"Well," Lori smiled and held up a couple of folded papers, "your intelligent girlfriend printed it out from Google."

"I guess I can consider myself lucky that I hooked up with someone so smart."

"Oh, I almost forgot." Lori twisted in the seat and took a folded one-hundred dollar bill from her front pocket. She opened the change tray in the dash and dropped it in, then closed it up, "This is from Daddy for the travel expenses."

"Is that a hundred dollars?"

"Yes, it's one-hundred dollars."

"It's only about twenty miles, each way."

"I know; I told him that, but like I told you, he's OCD. He started rambling on about travel expenses being more than just gas. It's oil, wear on tires, mileage depreciation on the car, on and on and on. So, I quit trying to argue with him and took it. I figured you could use the extra money, anyway."

"I just don't want any awkwardness with him."

"He's so absent minded, he's probably already forgotten about it. Take the money. It's not like you stole it."

As Gerald drove out of Hutsonville, Lori was quiet. "Do you remember that time when we were at Monical's? When you pulled me across the table and kissed me?" she asked.

"Oh yeah, I remember."

"I liked that."

Gerald smiled. "It was just a spur of the moment thing. I think I was just trying to throw you a curve."

"I liked it, because you took charge. I felt like a helpless damsel. I think women like to be dominated a little bit." Lori popped open the snaps at the bottom of her shirt, and tied the front corners together just under her breasts, revealing her stomach.

Gerald glanced over and saw what she was doing. "I can turn the air up, if it's too warm in here."

Lori shook her head. "It's not about comfort. I just thought I would show you a little skin." She opened a few snaps at the top of her shirt.

"You're feeling pretty frisky this morning."

Lori smiled, and then made sure her door was locked and leaned back against the side. "Well, it's broad daylight. You have to drive, and the folks are probably only five minutes behind us. I figure I can tease you mercilessly and still be safe."

"Women are wicked."

"Yes, we are," Lori whispered. She ran her finger over the knot in her shirt. "Do you want to see my breasts?"

"Uhm," Gerald stammered a bit. The question caught him off guard. "I'm driving right now."

"You can still take a quick peek. They're not some monstrous C-cups, like some of the girls have. Just a couple of B-cups," Lori looked down at her chest and then back. "They may not be huge, but they're very perky and nicely formed."

Gerald frowned. He felt conflicted. Her newfound sensuality was making him aroused, but he wasn't sure if he liked this new side of her. "Listen to this nice little National Honor Society girl talk. What would Mrs. Branson think?"

Lori took a pair of dark sunglasses out of her purse. "Every nice girl wants a chance to be naughty now and then." She unfolded her sunglasses and put them on. "Besides, haven't you heard? I'm not a nice girl anymore. I'm a birth control pill popping slut."

"Stop. Just stop all of it!" Gerald felt himself on the verge of getting angry. "I don't like you this way."

"Okay," Lori said with a slight quiver in her voice.

"And take off those sunglasses." Gerald began to realize he was being too harsh. He smiled at her, to take off the edge, "I want to be able to see your pretty eyes."

Lori folded the sunglasses and tucked them into her purse. "I don't know what I'm doing here, Gerald. These are uncharted waters for me. You're my first boyfriend. So I thought about it for a long time and I decided that I'm comfortable with anything above the waist. Do whatever you like upstairs but for now, don't go south of the border. Are you okay with that?"

"You said the other night that you would sleep with me."

"Yes, I did, but that was a mistake. I'm just not ready to go that far. Sorry, but you missed your window of opportunity on that one."

Gerald looked up the road for any oncoming traffic, and then glanced over at her. "Come here," he said softly, as he hooked the tips of two fingers around the knot in the front of her shirt, and lightly pulled her forward. With his free hand, he gently plucked at the knot until it came loose, then pulled it open to let the rumpled corners hang down. He went up the front of her shirt, and gently popped open the remaining snaps until the two halves of her shirt gapped open. He gently slid her bra up over her breasts, "I need you to unsnap your bra. I don't like the way it cuts into your skin."

"I will," she answered as she reached behind her back, "but you keep an eye on the road. I don't need you getting in an accident."

"That would be bad."

"Knowing my luck I would be unconscious and everybody would be wondering why my boobs were hanging out."

"You sure do expect a lot from me." Gerald smiled, "I'm supposed to drive and fondle your breasts at the same time."

"Suck it up, mister."

The Break-In

- The Sycamore Building was very old, and had become dilapidated, but it still stood as the tallest building in Terre Haute for all those years. -

Eddy parked the car on Fourth Street. He took a strange-looking tool out of the back. It was two feet long, and was shaped like a huge screwdriver with a bent tip. The wooden handle had a hole drilled in the end. A nine-inch loop of light cotton rope with the ends tied ran through the hole. Eddy slipped his arm through and pulled it over his shoulder, and then pulled his jacket over the top. He reached into the rear floorboard and took out a length of light chain. He looped it around his waist several times, and then fastened it in the front with a small padlock.

"What are you doing?" Tammy asked.

"I'm getting ready. The difference between success and failure is preparation."

"Where are we going?"

Eddy smirked, "You're asking a lot of questions." He pointed to the north. "Two blocks up that way. In case we need to slip away, I don't want the car to be too close."

As they made their way up the street, Tammy could see the tall brick spire looming before them. They rounded the last corner and the Sycamore Building stood at the other end of the sidewalk. Tammy looked up at it, "Is that it?"

"Yes, but don't point at it, and don't look up. Just act casual."

Tammy reached into her pocket and felt for her cell phone. Without taking it out, she pressed the button on the side to turn the volume all the way down. "What do you want me to do?"

"Stand in front of the doors to block me. I need you to face out toward the street and put your hands on your hips. Flare your elbows out to make your body wider. Try to look like you're waiting for a bus or something."

As Tammy waited, Eddy moved behind her and put the tip of his tool into the door jamb. He pried the door, bending some of the metal.

"How's it going?" Tammy asked over her shoulder without looking back.

"It's going to take a bit. Watch for cars. Let me know if any of them take notice of us, point at us, or slow down as they pass." Eddy adjusted his tool to a new position and pressed again. The brown aluminum frame of the door was starting to bulge. "One more and that should do it." Eddy positioned the tool at a new angle and put the tip behind the deadbolt, then leaned all his weight against the handle. With a screech of metal the deadbolt hinged outward and the door came open. Eddy glanced around quickly, then pulled Tammy's arm, "Let's go."

Tammy stepped inside and stood in the foyer. On the wall near the elevators was a rack of wooden boxes, each of which would accommodate stacks of legal-size papers. Under the open end of each box was a faded label. "What is this place?" she asked.

Eddy took the chain from around his waist. He used one end to make a loop around the handle of a door and padlocked it. "Years ago, this building had a bunch of bank offices in it."

Tammy looked around and saw a mailbox with a forgotten legal-size manila envelope inside. She discreetly slid the phone out of her pocket and dialed 911, then checked to make sure Eddy wasn't watching. Tammy slid the phone deep into the box, underneath the envelope. Her heart pounded in her chest. The light from the cell phone's screen made a faint glow in the back of the box. Tammy silently tried to remember how long the window would stay lit before it automatically went dark.

"Come here; I need your help." Eddy had the chain strung from one set of doors to the other. He was trying to stretch it enough that he could snap the other end around the handle of the second set of doors.

Tammy went to his side, "What do you want me to do?"

"I need more slack," Eddy handed her the end of the chain, then stepped back up to the door to inspect the latch. "When I pull the chain tight, you lock it down."

"Why are you doing this?"

"In case we get company, I want to buy us a little time." Eddy put his shoulder against the metal frame of the damaged door, and then strained to pull it shut.

Tammy moved the lock around, but pretended that she couldn't get it latched. She glanced over at the mailboxes. The cell phone was still glowing. "I can't get it."

Eddy cursed under his breath and pressed a knee against the frame to pull the door tighter to give her more slack. Tammy bit her lip as she worked the lock. She fumbled for a moment. "Just lock it!" Eddy scowled at her in a frustrated voice. "What's wrong with you?"

Tammy knew she couldn't buy any more time. If she tarried any longer he would know she was stalling. She snapped the padlock shut. Eddy walked over to the middle and yanked the chain, to check for slack. He pressed his weight against the door to test the width of the gap. Tammy glanced over at the mailboxes, saw the light on her cell phone wink out, and breathed a sigh of relief.

Eddy walked back to the elevator and stood next to Tammy. He studied the way she anxiously shifted her weight from side to side. "Are you okay?" he asked. "You seem a little nervous."

Tammy smiled, "This is my first break-in." Above the elevator door, she saw a half moon brass dial with numbers ranging from one to twelve. The needle was pointed toward one. Eddy pressed the button on the wall to call the elevator, and it opened almost immediately.

"Where are we going?" Tammy asked as they stepped inside.

"To the tenth floor," Eddy pressed the button that read "10."

"Why ten?" she asked.

"Because, that's the floor that lit up shortly after your old boyfriend went up there. I think the old doc lives on the top floor. I went past here a few other nights, and those are the lights that are mostly on."

"What are you going to do if he's up there right now?"

"Since the elevator was at the bottom, I'm guessing he's not here. He's probably at the station, doing his television show. I called the station last week, pretending to be a fan, and the lady told me that he usually comes in on Saturday to tape the show, a few hours before it's aired. If I'm wrong and he shows up, then I'll deal with it."

"Why are we here?"

Eddy smiled, "We're just going to have a look around. I want to know why Gerald comes here."

The elevator doors slid open on the tenth floor. Eddy stepped into the lab and found the light switch, then flipped it up. The room seemed crammed with all sorts of electronics and display screens. He motioned Tammy over to the window. "I need you to keep an eye on the street. Tell me if anyone pulls up or lingers out front."

Tammy went to the window and looked down at the pavement. A black and white squad car came down the street with its red lights flashing. She glanced back over at Eddy, "All clear."

"Well, keep watching." Eddy flipped on the overhead viewer. Gerald's DNA map came up on the screen.

"What is that?" Tammy asked.

Eddy shook his head, "I have no idea." He pointed to the wording in the lower corner. "That's your old boyfriend's name, though, so it definitely has something to do with him."

Eddy spotted a cage just beneath the screen, where a small gray mouse peered out from between the bars. "What is this?" Eddy bent lower to take a peek.

"What is it?" Tammy glanced down at the street to take another look at the black and white squad car with the doors open.

"It's a mouse, but it has these little posts sticking out of its head." Eddy twisted the wire loose and gently opened the door.

"What are you going to do?"

Eddy grinned. "I'm going to snap its little neck."

"Please don't do that, Eddy."

Eddy stared at her in disbelief, "It's a mouse! Why do you think they have mouse traps?" Eddy opened the cage door and grasped the tiny warm ball of fur in his hand then lifted it out. He positioned his thumb and crooked the index finger on each side of its skull. The mouse peered innocently back at him. "Just relax little fella," Eddy cooed softly, "I promise this will all be over quick and easy."

At the last minute, the mouse turned in his hand. Eddy scowled and jumped back, then put the side of his index finger in his mouth.

"What happened?"

Eddy looked at the broken skin on the side of his finger. "The little son of a bitch bit me!" Eddy began raking the stools away from the counter and stomping the floor, but the mouse scurried about too quickly and avoided his feet, then crawled under a cabinet. Eddy took a wooden pointer from the shelf beneath the projection screen, and got down on his hands and knees. "There you are, you little bastard!" He began jamming the pointer underneath the cabinet, but the pointer wasn't quite long enough to work well. Eddy banged his knuckles with each thrust. He stood up, "I need something longer."

"Eddy, what's the matter with you?" Tammy called out to him from across the room. "You're wasting precious time on a stupid mouse."

Eddy wiped finger on the side of his blue denim pant leg. "You're right," he agreed. "Good correction." Eddy still felt frustrated. "I sure would like to wring his damned neck, though."

Eddy walked over to the shroud-covered bell jars. He pulled the covering off the first one, but found it empty. He pulled the shroud off the second bell jar, to reveal a hairless rabbit lying on its side with wires hooked up to electrodes mounted in its skull. "Wow," Eddy commented quietly. "Now that is freaky!"

"What is it?" Tammy asked.

"I think it's Frankenstein's rabbit."

"Can I come and see?"

Eddy glanced down at the rabbit, then over at the window. "Alright, but just for a second. I need you to keep watch."

As Tammy came across the room, Eddy squatted down to look under the counter. "There's an air pump under here and a bunch of other stuff. I think it's some sort of life support system." Eddy stood up and grasped the top of the bell jar. "It's heavy." He pressed the top knob to the side. With a hiss, the bottom rim broke free and the jar tipped slightly. "That's it." He lifted the jar up and set it to the side. The rabbit made a twitch, and started to gasp for air. Several red bulbs in the console started to light up.

"I don't think it can breathe without the jar. Put it back. I think you're killing it."

"Don't be giving me orders." Eddy reached down and nudged the rabbit to roll it slightly. One of the leads turned on the post in its skull and flipped off. "I go along with what Charles Darwin said: If it can't survive on its own, then it doesn't deserve to exist."

The elevator made a ding as the pointer on the bronze dial over the door started to rotate left and move off of the number ten. "It's headed down." Eddy ran to the window and looked down at the squad car. "It's the cops. I should have had you stay at the window."

"What do we do now?"

Eddy pulled the revolver from the waist of his pants. "We can't hide. They know from the needle that the elevator was on the tenth floor." Eddy went to the opposite end of the counter and squatted down. "Get over here. There's only one squad car." Eddy cocked the hammer back on the revolver.

Tammy came to squat next to him. "What are you going to do?"

"Shut up and stay down behind the table," Eddy barked back. "And put your fingers in your ears."

<u>The Bowl</u>

- I have fought the good fight. I have finished the race. -

When the Mustang started to enter town of Marshall, Lori shifted back over to her seat and put her bra back together, then snapped up the front of her shirt. Gerald pointed up to the rear view mirror, "Isn't that your folks right behind us?"

Lori quickly whipped her head around, but no one was following them. "Stop that!" She swatted him on the shoulder. "You're going to give me a heart attack."

"Easy now. Don't disturb the driver. Can you check the map?"

Lori grabbed her printouts and looked them over. "Okay, you need to stay on this main road. This is Michigan Street. You'll go about six blocks, then take a left on Mulberry."

"About six?"

"The streets are all crisscrossed." Lori made an "X" with the flats of her hands. "Route 1 hits the town at a forty-five degree angle. In a few blocks, you'll need to turn left on Mulberry. Spruce is coming up soon. That's the last street before Mulberry, so when you see Spruce you'll know we're getting close."

"Got it," Gerald nodded.

"Okay," Lori pointed to a sign, "There's Spruce."

Gerald slammed on the brakes, and turned on the turn signal.

Lori caught herself on the dash, "No, no; you don't turn on Spruce. You turn on Mulberry. It should be coming up soon, crazy driver."

"Crazy navigator," Gerald canceled the turn signal and took his foot off the brake. "You're going to get me in a wreck."

"That's Mulberry," she pointed to the sign.

Gerald slowed down to take the turn.

"Take the next one," Lori instructed him.

Gerald shrugged and took his foot off the brake.

"What are you doing? You need to turn here."

"You said to go on to the next one." He pressed the brake pedal.

"You need to turn on this next one! Not the next next one. Turn right here."

Gerald was about to push the lever up, then stopped. "I can't turn right here; it's left turn only."

"That's what I mean, turn left right here."

Gerald pulled the turn signal lever down, made the turn, and glanced over at her. "Did you have anything to drink this morning?"

"Just some orange juice. Why?"

Gerald shook his head, "Never mind."

"There," she pointed to the left side. "That's the school right over there. Turn left right there."

"Okay. I will turn left right here." Gerald smiled and turned the left turn signal on, then pulled into the parking lot. "Any certain space you had in mind?"

"There's Mrs. Branson. Pull up next to her car."

Gerald pulled up and then turned to Lori and smiled.

"What?" Lori asked.

"I think I am in love with you. Because you are driving me batshit crazy."

"Shhh," Lori put a finger to his lips, "Mrs. B doesn't like profanity." Lori opened the door as Mrs. Branson came to the side of the car, "Hi, Mrs. B."

"Hi, Lori," she said as she leaned over the door glass. "I see you found it okay. Have you got our secret weapon all locked and loaded?"

"Oh, he's a handful, but I think we'll manage."

"Great," Mrs. Branson smiled. "I need to run in and help get set up. I'll see you inside in a moment."

"I don't believe it!" Gerald said, pointing across the parking lot. "Look who made it."

Lori glanced over to see a thin, awkward man in a tweed suit with a bowtie. "Is that Dr. Gauge? Isn't he the guy on television?" Lori watched him saunter toward the car. The suit seemed too tight and by the way he walked in his black leather shoes seemed to be uncomfortable.

Gerald stepped out of the car and went over to shake his hand, "What are you doing here?"

"I went into the studio last night and videotaped today's show, so I could be here to support you." Dr. Gauge's voice took on a regretful tone. "I never went to any of Tyler's football games and perhaps I should have. I decided maybe you were right. Keeping a safe distance might be the most comfortable thing, but it's not good for the soul. It's too late for me to make it up to Tyler, but a good scientist never repeats the same mistake."

"I'm glad you came," Gerald answered warmly. "It means a lot." As Lori stepped up, Gerald motioned toward her, "This is Lori, my girlfriend."

Lori smiled at him with recognition, "I watch your show sometimes. It's always very interesting."

"Dr. Gauge and Friends." He shook Lori's hand, clutching the end of her fingers with his thumb. "I'm at your service, ma'am, and pleased to make your acquaintance."

Lori smiled at his quaintness. As Dr. Gauge turned to go inside, Gerald recognized a couple getting out of a dark gray Chevy Malibu, "There are the folks."

"My folks?" Lori turned to look.

"No, my folks."

Christine stepped forward to give Gerald a hug, and cradled the side of his face with one hand. "I'm so proud of you, honey."

"Thanks, Mom," Gerald answered, smelling her vanilla-scented perfume.

"And you must be Lori," Christine held out her hand. "So you are the reason we hardly ever see our son anymore," she said with a smile.

"Well, he does require a lot of work."

Christine didn't seem to understand, "What sort of work, dear?"

Lori smiled with a faint hint of nervousness, "You know, I'm still training him to be a gentleman."

Christine reached over to Gerald and brushed the hair back from his forehead, "Well, nobody's perfect. I suppose there's always room for improvement."

Lori turned toward John, "You must be Gerald's dad."

"I am, indeed. Nice to meet you, Lori."

Lori slapped Gerald on the shoulder, "We'd better get inside."

Christine lagged back a bit to let them walk ahead. She leaned close to her husband and whispered to him, "This is the girl who thinks she needs to teach our son how to be a gentleman?"

"Ah, come on now," John put his arm around his wife's waist and led her inside. "They seem pretty happy together."

In the school theatre was a raised platform with a podium in the center. On each side was a table with four chars. As the Hutsonville team made their way to their seats, Gerald glanced nervously over at Lori.

"You'll be fine," Lori whispered as she touched his hand.

Mrs. Branson came up to the table for some last-minute coaching. "Remember, Gerald, you can't answer two questions in a row. The other three have only studied their specific areas. If there are two consecutive questions in the same area, you will need to step in and answer for them."

Gerald nodded, "I think I've got it."

The moderator stepped up to the podium and gave a brief overview of the rules, then introduced the participants for the first half. He called for a start of the clock, and then read the first question. "Our first toss-up question is: This president lost popularity in his party for his support of the Kansas-Nebraska act, which expanded . . . ."

Lori buzzed in, stopping the rest of the question from being read, "Franklin Pierce."

"Franklin Pierce is correct. That is 10 points for Hutsonville. The 5-point bonus question is as follows: Due to his unpopularity, Franklin Pierce was abandoned by his party, and was not renominated. Who was nominated in his place?"

The Hutsonville team conferred for a moment, and then Lori spoke into the microphone, "James Buchanan."

"That is correct. Another 5 points to the Hutsonville team. The score is now 15 to 0." The moderator turned over his next card. "Our second toss-up question is: To appease the South, this president supported the Compromise of 1850, which included the fugitive . . . ."

Gerald buzzed in, "Millard Fillmore."

"That is correct. Another 10 points to the Hutsonville team. The score is 25 to 0."

As the first half of the Bowl began to draw to a close, Gerald began to feel strange. The voice of the moderator reading the question became dim and faded in the background. He leaned forward and rested his fingertips on the table. He started to pant and become dizzy.

Lori leaned over to his side, "Are you okay?"

"I am sorry, but that is a foul by Hutsonville. Conferring with team members is not permitted during a toss-up. Hutsonville is excluded from the question. For the benefit of the Marshall team, I will reread the question in its entirety, and allow them to collaborate on an answer."

Gerald gasped and stiffened, then fell forward onto the table.

Lori stood up and bent over him, "What is it?"

"I can't breathe," he gasped out.

Most of the audience rose to their feet. Dr. Gauge pushed his way through the crowd, "Let me through. I'm his doctor. Please let me through." Dr. Gauge came up the steps of the stage and ran to bend over Gerald's quivering form.

The moderator spoke into the microphone, "Can someone call an ambulance?" Kevin and Eugene lifted Gerald's legs up on the table to help him lay down.

Christine rushed to his side and smoothed the hair back from his forehead. "Just breathe, dear."

"We'll take a brief recess," the moderator announced.

Gerald weakly turned his head, "I'm sorry, Mom," he gasped.

Christine's lower lip quivered. "I love you," she whispered back.

All of Gerald's muscles stiffened and shook. He looked up at Dr. Gauge, "Someone's in the lab," he choked out.

Lori rubbed Gerald's hand in her palms and tried to make sense of what he was saying. "What lab? What are you talking about?"

Dr. Gauge took a cell phone from his jacket pocket as he stepped away from the table and then began dialing the Terre Haute police department.

Gerald's bodily tremors began to slow. He looked over at Lori, "I'm so sorry. I love you and I should have told you."

"What?" Lori asked breathlessly. "What should you have told me?"

Dr. Gauge brought the cell phone down from his cheek and put his hand on Gerald's shoulder, "The police are already at the lab. Just hang on for a few moments."

Gerald began to feel lightheaded, "Not enough time." A haze past before his eyes, as he felt the life force starting to drain out of him. "I can feel it." His face moved to a slight smile. "It feels good. It feels peaceful."

Gerald's eyes stared into the distance. "Don't grieve for me, Dr. Gauge," he said breathlessly. "After all, I'm only a rabbit."

Gerald felt his mind race though a long dark tunnel. The body on the table made a quiver, then quit breathing and laid still.

The Shoot-Out

- All good things . . . . -

Eddy watched the brass needle slowly turn to the right as it approached the 10 on the dial. He took out a pair of foam ear plugs and stuffed them in his ears. He squatted low and looked over at Tammy. "Cover your ears and keep your head down!"

Tammy kept her fingers in her ears, and slid her feet out from under her to shift to a sitting position. Her foot kicked one of

Tyler's abandoned barbells, making it roll up against a stack of old books, then back toward her foot.

The door of the elevator slid open, but there was no one to be seen. Eddy aimed the revolver into the open doorway of the elevator and fired off a shot. On each side of the open doorway, a fist with a pistol in it appeared. Fire billowed from the barrels as the policemen blazed through their clips. The glass window behind Eddy and Tammy shattered into fragments that rained down on them with each shot. Tammy covered her head to shield herself from the shower of tiny crystals.

"Stop it!" Tammy screamed. "Please stop shooting!"

The room was quite for a moment except for the sound of two empty clips hitting the floor of the elevator, and new clips being jammed into place.

"Don't shoot!" Eddy yelled out, "I have an innocent girl up here that I have taken hostage."

There was no sound from the elevator but metal slapping against metal, as the policemen released the hoods on their Glocks to chamber the first rounds.

"You on the elevator. Answer me or I will shoot her now."

"We hear you," a voice from an unseen police officer came from around the corner.

"Here's what I want. Go down the elevator. Leave your squad car running with the doors open and back away. I will be down in ten minutes with the girl. When we drive off, I don't want to see another cop anywhere on the road. I will drive out to the country, ditch the squad car, and let the girl go."

It was quiet for a moment. Eddy strained his ears to hear them whispering in the elevator. "Do you hear me in there? In five seconds, I'm going to put a bullet in her, if you're not headed down."

"Alright. We'll do it. Just don't hurt the girl."

The elevator doors slid shut as it started down.

"Will that work?" Tammy asked.

"Leaving in a squad car? With all that radio and GPS equipment and a big number painted across the top? No way. That was just to buy us some time." Eddy smiled. "They think I'm stupid, and that we're going to walk right out the front door. We're going down the fire escape in back. I hope you can make it down ten flights of stairs." Eddy peered out through the window. "Find something to break out the rest of the glass. We have to get out of here before more cops show up. By the time they figure out we're not coming out the front, we need to be back in the Cadillac and on our way."

Tammy stood up and lifted the ten-pound barbell. Eddy turned around to see it in her hands. "That will work fine. Just a second." Eddy reached his arms behind his back to tuck the revolver into the back of his waistband.

Tammy swung the barbell with all her might, and struck him in the side of the face. Eddy staggered backward and fell through the open window, breaking away most of the remaining glass.

Tammy gingerly followed him through the window, stepping onto the wrought iron landing of the fire escape. She shook tiny fragments of glass from her hair and walked over to Eddy.

Eddy was lying on his back, staring up at the sky. He rolled over onto his knees and groggily came to his feet. He looked down at his arm. Blood was streaming from a gash down the length of his forearm. Eddy ran his hand over the wound, and then rolled his palm over to show a thick film of red, "Ah, I'm really bleeding bad," he said in a groggy voice. He rested a weak hand on the rail and glanced behind him to the square hole in the platform.

Tammy stepped up to him, "You can bleed in hell, you son of a bitch!" She grasped the barbell tightly in both hands, and swung it up in an arc. It caught Eddy squarely under the chin, knocking him cold. Eddy's body went limp as it fell backward through the square hole and dropped down to the next level. His body smacked against the metal deck of the next lower platform and was still. The revolver slid through the metal bars, then dropped another level and bounced off to the side. It fell the remaining stories, and then fired off a shot when it bounced off the pavement.

A few seconds later, two policemen appeared around the corner with their weapons drawn.

"Don't shoot!" Tammy called down to them. "He's unconscious. He fell down to the next landing. The gun is down there somewhere."

One officer knelt down to pick up the revolver, while the other one shouted up to Tammy, "You stay right there, miss! There are more people coming. We'll be up to help you in a moment."

Tammy dropped the barbell and sat down on the metal deck. She folded her legs up into a fetal position, then rested her arms on her knees and wept.

Before long, the entire area was flooded with the flashing lights of squad cars. Policemen moved through the lab taking pictures. An officer helped Tammy off the fire escape landing and back in through the window. They tried to ask her questions to get a statement, but she was too upset to be coherent. One level down, a medical crew gathered around Eddy and put him on a stretcher. They carried him in through the window on the ninth floor, and then wheeled him onto the elevator.

Tammy rode the elevator down, hanging onto the arm of a policeman for support. Just before she got into the police car, she glanced over to see Eddy being loaded into the back of an ambulance. He appeared to be unconscious. His skin was pale from the loss of blood.

As policemen milled around through the lab, one stopped to look at the rabbit with no hair. It was lying on a round, black wooden base that had holes coming up through the bottom. He hovered his hand over it and felt the air blowing up against his palm. One of the leads that led to a terminal in the rabbits head was still attached, but the other had slipped free. He reached down to squeeze open the small alligator clip, and then reattached it to the tiny node. He ran his finger around in the quarter-inch recessed grove that ran along the outer edge of the base, and then glanced over at the bell jar. He lifted the glass and set it back onto the base. The policeman wiped a few remaining fragments of glass off the smooth black surface of the table top, then left the room to step onto the elevator.

Under the bell jar, the rabbit's leg made a slight twitch.

Rabbit in a Bottle

Epilogue

That same day, Eddy Leach's hospital room was dark, except for the array of lighted equipment that kept him alive. Dr. Gauge slipped through the door and entered the room. He pulled a tiny penlight from his pocket and ran the beam over the bed. He found his way to Eddy's side, and clenched the end of the penlight in his teeth. Ripping open the pouch on a small alcohol pad, he swabbed Eddy's thumb. He tore open the paper envelope around a lance, and squeezed the stalk of Eddy's thumb in his fist. As blood gathered in the pad of the thumb, Dr. Gauge gave it a quick poke. He produced a pair of rectangular glass slides and gathered a few of drops of Eddy's blood. He placed the second glass over the top of the first, and then held it in the beam of the penlight to verify he'd taken an adequate sample. He slid the tiny panes of glass into a plastic sheath, dropped them in his pocket, and silently exited the room.

The follow up story, "Mouse in a Bottle" is available now.

Rabbit in a Bottle

Any resemblance to people living or dead is purely coincidental. Any similarities between happenings in this story and actual events are completely unintentional.

Special Thanks to:

Janey "Mrs. B" Branson
The family of Irvin Haak
Leslie Leighty
Marjorie McCain Strohm
Clifford Pensyl
Charles Eckert
Chalon Ray Titsworth
Eugene Crumrin
Kevin Boyd
Jennifer Foster
Scott Anderson
Randy Strohm

Monical's Pizza
Wabash Valley Heat & Gas
Wabash Coffee House & Antiques

Hans Berger – Discoverer of brain waves

Ian Wilmut - Rosilin Institute
Member of the the team that cloned Dolly the Sheep

Keith Campbell - Rosilin Institute
Member of the the team that cloned Dolly the Sheep

Charles Vacanti – Harvard Medical School

Vacanti's Mouse

Dolly the Sheep

www.ingramcontent.com/pod-product-compliance
Lightning Source LLC
Chambersburg PA
CBHW030032180626
46810CB00001B/331